Southern Exposure:

Crashpoint

Published by

Cheatham Works™

ISBN

979-8-218-85218-4

For the "Dirty Dozen."

Special thanks to JCB for starting me on this journey and to GT and SG for their guidance along the way.

Follow me online at briancheatham.net

Introduction

"Boss! Boss! You Okay?"

He could hear the words, but everything sounded muffled; as if a dense pillow had been shoved between his ears. There was a loud ringing in his head, and he felt dizzy; disoriented. His vision was blurred, and he could feel a warm wetness around his eye and down his cheek.

"C'mon, Boss! We gotta move!"

Through the fog of muted sound, he could hear the clattering of gunfire. From time to time a spray of dust and small chunks of brick peppered him as he struggled to come to his senses.

"Adams! Johnson! I'll cover; you get him the hell outta here!"

"Copy that," came the reply.

A pair of men shuffled to him and grabbed him under the arms. As they prepared to heft his body weight a third man swung his rifle over the small brick wall and began firing wildly.

They hoisted him up and began to drag him away. To where? What had happened?

In a vain attempt to carry his own weight, he put his foot down. The pain was excruciating. Why did his leg hurt so badly? He looked down at his foot, but in the darkness, he could only see shadows and shapes. Something wasn't right.

"Hold up, Boss. We've got you. You just hang on," Adams said.

They carried him around the corner and zigzagged down narrow alleyways while the sounds of combat faded in the increasing distance. After several minutes on the move his head began to clear.

"What happened?"

"Bad neighborhood, man," Johnson said, "They jumped us on the way out. We were moving so fast we didn't take time to clear the area first."

"Casualties?"

"Just you," Adams snapped with a smirk.

"So far, we're good," Johnson added, "Everyone else went ahead to the rally point. Then you had to dick around and get blown up."

"Yeah. Sorry about that. Wasn't on my 'To Do' list, you know?"

"Nothin' but a thing, Boss. You know that. Now we need to get to the rally point. Any sign of Simmons?"

Adams looked back over his shoulder, down the darkened lane.

"Not yet. He should be along soon. Can you handle him?"

"Yeah," Johnson replied, "We'll keep moving. You link up with Simmons and watch the back door. Don't screw around, though. We need to be out of here ASAP."

"Tell me something I don't know."

Adams slipped out and assumed a defensive position as the other two men continued to the rally point.

A couple of minutes passed before Adams could hear the rapid thump of footsteps approaching. He raised his rifle and watched the far end of the alleyway. A figure rounded the corner, rifle at low ready. Behind him came a shower of bullets, slamming into the bricks and splintering windows.

Adams reached into his dump pouch and produced his single smoke grenade. He pulled the pin and sent the cylinder hurtling toward the approaching figure. As it bounced along the asphalt a thick yellow chemical fog belched forth, filling the passageway.

Simmons broke through the bank of acrid smoke, coughing and cursing as he passed Adams.

"Damn! I hate surplus smoke! That stuff'll kill you!" he coughed as Adams peeled away and joined him.

"Yeah, well, you're welcome for the screen. Now shut up and find a hole."

The men scattered across the alley behind whatever cover they could find and waited for their opponents.

Gunfire erupted through the smoke. They were "feeling" the alleyway. Trying to get a response from the two men; anything that would give their position away or, better yet, kill them in the process.

Adams and Simmons sat still and quiet, waiting and watching through the haze. Finally, a cough. Quiet, but a cough, nonetheless. Someone was coming through the smoke. The humidity of the evening held the chemical blind firmly in the confines of the alley, creating an effective killing zone. A "fatal funnel" as it was often known. The problem was that the effect served both sides. It was best not to move and let them come to you…if they were that stupid.

A dark shape began to form in the yellow miasma. A figure carrying a rifle slowly emerged, sweeping the alleyway from side to side, searching for a target.

Finding nothing he called back into the darkness, "Nobody here. They must have moved on. C'mon! We can still catch them!" They were that stupid.

Shuffling sounds began to penetrate the amber vapor as more people pressed through to meet the first man.

Simmons looked at Adams who responded with a nod and raised his rifle. Both men opened fire, and a shower of bullets tore into the attackers. In a matter of seconds five figures lay across the pavement, dead or dying.

Adams signaled to Simmons to cover him while he checked the bodies. A nod was all he needed to know the message was received.

He carefully approached the fallen men and began to scavenge what he could from them. Ammo, magazines, weapons, anything of use or of value became extra compensation for the job. It was poor reimbursement, to be sure. These men weren't professional soldiers. They weren't even adequately trained. They were just heavily armed thugs.

Adams filled his dump pouch and pockets with what he could before motioning for Simmons to collect anything left. As they resumed their course to the rally point Simmons stepped over one of their assailants, still clinging to life.

"You gonna pay," he spat, "We'll find you. And when we do…"

"Well," Simmons said as he drew his sidearm from the holster, "We can't have that now, can we?"

Simmons pressed the trigger and sent a nine-millimeter hollow point into the man's head. He tucked the pistol away and caught up to Adams who was already at the far end of the alley.

The duo rushed down the narrow paths, scanning rooftops and intersections as they went. Just because it was quiet didn't mean it was safe. That was the mistake they had just made. That was the mistake that had gotten the Boss injured.

Up ahead Adams could see the rally point and the other members of the team. The area was quiet apart from the low rumble of the truck's engine idling. He could see Richards in the bed already tending to wounds.

He made for the truck and vaulted in as the others did the same. Simmons rushed to the driver's door and clamored in. With a lurch the vehicle was underway. Everyone tried to get situated and comfortable, but still alert and monitoring their route. With everything that had just happened, the last thing anyone wanted was to be caught in an ambush or roadblock.

As quietly and quickly as they could navigate without the headlights on, the group meandered through the side streets, desperately trying to make their way to open highway where speed would be an ally. Speed would give them distance and, in situations like this, distance was your friend.

Crouched low in the bed of the truck and frantically working by the glow of a small flashlight, Tom Richards produced a small tubular packet.

"Ok, Boss, this is probably gonna suck pretty badly but try not to move too much.

Adams, hold him steady," Richards said.

He carefully exposed the man's leg, cutting the pants with his Zero Tolerance knife. The leg was covered in blood and a dozen or more lesions, but Tom's main focus was the large hole punctured through at about mid-calf. It was a through and through, but it was larger than he expected.

Richards pried the wound open a bit and inserted the tip of the tampon, pressing it as deeply into the wound as he could.

"Shit! That hurts!" the patient shouted as Richards shoved the product deeper into the entry side of the wound.

"I told you it would probably suck. Now, shut up and lay still, you big baby."

"Ungh! If I could, I'd kick your ass right now!"

"Yeah, I know. Good thing you only have one leg," Richards smiled as he dug a small white bottle with a blue label and yellow cap out of the bag. After shaking it vigorously, he applied the powder across several of the smaller cuts, much to the other man's protests. Tossing the now empty bottle aside he snatched out a roll of bandages.

Working deftly with his blood covered hands he proceeded to wrap the leg tightly with layer upon layer of gauze.

A young woman peered out the sliding glass portion of the rear window; amazed at the swiftness of the triage carried out in the back of a moving truck.

"What is that stuff?" she asked, motioning to the discarded bottle.

"It's a powder coagulant for horses. Wonder Dust. Stops bleeding quickly but can't be used on a deep hole very well," Richards replied as he scooted away from the leg.

The pickup quickly lurched to the right, and the group was soon climbing the ramp onto the interstate. Everyone kept low in the back as the engine growled and the pickup increased speed.

"You okay?"

The girl stared at the men in the back before turning her gaze back to Richards.

"Yeah. I'm okay," she said softly, "Will he be alright?"

Tom looked at his friend lying in the bed, a considerable pool of blood under and around his legs, reflecting the glow of the few streetlights that still burned overhead.

"I hope so. We need to get him home. Soon."

"What's his name?"

Richards never took his eyes off his friend.

"Irwin. Scott Irwin."

Chapter One

Howdy Partner

April 6th

Scott walked briskly down the concourse of the Nashville International Airport toward the baggage claim area. The early morning flight left him drained and unmotivated, but it allowed him the time he would need to drop by the office to finish up some paperwork and meet with the partners at his firm. Williams and Donovan wasn't a huge company, by many standards, but they were a large enough group to have clients across the U.S. and even a few outside the country.

The partners had specifically asked him to come in and meet before taking the rest of the day off. They were somewhat cryptic in their request, but that wasn't terribly unusual. Considering some of the clients he had worked with, there was no telling what they had in mind for his next project.

As he strode through the crowded corridor, he passed a pair of ladies that had been on his flight. He recalled seeing them on the plane, but they had been seated several rows away from him, so he hadn't had the opportunity to meet either of them. As he got closer, he overheard their conversation.

"You see? I told you. They *do* wear shoes down here."

The second lady acknowledged the point with a convincing nod of her head just as Scott stepped alongside.

He fought the urge to comment about it but figured it was a waste of breath. Perhaps it was meant as a joke. Perhaps not. Perhaps it was just the ignorance of someone manifesting. Either way he had to grab his bags and get to the office.

Soon after he had collected his small bag, he was on his way to the parking garage where his BMW waited. The car was his pride and joy. Growing up on a farm just outside of Lewisburg, it was difficult to justify driving anything but a pickup truck. He had suffered the shame of driving his father's old hand me down truck from the age of ten until he left for college. By then it was so worn out he got an upgrade; to his father's next hand me down truck.

Pickups were all he had ever owned and when he finally got a "real" job as an engineer with Williams and Donovan he began to focus his efforts on getting a car. Not just any car, but a nice car; one that was as far removed from being a truck as he could get. He instantly fell in love with the little BMW Z4 as soon as he saw it.

As he dropped the bag and briefcase into the passenger side seat, an unusually warm late April breeze permeated the garage. It was a perfect day to put the top down. Besides, that would help him stay awake on the way to the office. The last thing he needed was to doze off in Nashville traffic.

Within a few minutes Scott was heading into downtown Nashville, among the high-rise office buildings and medical complexes that seemed to dominate the area. He pulled into the parking garage on the lower level of the "Batman Building" as it had come to be known and found his parking place.

The building was situated in the heart of the city's bustling central business district and was a recognizable icon due to the unique twin tower design extending from the upper floors skyward. From the offices on the 26th floor, Scott could see most all of the popular landmarks in the city, many of which were within walking distance.

He stepped out of the elevator and turned to his right, through the doors and into the pristine spaces of Williams and Donovan.

"Good morning, Mr. Irwin," Rachel Avery said with a broad smile. The twenty-four-year-old brunette was captivating. Scott had considered asking her out many times, but inter-office dating was frowned upon by the partners.

"Good morning, Rachel," Irwin replied with a smile of his own, "Anything I need to know before I go to see the big dogs?"

"Not that I'm aware of. Your mail is in your office, and I think there may be a package for you as well. How was Detroit?"

"Cold. When I landed it was 32 degrees and raining. When I left it was 26 and snowing. It feels so good to be back home.

"Well, I guess I'll see what's on the schedule for me next and then I am out of here for the weekend. Be good."

The smile returned to Rachel's face with a little bit of a blush.

"Can't do it," she said with a tiny hint of a giggle.

"Well, then don't get caught."

Scott quickly made his way to his office and dropped his briefcase on the desk. He debated taking off the jacket and tie but didn't have a chance before a visitor knocked on his doorway.

"Back already?" The voice belonged to Chad Stapler, one of Scott's friends from the Engineering Department.

"Yeah, I wanted to get finished early so I could take some time off and recuperate. Mr. Donovan called yesterday and asked if I could drop by before I took a day."

Chad smiled a knowing grin, "I don't think you'll regret the visit, man."

Scott faced his friend with a raised eyebrow, "What makes you say that?"

Stapler shrugged his shoulders with an innocent expression on his face, "Word is you are up for a promotion. Could be a big one."

Scott smiled. He had heard rumors like this before. Most times they were just that, rumors. Sometimes there was some actual truth to them. Either way, he had never been the root of the rumor. It was a bit uncomfortable.

"Yeah," Scott replied with a smile, "When they make me 'Grand High Mucka Muck' I'll believe it. Until then, I'm just a simple, mild-mannered engineer who wants to go home and sleep."

"Alright, man. Well, good luck."

Scott gathered a small stack of papers for his report on the Detroit project and shed himself of the jacket before making his way to the corner office. As he stepped into the doorway Cheryl, the executive assistant, smiled and told him to proceed into the conference room. The partners would be in soon.

Scott dropped his report material onto the large mahogany table and selected his seat. Within a few moments he heard approaching footsteps and stood to face both of the elderly gentlemen as they stepped into the room.

Ed Williams and James Donovan were both in their mid to late sixties. Both men had been in this business a long time and both were commanding figures. To look at them you would never assume that either had a casual side, but you'd be wrong.

"Good morning, Scott," Williams began, "How was your flight?"

"I'll let you know as soon as I wake up," he replied with a smile.

"Well, let's see if we can't wake you up a bit. We can't have you taking the rest of such a beautiful day off just to go home and sleep now, can we?" Donovan smiled. Scott almost wondered if James had been reading his mind.

The trio gathered their seats and got comfortable.

"Business before pleasure, folks. Bring us up to speed on Detroit, Scott," Williams said.

"As of yesterday, the project is running ahead of schedule. We have some issues with timing from a couple of subcontractors, but they are minor. If the weather holds out, we should be looking very good."

Scott continued his presentation with page after page of notes and supporting documentation about the office complex project he had been working on. Before long he closed his folder and leaned back in his seat.

"Very good, son. Thank you. It looks as though we are primed for early completion and a healthy bonus for being under budget and on time. That's what we like to hear," Donovan commented.

Williams nodded his head in agreement, "Once again, you have shown that you have the skills and drive for the job. I knew we had the right man when we hired you."

He shot a cursory glance at Donovan who quickly continued the line of thought.

"Scott, you've worked for us for, what, twelve years now?"

"Yes, sir. Something like that."

Donovan leaned back in his seat, "Every project we've sent your way has been accepted with confidence and completed in a timely and efficient manner. I think I can safely say that the two of us have been very impressed with your talents as well as your work ethic."

Williams nodded his head in agreement, "That's why we asked you to stop by this morning. The briefing on the project could have waited until Monday, but Ed and I wanted to talk to you about something a little more…important. To us, anyway."

"Sir?"

"Scott," Donovan began, "you are a talented man. You have a rare work ethic that many just simply don't have these days. You take projects personally, which makes you driven and attentive to details. Those are leadership qualities that Ed and I appreciate."

"We wanted to talk to you about utilizing those qualities in a more 'administrative' capacity," Williams continued, "You see, we aren't exactly spring chickens anymore and, well, in our old age we've begun to think about things like stepping back a bit. Possibly even retiring."

"Holy crap," Scott thought, *"Chad was right."*

"My wife has been bringing the notion up that she wants to spend more time with me before one of us dies," Williams carried on, "and, well, with Ed and his motorcycle, I never know if he'll make in to work or not."

Both men laughed at the suggestion of Donovan's biking skills being less than par.

"The point is, Scott, we'd like you to consider becoming a partner in the firm. That way, when we're not around, we can rest comfortably knowing that what we've built is in good hands."

"What do you say, Scott?" Donovan asked, a broad smile across his face.

After a second of collecting his thoughts, Scott finally replied, "Of course. It would be an honor. I appreciate your confidence in me, and I won't disappoint. Thank you. Thank you so much for the opportunity."

"Heh," Williams snorted, "Don't thank us too much just yet. Your first job is to go over the contingency plans with us and update them. We'll tackle that Monday."

The next several minutes were spent discussing Scott's new responsibilities and gleaning the benefits of the new post. His salary would get a huge boost, and a new office was already being planned for his occupation. It would be ready in just a few weeks.

Irwin was elated. He couldn't wait to tell his family over the weekend at the reunion. It was the perfect opportunity to share the promotion. He made a mental note to contact all of his friends as well so he could dump the news in their laps at the same time too. He wasn't one to brag, but this was a special exception.

Williams and Donovan had asked him to keep it quiet around the office until things were a little more prepared for his new position. He would take the rest of the day off and enjoy his weekend. They would make a formal announcement on Monday. Irwin was about to explode as he strutted past Rachel and out to the elevators.

"Good news?" She asked as he strode by grinning.

"Yep," was all he said.

"Wanna share?" she inquired.

He opened his mouth just a bit, eager to explain the source of his newly found pep but knew he couldn't.

"Nope. See you Monday," he smiled and turned for the elevator doors.

Chapter Two

A Rumble in the Distance

April 6th

Hundreds of people had already gathered outside the state office building. Sean Carter couldn't tell how many different groups were represented, but it seemed that all the major players were there. Dozens of signs waved above the crowd on both sides of the plaza.

Officially, the protest planned for the morning was to express opposition to increased property and sales taxes demanded by the governor. Off the record, it would address much more than just taxes. Many in the crowd, like Carter, couldn't care less about the cost of baby formula or how much property taxes jumped. He had no family and owned no property. He was there to help make sure capitalism died.

Sean, and several others that day, had come to the protest with a simple goal in mind: fight for what he thought was right. The stark irony that he and many of his associates never addressed was that the very government they opposed was what allowed them to hate it so much.

The police that they despised for being brutal and racist were the same ones charged with protecting them from the groups forming ranks on the opposite side at that very moment.

The system that they said was archaic and outdated provided the very source of income they relied on to allow them to participate in protests like this. By taking advantage of the system, the way he had for years now, Sean could effectively live off the government checks each month while spending all his time seething in his own hatred and sharing it with others of like mind.

A few yards away chanting began via the tinny sound of a bullhorn. The crowd began to push in tighter as a light mist began to fall. The bullhorn was soon drowned out by the growing echo of the multitude.

In recent months sales for the automotive industry had fallen so badly that most manufacturers had begun to scale back operations across the board. It wasn't "downsizing." It was straight out shutdowns and layoffs, no bones about it.

Cities like Detroit caught the brunt of the economic spiral as thousands of employees suddenly found themselves without jobs. The massive impact on the local unemployment system was more than it could bear. In an attempt to recuperate their sudden losses, the governor and other officials decided it would be prudent to increase taxes in an effort to offset the new costs of maintaining the populace.

The citizens had finally had enough. Already shackled to city, county, and state income taxes on top of their federal income tax burden, these new measures didn't just push limits, they broke them. As a result, people decided to let their leadership know they were not happy with things and, for the most part, decided to peacefully protest.

Standing beneath the shelter of an awning, Sean and his comrades watched the crowd move slowly closer and closer toward the police line that separated them from the state building. On either side of the street stood a small army of media representatives. Cameras rolled and microphones recorded the event for all the world to see and hear.

Carter glanced at his friend Bobby with a slight smile. He quickly reached in his pocket and pulled the small .38 Smith and Wesson revolver out, nervously checking the chamber to be sure he was ready. Their agenda would be heard today.

"Ready?"

Bobby returned a sly grin of his own, "Let's warm this party up."

They stepped casually out into the mass of people and began pressing their way toward the front.

Across the plaza the opposition had begun to move. Soon the groups stood toe to toe, and the chants of "unfair taxes" became obscured with radical shouts of racism and fascism hurled against shouts of capitalism and freedom.

Somewhere in the crowd, unseen by the cameras and unheard by the microphones, a punch was thrown. It was immediately followed by another. Like a raging virus the fight soon exploded on the streets as protest signs became weapons, and the blood began to flow from knuckles and broken noses.

Law enforcement moved in rapidly, but not quickly enough. Riot shields and helmets were quickly scarred by sticks and rocks as the crowd turned on the officers. In an effort to control the situation, tear gas grenades were lobbed into the mass, only to be kicked back and forth as they spewed their contents between the various factions.

Among the chaos Sean Carter produced his revolver and cocked the hammer back with a sinister grin. As he raised the weapon the officer directly in front of him turned to face him.

Time slowed as the man's face contorted from an expression of anger to one of fear when the barrel rose to his eye level. Carter pulled the trigger and the stubby barrel belched forth a 129 grain +P jacketed hollow point directly into the officer's face.

At over 900 feet per second, the man never stood a chance. He dropped instantly to the ground as his fellow officers spun to identify and address the new threat among them.

"There! Green jacket!" one yelled as the crowd began to scatter.

Carter quickly ducked his head and disappeared among the panicked protesters before other officers could reach his position.

"C'mon, man! This way," Bobby called as he turned down a nearby alleyway.

Carter quickly followed suit as the area became saturated with more tear gas and rubber crowd control bullets. Police were grabbing protesters left and right as they moved frantically to intercept their shooter. It was a losing fight.

Within a few minutes Sean and Bobby had managed to escape the area, tossing Carter's jacket in a dumpster as they passed by. Soon they were back at their apartment.

"Did you *see* that?" Carter was running on an adrenaline rush like he had never had before.

"Yeah, man. That'll teach those damn cops!" Bobby replied, still high on his own adrenaline.

"Too bad I didn't have time to kill more of 'em!"

"Next time, man," Bobby said, "Next time we'll take 'em all out."

Carter paced the floor anxiously trying to calm himself down. He carried the pistol in his hand, waving it indiscriminately as he walked and recounted the finer details of the event.

"Man, you should have seen his face! It was like…pure terror or somethin.' You could see it in his eyes, man!"

Bobby opened the refrigerator door and grabbed a pair of cans off the upper shelf. Returning to the living room of the tiny apartment he handed one to Sean who popped the top and slumped onto the ragged couch.

"So," Bobby started, "What's it like to have a man's life at your command?"

Carter thought for a second.

"It was awesome, man! This must be what God feels like!" He turned the beer up and took a long chug from the can.

That night the news on every local station carried the story about the protest gone wild and the death of the officer.

Descriptions of the shooter were announced, and a sketch was displayed, but it didn't favor Carter very much. At least he didn't think so.

"Sean," Bobby's voice called over the phone, "Sean, man listen to me."

"What Bobby? Why'd you wake me up, man?"

"Listen, I'm down here at the smoke shop and they said there were some cops in here earlier looking for you."

"What? When?"

"This morning. They are on to you, man. What do you want to do?"

"Let me think, alright? Get back here as quick as you can. And bring me some cigarettes."

Bobby knocked on the door a half hour later before coming in. When he stepped through the doorway, he found Carter sitting in the chair across the room from him with the revolver in his lap.

"How much cash you got?"

"I don't know, man. Why?"

"I've got a plan. I need traveling money."

Bobby looked at his friend with an odd expression.

"Where you gonna go? How much do you need?"

"I've got an uncle down in Tennessee. Worked for GM down there. I figure I'll go there and hide out until things cool off. I need enough for a bus ticket."

"I didn't know you had any relatives left."

"Yeah, well, we don't keep in touch much. Last time I saw him I was maybe twelve. It's the only option I've got."

Bobby studied the notion momentarily before tossing Sean a pack of cigarettes and heading to his bedroom, "Hang on. Let me see what I've got."

Chapter Three

Home Again, Home Again

April 7th

Lewisburg was not what you could call a "sleepy little town" by any real measure. No, it didn't have a bustling shopping district or large corporate office park. It was mostly a manufacturing town that had lost many of its manufacturers long before. The industrial park was largely warehouse space and, as for shopping, well, you might be surprised at what you could get at Wal-Mart.

Still, it was in an excellent location as far as logistics went. Roughly a one-hour drive would put you in Nashville or Huntsville, Alabama easily. Several other prominent communities were within that same radius with strong connections to the defense and aerospace industries, the automotive sector and medical fields.

During the Cold War, nearby Fayetteville was a hot spot for espionage since it was close to Redstone Arsenal and the Arnold Engineering and Development Center. To the west of Lewisburg was Mount Pleasant which was home to several large chemical companies.

Because of the proximity of all the adjacent industry and commerce, Lewisburg became more of a retirement town than anything. There remained a strong manufacturing core, with local industry filling the void of the companies that had moved out following NAFTA. Still, the largest volume of revenue came, as it had for over two centuries, from the agricultural base.

Arguably, one of the biggest cash crops in the area was marijuana. In fact, the little community had a reputation as "Little Tijuana" during the 1980's for the volume of drug trafficking that crossed the area. It remained a continual battleground for law enforcement.

Scott arrived in town that Saturday morning still carrying the excitement of his new promotion bottled up inside. He couldn't wait to tell his family. He came to a stop at the crest of a small hill in front of a Shell station and pulled into the parking lot. As he shut the engine of the BMW off and stepped out a city patrol car eased up alongside.

"I need to see some identification, sir," the voice called out the open window.

Scott smiled to himself and turned to face the vehicle, leaning down in clear view of the driver.

"Here you go," he said with a smile as he extended his middle finger, "Will that work?"

"That'll be fine, sir. Thank you for your cooperation," the officer replied with a chuckle.

Dave Browning had been a friend of Scott's since elementary school. Before accepting the responsibilities of adulthood, he and the rest of the "Dirty Dozen" were constantly into some form of mischief or another. Most of the friends had either entered military or law enforcement careers upon graduation. Scott and a couple of others were the exceptions.

"When did you get in town, man?"

"Just now. I'm going to grab a drink before heading out to the farm. You going to be available later today?"

"My shift ends here in a few hours. I'll be free. Where did you want to meet up at?"

"I thought we might grab a pizza, for old time's sake. How does that sound?"

The radio in the patrol car crackled with a stream of jargon that Scott didn't understand, but apparently Dave did.

"Sounds good. Hey, I have to go. If this is what I think it is, I should have a good story for tonight," Browning smiled again as he shifted the car into reverse, "Give me a call when you're ready to eat."

"Will do."

Irwin feigned a salute to his friend and turned back to the store. Within a few minutes he was back on the road and heading to the family farm.

The Irwins had been in the area for a few generations and owned several hundred acres of prime farmland between them all. Much of it was situated along the Duck River and could easily have been sold for development for a very healthy price several times before.

"I can always make more money," Scott's father liked to say, "I can't make more land." His stubbornness with finances was a gift from his father and grandfather. A genetic malady, some would say, passed down from father to son for generations. It had been a point of contention several times, but it had also been a saving grace for many in the community during the Great Depression and countless times since. From their abundance, they had always reached out to provide for others in need. Of course, there was always a profit to be made as well, so a delicate balancing act was always adhered to. After all, if you gave it all away, you wouldn't have any for yourself.

As Scott cleared the last bend in the long winding driveway, he could clearly see the family homestead ahead. The property contained a large two-story farmhouse with a garage attached to the right side. Behind the main house sat his father's workshop. It was a generous building that he had built with a basement level storm shelter underneath. The shelter had been used by Scott and his friends in high school as a private hangout where they had been known to fracture a law or two regarding legal age limits and alcohol from time to time.

Farther out back sat the barn. It was an older building, but still large enough to house all the tractors and farm equipment plus it provided a place to tend to the needs of the cattle and few pigs the family maintained. Across the pasture behind the barn was the tree line, where the property eventually met the river.

The wooded divide outlined the northern, eastern and western edges of the property, as did the flow of the river. It provided a thick, natural wind break as well as ample hunting grounds for the many deer and turkeys that roamed the area. Scott and his father had built a rather posh hunting blind up toward the northwestern corner for that reason. From the elevated room you could scan a good deal of the property in winter, and you could easily see the intersection of highways 431 and 96 in the opposite direction.

The farmhouse had been home to several family members over the years and was to be passed to him after his parents had no more need of it. Scott had mixed emotions about taking possession of the place for a couple of reasons. First, thinking of it reminded him of his own mortality. He would take over when his parents passed away or simply couldn't manage to stay there any longer on their own. Second, he had worked very hard to get out of the traditional family business of farming and to become an engineer, no, a partner in a firm. He was very proud of himself and the thought of leaving it behind to work the same soil he did growing up just didn't appeal to him.

He parked his car in front of the garage and to the side of the driveway so as to not block anyone else from getting in or out. As he cut the engine off his mother stepped out the back door and approached the little vehicle with a beaming smile.

"Hi, baby. Did you have a good trip?"

"Hi, mom. Yeah, everything went well. I'm glad to be back home, though."

"Me too. I worry about you having to travel like that. Especially places like Detroit. People get killed up there all the time, you know. That's crazy."

"I know, mom. But there's not a lot I can do about it. Sometimes you just have to go places like that," Scott smiled a sly smile, "Maybe that will change soon."

His mother caught the look and immediately knew something was amiss.

"Okay, what's that supposed to mean?"

"What?"

"You can't fool me, Scott Irwin. I raised you and I know that look. What have you got up your sleeve?"

Scott smiled and laughed, "I never could get anything past you. Just be patient. I want to let everyone know at once. Speaking of, what time is the party starting?"

"Well, your father is still down at the barn, but he's supposed to be coming up in a few minutes. I expect the first guests to roll in here in about thirty minutes or so."

"Okay," Scott said with a grin, "Is there anything you need me to do while we wait?"

"Well, if you want to go get your Daddy, that would help. You know how he is when he's working on something."

"I'm on my way."

Scott stepped into the barn and peered across the room. There, on the floor, was his father; stretched out under the PTO of the tractor with both sleeves rolled up and a pair of snips in his hand.

"Hey, Dad."

The elder sat up and almost bumped his head on the tractor, surprised to hear the voice of his son instead of his wife.

"Hey, bud. I didn't know you were here yet," he began scooting out from under the machine, "Your Mama send you after me?"

"You know it. She said folks should be here pretty soon. You might want to clean up a bit."

His father looked at his arms which were covered in grease, dirt and small blotches of blood.

"Yeah. I got some old fencing wire tangled up in the PTO this morning and thought it might be a good idea to cut it all out before I forgot. Gettin' old ain't no picnic."

He smiled and headed for the work bench nearby where a large bottle of hand cleaner sat beside a roll of paper towels. He quickly lathered up and wiped down with a dry towel before presenting his arms for inspection.

"Good as new," he proclaimed, "Now, I guess I need to go change out of these clothes before your mother sees how filthy I am and loses her religion."

"Use the side entrance. I'll run interference for you," Scott said with a grin. "That sounds like a plan, son. I like the way you think."

Just before noon the family members began streaming in. It was almost like a parade of pickup trucks sprinkled with the occasional SUV or sedan and each arrival brought a crock pot or other covered dish along. One thing about the Irwin family, they knew how to cook and didn't mind sharing the results.

Soon the kitchen was filled with so much food that there was no room to work and very little room to sit at the dining room table. Between the aunts, uncles, nieces, nephews, cousins, and kin nearly 60 people gathered for the feast and fellowship.

Stories about the "good old days" and relatives long passed filled the air for hours while a few of the men compared notes on their genealogy research in the den.

Scott's mother caught his attention and, without saying a word, he knew it was time for his announcement.

"Everybody," she called to the assembly, "Can I have your attention for a minute?" The chatter slowly began to subside as she gained their interest.

"Scott has some news he wants to share with everyone. I don't know what it is because he wouldn't tell me, but I know it has him pretty excited."

"Are you pregnant?" one of the cousins called from across the room with a hearty belly laugh.

"Alan, hush," she replied, "This is serious. I think."

Scott laughed as well, "It's OK, mom. No, I'm not pregnant. The big belly is just from all the food I ate earlier. It's a good thing we don't have reunions more often. I'd have to get a bigger car."

A laugh swept over the room as he prepared to make his announcement.

"I just wanted to take a minute and say 'thanks' to all of you who have encouraged me over the years. This family is an incredible source of strength and support that I have been deeply blessed to have behind me."

"You sure you're not pregnant?" Alan suggested again with a smile.

Scott returned the smile but never skipped a beat.

"Yesterday morning I was asked to meet with Mr. Donovan and Mr. Williams at my firm. My bosses, actually.

I was expecting them to give me a new project to work on, but instead they gave me an opportunity. They said that, thanks to my strong work ethic and attention to detail, they wanted me to take on a partnership at the company. I will be officially taking over the company as they retire.

"The characteristics they admired in me, the work ethic and all, I owe to you. So, it's because of this family and your help raising me and influencing me that I was offered this job. I just wanted to say thanks. So, thanks."

Almost as a single unit the family congratulated him on his accomplishment and began to ask him question after question about the responsibilities, and pay, of his new post. Scott Irwin was, if only for a moment in his family's eyes, the man of the hour. It felt good.

Chapter Four

Pizza and Crackers

April 7th

James Evans was the last to arrive at the local Pizza Hut that evening. His work schedule at the guitar plant in Nashville had him working quite a bit of overtime and most Saturdays as well. The pay was alright, but the real draw for him was that he actually loved what he did. Being a guitarist himself, getting to work for a global manufacturer in the heart of "Music City" was a dream come true.

He made his way to the corner booth where a cluster of thirty something year old men had gathered. Scott was at the corner on the right and Dave Browning beside him. Beside Dave sat Chris Davis, another Nashville resident and operations manager at his in-law's building supply business. Chris kept himself busy instructing Krav Maga when he wasn't chasing his kids around or tackling critical items on his "honey-do" list.

Next to Chris was Andrew Phillips. He was the financial guru of the group. Andy had worked in the banking industry for years, following in his grandfather's footsteps. The bank had changed hands several times since he first hired on, with bigger and bigger names on the sign each time, but he was still there.

James pulled up a chair beside Tom Richards and slid up to the table. Tom had been perhaps the most successful of the friends with his management position in a health care firm in Brentwood; a ritzy upper-class community that was almost a polar opposite to Lewisburg. He had achieved the rank of Vice President a couple of years earlier and had moved his family into a nice neighborhood on the other end of Interstate 840, close to Murfreesboro.

"What's up, guys?" James said as he picked up a menu.

"Waiting on you. Where have you been, man? We're starving!" Dave questioned.

"Yeah," Chris chimed in, "We were about to order without you."

"You should have," he replied with a grin, "I would."

"Still working Saturdays, huh?" Scott asked.

"All the time. I spend more time at the plant than I do at home lately."

"Well, I've been to your neighborhood and that might not be such a bad thing," Dave said flatly.

"How are things in the 'DMZ' these days?" Andy asked.

The neighborhood Evans lived in sat astride of the newer Germantown developments, with the Lexus and Infinity dealerships and Starbuck's coffee shops, and the lower income government housing of the Cheatham Place apartments. During his first night in the house, he and his roommate could clearly hear gunfire a few yards away. Later it was confirmed when the local news chopper circled, reporting a drive by fatality within 200 yards of their front porch.

"Everything is fine at 'The Ritz' for now. We have a homeless guy living in a tent behind us. They tore his condemned house down, but he wasn't ready to leave yet."

"The Ritz?" Scott asked with a bit of a puzzled expression.

Evans smiled, "It's where the 'crackers' live."

Everyone at the table chuckled. Though it was tongue in cheek, the fact of the matter was that in his neighborhood, Caucasians were definitely in the minority.

"You guys should come up and spend the night one weekend. We can hit all the downtown bars and restaurants. Then you'll see why I love living up there so much."

"No thanks," Browning said, "They don't make enough ammo or armor for me to stay in your neighborhood. That place is going to be a powder keg when things go sideways."

"Hey." Tom spoke up, "That reminds me; I got an email yesterday about the weekend deals at Palmetto State. They have some really good prices on 5.56 right now. Anyone want to get in on an order?"

Everyone at the table presented their opinion on the topic. A couple decided to join in on the sale and split the shipping costs while one or two others couldn't justify the expense at the moment.

"That's a really good price," Irwin chimed in.

"So, you want in?"

"Nah. I'm good," was all he would say.

"You're good?" Browning asked, "You mean you have enough ammo? I don't think *anyone* can ever have enough ammo." He smiled at his friend as he turned to look him in the eye.

"Well, I mean I could use some more, obviously, but right now I need to pass on ordering. That's all. I have some job changes coming up and, well, I just think it would be best not to order anything today."

"Uh huh," Browning muttered before turning his attention to Evans, "What about it James? How many cases do you need?"

Evans smiled.

"Oh, I *need* several. I can't afford any. Besides, at last count I had nearly 5000 rounds in the closet at 'The Ritz.' I think that will hold me over for a while."

Dave smiled at his friend, "Five thousand rounds? That's a good start. You're going to need every one of them to get out of that neighborhood."

Chris subtly, but effectively, changed the subject.

"Scott, you mentioned a job change. Are you leaving the firm?"

"No. No, nothing like that," Irwin could feel the pride and anxiety building inside, "I was offered a partnership the other day."

"Whoa! That's awesome!" Davis exclaimed, "Congratulations, man."

The rest of the assembly shook his hand and patted him on the back, congratulating him on his success.

"Yeah, congratulations!" Tom added, "When do you step into the big chair?"

"They are going to make an official announcement Monday," Scott said, "They already have things rolling on a new office for me. I'm still a little in shock, but I'm really excited for the opportunity."

"So, new office, new job…new pay?" Andy raised an eyebrow.

"Oh yeah. My base salary will take a huge jump. I'll easily be in the six-figure range starting next week."

Browning couldn't resist taking a jab.

"So, how many cases did you want to order again?" he said with a grin.

"I need to *get* a check before I can spend it," Scott snapped with a grin of his own.

"You know what you need?" James began, "You need a sexy secretary to go along with that new office."

"Are you volunteering?" Scott asked amid a collective chuckle.

"No," Evans quipped, "You don't want to see me in a pencil skirt. It's not pretty. But there is a waitress at the Peaks who is a business major…"

"That's okay," Scott said, "As much as I would love to have a secretary of my own, I don't think the partners are planning on spending that much to put me in a new office."

"So, what are your plans for the new money? Are you going to move out of the subdivision?" Tom asked.

"Well, I thought about trading in my Jeep. I like it, but it's four years old now and the new models are really nice," he said, "Then again, I wouldn't mind remodeling the living room and getting some new furniture. I really don't know.

"I'll stay where I am, I guess. Right now, I love my house. The neighbors are great and, well, it's home."

Dave Browning sat silently as Scott daydreamed about his new income and all the material things he could buy before long. After a few minutes he couldn't hold it any longer and had to say something.

"So, I gotta ask, how are you situated for food and supplies? I mean, your neighborhood is nice and all, but you're still in a densely populated area with a lot of people that *aren't* as well off as you. What happens when the government checks stop coming in? Can you get out? Are you prepared to bug in?"

"I know," Scott said, "There's always room for extra improvement. I'm doing okay, though.

"I can manage to bug in at the house for a few days without any problems.

"I keep a trauma kit in both vehicles, and I have a large first aid kit in the house. I have my pistol with me when I leave home and a pair of extra magazines within reach, just in case. I'm good."

James laughed, "Dave probably has more than that in his sock right now." Browning just smiled.

"How many firearms are you carrying right now?" Chris asked Dave.

"Well, I have the Glock 22 with two spare mags, the Smith .38 is in my pocket with a pair of speed loaders, and I have the Seecamp in an ankle holster with a pair of mags in my vest pocket. Plus, my Zero Tolerance knife, my Spyderco Military and a Grab N' Stab in the small of my back."

"What? Nothing in your other pants pockets?" Andy chuckled.

"That's where I keep my tourniquets and bandages. Plus my keys and wallet. Wouldn't get far or do much without those," he smiled again.

"Well," Scott said, "I'm not carrying *that* much, but I do have my Glock and some extra magazines in the console of the BMW."

Dave looked at his friend, but spoke to the whole group, "Guys, I know you think I beat you up about this, but something's about to break loose. Every day I see and hear more and more things about how the economy is going. There are a lot of things we get over the wire at the department that make me scratch my head and wonder.

"Homeland has been active in sending out a lot of paperwork concerning 'terrorist cells' and how to identify potential terrorists. Some of the descriptions they include could easily apply to any of us here.

"The economy is sliding sideways more each day. I wouldn't be surprised if it all fell apart soon. Very soon.

"Andy, you're in the banking business. Have you seen anything odd lately?"

"Well, recently the interest rates have been really volatile. I do a lot of property assessments and it's difficult to pin a value to something because the dollar has been getting more and more unstable. I've overheard some of the higher-ups mentioning bond dumps and even economic collapse once, but they are more in tune with that than I am. All I do is push paperwork."

"We have had some trouble in the building industry too," Chris commented, "Price fluctuations on building supplies are crazy right now. We set a stable price, but our profit margin could be thick or thin depending on what day it is lately."

"I know, I know," Scott said, "Things are looking rough and there's always a chance that it can fall apart. Right now, I just need to focus on prioritizing what I *have* over what I *might* have to have. Besides, we've all been expecting the world to turn inside out for years, and it hasn't happened yet."

"Don't forget," Dave replied, "it wasn't raining when Noah built the ark."

Chapter Five

Patterns

April 9th

The announcement of Scott's promotion was the first thing on the agenda Monday morning. As he stood before his coworkers beaming with personal pride he couldn't help but look over at Chad Stapler who was grinning with the most ridiculous smile on his face. Chad mouthed the words, "I told you," and gave Scott a 'thumbs up' gesture.

Across the crowd was Rachel who was smiling as well. She was gorgeous and the smile on her face only made her more so. Scott swelled with pride as Donovan raised his hands and quieted the applauding group.

"I know Scott is very excited to accept this position and we are all very excited that he has accepted it as well. Now we have some work for him to do so, ladies and gentlemen, if you would excuse us, we'd like him to earn his new pay."

A subdued chuckle passed over the crowd and everyone began slowly making their ways back to respective desks and cubicles. Several stepped up to shake his hand and pat him on the back.

One of them was Rachel.

"So," she began with her brilliant smile, "Wanna share *now*?"

Irwin laughed, "I was asked not to say anything. I didn't think it would be a good idea to start off my new job by not following the boss's orders."

She gave him as close to a bear hug as she could muster with her petite frame and turned toward her desk.

"Congratulations," she said as she strolled away.

Mr. Williams stepped up and put a hand on Irwin's shoulder.

"Alright, son, let's get you to work."

Irwin smiled at the man as the three partners headed for the conference room.

When they entered the room, they found that Cheryl had already compiled copies of the current contingency plans for each if the men as well as some supporting documents and even refreshed the pitcher of ice water at the corner bar.

"Scott, could you close the door? Thank you," Williams said.

Donovan sat in a chair at the far end of the table as Williams poured himself a glass of water and made his way to an adjacent seat.

"Have a seat," he said gesturing to the chair closest to his own, "Hopefully this won't take long."

Irwin noticed the tone and expressions on the faces of both men as he sat down.

"Is everything alright?"

"The company is fine, Scott," Williams began, "but there are some things going on that we wanted to discuss with you. Seeing as you are now a partner in this organization, we wanted to talk to you about a developing situation that has both of us deeply concerned. If it doesn't bother you, it should."

"Scott," Donovan picked up, "James and I have been in this business for a long time. We've had clients all over and we've seen how money and politics work, for good and bad. Right now, we are seeing some shifts that, well, are a bit too familiar to us."

"I'm not sure I understand," Scott replied.

"Back in the late 1990's we took on a job for a large office building in Buenos Aires. It was to be a multi-story structure with parking and a sizable, landscaped plaza out front. Not too far from the Rio de la Plata. Some of the office space was to be used by the city government for smaller departments, but the majority was commercial space," Williams interjected.

"Now, at the time, the Argentina economy was the third strongest in the world. It's a food producing country and relies heavily on agriculture and livestock exports. Tourism was a strong secondary revenue generator.

"Anyway, we began the project in, what, 1998?"

"That sounds about right," Donovan replied.

"The people of Argentina had already been struggling with their economy before then, but due to some fancy legislation, they reinstated the peso as the official currency and helped to strengthen their situation a bit.

"Their biggest shot in the arm came from the IMF, the International Monetary Fund, who pumped billions of dollars in to keep the country afloat through a series of loans.

Rather than managing the IMF funds and repaying the loans, the government went on a spending spree, keeping the illusion that the economy was booming alive for the people.

"Massive amounts of tax evasion and money laundering added more fuel to the fire and the central bank was even caught up in it. Countless millions were moved to offshore banks where it crippled the local economy even more. Still, the IMF continued to lend.

"In about 1999, the Brazilian Real was devalued, impacting the Argentinean export industry heavily. Their GDP dropped and the country went into a recession. Rioting and protests were already happening across the country because of labor issues and fuel costs.

"In 2000-2001, the beef industry had a huge hoof and mouth issue that was another blow to their economy. That was followed by a massive strike and rioting over proposed government spending cuts. By this time our project was well under way, and we had invested heavily in it."

"Understand, Scott, this was early in the life of the firm, and we didn't tend to watch the world situation as closely then as we do now," Donovan added, "As long as they paid the bills, we would gladly take the money. We didn't realize how much of it was just passing through from the IMF."

"Exactly," Williams continued, "Economic stability had given way to stagnation and no matter what they did, legislation wouldn't turn it around. Finally, around December 2001, things broke loose.

"In the rioting that month over two dozen people were killed across the country. Martial law was imposed, and bank accounts were frozen. All economic activity essentially stopped. Unemployment was over 15%, the peso had been devalued at least once, the country was in a recession, taxes weren't being paid in, and the country's credit rating had been downgraded significantly. They still had enormous amounts of debt owed to other nations and the IMF, but nobody was even trying to pay them off.

"Across the nation, but especially in the larger cities like Buenos Aires, people hit the streets in noisy protests. At first it was all about voicing their frustrations. It wasn't long before they targeted banks and foreign companies, especially American and European ones."

"Our site manager contacted us one morning and said the entire job had been torched. In the rioting, the equipment, mobile office, prints, everything was lost," Donovan said, "We were too small to reinvest, so we had to cancel the project. We wrote the whole thing off, but it cost us significantly."

"The country was in turmoil. The president just…quit. They were paying executives and high-ranking officers with IOUs and cutting salaries everywhere. It was insane."

"And you are seeing the same things here? I've never really noticed."

"Not exactly the same things, but there are a lot of similarities, Scott," Donovan continued, "The U.S. credit rating has already been lowered, and we are teetering on another downgrade. Our debt is ridiculous. The U.S. owes the Chinese alone billions just in interest for buying up our debt over the years. We haven't made any efforts to repay any of it, either.

"Unemployment is as high right now as Argentina had then and it is growing every day. Just in the aerospace and automotive industries we are seeing massive sales slumps that are resulting in thousands of lost jobs across the country."

"Not to mention that we are beginning to see protests about the economy and taxation turning into riots as we speak," Williams leaned back in the leather chair, "And don't forget about the politically motivated folks that are seizing these opportunities to promote their agendas."

"Hmm," Donovan grunted, "These are the times when all the politics come to a head. This is the kind of environment where you see people screaming for a return to a normal routine while the fascists, communists, socialists, and anarchists are screaming for 'reform' or 'diversity' or whatever the PC catchphrase is of the day."

Scott considered the information. He hadn't really been looking at a big picture. Oh, he watched the news every day. Well, he had it on to catch the traffic and weather reports, anyway. But he hadn't paid much attention to the economic reports or the political scene for years. The media had become so biased that it wasn't as much "news" as propaganda anymore.

"So," he said finally, "Where does our meeting today fit into all this?"

The older gentlemen smiled. Donovan motioned to the packet of papers before Irwin.

"Let's take a look, shall we?" he said.

"Since our experience in Argentina all those years ago, we have been trying to maintain a contingency plan for the firm. Things to have in place in case anything were to happen, you see?"

Williams interjected, "While we can't plan for every situation, we try to at least have something for most of them, the biggest or most likely, anyway.

"We have backups of all project data stored off site at a secure location, in case someone decides to burn down the office building. We want to look into alternate office space in case something were to happen to the main building here, like an earthquake or tornado."

Scott halfway smiled as the word 'earthquake' came out in conversation, but then he quickly recalled the New Madrid quakes of 1811-1812 that remained the most powerful quakes on record in the U.S. That wasn't too far away, as the crow flies.

Williams continued, "What we mainly want to address are the plans surrounding the current economic situation. What has changed? What can remain the same? What other options are available now that might not have been last year.

"That's where we are going to rely on you, Scott. A fresh perspective, so to speak. We'll address all the other points, of course, but we mainly want to look at this section here."

Williams folded open the binder and indicated a page with a heading in large bold print that read "Economic Contingency."

For the next several minutes the trio discussed their options and a number of "what if" scenarios. Finally, Donovan looked at Scott and, with a slight squint in his eyes, said, "Well, what do you think, partner?"

Irwin smiled and leaned back in his seat with his hands clasped in front of his chin.

"I like the idea of taking the data storage out of the building. Getting all of our files backed up and off site is good. I would suggest we look at a virtual storage option as well. Nashville has flooded before, and if we are worried about riots like you mentioned, buildings can burn. Virtual data can be accessed online from your home if you need to. That also provides us with an option to not have an office space, if something happens to this one. Or if we can't get to this one.

"Rather than having Cheryl and Rachel call everyone, we should look into a broader alert system. Something like a company alert text to all the employees would be perfect. We could also piggyback an email message advising everyone to whatever emergency we have. Texts use less data than a phone call, and they can be delivered more reliably during times of emergency when you might not be able to get a call to work.

"I'd also say that we should look at a company like Regus for a backup office location. It might not be as convenient as where we are, but if we had to meet clients or something, they specialize in providing backup office space on a lease basis. It's not too expensive, and they are usually fully furnished and wired for business needs. I think they have several places here in Middle Tennessee around Nashville, Franklin and Murfreesboro.

"I read an article once about a startup that had to recover following a hurricane. Their offices were destroyed and many of the employees lost their homes as well. The company actually had set up each employee with a company credit card with a $500 limit or so that they could use for emergency needs. It wasn't for a shopping spree, but they could use it for travel costs or supplies and so forth. They also allowed employees to have time off without using vacation days to deal with the situation they were in."

"I like the idea of an 'emergency fund' for the employees, Ed. What do you think?"

"I have to admit, that's a nice take on it. We'll need to look into the finances and see what we can do there, but I like it. I like it a lot."

"I also like the mass text alert idea. See? This is why we need young eyes on the problem," Williams announced, "That would only take a fraction of the time to let everyone know what's going on."

"I couldn't agree more," Donovan added, "Let's get to work on these new ideas and see how we can implement them ASAP."

Chapter Six

Travel Plans

April 27th

Denise Shelby packed her flip flops into the small carry-on bag and headed out the door to the street below. Waiting in the small convertible was her best friend and co-worker, Amber Espinoza. The two had known each other for a number of years through their mutual employment at a local medical clinic. Amber was a registered nurse, and Denise was working on her nurse practitioner license. Between her work and class schedules, she was exhausted and desperately looking forward to the vacation she was about to embark on.

"I wish I could go with you," Amber said as she started the car, "It's going to be crazy while you're gone, I just know it."

Denise smiled at her friend, "You can handle it. I have confidence in you. Besides, I'll only be gone for a couple of weeks. Then you can tell me what I have missed, and I'll tell you all about the beaches and cabin boys."

The pair had a good laugh as they headed to the airport. The airfare and hotel costs of this vacation had almost entirely depleted her savings, but Denise knew if she didn't get away for a while it would begin to show at work. When you are supposed to be caring and compassionate, snappy and irritable often didn't work very well.

All around the Los Angeles area the economic turmoil had left its mark. Protests took place almost daily and crime was on the increase. Emergency teams and first responders were stretched thin everywhere.

Denise and Amber had both taken their jobs with a smaller clinic due to the overwhelming workload at their respective emergency rooms, but even at the clinic they had been seeing an increase in cases that should have been seen at a more fully equipped facility.

After several miles of congested traffic, they finally exited the freeway for LAX. The airport was an amazing complex of lanes and aisles that seemed to twist and turn in every direction possible.

Amber pulled up to the curb and Denise stepped out, shifting her sunglasses to the top of her head as she headed for the trunk. As she removed the bags she could hear Amber call back to her.

"I still can't believe you have everything you need in those. Are you going 'clothing optional' or what?"

"No," Denise replied with a smile, "But sandals and swimsuits don't take up much room. And that's about all I plan on wearing for the next two weeks."

"What if you have a dinner date? You gonna wear your bikini?"

"I'm not looking for a boyfriend, Amber. I'm looking for a break. Besides, I have a couple of sun dresses if I need them."

Denise walked back around to the passenger side door.

"Well," she began, "I guess I'm off. Take care of everything while I'm gone."

"I'll do my best, but you know I don't have a green thumb. I can't guarantee the safety of your houseplants," she said with a smile, "Be careful. Call me if anything changes with your flight home."

"I will. And, thanks for everything. I'll have a margarita in your honor."

She stepped onto the sidewalk as Amber pulled back out into traffic and drove away.

As she made her way to the airline terminal, she was keenly aware of the tension in the air around her. Even here, in the airport, people were talking about the economy and how much their flights had cost them versus the same flight a year ago. Even a month ago.

Denise had tried to be frugal with her planning by booking her trip several weeks in advance. She scheduled a flight with extra layovers to cut the price even more, but it was still expensive. She packed light to avoid having to check baggage and had chosen her hotel carefully to minimize cost while still maintaining security. She had heard that in many Caribbean countries there were areas you just simply didn't want to be as a tourist, especially as a single woman.

Her flight would take her from LAX to Memphis where she would have a layover of a few hours before continuing on to Nassau. The return flight would be the reverse. It was less than convenient, but it saved her a lot of money compared to a direct flight. Besides, she didn't mind all that much. After all, it was still time off from work.

As she finally stepped up to the counter the girl on the other side began the typical line of questions about whether anyone else had handled her bags and if she was carrying anything of a restricted nature.

She then opened the bags and began to rummage through to verify that there was no contraband within and promptly handed Denise her boarding pass. Next up was the security screen.

After standing in line for what seemed like an eternity, Denise was finally able to have the privilege of going through the full body security scanner. In recent months, due to the increased global tensions and domestic rioting, the TSA had felt it necessary to step up the frequency of the use of the notorious machines. Rather than a random sampling, now every potential passenger had to step into the zone and be reviewed. Denise was not the least bit comfortable with the prospect but complied anyway.

As she stepped into position in front of the scanner wall, she could "feel" the eyes of the operators as they scanned the image on the screen. She wanted to put her arms down and shield herself from their prying eyes, but she knew that would only complicate her trip and she had no desire to stick around any longer than she had to.

When they finished, she was instructed to step over and collect her bags. As she did, she noticed the primary operator smiling at her, like the kid next door who had peered through the window and seen her changing clothes without her knowing. She felt dirty. Almost as if she needed a shower to wash the groping eyes off her.

As much as she wanted to protest, she knew what it would gain her. At least she wouldn't have to deal with the embarrassment again for a couple of weeks. Maybe they weren't as seedy in Nassau. Maybe they wouldn't even have the same equipment. Then again, they probably did.

Not soon enough her flight began boarding. She produced her pass and hastily made her way down the ramp to the aircraft. Shuffling down the aisle, bags bumping off every row of seats she passed, Denise finally found her assigned seat. She quickly stuffed her belongings into the overheard compartment and slapped the door closed.

Dropping into her seat she began to think of her destination and how nice it would be to not have the stress and deal with the people for a few days. She loved her job, but had to admit that sometimes patients, and people in general, could be a little…difficult to deal with.

Soon the plane began to taxi down the runway and as it lifted clear of the asphalt, she could almost feel the anxiety begin to fade away. The next couple of hours were a blessing as the aircraft slipped from the west coast to the Memphis International Airport. There she had a layover of a couple of hours before changing airlines for the rest of the trip into Nassau.

Before she knew it the plane was pulling up to the terminal at Memphis International. Despite the recent remodel of the facility and all the conveniences, she didn't particularly relish the idea of sitting there waiting for the next leg of her trip.

"It's a small price to pay," she thought to herself as she walked down the jet way and headed to the baggage claim area. Along the concourse the massive monitors displayed flight status information and other information to help direct passengers and crew to their next destination in the massive facility. Some were tuned into entertainment and news programming to help those, like Denise, with time to kill.

After collecting her bags and boarding pass, she made her way to the terminal to await the next flight. She watched a little of the news broadcast on the monitor across from her seat but quickly became uninterested. The main topic, practically the only topic, seemed to be the economy and related social unrest. That was exactly why she was going on vacation. Rather than listen to the media bias and bad news she rummaged through her purse and pulled out her phone and a pair of ear buds.

She was sitting quietly, listening to her playlist on her phone, when her flight was called to board. Pulling the ear buds out and grabbing her bags she made her way to the gate.

Again, she headed down the jet way and boarded her plane. She promptly found her seat and stowed her bags. This time she hadn't managed to secure a window seat as she had from LAX. That was okay, though. It kept the anticipation of seeing the crystal blue waters and sandy beaches more of a surprise.

Chapter Seven

The Shopping Trip

April 29th

As Scott pulled into the parking lot at The Outpost, he noticed that his was one of only a couple of cars there. All the other vehicles, and there were several, were trucks, Jeeps, 4x4 Blazers and Broncos, and the like. His BMW looked a little out of place. No, it looked a *lot* out of place.

Davis and Evans had planted the bug in Scott's ear about stepping up the preparedness cache, but the meeting with Williams and Donovan really got him thinking about his situation. Over the past couple of weeks, he had been picking up extras at the grocery store and making side trips to the local outlet stores to increase his supply cache.

Browning had mentioned this store as one of the places he could look into as an additional resource. He thought it best to check the place out on the way home after work and see what they had to offer. Both Browning and Evans spoke highly of the place, but Browning was such a regular customer he even had a specific contact for Irwin to talk to.

Growing up on a farm in the area, Irwin wasn't ignorant of the possibility of floods and tornadoes and was more than adequately prepared for a short-term emergency like that. What his friends and co-workers had been talking about was definitely not a short-term emergency. Argentina struggled for decades with an economy in the toilet and a rampant social situation. They still did, as a matter of fact.

Things had stabilized, but there were areas in Buenos Aires that were still considered "Zona Liberada;" almost like a no man's land where law enforcement won't go. At least, not without armored vehicles.

He stepped through the door and was met with a visage of everything firearm and tactical he could conceive. Shelf upon shelf of magazines down one aisle and an extensive array of holsters and belts down the next. Tactical gear filled an entire wall. Around the corner was a full wing dedicated to ammunition and reloading needs. The third wing of the T-shaped building was the actual gun shop. It was full of everything from the simplest Cricket .22 training rifle to an assortment of Barrett's latest offerings.

"Can I help you find something?" a young lady asked as Scott stood there, amazed by the volume and variety of product.

"Uh, I'm looking for Frank?"

"Of course," she said, "Just a minute and I'll get him. I think he's with a customer right now."

As the young lady stepped away Irwin noticed she was carrying a 1911 in a Kydex holster on her hip. Then he noticed that all the employees were carrying some form of sidearm or another.

She approached an older staff member who was working with a customer on a pistol sale, by the looks of it.

Words were exchanged and she was soon on her way back to Scott.

"He'll be with you shortly. Meanwhile, is there anything I can help you with?"

The petite girl smiled brightly at him. She could tell he was a bit out of his element, but not uncomfortable.

"Oh, uh, I don't know. It's been a while since I've done any shooting, really. Work usually takes up all my free time," he stammered.

"Sounds like you need a better job," she giggled, "What brings you in? Trying to get back into a regular shooting routine or just stocking up on supplies?"

"A little of both, I guess. A couple of friends of mine suggested talking to Frank about getting some items together."

Again, the smile returned to her face. She was actually a very attractive girl. And, there was something kind of attractive about the way she wore that pistol, Scott thought.

"Well, he is definitely a good one to talk to about things like that. We have a lot of really good deals going on right now. I'm sure he will point you in the right direction.

"He seems to be finished now. I'll leave you with him, then. It was nice meeting you…."

"Oh, Scott. Scott Irwin. Sorry."

"It was nice meeting you Scott. I'm Natalie. If you need anything and Frank isn't here, just ask for me and I'll take care of it. Okay?"

"Absolutely," he said with a grin.

Soon an older man walked up and extended his hand.

"Good afternoon, sir. How can I help you?"

"A couple of friends of mine suggested I talk to you about putting some items together for an emergency situation; Dave Browning and James Evans?"

"Oh, yeah. I know both of them. Browning has been a customer of ours for several years now. Hell, if we worked on commission, I could probably have retired by now just from his sales," the gentleman smiled broadly, "What are you looking for, specifically?"

"Well, I have a 9 mm Glock pistol and an AR-15 that I could use ammo for. But mostly I could use some long-term items. Food and things, mainly. They said you could help with both."

"Alright. Let's start with ammo. That is selling out faster than anything else we have at the moment and I'm afraid it won't be long before the feds regulate it out of availability."

"Why is that?"

"It's easier to keep control of an unarmed public," he said bluntly.

Frank led him a few steps away into the ammunition wing. Pointing to a large box he said, "This is the 5.56 we have today. It's 1000 rounds of 55 grain Full Metal Jackets. We just got these in, and they are on sale right now, so it's a really good deal. Brass cased and Boxer primed, so you can reload them if you need to."

Reload? Scott wondered if he would ever even have time to fire them the first time. He didn't even have a reloader. What did he care if they could be reused?

"Over here," Frank continued, "is the 9 mm. Again, we are running a special on it right now, so you'll get a pretty good deal on it, too. By this time tomorrow, most all of this will be gone."

"Gone?" Scott seemed surprised at the word.

"The way we've been selling ammo, I'll be surprised if we have any of this left tomorrow.

We have a ton of that 5.56 in the back today, but it will be sold out by the end of the week.

Guaranteed."

"There's that much of a demand?"

Frank looked at the younger man with a curious twist to his expression.

"You don't watch the news much, do you, son?"

Scott felt a little embarrassed by the question, but Frank did have a point. If it hadn't been happening at Williams and Donovan, he hadn't been keeping up with it until very recently.

"No, I guess not," he said shyly.

"The economy is tanking, social discord is all around, and we've got a lot of people pissed off about it. Rumors have been growing about a major financial slip being imminent. Some say there's no stopping it now.

"People are getting worried. Hell, even on the state level the legislators have been kicking around the idea of a state currency system again. Nobody trusts the dollar anymore. It's all gonna break loose. Not a question really of 'if' as much as 'when' at this point."

Scott suddenly remembered a saying from an old Indian friend in college; "If seven people tell you that you have a tail, you have a tail." Meaning if a lot of people are telling you the same thing, it's probably true. Could they be right? Could the failure of the U.S. dollar be looming? If so, Scott was not prepared, and it hit him like a brick in the face.

The man led him over to a set of metal shelving that contained dozens of Wise, Provident Pantry, and Augason Farms brand food pails and cans. He picked out a two-month supply, the "Essential Package," of various selections, which were individually packaged in Mylar pouches inside the pails. The shelf life was 25 years under ideal storage conditions, and preparation of meals was simple and quick.

"Say, it looks like you are pretty busy, and I don't want to take up your time. You probably need to get back to your customers…"

"I'll get your items from the back. Sit tight."

Frank disappeared into the stock room and returned a few minutes later with a cart full of boxes and pails. They rolled it out to Scott's BMW and stuffed everything in the tiny trunk.

Scott caught Frank eyeing the little sports car with a look of, well, contempt.

"Not much for hauling stuff, is it?" he finally said.

"Well, this wasn't exactly on my 'to do list' when I left home this morning. Next time I'll know to bring my Jeep," Scott said with a smile. He felt a little more vindicated in the presence of all the other vehicles in the lot when he mentioned he had something similar at home.

"By the way, you have a nice shop here, but it's a bit out of the way for me. Is there anywhere closer to Franklin I could get stuff? You don't have another store over there, do you?"

"Nope," Frank said outright, "As far as I know, nobody else around is a one-stop for this variety of items. About the closest other place you'll find might be The Armory of Nashville or Franklin Gun, and I don't think they carry the food and survival gear. If you need anything else, give me a call. We'll get it to you, one way or another."

With that the men shook hands and Frank returned to the store. Scott headed home with his trunk, and his mind, full of things.

He needed to dig out his rifle and clean it. It had been in storage for a long time and could probably use a thorough inspection. He needed more magazines for it. Where were his magazines, anyway? What about his Glock? Should he get extra magazines for it too? A holster. He needed a new holster for it. Didn't he?

He had two months' worth of food in the trunk of the little car. That would be enough, right? The partners said Argentina's problems ran for years. Could that happen here? He needed a bigger food supply. He had canned food in the cabinets at home. Would that be enough? What about water?

Scott's mind raced. He was letting himself get overwhelmed by the sudden realization that he was, in fact, not ready for this. Despite him telling everyone for years he was, he now began to realize that he was severely lacking. He was so caught up in thought that he nearly missed his own street. He quickly corrected course and pulled in his driveway. As he opened the garage door and pulled in beside the Jeep, he noticed some of his neighbors were out in their yards.

"What about the neighbors," he thought, *"Should I say anything to them? Nah. They'd think I was crazy. What if they aren't prepared? Should I stockpile food and supplies for them too?"*

He closed the door behind him, shutting out the rest of the world while he unloaded the trunk and found places for his new supplies. Not wanting to be ridiculed for his purchases, he decided it would be best to lock them away in the hall closet.

Over the next week, Scott began to watch the financial reports himself and made almost daily trips to the local Sam's Club and Costco stores where he bought rice, beans, and various other items to put away in his growing emergency stash. Soon the closet was full, and he moved it all to the guest bedroom closet. If he needed to, he could always put it upstairs in the bonus room above the garage, but that would be inconvenient, so it was a last choice.

Cases of bottled water were stored under beds and in garage shelves. That didn't look suspicious because many people didn't like tap water with all the chemicals and additives. Maybe the volume of bottles would raise an eyebrow, but he could explain that away by being frugal and getting stocked up while they were on sale.

He began driving the Jeep more frequently because he could carry more supplies within the larger, 4-door space. It still wasn't his daily driver because, to be blunt, it didn't get good mileage. For all their off-road capabilities, Jeeps, the traditional style Wrangler models, anyway, lacked any kind of aerodynamic styling. Driving one on a windy day down the interstate was akin to driving a billboard in a hurricane. All that wind resistance burned fuel. Irwin's BMW sipped gas compared to the way his Wrangler chugged it.

With each day the financial crisis worsened, but at least Scott was making headway into being prepared. It was costing more each time he stocked up on an item and some things were beginning to get scarce, but he was able to at least put things of value back. On the weekend he decided to relocate some of his booty to the family farm back home. He was running out of discrete hiding places for some of it and just didn't feel good about leaving everything in one place, to be honest.

His father helped him unload the Jeep in the workshop. Years earlier the patriarch had built the building for his own emergency needs following a tornado outbreak. The floor was concrete with a storm shelter built into the ground beneath and there was plenty of extra storage room with the large shelves that lined the interior and walls for Scott's meager supplies. He marveled at the stockpile his father maintained.

"Two is one and one is none," he said with a smile, "What has you suddenly interested in emergency planning, son?"

Scott stopped for a second and smiled, "Honestly? I had a meeting with the partners at work, and they basically echoed what Browning and the guys have been saying for years. I started watching the news and keeping up with things myself and, to be blunt, I think they're right. Everything is pointing to a major economic problem. Soon."

Ben Irwin smiled at his son, "Yeah, I know. C'mere, I'm gonna let you in on a family secret"

He walked over to a door on the opposite side of the room and motioned for Scott to join him. Producing a key he deftly unlocked the door and flipped on a light switch.

There, before Scott's eyes, was an entire room of first aid supplies, boxes of ammunition, bottles of water, and cases of food. Most surprising of all to Scott was the fact that a good stock of ammunition was 5.56 mm. He shot his father a curious glance.

Placing a finger to his lips in a gesture of silence he pointed to the ground beneath their feet.

"What Mom doesn't know about is down in the storm shelter. I have some rifles and magazines tucked away. She never goes in there, so she hasn't seen them."

"What about the rest of this? Does she know you have a cache in here?"

"Oh, yeah. Shoot, boy, she helped stock most of this stuff. That mother of yours can work a coupon to death and she managed to get most of the household stuff in here for a screaming deal. She doesn't know about the guns, though. I'd kind of like to keep it that way, if you know what I mean."

Scott smiled at his father and his "dirty little secret" before a thought occurred to him.

"Were you going to tell *me* about any of this?"

Ben laughed, "I figured if it all went sideways, you'd be back here anyway, so, yeah. I just didn't want you to think I had lost my mind or anything. Everything has been going so well for you I figured I'd just quietly keep things ready, you know, just in case. That way if anything *did* happen, you'd be taken care of too."

"Always looking out for the family, huh, Dad?"

"That's what we do, son. That's what fathers are supposed to do."

Scott's dad took him down into the storm shelter where the spacious room was also lined with shelves of food, water, first aid supplies, and ammo. In the corner hung a trio of brand-new AR-15 rifles. Each was a mid-length configuration with an 18" barrel and flip up sights. One was equipped with a holographic optic. An EOTech, Scott thought. He had never used one but had heard his friends talk about them and the AimPoint brands very favorably.

"Got enough of them?" Scott asked.

"Like I said, two is one and one is none," came the reply, "You got a rifle, son?"

"Yeah," Scott said, I have a 20" AR. I need to get it out and sight it in. It's been a while since I've been to the range."

"I'd suggest you pick up another one, if you can. I had a fellow tell me years ago that your pistol is the gun you use to get to the rifle you shouldn't have put down to start with. Smart guy. He'd been through enough to know it was true, too."

Scott considered the logic. A handgun was better than nothing, but a rifle was more accurate over distance, easier to learn, and more versatile for more applications. On top of that, the AR platform was incredibly adaptable. With only a few minor modifications you could change caliber, barrel length and weight, stocks and grips, sights and optics. You could even quickly change the whole configuration from a rifle to a pistol or short barreled rifle, if you needed to. Of course, that got into the NFA realm and a lot more paperwork with the government, but it could still be done.

Thanks to some assistance from his friends, he managed to secure a second AR and extra magazines which he kept in the Jeep. It was a pistol model, so it was very compact, but he hadn't had the chance to take it out and run it yet, so it was more for intimidation at the moment than accuracy. He hoped the economy would hold out for a little longer so he could be ready.

That wasn't meant to be.

Chapter Eight

The Slip

May 1st

It started quietly, the way most disasters do.

Three days before the official rollout of FedCoin, a mid-level security engineer at one of the system's private contractors submitted a request for medical leave. Stress, he said. The timing wasn't questioned. The team was overworked, deadlines were brutal, and nobody wanted another resignation before launch.

What no one knew was that, just days earlier, he'd accepted an anonymous payment routed through an offshore wallet. His final act before leaving was a single line of code; a silent gap in the wall that would let someone slip in without tripping alarms.

When FedCoin went live, everything worked as expected, at first. The Federal Reserve's new digital currency promised instant transactions, traceable payments, and stability in a shaky market. Within hours, millions of accounts across the country were converted to digital balances. For a moment, it looked like progress.

Then came the slowdown.

Transaction nodes began dropping offline without warning. Small banks reported that balances weren't matching their ledgers. A few flagged it as a synchronization bug, but within minutes, central servers began pushing corrupted updates through the network.

By midmorning, reports were flooding in.

- **08:15 EST:** Federal Reserve announces "temporary maintenance."
- **09:02:** Major retailers report failed payment authorizations.
- **09:47:** Trading platforms suspend all digital transactions.
- **10:22:** Regional banks lock out online accounts to prevent withdrawals.

At 11:15 a.m., the first confirmation came in from the cybersecurity team: the breach was real. The open port wasn't a glitch. Someone had come through it.

Within minutes, every account linked to FedCoin, personal, business, or government, was compromised. Whole blocks of digital currency were rerouted to anonymous addresses before the network could be shut down. When the system finally went dark, nearly half of all converted funds had vanished into data fog.

The media called it the largest cyberattack in American history. Officials blamed a foreign power. Congress demanded hearings. The Fed promised restitution. But the truth, that a single contractor had left a door open, and someone had paid him to do it, never made it into the press briefings.

The crash spread faster than anyone predicted. Without access to liquid currency, trucking companies halted shipments. Stores closed within days. Fuel reserves were locked behind frozen digital accounts. And in less than a week, the phrase *"when the money stopped"* became shorthand for the new reality.

No one knew exactly who had done it, or why. But everyone agreed on one thing: **the day the screens went black was the day everything slipped.**

Many of the volatile industries, particularly the automotive and aviation sectors, had already seen considerable drops in sales. Tens of thousands of employees were already laid off indefinitely and the situation only grew worse. Unemployment shot to over 25% within a week.

Amid all the financial chaos, the stock market buckled and crashed…again. It hadn't recovered from the previous crash that followed the lowering of the U.S. bond rating. Once again, the United States was in a full depression, except it was far worse than the Great Depression so many years before.

The degree of impact felt by the public varied from region to region. The Northeast and California were lost causes. Dependence on government checks in some places was over 30% before everything went off the rails. Suddenly over a third of the population couldn't afford to pay for medicine, groceries, or utilities.

Places like Detroit, Chicago, New York, and many cities in California soon faced rioting on grand scales when EBT cards stopped working and checks stopped coming in the mail. Crime, all crime, but especially violent crime, began to increase. Unfortunately, in areas like these, it flourished.

Many of the larger cities had chosen to adopt heavy handed gun control legislation making it difficult or even impossible to own a firearm or get a carry permit. Without the ability to defend themselves, the citizens were at the mercy of the criminal elements.

As a response to the dwindling supplies of food and fuel on the roads some areas had also imposed anti-hoarding laws to prevent anyone from storing large amounts of food or water. Resources such as that were meant to be available for everyone in the community and not just for those with the foresight to be prepared for a bad situation.

Across the Midwest, the conditions varied with larger cities suffering while smaller, rural communities weathered the storm much better. The smaller towns were less reliant on federal funds and were typically more self-sufficient.

Texas, Arizona, and the Southern States fared much better still. These areas felt the pain, to be sure, but with far less government per capita and a greater degree of self-reliance, problems were far less widespread.

Texas still had immigration issues, as did Arizona, but more often than not it flowed the other way, back into Mexico. Many found that it was safer to return home than to stay in the U.S. simply because the violence and poverty here became worse than it was there. The cartel wars had left the criminal organizations badly weakened and finally outnumbered and outgunned by the "Federalis."

The Southern States, as they became known, had maintained a well-developed infrastructure of power generation and distribution thanks to the TVA network. Since so much land was still dedicated to agriculture, food shortages were less of an issue. Of course, there were exceptions.

Like their counterparts in other areas of the country, places such as Memphis, Atlanta, New Orleans, and Birmingham saw extreme rioting and violence. Of course, many of these locations were already hotbeds of crime even in good times, so it was no surprise when things got worse. In many places the Federal Government was firmly in charge. In other places, like the Southern States, it was essentially ignored.

For many years prior, states like Tennessee had been flexing their Tenth Amendment muscle and taking back the rights given under the Constitution. Laws such as the Firearms Freedom Act had been passed stating that firearms and ammunition manufactured, sold, and possessed in the state were not required to have a serial number or 4473 form completed per ATFE requirements since they didn't cross state lines. Previously the law hadn't been challenged because of the far reach of the agency, but now it, along with the rest of the Federal Government, was so broke they couldn't afford to pursue action.

Tennessee had also passed legislation exempting the sale of printed currency, coins, and bullion from sales tax. What this did, in a very subtle way, was to remove these items from being "commodities" and re-establish them as "currency" in a legal sense. This essentially allowed the public to have an option, by law, to use something other than Federal Reserve notes as acceptable currency under Article 1, Section 10 of the U.S. Constitution. Basically, the state had taken measures to put itself back on the "gold standard" even though the federal government refused to.

Despite the hopes and dreams of many in the South, the opportunity to stand toe to toe and re-fight the "War of Northern Aggression" simply couldn't happen. There was no power to resist and no authority to buck. It was a simple shifting of strength in these areas from a powerless central government to a leaner, more functional state government that could better meet the needs of the people..

Most people just wanted crime under control and a return to normal life. Open war, like during America's Civil War, would be devastating and divisive. It was bad enough anyway; nobody wanted it to get worse.

Following the examples of Montana and Idaho, Tennessee overruled agencies such as the BATFE when it came to matters of law enforcement. Officially, the agencies still had authority, but without funding to support them, they were toothless lions. Local law enforcement was no longer required or expected to assist them with raids or investigations, and federal agents could actually find themselves on the wrong side of the law if they overstepped their bounds.

Like Texas, Tennessee changed the name of the National Guard to State Guard to reflect the loyalty of the organization to the people of the state. It was merged under the state's War Department with the Tennessee Defense Force, a volunteer organization that used to be known as the Tennessee Militia. The responsibilities remained mostly unchanged for both divisions, with the TDF acting as support should the Guard be called up.

"Loyalists," those loyal to the Federal Government, and "Patriots," groups who swore allegiance to the Constitution, saturated all branches of the armed forces and law enforcement. The presence of the two groups was enough to keep level heads in charge most of the time. Yes, they would disagree, but they both knew better than to start a war.

Due to the conditions in many federally controlled areas, refugees became commonplace as word of stability and even opportunity in Texas and the Southern States spread. Legislators worked frantically to address the sudden influx of people.

Reflecting on experiences with natural disasters in recent years, Tennessee quickly moved to annex the General Motors facility in Spring Hill and the Nissan facility in Smyrna to be used as improvised shelters. Both locations contained massive buildings, and the Spring Hill site was actually used as a working farm in addition to an assembly plant. TEMA, the state level office of emergency management, swept in, securing the facilities and began overhauling them for use right away.

Since they already had acres of covered and climate-controlled floor space on top of medical and dining facilities, the plants required little to begin accepting refugees. In addition, the GM plant would be used as an agricultural resource to provide work and a renewable food source to local communities. The state would not simply provide free food and shelter. Evacuees would earn their keep.

Most of the Japanese Nissan employees were ushered home immediately even before the events of May unfolded, so there was little resistance from corporate executives concerning the use of the facility. The General Motors plant, however, was heavily disputed. In the end the needs of the public outweighed the financial desires of the company and the state refused to budge. With no production taking place at the facility, the state saw no grounds to simply let the massive structure sit idle while there was a public need for it. The company was overruled.

Before long tables were hastily set up at rail and bus stations and airport terminals to catch anyone fleeing the chaos of the harder hit areas to better control the flow of refugees.

Chapter Nine

Tennessee Welcomes You

May 12th

Denise gazed out the window of the aircraft at the world below. From 40,000 feet things were so peaceful and calm. It almost made her dread getting back to the reality that awaited on the ground back in California. She had spent the past two weeks avoiding the news and refused to talk about things of a stressful nature. It was awesome.

She couldn't avoid it all, of course. Try though she did, the news of and the turmoil that had followed were topics she couldn't escape or ignore.

When she arrived back at the airport, the girl at the terminal informed her that her ticket price had increased due to the devaluation of the dollar, despite the fact that she had bought her ticket long before any of this happened. After a healthy argument an older gentleman tapped Denise on the shoulder.

"Honey, not to be to blunt, but they have us all by the short curlies. I've already had this argument three times today. You won't win and the only other option is to stay here and find a job." Denise was infuriated. To pay the increase was outright robbery, but she had to go home. They even refused refunds, and they wouldn't negotiate. If she tried to book a different flight with a different airline, she would lose the money she had paid for this ticket anyway and the other airlines had all increased their ticket prices as well. It was a maddening, losing situation at every turn.

Producing her debit card she reluctantly handed it over to the attendant. The girl swiped the card with a cringe and handed it back with a sheepish, "I'm sorry. I just work here."

Denise understood that the increase wasn't the young lady's fault. Still, she represented the company that had just duped her of her savings. When it came time to finally board the plane she was still fuming. All the relaxing had been for naught.

As the aircraft drew closer to the layover at Memphis she had calmed down. Soon enough she would be back home and on the job. Her first priority would be to rebuild her savings as fast as she could. At thirty years old she still had plenty of time before retirement age rolled around, but that didn't mean she couldn't be frugal and use her head. By what she had heard of the economy, she would need every dime to retire.

"Ladies and gentlemen," the overhead speakers crackled, "This is your captain speaking. Due to some problems on the ground in Memphis, we are being diverted to Nashville. The airlines are working now to coordinate the layovers and flights as we speak. On behalf of the airline, I apologize for the inconvenience."

Denise slumped back in her seat. What else could possibly happen? What did that even mean?

One of the flight attendants was making her way down the aisle when the gentleman from the terminal flagged her down.

"Excuse me, ma'am," he began, loud enough for everyone around him to hear his voice "What does that mean? Problems on the ground in Memphis?"

The attendant looked around the cabin and chose her words carefully, "From what we have been told, there has been an incident on the ground at Memphis. For safety reasons, they have closed the airport and are diverting all incoming traffic to nearby locations."

"Was there a crash?" Another voice called.

"No, there wasn't a crash. The information wasn't specific. We only know that there is an ongoing situation in Memphis that is a security concern, and they have closed the airport."

"Was it a terrorist attack?" Some else called out.

"I really don't have any more information, ladies and gentlemen. I am sorry to be so vague."

She resumed her walk toward the rear of the aircraft as a flurry of whispers spread through the cabin.

About forty-five minutes later the plane was on final approach to Nashville International airport.

Denise made her way to the baggage claim area and found herself among a growing crowd of passengers that were being funneled this way and that by security and airline personnel.

"*This must be the mess from the redirects and layovers. Great,*" she thought to herself. She stepped in line and slowly made her way to the table at the head of the line.

As the young couple in front of her stepped up with all their baggage she overheard the woman at the table begin asking questions.

"Name?"

"Tom and Brenda Johnson."

"What flight were you on?"

"American 1136 from Phoenix."

The woman began flipping through pages in a binder.

"Destination?"

"Nashville. We just want to go home."

"You live here?"

"Yes, ma'am."

"May I see your driver's license?"

Tom reached into his pocket and Brenda began to dig in her purse. Soon they both produced their identification and handed them to the woman who looked them over intently before smiling and handing them back.

"My apologies. We are having to screen all passengers because of the recent events. Have a nice day." She motioned to the exit with a slight smile. The young couple collected their bags and quickly made for the exit.

Denise stepped up to the counter and began fishing out her license as the woman started with the questions again.

"Name?"

"Denise Shelby."

"And what flight were you on?"

"American 421 from Nassau. We were supposed to go to Memphis…"

"Yes," the woman said without taking her eyes from the pages, "I heard about that. What was your destination?"

"Los Angeles, after a layover in Memphis," Denise looked at the pages. It was a passenger manifest for incoming flights. The lady's finger was resting on Denise's name.

"Oh. I'm sorry to hear that. Can you please gather your things and follow this guard? He will show you what you need to do next. Thank you, dear."

"I don't understand. Is there a problem?"

"Flights to California have all been changed up. We are trying to accommodate everyone as best we can. He is going to take you to the people that are handling that. Next."

Denise collected her tiny bags once again and stepped over to the guard, "I guess I'm supposed to follow you."

"Yep," he said flatly, "Sorry for all the trouble. Maybe it won't be too long before you can get home."

He began escorting her through the facility very casually, as if he'd done this a thousand times before. Perhaps he had. Probably that day, by the look of the crowds everywhere.

"So, what's going on? Why couldn't we go to Memphis?"

"You don't know?"

Denise shook her head, "All they told us was there was a problem on the ground, and the airport was closed."

The guard grunted smugly. His gaze never broke from the aisle ahead.

"Memphis is a war zone. The last I heard the airport was burning and a lot of folks were hurt and killed. I heard the Guard was called out to get things under control."

"The National Guard? Who attacked it?"

"State Guard," the massive figure corrected, "Tennessee doesn't have a National Guard anymore. As for who, well, people do funny things when they're tired, hungry and pissed off."

The duo reached another table at the head of another line of passengers. Denise slumped her shoulders in frustration.

"Here you go," the guard said as he extended his hand toward the desk, "Good luck, Miss."

A sympathetic smile broke across the man's dark brown face as he turned back down the aisle and made his way back to the first line.

As she finally stepped up to the table, she was again asked a series of questions about her destination and identity.

"I am sorry for the inconvenience, Miss," the skinny little man said, "It's a terrible thing that's going on everywhere."

"What, exactly *is* going on? Why is all this necessary?"

The little man glanced over the top of his glasses at her with a slight look of surprise, "You don't know? Have you been hiding under a rock?"

"Well," Denise began, "Actually, I've been hiding on a beach avoiding the news for two weeks."

"You should have stayed there," the little man said with a smirk, "I would have."

He began to recount the news of the Slip and how the people had turned to protests and then rioting when they couldn't afford to live. He explained how the airports in Memphis and Los Angeles were prime targets for terror attacks that spun off from the riots. The violence had gotten so bad in California that they couldn't get any airline to fly in, and none had come out for days.

"So, what am I supposed to do? I can't just sit here in the airport until this all blows over," Denise felt her frustration growing by leaps and bounds.

"We have set up a location for people in your situation. Now, it's not ideal, but you will get fed and housed and all your basic needs met until such time as we can get you home, okay?"

"What? A refugee camp or something? Really?"

"Do you have any special skills, Miss Shelby?"

"I'm a nurse. I've been working for my Practitioner's license," she said.

The little fellow sat upright in his chair, "Oh, really? Well, that makes a difference."

Denise perked up a bit. The tone in the little man's voice was the first hint of something positive she had heard since boarding the plane in Nassau.

"How so?"

"Well, we have had a shortage of medical staff everywhere for a number of years now, but with recent events it's gotten worse. If you are interested in working while things are so crazy, I can get you in a position today in Spring Hill. All your basic needs will be taken care of, and you'll actually get paid for your work. What do you say?"

Denise considered the situation. She didn't want to be here in a camp, but from what she had been hearing she didn't want to go home to the chaos there either.

"I don't guess I have much of a choice, do I?"

Chapter Ten

A Good Place for a Stickup

May 18th

Andy Phillips stood up from his desk in the basement level of the bank in Columbia with a small grumble and a big stretch. Over the years he had worn many hats at the institution and today was a chance to return to one of them he had worn early in his career: ATM maintenance.

Years ago, he and his company sidekick had the responsibility of taking sacks of cash around to all the area ATMs and filling the machines. It was dangerous work carrying tens of thousands of dollars' worth of currency around, especially when the bank frowned on carrying a weapon for defense and it was near to impossible to get a police escort. Despite policy, Andy typically carried anyway.

With the failure of the economy the bank had let many of its employees go in order to cut operating costs and had terminated the contract with the armored car company that had taken over the task of refilling the machines. Now it fell back on Andy's shoulders to make sure they were adequately loaded with worthless currency to last through the weekend.

With a grunt he hefted the bag of $40,000 in twenties onto his shoulder and met his partner at the van. They would travel around town and check the operational condition of the ATMS, repair any issues they could, and restock the money. His sidekick, Brad, knew that Andy usually went armed, but didn't say anything. He felt better knowing that they at least had a chance of protection even though their employer decried it.

Columbia proper lies a few miles west and north of Lewisburg and is a much larger city by comparison. It also has a larger criminal base and has always had a bigger problem with crime. While Lewisburg was mostly manufacturing, Columbia was mostly retail and commerce. When the economy tanked, a lot of stores closed, and a lot of people lost jobs. Crime had shot up exponentially in the past several weeks. It was so bad that Andy, along with many of his coworkers, had been seriously entertaining another line of work. His concern was that he lacked any marketable skills for anything but banking.

As they approached their third ATM stop of the day, he scanned the neighborhood before stepping out of the van. Brad cautiously got out on the other side and hovered near the door for a minute before approaching the machine himself. It took both men to access the money box, which was fine since one could act as a lookout while the other loaded the cash into the machine.

As the two turned their keys and opened the dispenser they failed to notice a vehicle pass and slow just down the street. Traffic was light, but steady in the area, so a single passing car didn't garner much attention. Besides, they were wanting to finish the task at hand and move. Staying in one spot with large sums of money made them nervous.

The car turned around in a small parking lot and the occupants watched for a brief minute before deciding to make their move. Both men at the ATM were busy and distracted and they clearly had a sack full of money.

The car eased out into the street and began to approach steadily. They didn't rev the engine or speed up, because that would draw unwanted attention. Within a few seconds they were almost on top of the bank men and the passenger produced a pair of handguns from under the seat, hanging them out the window as they came closer.

"I swear," Andy started, "If these people don't start backing off when we do this job I'm going to start shooting."

"I know. It's like they can't wait to get in here and pull money out whenever they see us working on a machine. They probably don't even have anything in their account to pull out. I know I don't," Brad added.

As the vehicle got closer Brad looked over Andy's shoulder and spotted the passenger working his head and shoulders out of the window.

"Oh, shit."

Andy turned to face the vehicle and immediately knocked Brad to the ground with the heft of the cash bag.

"Get down!"

Andy dropped and scooted as close to the van as he could while Brad scrambled to get to the side door.

The assailants opened fire as they rolled to a stop only a couple of yards from the van's front bumper.

Andy leapt into the front seat of the van and drew out his weapon, a compact Springfield Armory XD in .40 caliber.

"Why did I come in today?" He muttered.

Rounds began pinging off the front of the van and deflecting off the sloped hood and windshield as he rolled himself back into a position where he could return fire. The van was parked at a slight angle to the attacker's car, so he crept quickly between the front seats and flopped into the floor next to Brad in the center section.

"Call the cops."

"What are you going to do?" Brad asked as he fumbled for his phone.

"Probably get fired. But at least I plan on being alive when it happens."

The passenger side door opened on the car as the shooter stepped out and began to look the van over. Andy dropped to the ground through the open passenger side door and could clearly see the man's feet on the pavement. A well-placed shot quickly shattered his left ankle as the fury of 155 grains of full metal jacket met flesh at over 1100 feet per second.

The man dropped instantly to the ground, losing his grip on one of the pistols. He rolled his head around, looking under the van where his eyes met Andy's. As he swung his second pistol up Andy pressed the trigger a second time. The second round drilled a small hole directly through the bridge of the man's nose, scattering gray matter across the street behind him as the driver emerged from the car.

Suddenly the van was being riddled with gunfire as the driver moved to check on his associate. Scooting behind the added protection of the engine and suspension of the van, Andy waited for the inevitable reload.

In a rage, the man emptied his magazine and screamed at the van. He dropped his gaze to retrieve another magazine so he could finish the job and take the money which gave Andy the opening he needed.

In a single, fluid move, he rolled onto his knees and drove himself upward, rising over the fender and acquiring his target. The driver saw the flurry of movement out of his peripheral vision and tried to bring his own gun to bear, but it was too late.

Andy's first round clipped the man's left shoulder, shattering the scapula and severing blood vessels and tendons. The second shot punctured the left lung and took a considerable piece of rib with it as it buried deep in the chest cavity. As the driver reeled from the impacts he swung the pistol up, losing his grip with the injured arm before he could successfully seat the magazine and chamber a fresh round. The magazine slipped out of the well and fell to the ground just as Andy's third and final shot found its mark at the center of mass.

Andy's tunnel vision kept him from hearing the moans coming from the van for a few seconds as he was focused on the bodies before him. Shaking himself back into the world he scanned the area, looking for additional threats before holstering the XD and moving to the side door again.

Clutching his leg with his phone lying on the floor beside him was Brad. His face was covered with tiny scratches where the window glass had peppered him and daylight shined through a pair of holes in the van's driver's side sliding door.

"He shot me," Brad said, "He shot me through the damn door!"

"It's alright," Andy replied, "Can you reach my bag over there?"

Brad dragged the small backpack across the floor of the van and immediately turned his attention back to his leg.

Andy produced a small packet and opened it up to reveal a pack of Quick Clot gauze and a pair of EMT shears.

"I hope you aren't too proud of those pants," he told his partner as he grabbed the scissors.

Peeling Brad's hands off the wound he quickly split the pant leg open and inspected the injury.

"You're gonna hate me for this now, but you'll thank me later," he said as he began shoving the gauze into the wound.

In the distance the sound of sirens was getting steadily closer.

"You knowingly violated policy and carried a firearm on the job! I don't *care* if you saved your lives! You broke the rules, Mr. Phillips, and that is unacceptable. You should have just let them have the money and walked away!"

The branch manager was beyond angry. He was irrational. Andy was straining to keep his temper in check, but the more the man ranted the more his ire grew.

"You idiot," Andy finally blurted out, "They were going to kill us anyway. It didn't matter about the money. They came up with guns out. If I had walked over to the car and handed the cash to them with a smile and a handshake, they would have still shot me in the face."

"It doesn't matter. You still violated bank policy in the matter."

"Yeah, and you're a dumbass."

"Mr. Phillips!" the man demanded, "I'll have your job if you don't apologize for that remark!"

"You can have the job. You'll have my resignation and my foot up your ass before you get my apology. Which one do you prefer?"

As the pair exchanged verbal blows the on-call physician and one of the officers walked into the room.

"Mr. Phillips," the doctor began, "everything looks fine. You just have some minor injuries, but you should be fine. Thanks to your quick action out there you managed to save Mr. James' leg. I'm impressed.

"We have some paperwork for you, but you'll be free to head home in just a little while."

"Thanks, doc."

The officer stepped up and shot a stern look at the branch manager before addressing Andy.

"Mr. Phillips, we've spoken to witnesses and Mr. James concerning what happened out there and we will not be pressing any charges against you. As a matter of fact, if it hadn't been for your actions, I have no doubt we would have had a much worse situation today.

"You might be interested to know that those two were already being sought in another crime from earlier this week. A particularly violent home invasion that left an entire family in here, a couple of floors up. We don't know yet if the little boy will live or not," he glanced at the manager again as he turned to walk out.

"You can pick up your weapon at the station when you are finished here. Oh, and, off the record, thanks. I wish there were more folks with the balls you've got."

The branch manager cleared his throat as he tried to carefully choose his next words.

"Perhaps we should discuss this later, when we've both had time to cool off a bit. Why don't you take the next few days off and we'll talk about your future next week?" Andy slipped from the exam table onto the floor.

"My grandfather was on the board of this bank from the start. I've worked here since I was in high school without a single blemish on my record. Despite you and the other idiots putting incompetent people in positions of authority that couldn't otherwise find their ass with a guide and a GPS, I have kept my mouth shut and carried on. Today I stopped something bad from happening. Today I did something most people would be proud of. I saved a man's life, and I stopped two violent criminals in the process.

"My future? My future is not with your bank."

Chapter Eleven

Vacation Days

May 21st

Tennessee was never a place to catch on quickly to fads or popular culture. By the time it got here something new and catchy was usually sweeping the nation. Legislation was the same way as was the mayhem of the rioting. Things just took longer to gain ground here and longer to leave once it did.

Following the events of May first, projects at the firm suddenly began to slow down, and even stop. Many clients had decided to err on the side of caution and put a hold on completing things until they knew more of what the future held in store.

As a result, the office became more of a meeting place than a workplace. With nothing to do the employees would gather in the break areas or around cubicles and discuss issues. Mostly they talked about the economy and how bad things were getting.

Scott tried to keep himself busy with paperwork, but even he couldn't ignore the fact that things were at a standstill. He gathered some papers and headed to Rachel's desk.

"Rachel," he said as he plopped the files on her counter, "Can you make sure these get filed for me? I have to go work up a status report for Ed and Jim."

Ed and Jim. It still sounded strange to use the men's first names, but they insisted that he do so since he was now on their level.

"I'll take care of it for you," she smiled, "It's not like I have anything else going on right now."

Scott looked across the room to the corner where his new office stood, still unfinished.

"Don't worry," Rachel said as she collected the papers and stepped around the counter,

"You'll be in there soon enough."

She smiled again and headed down the aisle toward the project room.

"Scott!" Ed called from the other end of the aisle. Irwin turned and saw him gesturing to meet with him.

As he got closer Ed patted him on the shoulder and said, "If you have a second, we need to discuss some items."

"Of course."

Inside, already sitting in one of the high-backed leather chairs, was Jim; newspaper in hand. "Good morning, Scott," he said as he folded the paper up and tossed it on the corner of Donovan's desk.

Ed closed the door and headed for his seat.

"Pull up a chair, Scott," he said as he scooted up to his desk, "This won't take too long. We just need your opinion on something."

"Okay," Scott said as he settled into the plush leather chair, "What do you need?"

"Have you been keeping up with the news lately?"

"Yes. After our talk a couple of weeks ago I started watching things a lot more closely. I've tried to stay on top of the financial reports every day and the outlook isn't good."

"That's our opinion as well," Williams commented, "which is why we've decided to have an impromptu meeting to discuss things here at the firm."

Ed leaned back in his chair and folded his hands across his chest as he spoke.

"As the decision makers of the firm, we have to look at the big picture. We prefer to keep our employees working, but we also have to keep the firm viable as well. With the economy in its current state, those two concerns don't work very well together."

"I agree," Scott said. He was beginning to put things together in his mind even as Williams carried on the conversation.

"We've been discussing the options on the table and the two of us are inclined to believe that it might be in the best interest of the firm to close down operations…temporarily, of course…until the economy stabilizes. We wanted to know what your opinion is and if you see any options that perhaps we don't."

Scott leaned back in the chair for a bit, trying to think of anything that might keep the doors open. They couldn't really scale operations back because the clientele was too scared to press ahead on projects. They couldn't push the clients either. That wouldn't look good for the company. Every scenario he could think of just didn't solve the problem. The only option seemed to be stopping and waiting it out.

"I can't think of a thing," he finally said.

"So, are we in agreement? We will discontinue operations for the time being and see where this economic tragedy goes?" Williams leaned back in his seat, measuring the expressions on the other faces.

Irwin and Donovan both nodded in agreement.

"I'll have Cheryl put together a press release and submit it to the papers and our webmaster. Scott, can you make sure that everyone knows to contact their respective clients and pass the word to them?"

"Absolutely, Jim. I'll take care of it."

"I'll address the troops," Ed announced, "Scott if you want to follow me, we'll just make an announcement here in a little while to everyone at once. Say, in about thirty minutes?"

"That will work for me. When will the shutdown be in effect? How long do we want to give everyone to prepare for it?"

The elder pair looked at each other, considering the use of the term "prepare" in the question. They needed to be sure everyone had an opportunity to be ready for the rough road ahead.

"Two weeks?" Ed asked Jim.

"Yes, I think that would be good enough. We'll cease operations here in two weeks, but we can afford to pay everyone until the end of June. Well, unless things get worse."

"Alright, then," Scott said as he stood, "Give me a call when you are ready to make the announcement."

The trio split up and Scott began spreading the word among the employees about the meeting. He decided it best not to reveal details, but to simply ask everyone to meet in the main conference area.

About half an hour later the entire Williams and Donovan team came together in the large expanse of the office at the far end. The open area had been set aside for this purpose; assembling the team for parties, promotion announcements and the like. It had always been associated with good times and positive messages. That would change today.

Once everyone was gathered, Ed stepped to the center of the group and raised his voice.

"Can I have your attention? Attention, please."

The conversations subsided as consideration turned to the gentleman up front.

"Thank you all for taking a moment to listen to what we have to say. I'll be brief and then Scott has something he needs to tell you as well.

"Now, I know you have all been affected by the recent economic landslide that we've had here in the U.S. Jim and I have been watching things carefully, as have Scott and most of you. There is no surprise here, folks. The economy is deep in the toilet. We feel it's going to get worse before it gets better.

"Due to that fact, our client base has decided it is in their best interests to put projects on hold. I don't blame them. It would be a bad business move to continue most of our projects at this time. So, what does this mean on a personal level?

"In light of the current situation, Jim, Scott, and I have discussed our options. We feel that it is in the best interests of Williams and Donovan to stop operations, temporarily, until the economy has had time to recover and our customers feel comfortable resuming their work."

A light whispered murmur passed through the crowd; almost phantom-like as it could be heard, but a source couldn't be discerned.

"Please, let me continue," Donovan said, "We, the partners, want you to understand that this decision is not made out of hand. We've considered every possible option we could think of that would ensure a paycheck for everyone today, but also a job tomorrow. This is the best option we feel we have to guarantee both.

"So, effective in two weeks, this firm will cease all operations until such time as the economy can support our work again.

"Now, you know that Jim and I have always said this group was like extended family to us. You also know that we feel like family should take care of each other. So, we have agreed to loosen the purse strings a bit. Every employee will be paid a full salary until the end of the month of June. I would strongly suggest that you use the advances wisely, since the future is very uncertain right now. Boys and girls, set your houses in order. Scott?"

Donovan stepped aside and Scott took center stage. Following a hard swallow and a caring gaze across the faces of the staff members, he spoke.

"Well, this isn't how I imagined my first big speech to the team. I was hoping it would be more positive and upbeat, but you play the hand you're dealt, I guess.

"As soon as we disperse, I need all project leads to contact your respective clients and let them know that we will be stopping operations. Someone will be here to answer questions, but we will not be fully staffed until this all blows over."

In his mind Scott wondered if it would ever blow over. Could there be a reboot to the economy, or would there be something new to come out of all this?

"If you have any questions, please let me know. I'll answer them the best I can. If I can't answer them, I'll find someone who can.

"Guys, I know this is a hard blow to everyone, myself included. We will get through this. It has been a pleasure working with you all so far. I am looking forward to working with you more when this is all over. Stay alert. Play it smart. Take care of yourselves. If you need me, call."

The group began to shuffle away, back to the desks and cubicles that each called home for a few hours each day. There was a solemn feel to the room that didn't exist before the announcement. It was strange; everyone knew what was coming, but to have it actually, formally announced, was devastating. Scott began to realize that the office was a microcosm of the world outside.

For generations, people had looked at bad news with blinders on. If you don't acknowledge it, it will go away. If you ignore it, it didn't happen. Then, when the facts can no longer be ignored, those same people run to their "safe space" and cry; desperate for a return to the normal routine, but unable to get back there. They shut down and become utterly useless. He was already seeing this happen among his coworkers.

As he made his way back to his desk, Scott could hear the panicked calls home and the desperation in the voices of several people as they passed the news to family and friends.

There were a few that seemed to be taking it in stride, but most of those were acting like it was a minor issue. After a couple of weeks off with pay, the world would right itself and everything would be fine. Scott recalled how that similar attitude was popular at the outbreak of the Civil War. People would actually gather at the battlefields to picnic and watch the war they thought would be over in a few weeks like it was a football game or something.

As he passed Chad's office, he noticed the man sitting, almost dumbfounded, and staring blankly at his computer screen.

"You okay, man?" Scott asked.

"Hmm? Oh, yeah. I'm good," he said as he turned to face Irwin, "You really think it will get worse?"

"I don't know. I hope not. But I tend to hope for the best and prepare for the worst, then take what comes," it was at least partially true, Scott thought.

"You think I should cancel the order for my new golf clubs?" Chad asked.

"Yeah, I think I would."

Chapter Twelve

Call for Help

May 23rd

As Scott shut his terminal down, he stood and grabbed his jacket. He made his way down the main aisle, through the darkened office space toward the partner's offices. The workplace was almost devoid of life, save the corner offices where Ed and Jim remained. Almost all the other staff had gone home. He could hear Rachel putting her things away and getting ready to leave as Cheryl was speaking to the partners.

"I'm heading home," he said with a slight yawn, "I'll see you all tomorrow."

"Be careful out there," Ed replied.

"Be very careful," Jim said, "Things are starting to go sideways." He motioned to the television on his office wall. The images were from one of the local stations, apparently from one of the news helicopters.

Scott leaned in a little to better see what was happening. There, on the screen, was a crowd of people in the street amid burning cars and broken glass. It looked like one of those scenes from the Rodney King riots years ago.

"Is that happening here?" Scott asked, a mild tone of disbelief in his voice.

Williams gestured to the window where the glow of flames could clearly be seen across town.

"People stopped getting their money and there are a lot of pissed off folks out there that want their government funding. They are taking it out on anyone who comes close. Keep your head on a swivel, Scott. If you can't come in tomorrow, don't worry about it."

"You think it will get that bad?" Scott was still stunned that something like that could happen in Nashville.

Ed stepped into the conversation.

"Son, downtown Nashville has always had a high crime rate. Now they just have an excuse. It will get worse before morning. Hopefully everyone will have their frustrations vented by tomorrow and they'll cool off. Honestly, I'm not that optimistic, but I've been wrong before."

"Stick to the major streets and interstates as best you can. Those are still moving smoothly, right now. That'll get you home without taking you directly through harm's way…for the most part," Jim suggested.

"Alright," Scott muttered, "I'll let you know if I can't make it tomorrow. Goodnight, everyone."

Scott clutched his jacket a little tighter and headed for the elevators. Rachel was already waiting at the doors when he arrived.

"I thought you'd already gone," he said.

"I wish," she said with a tired smile, "I stayed a little later so I could get some extra project files finished up for Cheryl."

The elevator doors slid open, and Scott motioned for Rachel to enter the little box.

"Did you see the news broadcast in Jim's office?"

"Cheryl told me what's going on. Surreal, huh?"

"Yeah," Scott thought about his route home. Then it occurred to him that Rachel lived just a few miles away from Franklin herself.

"Um, not to be nosy," he started, "but are you going to be okay on your drive home? You live out toward Leipers Fork, right?"

"Yeah. Actually, between Leipers Fork and Franklin," she smiled again, "I think I'll be fine. I usually take I-65 down and then cut across Concord Road and bypass Franklin."

"You said 'usually.' Are you going a different route today?"

"I need to grab a few things before I go home, I'll stop by the grocery store before I head out of town. It shouldn't take long."

She smiled at him with a little twinkle in her eyes.

"Don't worry, Mr. Executive. I'll be fine. Thank you for worrying about me, though."

Scott felt a little embarrassed. She knew he was interested in her. Just then the doors parted, and the couple stepped out.

"Well," he said, searching for the right words, "Um, I guess I'll see you tomorrow. Right?"

"Yep."

"Okay. Be careful. If you need me, just call. I'm not that far away. I'll be there in just a few minutes," he patted his pockets fumbling for a business card or scrap piece of paper, "Hang on and I'll give you my number."

"I already have it in my phone. I have everyone in the office added to my contacts. Don't worry. I'll call if I need anything," She sheepishly grinned, "You be careful too. I want to see you bright eyed and bushy tailed tomorrow morning, young man."

They parted ways and headed to their cars. As Rachel pulled out of her parking place Scott couldn't help but sit and watch her until she disappeared from sight. He was genuinely worried about her. She would be fine, though. Nothing ever happened in Franklin like it did in Nashville. Besides, she lived outside of town in the country. Nobody would ever go out that far to cause trouble.

He started the BMW and pulled out onto the street. As he reached the elevated overpasses of the interstate he could see several columns of smoke across the city. Much of it was around the western downtown area, but some was to the south, probably around the fairgrounds. That was in Berry Hill.

That part of town had a very poor population and was prone to high crime rates anyway. Scott was sure that with the cessation of money coming in, many of the residents there were probably on a tear. Unfortunately, his route home carried him along the western edge of those neighborhoods. Maybe it hadn't gotten out of hand yet. Maybe he could just cruise right through and go home. Maybe, but no.

Despite it being after rush hour, traffic was unexpectedly light when he first got on the interstate. There was usually a little more to fight with even at this hour. Most of the commuters had probably stayed home or left early when things began to develop. That made sense to him.

As he neared the Wedgewood exit, he noticed people running across the interstate with baseball bats and sticks. A few drivers had been dumb enough to stop on the road and now their vehicles were ablaze as rioters filled the surrounding streets. He didn't want to run anyone down, but he didn't want to wind up like the others either.

Seeing the approaching sports car, a group of angry people gathered along the side of the road and began moving toward Scott. He stomped the pedal and began to accelerate, hoping nobody would be stupid enough to jump in front of him.

Rocks, bottles and other debris hurtled toward the little car, but amazingly nothing found its mark. He bolted past the area and headed farther south, scanning the damaged and smoking remains of vehicles as he passed; hoping none of them were Rachel's. Behind one car he thought he saw someone lying on the ground, but he passed so quickly he couldn't be sure.

As he scanned the roads, he saw a police car engulfed in flames as the lights still tried to flash atop the roof. Everywhere around it was debris and flames. The area had gone nuclear over the course of the past few hours.

Within a few seconds he could see the overpasses of the I-440 interchange. All around it sat abandoned cars and a couple of box vans. A tractor trailer lay flipped on its side against the exposed stone wall of the northbound lanes.

Scott was so distracted by the imagery that he almost didn't see the Molotov cocktail dropping from the overpass above him. Catching it out of the corner of his eye he jogged left, narrowly missing another car as the 40-ounce beer bottle smashed into the windshield of the car behind him. A pileup ensued and cars scattered across all lanes under the bridges.

"This is crazy," Scott muttered under his breath, "These people have lost their minds!" His phone rang, startling him as he tried to desperately navigate the growing combat zone.

Pressing the button on his steering wheel, he opened the call over the Bluetooth connection.

"Irwin," he said with a tense voice. He was already doing nearly 90 miles per hour and was considering pushing the little car harder.

"Scott!" The voice on the other end was James Evans, and he sounded desperate.

"James? What's up? You okay?"

"Hell no, man! My whole neighborhood has gone to hell and I gotta get out of here!"

"I hear you. I'm on 65 trying to get home now. There are pissed off people everywhere!"

"Man, I hate to ask, but is there any way you can pick my ass up?"

Scott's heart sank. He didn't want to go back through all that again. He could be home in just a few minutes. In the background, amplified by the surround sound speakers in the car's cockpit, he could clearly hear shouting and gunfire from Evans' neighborhood. It sounded close.

"You can't get out?"

"The sons of bitches have blocked the streets. I can't get the car out across the ditches and vacant lots without getting stuck and I don't think anybody is going to offer to help me push it out."

"What about your roomie, he's got a truck, right?"

"Yeah, but he's also in Honduras. The truck is at the airport. Besides, I don't have a key for it anyway."

Scott struggled with the decision to go back through town and into the chaos that was his friend's neighborhood. Why the hell did he have to live there?

"Alright," he finally said, "Get what you can carry and make your way out the back and down the ramp to the interstate. I'm not coming up to the house, so grab what matters most and meet me there. Got it?"

"Got it."

"You'll have to leave a lot behind. I'm in the Beemer. No room for totes full of gear."

"No worries. Just hurry up and get your ass over here."

"On my way. Move your ass."

Scott ended the call and headed for the Armory Drive exit. He crossed over Interstate 65 and then doubled back, all the while cursing under his breath. It infuriated him to know he had to go all the way across town to get Evans, but he also knew if he didn't Evans would probably be dead soon. At the very least he would be beaten nearly to that point and the house ransacked. The last time Irwin had been there, Evans had quite a lot of gear and ammunition stocked in the little residence. His roommate and landlord, Tim Willis, was in a similar shape.

Tim was an engineer as well, but he traveled a lot overseeing power generation and water purification projects in third world countries. His latest project must have taken him abroad before things went haywire. All that gear, ammunition, radios, and firearms would have to be sacrificed to get Evans clear of the area.

"*What a waste*," Irwin thought as he accelerated toward downtown and the Wedgewood area again. Though the highways were becoming thick with rioters and abandoned cars, they were still more passable than most of the side streets that Irwin could see.

As he weaved his way through all the debris on the road, he noticed a figure step out from behind a truck in the southbound lanes, behind the concrete dividers. Before Scott could react, a large rock smashed into the backend of his precious BMW.

"No!" He shouted, "You sons of bitches!"

He blasted through and soon was swinging around the western half of downtown on I-65. The on ramps at Charlotte and Church were packed with vehicles and ambulances as people crammed themselves onto the pavement trying to get out of the central downtown area. Scott slowed considerably as he navigated the thick traffic.

He finally made the sweeping bend where I-65 and I-40 split, bringing him within a few seconds of Rosa Parks Boulevard, the exit to go to Evans' house. To the right, the neighborhood burned. To the left, in the Germantown area, he could see a heavier police presence, attempting to form a defensive line.

Scott pulled to a stop on the edge of the ramp, scanning the area for his friend. Irwin left the car in gear and proceeded to call Evans.

Half a ring later Evans' voice came over the phone, heavily winded and distressed.

"Where are you?" Evans said in a breathy whisper.

"I'm on the side of the ramp. Where are you?"

"Okay. I see you. Pull over at the old gas station. I'll meet you there."

The line went dead as Scott began cursing under his breath again. He shut the headlights off, easing up the remainder of the ramp and into the fenced in parking area of an old gas station that had last seen glory as a car repair business. Some of the failed repairs still littered the parking lot.

Evans appeared around the back corner of the building, with a rifle in his hand and another slung over his shoulder. In his other hand he carried a pair of ammo cans. He crouched as he ran, exposing the backpack he had slung over his shoulder.

Irwin popped the trunk, and Evans began shoving things in. He slipped alongside the car and opened the passenger side door, plopping unceremoniously into the leather seat.

"Get out of here. Fast," he said flatly.

"Did you get everything you needed?"

"I got everything I could. The rest goes with the contingency plan."

"The what?"

The front door to "The Ritz" burst open as a pair of young men entered waving pistols from side to side. They checked the front room and began moving toward the back of the small house as additional men entered the front door.

Around back the privacy fence, which had dozens of carpet tack strips nailed along the inside top edge, shredded fingers trying to gain entry. Soon the wooden gate was bearing the brunt of an increasingly angry assault. After a heavy battering, it gave way and more people entered the back yard, torching Evans' car as they went.

On the kitchen table sat a little note that read: *It's all yours. Enjoy it while you can.*

From the back bedroom a voice called out, "Hey, man! Look here! I done found the shit!"

As the second man entered the room, the first lifted an ammo can, tripping the switch beneath and completing the circuit under the table. The room erupted as several pounds of carefully concealed jugs of black powder ignited via the exposed filaments of small incandescent bulbs.

The tiny house shuddered and crumpled, trapping everyone inside and showering the backyard with debris.

"What the hell was that?" Scott shouted as they sped away down the interstate once again.

"Contingency plan," Evans said.

Chapter Thirteen

Shoot and Move

May 23rd

"You blew up the house?" Scott was almost shouting as they barreled down the interstate.

"After our meeting with you back in Lewisburg, Tim and I decided it was time to start slowly bugging out. He moved pretty much everything he had back to his family farm in Wheel, and I started carrying stuff back home to my dad's place. The only things left behind were some ammo crates, old radio equipment and furniture. All the important stuff has been gone for days," Evans said.

"But why blow up the house?"

"If we had been caught there, they would have killed us. Eventually, we would have run out of ammo or time, or both. They had already been sending people to case the house over the past few weeks, so they expected to at least get radios and electronics. That house was a target. We just turned it into a baited trap. The way we looked at it, we were living up to our part of the 'Golden Rule.' We were doing unto them what they would have done to us."

"That's crazy. You've lost your mind, man."

Scott turned his attention back to the drive ahead. Zigzagging through the maze of vehicles and debris they approached the Broadway exit.

"Hang on, I want to try something," Scott said as Evans clutched the rifle.

The BMW slipped off the crowded asphalt and raced up the ramp onto Broadway. There was considerable traffic, but it was predominantly headed toward the interstate; the opposite direction Irwin was going.

They followed Broadway until they reached the West End Avenue split and veered right. West End would take them away from all the Vanderbilt hospital complex and farther away from Wedgewood.

Though he had to travel at a slower pace, he was able to cover more ground since the area was more affluent and had far fewer people trying to block the roads and carjack vehicles.

Within a few tense minutes, they were able to pick up on I-440 and swing back toward I-65. Police cars passed frequently, their lights and sirens tearing through the evening as law enforcement tried desperately to gain control over a worsening situation.

From I-440 they swung down the ramp onto I-65 and were immediately back in the log jam of cars and trucks headed south. Weaving and dodging through traffic, even using the shoulder frequently, Irwin was gradually approaching Harding Place. He felt a little better since the bulk of the violence was behind him, but he could still see emergency vehicles on the side roads everywhere and there were numerous accidents up and down the interstate.

Franklin Pike was a parking lot. Hundreds, perhaps thousands, of cars had tried to use the surface street to bypass the clogged interstate only to create another jam on a smaller avenue. It would take much longer to go that way than using the multiple lanes Scott had chosen, and that was moving slowly enough.

Finally, he slipped off the interstate at Old Hickory Boulevard and made it onto Highway 31, which took him through the wealthy Brentwood area and directly into Franklin. From there he could connect to Highway 431 and go almost all the way to the house.

Other than thick traffic, the remainder of the drive was fairly uneventful. Franklin typically had traffic issues, but they were never as bad as Nashville on any given day.

"So," James began, "What's the plan?"

"I figure we will go to my house and ride out the rest of the evening. See what it looks like tomorrow."

"Alright. What if tomorrow isn't any better?"

"One day at a time, man. I've got food and supplies stashed at home. We can hold out there
for a little while."

The duo finally reached Highway 96 where Scott turned right for a few yards before crossing into the northern end of his subdivision. Within a few minutes, they were pulling into the driveway at the end of Battery Court. A wave of relief swept over both men. The garage door began to open, exposing Scott's 4-door Jeep and several shelves of bottled water and pails of food. He pulled in beside the Jeep, parking the little car in its traditional spot.

Scott got out and began to survey the car's exterior. As he reached the rear quarter panel the massive dent was all he could see. His beloved BMW was scarred.

James proceeded to remove items from the trunk but noticed his friend's somber expression and peered around the side of the vehicle.

"Damn. That's a dent!" he said, "Sorry about that, man."

Scott tried not to dwell on the damage, but it was huge. He'd have to call his insurance company in the morning and see if they would cover something like this. He didn't know if social unrest was part of his policy or not.

"I'll pay for the repair," Evans said, "It's the least I can do after what you risked coming for me."

Irwin pressed the button on the garage door opener and sealed the room up once again.

"If you want, you can just load your stuff in the Jeep," he finally said, "We'll head down to Lewisburg tomorrow and I'll drop you off at your dad's house."

"Thanks. I appreciate it."

Both of them went inside the house and sat down. Scott still wore his white shirt and tie from work, though it bore some unsightly sweat stains now.

"I think I'm going to grab a shower," he said finally, "I just want to go to bed."

"I hear you. Where should I take my clothes and stuff?"

"Down the hall, first bedroom on the left. It's all yours," Scott said as he headed toward his own bedroom.

As he gathered some clean clothes, he thought he could hear a faint popping sound outside.

Not terribly close, mind you, but close enough to hear.

He laid his cell phone on the bed and proceeded to empty his other pockets. Dropping his keys on the night stand his phone abruptly rang. It was his father.

"Hello?"

"Son?"

"Hey, dad. What's up?"

"We've just been watching the news reports from Nashville. Are you okay?"

"Yeah," he said with an exasperated sigh, "I had to go pick up James and we just got to the house a minute ago. We're both fine."

"That's good. I'm glad to hear it."

"Yeah. Say, I'm going to grab a shower and get some sleep. We'll be heading to Lewisburg tomorrow. I'll see you then, okay?"

"Okay, son. Get some rest. Be careful."

He ended the call and tossed the phone back on the bed. Irwin grabbed his clothes and headed for the master bathroom. Just as he reached the doorway the phone rang again.

With a grumble he turned back to look at the device, debating whether or not to answer the call. He decided, given the current situation, to go ahead and postpone the bath.

He looked at the screen, not recognizing the number, and was hesitant to answer but decided to anyway.

"Hello?"

"Scott?" The voice sounded familiar, but there was considerable background noise, and the caller was nearly whispering.

"Yeah?"

"It's Rachel. Are you in Franklin?"

"Yeah, where are you?"

"I'm trapped near the Piggly Wiggly on Columbia Avenue. Hang on."

Through the speaker on the phone Scott could hear the familiar sounds of indistinct shouting and gunfire. It was a repeat of the call he had gotten earlier from James.

"Scott, I need you. I'm scared and I don't know what to do. There are people all around and they have guns and weapons. They ransacked the grocery store and started beating people up…," the agitation in her voice grew as she spoke. Scott could tell she was crying into the phone.

"Shhhh," he said, "Calm down, okay? Look, you need to stay quiet and still. Where can I find you?"

"I'm hiding at the old Boys and Girls Club building on Columbia Avenue. Please hurry, things are getting crazy out here."

"Okay, that's the big building beside the Carter House, right?"

"Yeah."

"Can you go to the police station? It's on the other side of the shopping center from you."

"It's on fire. I heard a lot of gunshots coming from there too. Please hurry."

"It's what?" Scott's voice echoed through the hallway of his home, prompting James to come running.

"Did you say the police station is on *fire*?"

"Yeah. I gotta go. There are people coming this way. Please hurry. I don't know what's going to happen if they find us here."

Rachel abruptly ended the call, leaving a stunned Scott Irwin holding the phone.

"Unbelievable," was all he could mutter.

"What's up?"

"Grab your shit. We have to go."

As they loaded their rifles into the Jeep Scott briefed James on the call and they decided on an approach to the area. One word continued to echo in Scott's mind from the call: "us."

They piled into the vehicle and opened the garage door again, peering back out into the night with a pair of loaded rifles and pistols and ammunition to spare.

Scott opened the center console and checked the AR pistol. He pulled it out, unfolded the buffer tube and attached the barrel, then slammed a magazine in and ran the bolt. Hearing the mechanical slam of the operation, James looked at his friend with a grin.

"Ooh! New toy? When did you get that?"

"I've had it for a couple of weeks, but I haven't had time to run it yet. Everything went sideways before I could get it to the range."

"Well, there's no time like the present."

"Yeah, I guess," Scott muttered as he started the engine, "I just hope I don't have to actually *hit* anything with it tonight."

They pulled out of the garage and began making their way through the twisted side streets of his neighborhood. A few minutes later they were on Lewisburg Avenue and were about to cross over Columbia Avenue. Scott slowed, using the emergency brake to keep the taillights off, before making the turn onto the cross street and killed the headlights. To his right he could see the glow of flames from the direction of the police department and all around the neighborhood gunfire popped endlessly.

He sent Rachel a quick text for her to be ready and then hit the gas. The Jeep bounced across the intersection and onto the dead-end street of West Fowlkes. James watched out the passenger side window with his rifle at the ready, but all he saw was destruction.

The Piggly Wiggly parking lot was littered with cars, shopping carts, garbage and debris, and about a half dozen bodies. Many of the lights had been shot out, making visibility difficult, so he couldn't tell if the bodies were dead or just unconscious. They didn't have time to find out either.

Scott turned left, through the massive chain link gates that surrounded the old two-story building. A thicket of trees obscured the neighborhood and the Carter House to the south while a dense patch of overgrown shrubs lined the sides of the building. He stopped on the south side and scanned the gravel parking area for movement, the small AR firmly in his grip.

James unbuckled his seatbelt and said, "Keep it running. I'll take a look."

He hopped out and began to scan the area calling Rachel's name as loudly as he could without screaming it. Finally, the bushes near the building rustled as a pair of figures emerged. Rachel was in front and behind her came a second girl. A blonde wearing a flannel shirt that showed off an incredible amount of cleavage, and tiny tan shorts that showed off even more.

"Scott?" Rachel called to the Jeep.

"Get in. We have to move," he replied.

James jumped in and assumed his position in the passenger seat again as the girls quickly leapt in the back. A brilliant flash bathed the area in a bluish white light as one of the nearby transformers exploded, most likely from being shot out.

As they sped toward the gate on the Columbia Avenue side, a pair of figures appeared on the sidewalk across the street.

"Get down!" James shouted as Irwin turned the vehicle to the right, exposing himself to the armed duo.

As if time had slowed down, he could see the men raising weapons, one a rifle and the other with some sort of bottle. Irwin jutted the pistol out the window and fired three shots, scattering the would-be attackers as the rifleman fired his own volley. Neither man hit their marks.

The bottle arced high in the air and fell to earth, breaking apart in the middle of the road with a flash of flame. Too far away to be a threat to the Jeep or its occupants, but a sign that these people were serious in their determination to hurt or kill.

As they cautiously made their way through the narrow side streets James and Scott tried to keep a watchful eye on the yards and houses on either side. James commented on how the area around the police station was nearly devoid of activity, save the men on the sidewalk.

"I was at least expecting to see some sort of police presence. Anything, you know?"

"Things started getting quiet not long after I called. We could hear all the shouting and shooting getting farther away, like it was headed back toward the interstate or something," Rachel said.

James turned around to face the ladies in the back seat. It was then that he saw the face of the second girl.

"Whitney?"

The blonde looked at him with an expression of confusion for a second.

"Yeah?"

"Are you okay?" he asked with a sly smile.

"I guess. Do I know you?"

"I'm James. James Evans. I come into the restaurant a couple of times a week. You've been my server a few times."

She looked at him for a second longer before it registered.

"Oh! Yeah, you work in Nashville, right?"

"Yep. This is my friend Scott Irwin."

Scott glanced in the rear-view mirror briefly with a nod.

"Hey."

"Hi."

"Scott, do you remember Whitney? She's a server at the..."

"Peaks, yeah, I kind of figured that out from the clothes and all. Did you just get off work?"

"Yeah. I was going home to put on some actual clothes and needed to grab a couple of things at the store. Then all this happened," she stared out the window, "Where are we going, anyway?"

"Back to my place for the night. Don't worry, there's plenty of room for everyone. We'll get a fresh perspective in the morning."

As they approached Scott's subdivision they could make out a glow in the distance.

Chapter Fourteen

The Battle of Franklin

May 23rd – 24th

The flames from the massive Church of the City campus could probably be seen for miles.

The structure was totally engulfed along with many of the homes nearby.

Scott turned left onto South Royal Oaks and passed the gated Burghley Place subdivision. Many of the homes there showed signs of vandalism and a couple had flames lapping at the windowsills. The gates were smashed down and an older model Toyota SUV sat astride the tangled iron bars.

His heart began to pound as he thought about his home, just through the trees to the north of Burghley Place and the south of the church. It was sandwiched between a bad spot and a worse spot.

He could see, as did the others, several people running up and down the sidewalks and across yards, looting, fighting, and vandalizing anything that got in their way. The world had finally lost its mind and the destitute had unleashed on the gainful.

Scott made the final turn and stopped cold at the end of his cul-de-sac. His neighborhood was in chaos. Every house was in shambles. He slowly crept down the street with his pistol pointed out the window.

"What are you doing?" James demanded.

"It can't be. It just can't be," Scott stammered, "Everything. Everything I had. It was here."

He slowed in front of the burning hulk of his home. The garage door had already dropped from the framing, exposing his beloved BMW inside. The car, or what was left of it, sat in its spot, flames boiling out the convertible roof as chunks of drywall and joists dropped on top of it all.

"My car. I loved that car," Scott carried on. He put the Jeep in Park and stepped out into the street. He was so fixated on the scene before him he almost didn't hear James.

"Heads up! We've got company!" James called to his friend, shaking him back to the moment.

Around the corner of his closest neighbor's house stepped a small cluster of people. He couldn't tell who they were, but he could tell they were not in a good mood.

As the group approached, Scott recognized one of the closer men as Robert Haverson, a business owner a couple of houses up from his own. With him were his wife, Sandra, an older lady from up the street, Mrs. Davis, and a younger woman who had only recently moved into the neighborhood.

"Bob? Bob, are you okay?" Scott asked with the little AR dangling at his side.

"It's all gone, Scott," the man said, "They destroyed it all. They beat the piss out of me and

Phil down there and left us for dead, then stole our stuff and set the houses ablaze."

"Who? Who did this?"

"I don't know who they were, Scott. All I know is they have a real problem with successful people, and they are on a rampage tonight. They all had masks and were wearing black clothes. I couldn't tell who anyone was."

"Which way did they go?" Scott asked. His anger was getting the best of him.

"They headed over toward the interstate. There's a lot of them, Scott. They have guns and bats and…" the man glanced down and finally saw the pistol in Scott's grip, then turned and saw Evans with his rifle at low ready.

A few hundred yards to the east, past Highway 431, the sky suddenly changed from nearly black to brilliant orange. One of the gas stations closer to the interstate had just exploded.

Immediately following the eruption, they could hear car alarms blaring as the inventory at the Dodge dealership took damage. The Ford dealership was next on the hit list as the mob sought out financial justice.

"Do you have a vehicle that still runs?"

"I think my Land Cruiser is still in decent shape," a petite lady said from the back of the group.

"Alright. Let's go see what we're dealing with. James?"

"Yeah, boss?"

"Keep an eye on things here. I'll be right back."

Irwin stepped to the Jeep and retrieved a fresh magazine from the vehicle, shoving it into the front left pocket of his slacks. He turned to the small group.

"Okay, Mrs. Davis, you and I are going to check on your vehicle. Bob, you're with us. The rest of you stay here with James. If it runs, we'll be back and then we will get out of here."

The three figures disappeared into the darkness of shadow, away from the glow of the flames boiling from Scott's home. They quietly made their way back to Davis' home and slipped into the garage.

"Where's your husband, Mrs. Davis?"

"He had surgery earlier this week in Nashville. I was going to go see him in the morning when all this happened," the elder lady became somewhat quiet before admitting, "I'm scared to death. I've seen a lot of things in my time, but I've never been this scared… not since the 60's when we lived in Birmingham, anyway."

As they got closer to the house Scott could hear voices coming from inside. The rattle of dishes and glass breaking were clear and distinct.

"Anyone else supposed to be in your house?"

"No. Nobody except the cat."

"Okay, you stay right here. I'll check it out. Do you have the keys?"

Mrs. Davis reached into her pocket and presented a pair of keys to Scott. He quickly tucked them away and headed to the house.

Irwin eased up beside the house and slowly peered into a window at the side. He could see shadows of movement inside but couldn't tell who it was or how many. He could hear two voices, but there could easily be others.

Slowly Irwin made his way around the house to the back door. Stepping up beside the garage entry door, he looked in. There was the Toyota, and it appeared to be in good shape. The door from the garage into the house was wide open and he could see movement down the hall.

He gripped the doorknob and began to turn the knob, having to exert considerably more force on it than he anticipated. It struck him as almost funny how the house was listed a few years earlier for over $400,000 and still suffered from the same problems as the old farmhouse did back home.

Just as the door opened with a muffled "pop" a figure approached the garage. The man was clad from head to toe in black and was carrying a sizeable box of jewelry and electronics. He headed directly for the vehicle and opened the back door, sliding the box in before heading back to the hallway. On his shoulder, Scott could make out a small circular patch with a white circle and what looked like a knife with a red point. He couldn't be totally sure. It didn't matter. These guys, whoever they were, had crossed the line.

Scott slipped quietly into the garage and made his way to the door. A few seconds later, one of the intruders stepped out and Scott pounded the slender figure across the side of the neck, sending him crashing to the floor. The strike to the Vagus nerve was rapid and powerful, but not lethal. These scumbags weren't worth going to jail for.

Hearing the ruckus, the second burglar called out, "You alright? What'd you do, fall?"

Getting no response, he began to make his way to the door. As he stepped in and looked at the crumpled figure on the floor he laughed.

"Dumbass. What did you do? Fall down the damn steps?" As he stepped onto the landing at the top of the steps in the garage, he caught a sudden flash of movement from his peripheral vision.

Before he could react, his vision flashed white and he crumpled to the floor on top of his friend.

The simple, but effective, move was quick and quiet, but there was no guarantee how long the men would be unconscious. Scott decided to take advantage of the moment and quickly grabbed some cable ties from the tool bench at the back of the garage. He zip-tied the men's ankles and wrists, then propped them against the posts of the landing where he used the last of the ties to secure them to the structure. Finally, he yanked the masks off of their heads and snapped a few quick pictures of the two men. He could pass these along to police who could handle their arrest and prosecution later. For now, it was time to get the SUV and move. He opened the garage door and started the engine, moving the vehicle quickly to the street and down to where the others waited.

"Get in," he said bluntly as he rolled to a stop.

The other two clamored into the truck and they rolled back down the street to Scott's house,

or what was left of it.

As they slowed to a stop Irwin noticed that Evans had his rifle squarely pointed at him. He rolled the window down and jutted his arm out.

"It's me," he called, "Stand down, man."

Evans lowered the rifle as Irwin put the vehicle in Park and got out.

"Time to move, everyone," he said, "Mrs. Davis, do you and Bob have any place you can go for the night?"

The pair looked at each other curiously for a minute.

"I have a daughter in Columbia. That's not too far away. We can probably stay there for the night. If that's okay with you, Mrs. Davis," Haverson said.

"Oh, that will be fine with me, if it's okay with her."

"Well, if nobody has any objections, I'd suggest you make tracks as soon as possible. Don't worry about getting anything from your homes. These people are coming back, and they seem to be organized in some way or another. It's not just a mob of angry people."

"How do you mean, Scott?" Evans asked.

"Patches on their sleeves. Looked like some kind of group or organization. I didn't get a good look at it, but I have pictures of the goons in Mrs. Davis's house," He stepped over to his own vehicle and opened the driver's side door, "Saddle up folks. It may be a long night."

"Are you going to follow us to Columbia, Scott?" Haverson asked.

"No, sir. I'm heading to Lewisburg. I already have my plan laid out. Good luck to you all. Be careful out there."

The two groups took their positions in the vehicles and began to head out of the subdivision. Scott followed the first vehicle as far as South Royal Oaks Boulevard where they turned right and headed toward Maury County.

Scott watched their taillights disappear as he sat at the intersection.

"What are you waiting for, man? We need to get out of here."

"Gas," was all he said.

"What?"

"I'm gonna need gas in this thing."

Chapter Fifteen

Pay at the Pump

May 24th

"No, man," Evans began, "You gotta be shitting me. You seriously want to get gas? Now? Here?"

"Isn't there someplace along the way we could stop?" the tone in Rachel's voice was nervous and distressed, "How much do you have?"

"I might have enough to make it home, but that's about it. I have been driving the BMW a lot more this week, so I filled it up on the way home yesterday. I haven't driven the Jeep in a couple of days, and I was planning on topping it off this weekend," Scott was evaluating his options as he sat there, burning more fuel and wasting time.

He didn't notice that the group from the Burghley Place area had been on the move and were now approaching his Jeep from the rear.

"Look, I'm just thinking that if the station at the interstate ramp is still in good shape, we could grab a few gallons to be sure we don't have to walk and be on our way down 65, okay? I don't think any of us want to walk tonight."

Rachel spoke up from behind him, "No, none of us want to walk, Scott, but there must be another gas station along the way. Do we have enough to make it to exit 46? There are three or four stations there."

"Guys…," Whitney said softly.

"Yeah, we could probably make it that far, but I'd feel better starting off with a full tank if we can. That way if something happens and we have to change plans…"

"Guys!" Whitney exclaimed, "We need to go…somewhere…now!"

James looked back at the girl's anxious expression, and he realized what had her so upset. Around the curve in the road behind them he could see shadowy figures mingling among the bushes and landscaping.

Scott switched his gaze to the side of the vehicle where he saw another figure low-run to an adjacent building. He could clearly see the rifle in the man's grip.

They began to spread out and advance on the Jeep and its occupants.

"Get 'em," someone shouted as bottles, rocks and other items hurtled toward the four wheel drive.

James brought his pistol up and pressed the trigger as Irwin stomped the accelerator. The Jeep swung hard to the right amid a flurry of gunfire and hurtling debris, both incoming and outgoing.

The round went high, completely missing the crowd, but it got the point across well enough.

The group scattered across yards and parking lots as James dropped back in his seat.

As they began to pull away, he could hear more gunfire behind him. Evans hung his head back out the window and began returning fire, not really seeing who he was shooting at, but more as a covering fire to help them get away. The Jeep lurched and bounced as they raced southward. Finally reaching the Peytonsville Road intersection, they swung into a gas station on the opposite corner. Scott jumped out and headed for the pump.

Inside they could see the attendant staring wildly at them. He was clearly nervous and that, in turn, made them nervous as well.

Scott quickly filled the tank and put the cap back on as the man stuck his head out the door.

"You don't need anything else, do ya?"

Scott looked back across the vehicle at the man, "No, sir. We just needed some gas. We're going home now."

"Good. I'm shutting down and getting the hell outta here myself. You folks be careful."

With that the man stepped back through the door and locked it behind him. As the Jeep turned to head back down Lewisburg Pike Scott noticed the interior lights go out.

It was time to go home.

Scott decided to stick to Lewisburg Pike for the drive in. It would be less travelled than the interstate, though it would be a slower speed, but it would carry him closer to the family farm. The farm was situated about 5 miles outside of Lewisburg proper and was very secluded. He punched up a call on Bluetooth to let his parents know they were on the way and bringing company.

"Slow down when you get to Pottsville," his father warned, "They have a security checkpoint up there."

"Security? For what?"

"Sherriff's Department set it up to screen troublemakers out. We've all been listening to the scanners and news reports. There are a lot of people on the move out of Nashville and Franklin because of all the rioting. Show them your license and tell them where you're going. I'll make a call to let them know you're on your way.

"Since you have four in the car, I'm guessing you are in your Jeep?"

"Yeah, I lost my BMW. And the house."

Scott's father almost asked for details, but thought it best to wait until he knew they were all safe.

"Well, you're almost home. You can fill me in when you get here. I'll have your mom get some dinner ready for you."

Dinner. Scott hadn't even thought about eating. Everything had been so chaotic he forgot that the last meal he'd had was several hours before.

"Thanks, Dad. I'll see you soon."

"Be careful, son."

Scott ended the call from the Jeep as his father began dialing from home. Operating such a large farm in an agricultural community had served to keep the Irwin family in contact with numerous people in official capacities. The county and city mayors as well as many of the council members and commissioners were long time friends of the family, as was the Sherriff and the Chief of Police.

Within minutes, word was out to the checkpoint to be aware of the group coming in and their destination.

Soon the Jeep approached Pottsville, a small community just along the line between Marshall and Maury Counties. Its primary claim to fame was Marcy Jo's Meal House, a small restaurant directly at the intersection of Highways 431 and 99. Scott began to slow down and look for the checkpoint.

As he rounded the bend of the road, he could see the flashing lights around the intersection ahead that led to Chapel Hill. A considerable line of cars waited as officers checked each vehicle and its occupants.

Finally, the Jeep pulled up to the first officer and Scott rolled his window down.

"Identification and destination," the officer said as he scanned the back seat with his

flashlight.

Scott produced the small card and announced his name. As he was pointing to James the flashlight panned across the cabin to hit Evans in the face.

"This is…" he started.

"James Evans! What are you doing, man?" the officer said with a smile.

Peering through the glare of the beam James asked, "John? Is that you?"

"Yeah. Things getting pretty shitty in Nashville, huh?"

"You wouldn't believe it if I told you," he replied, "We're trying to get to Scott's family just down the road."

"Yeah, we got word from dispatch earlier to expect Mr. Irwin and some friends. I didn't know you'd be in here with him. Say, you bringing any guns or ammo in?"

Scott and James exchanged glances, unsure if they should say anything about the full-sized rifles they had tossed in the rear or the pistols under the seats and holstered under shirts.

"Why? You guys confiscating them?"

"Well, I'll tell you like this; if *you* have some, hang on to them. Things aren't just getting shitty in Nashville. I'm not going to ask again, so you folks just be on your way. Be careful out there."

"Okay," James replied, "Thanks, John."

The officer waved the vehicle forward and stepped up to the next in line. As they pulled away, they noticed a pickup truck on the shoulder with officers rummaging through the interior. On the ground, face down in the gravel, lay who they assumed was the driver; hog tied with zip-tie cuffs and apparently not very happy about it.

Just around the corner they crossed the Duck River at Hardison Mill and soon turned left toward the farm. Travelling the narrow black top road was a stark contrast to the surface streets of Nashville and the interstates they had been on. It was so quiet. No fires, no abandoned vehicles, no rioters. Just quiet.

The Jeep pulled in at the garage and all four occupants rolled out. James and Scott began removing weapons and ammunition from the vehicle while the girls surveyed their surroundings.

Scott turned to Rachel and held out one of the rifles.

"Would you mind carrying this in for me? I have to get this ammo crate and these pistols."

She reluctantly reached out to collect the firearm with a painfully uncomfortable look on her

face.

"You okay?"

"Um, I'm not a gun person. I really don't feel comfortable holding this thing. What if it goes off?"

"As long as you don't put your finger here," he said pointing at the trigger, "you should be fine."

She shot him a look as if she were about to be nauseous but accepted the weapon anyway.

Scott removed the ammo box from the vehicle and said, "I'll tell you what, you take the box, and I'll take the rifle if it bothers you that much. But tomorrow, you're going to learn to shoot."

Rachel smiled and happily grabbed for the box before she realized how much it would weigh. With a resounding "Oomph" she bore the mass and began waddling toward the front porch.

The group gathered at the door and, as Scott was about to knock, the door swung open. Ben Irwin stood before them with a broad grin and a revolver on his hip.

"Thank God, you made it. Come on in. Supper's almost ready."

The weary quartet entered the room stacking rifles and ammo as they went and plopped down on the couches and chairs. As Whitney entered the doorway Ben's eyes popped a bit and he cut a glance at his son. Scott just smiled. He was already thinking the same thing: what will mom say?

"What's with the hog leg, Dad?" Scott said, gesturing to the .357 Magnum his father carried.

"Oh, well, you can't be too careful. Even out here. Police are thin enough on a good day. Lately they've been stretched to the limit. Lots of trouble since things turned bad.

"Who have you brought with you, son?"

Scott slumped back in the chair and began to make the introductions.

"Well, you know James. I had to pull him out of his neighborhood before his house exploded."

Ben's eyes popped again, "Okay, I want to hear that story later."

Scott smiled, as did James.

"This is Rachel Avery," he continued, "She is the receptionist at work. She and Whitney here ran into some trouble at the Piggly Wiggly, so we picked them up too.

"Last, but not least is Whitney…I'm sorry I have no idea what your last name is."

"Anderson," she said with a smile.

"Anderson. She's a server at Twin Peaks in Cool Springs."

Just then Carol, Scott's mother, entered the room with a big smile and announced that supper was ready. As they stood to go wash up and eat, she caught herself staring at the scantily clad blonde and then to her husband who just smiled.

They gathered at the table and enjoyed a home cooked meal like none before. Maybe it was the stress. Maybe it was the exhaustion. Maybe it was the fact that none of them had eaten for several hours. Maybe it was just that good to begin with. It didn't matter. They were alive and it was delicious.

After supper, they exchanged stories of the events of the day and updated the family on how things were falling apart in the bigger cities. Carol, the ever-present mom, asked if anyone needed any medical attention or had any injuries to speak of. They were all unscathed, besides some scratches and scrapes.

Carol turned her attention to Whitney. She couldn't stand it any longer and had to ask.

"Honey, do you need some clothes or anything? I might have something a little…warmer you can fit in."

"I'd appreciate it. Thank you."

Chapter Sixteen

Homecoming

May 25th

Rachel sat behind the folding table as Scott lectured her on the basics of firearm operation.

She was, at the very least, nervous about pulling the trigger for the first time.

He was trying his best to be supportive and encouraging but not water down the importance of learning the skill, for her own benefit, since the world had suddenly changed.

"I'm just really nervous, Scott. I've never shot a gun before. Those things kill people!"

"How many people did you see get beaten last night? How many people attacked us with bottles, sticks, rocks, and baseball bats yesterday? Those would have killed just as much as a rifle or handgun. They are all just tools and objects, until they find the wrong hands. It's the hands that kill, not the object."

"Okay. But I'm still nervous."

"That's okay. That's good, actually. It means you are aware of what you are doing, and you are paying attention. You're less likely to go all macho and do something stupid. That's why women are typically easier to teach to shoot than men. We already know it all," He cracked a reassuring smile that she reciprocated with that twinkle he loved to see in her eyes.

He worked with her most of the morning establishing eye dominance and sight picture, then moving on to grip and stance. Finally, he got her to shoot from a rest. She jumped and dropped the rifle to the tabletop covering her mouth as she did. She had missed the target entirely, but Irwin simply smiled.

"You okay?"

"Yeah," she said, "I just wasn't expecting it to jump like that. Did I hit it?"

"Not by a mile," Scott said with a grin, "Are you ready to try it again?"

"Yeah. Yeah, I am," she said with a look of grim determination.

On it would go through the afternoon. Rachel became considerably more comfortable with the prospect of shooting, but Scott doubted she would ever have the discipline to pull the trigger on another human being. He hoped she would never have a reason to.

Back at the house Carol and Whitney prepared for a trip into town. The younger girl came downstairs still wearing the jogging suit that Carol had pulled from storage. Carol could instantly tell she had shed herself of under garments.

"Would it be possible for me to wash out my things today? I can't stand wearing the same underwear for days. It just makes me feel nasty."

"We'll do a load of laundry when we get back. We'll be picking up some items for everyone else while we're out, so we might be gone a while. Are you comfortable in that?"

"It's fine," she said, "At least it has more material than the outfit they make us wear at work." Both of them chuckled.

Despite the suit having more fabric, it was incredibly snug on the buxom lass and, in a way, was actually more revealing than the shorts and flannel top. Particularly so when she was going commando.

Carol snapped up the list of items they would need from town and began heading to the truck. As she left the kitchen, she grabbed a Smith and Wesson J frame and tucked it in a side pocket of her purse. Whitney gave her an odd look.

"Times have changed, dear. We have to change with them," was all she said as she pushed open the door and stepped outside.

In the distance, toward the river, they could hear Scott and Rachel on the firing line. James was at the barn with a rifle slung over his shoulder talking on the phone to his father before helping Ben with chores. Whitney was a bit thunderstruck. She had never imagined herself in a compound like this before. She just wanted to go home. To her apartment and her classes and her clothes and her job that paid really well when she showed too much skin. She didn't want to be here…wherever "here" was.

"I'm fine, dad. No, we made it out fine, but there were a couple of close calls. Is everything okay at home?"

Evans' father was more concerned with his son's current health and safety than anything around the house. He admitted that there had been no trouble out that way but was eager to see James. Word had spread about a considerable problem in Shelbyville concerning the immigrant situation there.

In recent years the population of Somali refugees had exploded in the small town with many occupying a specific corner of public housing. Police would often refuse to patrol there before things went off the rails. Now the refugees were pushing Sharia Law into the community with impudence. It had gotten bad. At least that's what the rumors said.

Reports on the radio had begun to surface that TEMA, the emergency management branch on the state level, had begun accepting refugees at the recently annexed and refurbished GM and Nissan facilities. Resources were being diverted to the locations to provide medical aid and necessities as well as security. Soon, individuals and families from federal regions filled the facilities.

News reports in the federally controlled areas were deftly scrutinized and sanitized. No reports were allowed to air that presented the facts that the federal government was losing ground in places all across the country. It wasn't so much a secret as just something that wasn't to be discussed. Due to this simple measure, many people still blatantly held on to the notion that things were still essentially normal and everything would shake out in a few days.

"So, Whitney, tell me a bit about yourself," Carol said as the old pickup bounced along the blacktop lane.

"Well, what do you want to know?"

"Where are you from? Are you still in school? What are your dreams and aspirations?" The last question seemed a bit inappropriate after it rolled off Carol's tongue considering the current state of affairs. Perhaps it was a subconscious glimmer of hope.

"I grew up just outside of San Diego. I moved here a few months ago because I wanted to get into the music business. I'm enrolled in classes for business management right now, but my work schedule makes it tough to balance it all."

"Oh, so, do you sing?"

"Oh, no. No, I don't have any talent at all. I'm a horrible singer. I love music, though, and that's why I thought about the management route. I still get to be part of the business, but I don't have to step in front of a microphone."

"Well, I know Scott has a friend from high school with some musical connections in those kinds of circles. He might be able to get you some pointers or maybe even names. I hear it's a very competitive business."

"Yeah," Whitney sighed, "I'm not even sure if it *is* a business right now."

The trip into town was very mundane with a systematic approach. They didn't shop so much as just bought. Fresh clothes for the visitors, nothing flashy, but everything functional, a few food items that they couldn't produce on the farm, and some small medical items. As Carol stepped up to pay at each of the small, locally owned stores Whitney noticed she used a curious-looking card or strange printed currency.

When they got back into the truck she asked, "What was that you used to pay for everything with? It wasn't regular money or a VISA card."

"Oh," Carol began, "That's something we started using a few years ago. It's called Marshall Money or LewisBucks. The idea is that it's like the old days when local banks printed their own money for use in the local economy. It's all based on local commodities and such, but you can convert regular dollars into local dollars. The bigger stores won't accept it, but that helps the smaller ones compete. It's worked pretty well so far, plus it gives the buyers a little discount for things. The local banks and city and county government decided to go with it a few years ago when things looked a little ominous. I'm glad they did."

"I've heard of that. I think there was a place in California that did that years ago. Maybe one up in New England too. Huh. I've never actually seen it used before."

"Well, right now the local money is considered more valuable than the greenbacks we've all relied on for so long. It's kind of strange paying for things with locally printed money, but it works."

"Is that why we had so many items loaded up when we came in?"

"Yes," she said, "In addition to the local currency it also works as kind of a barter tool. You bring in a product or a service and you get the value converted into local money. You can pay for repairs or food or whatever you need as long as the supplier accepts the money. Not everyone does, but most do."

Browning spotted the pair just as they were about to pull out onto the road and head back to the farm. He quickly hit his blue lights and pulled alongside.

"Good afternoon, Mrs. Irwin," he said as he flipped the lights off, "Sorry about the light show, but I wanted to get your attention before you slipped off."

"My, David, you scared me to death for a second. I thought something was wrong."

"No, nothing wrong. I just wanted to check on Scott and James. I knew they were coming in last night from the radio traffic. Did they make it alright?"

"Yes, they brought company as well. Rachel Avery from Scott's work and this is Whitney Anderson. She worked at a restaurant up there near the mall."

"Hello," he said as he looked the young lady over, "I'm going to assume they ran into some problems getting out."

"Oh, yes. It was terrible to hear the stories they told. But they're home now. I'm just glad they're all safe."

"Me too," Dave said with a smile, "Say, can you do me a favor? Tell Scott I'll be calling him later. I have a couple of things to talk to him and James about."

"I will. Be careful."

Browning smiled at the ladies and returned to his patrol as the truck once again resumed its course.

Chapter Seventeen

Love at First Fight

May 25th

"C'mon, man. Hand it over and we'll leave you alone."

The older man stood firm with a look of absolute defiance in his eyes.

"You little punk. You'll have to come and get it. I've earned everything I've got. Assholes like you are why the country's in the shape it is. You think everyone owes you something."

"Shut up, old man. I don't need a lesson in politics. I just want your stuff."

Sean Carter inched closer to the older man who drew his clenched fist back, prepared to swing.

"Is there a problem here?"

The voice carried from across the area with a slight echo. A younger man stepped from the shadows to Sean's left. Alan Land wasn't a large figure, but he was in very good physical shape and was hardheaded enough not to know when to back away from an unfair fight.

Carter squinted as he eyed the newcomer. He wasn't a guard, that was good, but he was a witness. That could be bad.

"No, no problems here," Carter replied, "I was just trying to negotiate with this gentleman for a ring. Clearly, he is rather attached to it."

"Then I'd say the negotiations have failed, wouldn't you?" Land said as he jockeyed for an advantageous position, "Maybe it's time to part company."

"Yeah," Carter replied as he cut his eyes back to the older man, "We'll talk more about it later. I think I can make you an offer you'll find pretty hard to resist."

Carter and his friends slowly moved back down the aisle to the main area of the Spring Hill Refugee Center.

Over the past several days he had become somewhat of a celebrity among the entitlement groups and politically left people that had come to call the facility home. He wasn't afraid to strong arm his way to get things that others couldn't. If you were in his circle he didn't mind sharing them, either. He always knew he could get payback in one form or another.

He and his friends were the first at the facility to form a "gang" and they knew the guards were prohibited from the use of excessive physical force to keep them in line. After all, the facility was supposed to be a humanitarian effort on behalf of the state. Nobody wanted to tarnish the image with violence from another oppressive government installation.

They had been subtle with their extortion and assaults but were getting more aggressive as more refugees entered the facility every day. The site administrators insisted that if you remained there you had to provide some form of compensation to offset the cost of your upkeep.

Many of the refugees worked on the farmland, prepping and planting crops by hand or maintaining the tractors and implements that were abundant. Some were happy to give back in exchange for their food and shelter. Sean and his associates despised it. It wasn't their fault the system had failed, and they felt it was only right that the system should be responsible for their survival, without expectations.

Of course, there were courses offered, for free even, to allow refugees to learn skills to become more valuable members of society, but why should he? If the system wouldn't take care of him and his friends, then the others in here would simply have to. Protection was the new business, and he was the sole provider. Of course, he was essentially the main reason for the need of protection, but that was just semantics.

Through a few connections Carter had managed to establish a rather successful trade program to get things otherwise unavailable, or even prohibited, inside the facility. He or his friends would steal from other refugees and trade with some of the less honorable guards for drugs, alcohol, or whatever the need was. The guards had easy access to the outside world and would typically turn a blind eye to the contraband for a cut of the booty.

The facility was so large that there were thousands of places to hide items and as long as he worked with the guards, they would overlook those areas. It wasn't a perfect arrangement, but it worked.

From time to time they would collaborate and arrange for a "find" of contraband to let the administrators know that the guards were all doing their part to keep the facility clean. Nobody seemed to question *how* things got in. They were just content to see that the staff was holding up their end of the arrangement and keeping a lookout for things.

The Spring Hill facility was over 40 acres of climate-controlled space that spanned three main structures. Each building was originally connected to the next by an overhead conveyor system. From the northern end the paint and body systems building provided stamped metal parts and assemblies to the general assembly building. From the south, the powertrain building provided the engines and drive train components. Everything came together in the central general assembly building where the bodies would "marry" to the chassis and drive train. The interiors, doors, windows, seats, and everything else would be added to the vehicles and the finished cars would be deposited out the back of the plant. During its heyday seeing the facility in full swing was an impressive sight.

Many people have the misconception that automotive plants are highly automated, and robots do the majority of the work. That was never the case at Spring Hill. The vast majority of the work done was manual labor. The Smyrna facility was surprisingly similar in that respect, though much larger in scope and capability.

Leftovers from the Saturn days saw massive amounts of equipment in storage in the basement level of the powertrain building. The area was unused for production and the cost to clear out the equipment was prohibitive, so it was left in place and the level relegated to use as a storm shelter. This was one of Carter's favorite places to conduct "business." It was isolated, remote, dark, and large. Very large, actually. It was a perfect lair.

The three main buildings were supposed to be divided into social zones, with married couples and families occupying the general assembly building, single men in powertrain, and single women in body systems. This was intended to minimize the chances of assault or abuse between occupants.

The sheer size of the facility and limited security resources often proved an Achilles heel, and men and women were frequently seen slipping in and out of the sectors unopposed. Many times, it was with the assistance, or encouragement, of the guards themselves. Single occupants would often meet during work shifts and slip off for a little rendezvous when heads were turned.

Sean and a handful of his cronies stood by watching as the work shift returned from the fields. A dirty, sweaty bunch of men headed in from the brightness of the 77° May warmth outside. In a few weeks their efforts would pay off with truckloads of lettuce, cabbage, tomatoes, and other vegetables to feed the refugees and supply the local community. Carter couldn't care less about that.

What he did care about was a curious looking individual that strode in with the crowd.

The young lady had tucked her hair under a cap and mingled with the mass of men as they headed for the building. Beside her was a young man of about the same age. There was little doubt as to why she was there. Still, she was in Carter's turf, and he made his mind up quickly that there would have to be a fee for that access.

He and his men followed from a distance, cautiously stalking the couple as they stealthily left the more crowded areas in search of some privacy. They finally settled on a spot toward the back of the building in a dark corner of what used to be a machine shop.

Carter gave the pair a minute to get comfortable before letting his presence be known.

Stepping from behind a large piece of equipment he smiled at the slender young lady.

"Good afternoon, folks. I hope you don't mind me popping in like this, but I thought I might let you know that you are in my spot."

The pair looked at him and then at each other.

"What?"

"My spot. This whole area, this whole building, actually, is my spot. Now, I don't mind you using it…for a small fee, of course."

"We'll just be leaving. We don't want any trouble," the young man started, "C'mon. We'll find someplace else."

Carter stepped in to intercept, "You see, there's the problem. There's not anywhere else to go. This is all mine, and you've already trespassed. Now you just have to pay the toll."

"What is it you want? Neither of us have any money or jewelry," the girl spat.

Carter cast a leering gaze at the girl and cracked a smile, "I think you can figure it out."

"No. I don't think so," the young man said sizing Carter up.

A few yards away a muffled metallic thump echoed through the forest of abandoned equipment.

"See, you're thinking you can take me right now," Carter began, "That's where you're wrong.

My friends are right over there and if anything happens to me, well, I wouldn't want to be you." Carter stepped in a little closer, pressing the point as the girl cringed.

"Son," a voice called from behind Carter, "We really need to work on your social skills."

Alan Land stepped into view holding a sizable wrench, catching Carter off guard and confusing the couple briefly.

"You."

"Yep. It's me again. The pain in your nasty ass," the man approached Carter, casually swinging the wrench as he did, "Like I said, we clearly need to work on your social skills. I think it may be time for lesson number one."

The rage began to swell in Carter's mind as he considered his next move. He was, essentially, unarmed and at a disadvantage. He needed to take the fight to the man and catch him off guard.

That wouldn't be easy. Unable to contain his anger any longer, Carter bum -rushed Land.

Land snapped into a slight crouch as if he had suddenly become a catcher in a ball game of sorts; ready to receive the incoming Carter and all his fury.

"You little piss ant! I've had enough of your shit!" Carter yelled as he plowed headlong toward his adversary.

Just as the pair were about to make contact Alan stepped aside and brought the wrench down on Carter's shoulders, knocking the breath out of him and sending him cartwheeling to the floor.

Shaking it off and regaining his footing, Carter spotted a piece of threaded pipe on a cart nearby. Grabbing his newfound weapon he jumped back into the fray. The young couple saw an advantage and headed for the nearest exit.

Carter lunged at the man, slapping the pipe against the wrench as both men jockeyed for an advantage.

Sean pressed the fight hard, finally pinning his adversary against a column. Grappling with each other, neither could bring their implements to bear without exposing himself to a response. Finally, in an almost desperate move, Carter slammed his forehead into Land's own. He saw the eyes roll white briefly and took the chance of stepping back to finish the fight with a blast from his pipe.

The half step was all that Alan needed to bring his knee violently upward, crushing Carter's testicles.

Sean was already mid swing with the pipe, but the sudden jolt of pain threw his aim off. Rather than striking

Land in the head, the pipe slammed his upper arm, breaking the left humerus before slipping from Carter's grip.

The wrench simultaneously swept up from Alan's right side and engaged Carter's shoulder, glancing off and impacting his head on the left side. Both men, dizzy from their injuries, fell to the floor as footsteps rapidly approached from various directions.

Carter woke in the main medical center in general assembly a few hours later. He had a large bandage on his head and a splitting headache to go along with it. As he looked around the room, he saw one of his men on another bed with an I.V. trailing down to his arm and an even larger bandage than his own wrapped around his head.

Hearing footsteps he turned his attention to the door where his blurry vision began to focus on a slender 5'4" brunette that had entered the room.

"Well, did you finally decide to wake up?"

"Huh? How long have I been out?"

"Just a couple of hours. You have a pretty nasty lump on your head. How do you feel?"

Carter processed the situation, his attention returning quickly to the attractive 30-year-old at his bedside.

"Like sh…crap. You should see the other guy."

"I did," she replied with a smile, "You boys certainly play rough. What was it? A girl?"

Carter stared at the nurse's face, absorbing every curve and nuance he could. She was stunning.

"Um, yeah. Something like that."

"Well, I hope both of you learned a lesson. Fighting doesn't accomplish anything. Now here you are with a concussion and a badly bruised shoulder and he's out with a broken arm.

"Security will be here in a little while to talk to you. They will have some paperwork for you, too. I have to go check on another patient now. If you need anything, I'm Denise. In the meantime, don't get up and don't try to move. I'll be back to check on you soon. Okay?"

Carter nodded his head. She smiled and turned toward the door. She was gorgeous.

Chapter Eighteen

Social Responsibility

May 26th

"What are we supposed to be doing?" Evans' concern was mirrored by Irwin's own.

"Beats me. Browning just told me to bring you into town and meet him at the police station this morning at 9:00. Something about needing some help."

"Help as in personal help or help as in police help?"

"You know as much as I do at this point, man. We'll find out in a minute."

As the Jeep pulled into the parking spot just in front of the station steps they could see Dave Browning inside, leaning against the dispatcher's window. He smiled and approached the door.

"I was beginning to wonder if you were coming or not," he said with a smile, "Andy's already inside."

Scott looked at his watch, "We still have six minutes. What's the rush?"

"Come on in and we'll cover it in a few minutes."

The trio entered the building and turned to the right, down the short hallway and into the courtroom area.

The room was spacious but sparsely decorated. It was used mainly for traffic court and similar purposes, so it lacked the formality of a regular courtroom. There were no elegant wooden panels along the walls or proper bench.

There was no jury box or reporter's table. It was mainly just a large room with tables and chairs that could be arranged in a courtroom configuration when needed. Today it was more like a classroom.

Around the room about two dozen people sat behind folding white plastic tables. Scott didn't recognize many of them, but he hadn't actually lived in Lewisburg for a while.

"Grab a seat, guys," Browning said, "The Chief will be in soon and we'll get started."

Evans and Irwin pulled up a pair of chairs beside Andy Phillips at one of the front tables as Browning slipped back out the door.

"Well, that was informative," Evans quipped.

"Tell me about it," Irwin replied, "I wonder what he has up his sleeve. Why do we need to see the Chief?"

"Auxiliary service program." The voice came from a young man at the table behind them.

James and Scott turned to face the man, who extended his hand in a friendly gesture.

"Dale Simmons," he said with a smile, "I wasn't trying to eavesdrop, but it's just really quiet in here."

"Scott Irwin. This is James Evans. Good to meet you, Dale."

"Good to meet you, Dale," Evans said as he shook Simmons' hand.

Irwin looked at Phillips curiously.

"We've already met," he said with a smile, "You get to be more social when you're on time."

"Auxiliary service program? How so?" Irwin asked.

"Well, I was told that with the recent economic situation that there has been a jump in crime, even around here, and they are looking for people who are willing to supplement law enforcement since they are keeping the patrols busy. I'm thinking they are looking for administrative people, but I really don't know. I said I'd be interested in helping out since I have nothing better to do."

"What were you doing before all this?"

"I worked at the auto plant in Spring Hill. My family and I moved here a few years ago from Seattle. It was just too expensive to live there after they jumped the minimum wage and all. Of course, nobody is building cars right now, so I have just been looking for something to do."

"Must be tough having to support your family these days without a steady income," James commented.

"It hasn't been too bad. We had some savings built up, so that's helped a lot. Of course, I'll be glad when things get back to normal and all this blows over." James and Scott shot each other a quick glance.

"You think it's just a passing thing? The economy, I mean?"

"Sure. I mean, why wouldn't it be? It's like the Great Depression, right? We'll manage through this rough spot and then, in a little while, the government will rework some legislation and pull us back out of it. That's the way it's always worked before."

One of the other men in the room snorted a little at Simmons' comments. Scott shot the man a glance but said nothing.

"You don't keep up with the news much, do you Dale?" Evans asked.

"Oh, yeah. I listen to the radio every day. I know there's been some trouble here and there, but it's not like we're on the brink of collapse or anything."

"Ever talk to anyone back in Washington?" Phillips queried.

Dale was about to answer when the double doors swung open and a group of uniformed officers entered the room escorting the Chief of Police and the Sheriff. Among them was Dave Browning.

The group spread out across the front of the room, facing the group at the tables while two of the officers remained at the doors for a security measure.

"Good morning, folks," the Chief said as he leaned against a table at the head of the room,

"I apologize if I have kept you waiting this morning. It's been a bit hectic around here lately." He scanned the faces of those in attendance before continuing.

"Let's just get right into it, shall we? The reason you have come here this morning is because you have expressed an interest in helping out local law enforcement in a time of need. With the recent economic developments Lewisburg, and Marshall County by extension, has seen a phenomenal increase in local crime.

"Now, we don't have serial killers running loose or anything like that, but we have other issues that demand our attention. We have increased patrols and established a presence at all major roads into the county to try and better control who is coming and going within our borders. We feel this is a positive and necessary effort to provide security and safety for our communities.

"The unfortunate side effect of all this increased patrol work is that we are shorthanded in a number of areas," he looked at a pair of ladies in the group, "not the least of which is administrative."

Scott looked at Dave Browning with an expression that clearly indicated no intention of taking on a paper pushing job. Browning returned the gaze with a smile and a single finger indicating patience.

"Some of you have been brought in by recommendation based on your knowledge or experience as candidates for a different type of supplemental program that the Sheriff's office has been working on with the city PD. I'll let Sheriff Daniels elaborate more on that."

The elder officer stepped up front and center and assumed a similar, casual posture.

"Okay. It's no secret that crime here is on the increase. It is everywhere. Our people are stretched thin, as the Chief just said. What we are developing here is essentially a backup team to supplement and support our officers. Some of you have administrative backgrounds, and we need that to be sure. Others have some military or law enforcement experience. We need that too.

"We are looking for people that can act as an extension of the department's existing force.

You will be asked to deliver summons or other legal paperwork, act as security for court proceedings, and train with our officers regularly. You will not be officers…officially. You will be deputized reservists under the direction of an oversight committee of myself, the Chief, and the city and county mayors. You may be asked to accompany our officers on raids or emergency calls to provide backup security, crowd or traffic control, or other services. That will be rare, but you will be trained for that.

"Understand that this is a voluntary post and you are free to leave right now if you are not interested. If you choose to participate, we do not have a budget in place to pay you. We do, however, have negotiations in place with several local businesses and services that have agreed to support you with what you need, within reason, in exchange for your service."

The gentleman looked over the group carefully, scanning each face present for an indicator of intent before settling on Scott and James. He immediately recognized Ben Irwin's son and gave a slight nod.

"Questions?"

After a brief moment of silence, a voice finally emerged from the rear of the room.

"Will we be provided with uniforms, equipment, weapons, or badges? How will people identify us as law enforcement?"

"We have an arrangement with a local business that will provide us with shirts that will have an embroidered badge on them. They will also bear your name on the right chest. That will have to work for a uniform for the time being.

"We will have a limited amount of equipment available, such as handcuffs and pepper spray. Any firearms will have to be your own. It's a liability issue for one thing and a training issue for another. We made sure that everyone in this room already has a concealed carry permit, so we know you can at least pass that requirement. If you choose to participate you will be further trained in weapon handling and maintenance with our SWAT team."

"Is this legal?" A lady on the opposite side of the room asked.

"Ma'am, right now, the legality of a lot of things in our nation are in question. We have the legal authority to deputize civilians to act in a support capacity. We do not have the authority to create officers out of thin air. That's why you will be an 'auxiliary' group."

"How long will these positions be needed?" Dale asked.

"I wish I knew, son. As of right now, they are open ended arrangements. We have no reason to suspect that there will be any need to close these positions any time soon." A slight murmur washed over the group.

"What if we decide we want out?" another asked.

"Inform one of us. It's that simple. We are asking for your help, and we appreciate your interest. This isn't a complicated deal, and I personally like that. Let one of us know, bring in your uniforms and equipment and we'll take care of the rest."

"Any chance this will be offered to others later?" Scott asked; the rest of the 'Dozen' sprang to mind.

"Possibly. It depends on the need and the interest. I hope that things will stabilize soon, but I have to be realistic about it. I doubt the country we all knew five years ago will ever be back. I'm afraid what we're seeing right now is the start of something altogether new."

After a minute or two of mumbles and suppressed comments, the snorting man spoke up.

"Sheriff, just how bad is it, really? I mean, we listen to the news and all, but I get the feeling that a lot of it has been sanitized. If it's bad enough to ask for civilian help here, how bad is it everywhere else?"

Dale's attention was fully engaged at the question.

The Sheriff shifted his weight a bit, as if trying to approach the question delicately, but not sugar coat it.

He shoved his hands in his pockets as he paced out into the room a little and became more intimate with the group.

"Folks, there's no point in lying about it; especially since we are asking for your help. If we expect to work together there needs to be a clear understanding of where we stand on all this. So, here it is, in a nutshell.

"Law enforcement hears things that a lot of people outside that circle don't. We are privy to information that doesn't get put on the news or in the papers. What we've been seeing and hearing lately is that our country has essentially fallen apart.

"As bad as things are around here, we are doing much better than most. Reports out of California, New York, and some of the larger metropolitan areas are…unreal. Nashville, Metro Davidson County, Chattanooga and, to an extent, Knoxville, have all seen the worst rioting on record. Memphis is a war zone. I have a friend from my academy days in Shelby County that was feeding me intel on their situation. I haven't heard from him in days. I assume, given their social unrest, he is probably dead. Please remember that Shelby County has been expecting a situation like this since Martin Luther King was shot there in the '60's. If they've not been able to keep it under control, it's bad."

Dale became increasingly uneasy in his seat as the officer recounted the status of the nation.

"Most of the logic behind the reporting is to keep it quiet and prevent an escalation of events. Ignorance is bliss. The feds think that's the way to maintain control; keep everyone in the dark and feed them rainbows and unicorns.

"Meanwhile, we are hearing that the same government that is controlling the media feed is also rounding up political opposition and 're-educating' them. It's like a page right out of World War Two Europe."

Dale couldn't stand it any longer and spoke up.

"So, if the rest of the nation is in such bad shape, why is everything here better? Shouldn't we see the same levels of social unrest as the rest of the country? Why aren't there camps for political prisoners around here?"

"Mainly because the people of Tennessee, Texas, Alabama, and most of the other southern states basically told the feds to piss off. You will still see federal agencies and operations going on, but they don't have the teeth they did. For the most part, they have lost authority here and nobody will support them. We take care of our own. Always have."

Dale slumped back in his chair as his mind began to return to Washington State. He hadn't heard from his family in a few days. Maybe he should try to call again or something. He knew utility services up there were spotty, but he needed to know that things were okay.

When the meeting finally broke up Scott and James turned to speak with Dale.

"You okay, man?"

Simmons looked as if he had just narrowly missed being hit by a truck.

"Yeah. I just hadn't heard all that. I've been listening to the news reports and all. I've been believing them. That everything was rough, but not *that* rough, you know?"

James looked him in the face with narrowed eyes as Browning approached the trio, "Do you have anywhere to be right now?"

"Nope. Like I said, when the plant shut down, I didn't have anything to do. Why?"

"I want you to hear something," James said as he looked to Browning.

Dave glanced at his watch and said, "Follow me, fellows. I think I know what you are up to."

They left the room and made their way out back of the building where Browning's truck sat. Unlocking the door, he reached in and flipped on a Yaesu FT 1900 radio. Fumbling with the controls for a minute he began to pick up chatter across the small mobile HAM radio.

"This is a guy somewhere up in Michigan. I don't know exactly where since he won't transmit his exact location, but he does a regular update on this frequency every morning at around 10:00 our time. He stays on the move, but he reports what he sees and hears. There are a lot of folks like this across the country."

The group listened closely as the static filled airwaves crackled with reports of political roundups across parts of Detroit and Flint and a large "re-education" camp being established somewhere close to Worden.

After a few minutes the operator signed off. Browning explained that the traffic was short to minimize the chances of being triangulated on.

"What does that mean? I'm not a radio guy."

"Basically," Browning started, "if he transmits from the same location for too long of a period, other operators can monitor his signal strength to establish where he might be. If you get three or more operators, they can go from a general to a more specific area. If he stays in the same spot, they can narrow it down and find him. Then he's removed as a political dissident."

"Do you ever hear anything from the Northwest?"

"Every now and then. I can't get much on this radio. It's just not strong enough and sitting here the buildings block a lot of traffic too."

"I have radio equipment from the Ritz, but I haven't had time to set anything up yet. It's on the list, I just haven't gotten that far yet," Evans added.

"My base station is up and running at home," Browning said, "I listen to it practically every night. You hear some interesting things from all over."

"I wish I knew what my family was dealing with up in Seattle. Really. Any chance you could keep an ear out for me?"

"Sure. I'd be glad to."

Chapter Nineteen

A Wee Small Voice

May 28th

Monday morning began the first day of training with the local police department. The auxiliary volunteers were divided into administrative and tactical support groups. The administrative group began with hot coffee and an overview of the codes used in the local radio communications system.

The tactical group began the cool morning in a similar classroom setting going over the do's and don'ts of traffic control and relative crowd control. The general feeling was that most of the assignments would revolve around checkpoints initially.

The group took a break around 10:00 to stretch legs, refill coffee cups or grab a snack before continuing on with the course of study. They didn't weigh the class down with a lot of the legalities of law enforcement, because that simply wasn't what it was for. These people weren't there to kick in doors and arrest anyone. They were to help control traffic around crime scenes and serve warrants, if needed.

Browning stepped into the room and approached James, Andy and Scott directly. They were off to the side chatting with Dale when he approached.

"Morning, fellows. Learning much?"

"I'm learning how much your job must suck," came Andy's reply.

"You have no idea yet, son. Wait until you get started," he smiled, "Say, have any of you heard anything from Tom?"

Scott and James looked at each other curiously.

"No," they replied in unison.

"Why?" Andy asked, "Have you?"

"No," he said flatly, "that's what has me concerned. We got a report of some wild stuff going on up toward Murfreesboro overnight. One of these extremist political movements has taken over the college campus in a big way up there and last night they went on a tear across the city. We hear that the 'Boro is essentially on lockdown, with all the major roads and interstate access cut off. Lots of people hurt and more reports coming in. I don't know if they made it out before it went off the rails or not."

"Doesn't he have a radio? One of those handheld Baofengs?"

"Yeah," James said, "He and I ordered a couple of those at the same time to save on shipping costs when they were on sale a couple of years ago. You know, just to toss in the 'go bag' if we had to bug out and needed comms."

"Hmm," Dave mumbled, "At this distance he would be hard pressed to transmit directly here without a repeater. Maybe they've gotten out and he just hasn't been able to make contact."

"Can you contact anyone at the PD up there and verify?"

"They have their hands full enough as it is," Dave said, "I'm not going to ask them to run a wellness check while they're dealing with that mess."

"On that same note, has anyone heard from Chris?"

"Yeah," Browning replied, "He's still in Nashville right now. He's having a hard time convincing his wife that they need to be leaving. She's in denial that things are as bad as they are up there. He caught me on the HAM last night. Nashville's in bad shape. You guys did well to get out when you could. It's not as bad as Memphis or Birmingham, but for Nashville, it's bad." Dale cleared his throat subtly.

"Simmons?"

"You didn't happen to hear anything from my old stomping grounds, did you?"

"Sorry, man. Not a peep last night. I have a few freqs I monitor from different regions, but catching something on air is kind of a crap shoot."

"Freaks?"

"Frequencies. Sorry. Not like weirdoes. If I hear anything, you'll be the first to know."

"Okay," he said quietly, "I appreciate it."

The instructor stepped back into the room and asked everyone to take their seats once again. In his hand was a small stack of index cards that contained all the call numbers for the common codes they would use on the radios. For the next couple of hours, they would be learning how to use the established communication system for the department and how to respond to calls from dispatch or officers in the field.

When they finally broke for lunch the four men decided to grab a bite at one of the locally owned establishments. Chain restaurants dotted the small city, but their inventory levels were constantly changing and usually low to begin with. Since the economic bomb the delivery trucks that brought the frozen patties and premixed ingredients didn't show up regularly, if at all. Most days they wouldn't even open the doors because they didn't have the supplies to cater to customers.

Some of the resourceful local entrepreneurs had managed to lock in arrangements with area farmers and secure a source of meats and vegetables for business to continue. Granted, most could only open for one meal a day, but that was usually enough to justify the effort since they got all the overflow from the franchises that couldn't unlock their doors. Still, the food was good, fresh, and with the local currency, affordable.

They piled into Dave's truck and headed down to the Gizmo for some sliders. The little shop had been around since before any of the men had been born and offered the tiny square hamburgers much like the ones to be had at a White Castle or Krystal. As they made the short drive, they listened to the HAM radio to see if any new information was to be found.

Nothing met their ears but silence.

As he pulled in beside the burger joint Browning asked the others, "Okay, so are we splitting a bag or what?"

"That's fine with me," Evans said, "I'm not that hungry."

"That'll work," Irwin answered.

"What do they have?" Simmons asked, "I've never eaten here before."

"Sliders," Andy offered, "that's it. Not a very elaborate menu, but they're pretty good."

"Oh, okay," Simmons said with a tone of disappointment.

Phillips smiled at the man, "Trust me."

The four men exited the vehicle and stepped in the confines of the small structure. Directly across from the front door stretched a counter and a couple of feet behind that was the griddle. A man worked the grill at a fever pitch which was covered with small square beef patties as an older lady commanded the cashier's station.

"Why David, I haven't seen you all week," she said with a smile, "and you brought company this time!"

"Hey, Mrs. Sally. I know. We've been pretty busy lately, so I haven't had time to swing by, but today is the exception. We'd like to split a 24 bag, please."

"Yes, sir. Dan will have those ready for you in a minute," she said with another smile as she cast her gaze across the other members of Browning's party.

"Oh, my," she said, "Are you Scotty? Ben and Carol's son?"

"Yes ma'am," Irwin replied, "It's been a while since I've been in."

"Yes, it has," she said, "Tell your parents that I said a big 'thank you' for the vegetables. We have had more compliments about the onions and pickles they bartered with us than any we've used before."

"I'll be sure to. Thank you."

After a few minutes the burgers were bagged up and the four men headed to a small picnic table outside to enjoy their meal. Rounding out the feast was a gigantic order of fresh French fries and paper cups of tea, sweet and unsweet alike, with the water Dale opted for.

The building was situated on the crest of a small hill near the county square. Without much movement, one could sit at the table outside and see the courthouse and two thirds of the square to the east and nearly a mile down West Commerce Street to the west. The parking lot was formerly shared with two other businesses in decades gone by, both of which had long been scoured from the landscape. Only the Gizmo had remained. With nothing around the tiny structure Evans decided to take advantage of the clear surroundings and pulled a small radio from his bag in Dave's truck.

Attaching the whip like antenna to the tiny Baofeng UV-5R Evans quickly turned it on. He began to scan the stored frequencies until he found the local repeater and set the device on the center of the table. Dale noticed a shimmering wave of mirage above the concrete tabletop as he looked at the radio.

"You know," Dale began, "I've lived here for nearly five years and I still can't get used to the weather here. I don't see how you stand it."

The other three chuckled lightly before Scott added his own insight.

"I've lived here my whole life. You don't ever get used to it. You just learn to be adaptable."

"Welcome to Tennessee," Evans quipped as he wiped his chin, "If you don't like the weather, wait a few minutes."

"I guess," Simmons replied, "It was, what, fifty degrees this morning? It's got to be over eighty out here now."

"Seventy-nine. You forget about the humidity," Browning added, "That's what gets you here. The heat is bad, but the humidity is oppressive."

"Wait until July or August," Phillips chimed in, "It'll be triple digits on the heat index by this time of day."

"Oh, yeah. I know."

The tiny handheld radio crackled a little bit and a faint voice could barely be heard through the static. All five men stopped talking and leaned in toward the radio trying to comprehend the message that was straining to come through.

"Did you get any of that?"

"Nope," Dave said as he focused on the speaker.

"You don't suppose it could have been Tom, do you?" Evans looked at his friends with hopeful curiosity.

"I don't know. He could be hitting the repeater, but he'd have to be on a handheld or barely in range to be that broken up. I couldn't hear enough of it to catch the voice," Browning said.

"He has the MCARS repeater frequency programmed in his radio. We all have the same freqs set up in our radios as a core selection. Tom, Chris, and I set ours up with additional local frequencies for police, fire and emergency services in our areas," Evans commented.

"MCARS?" Dale looked confused.

"Marshall County Amateur Radio Society. It's the local HAM group. They own the repeater and monitor the network access through it. It's under the oversight of the Emergency Management office here in town."

"Oh, okay. This is all kind of new, you know?"

"Don't worry about it, Dale," Scott said, "I've had my Technician License for a couple of years now and I'm still at a loss most of the time."

"Yeah, well, you'd learn more if you'd come to the meetings, you know," Andy shot

sarcastically.

"I've been a little out of town for the past few years, in case you hadn't noticed," Irwin popped back with a grin.

The radio crackled again, but the voice was so faint that it was little more than a washed-out murmur in a sea of static. That was the last mysterious transmission that they would hear that day.

Chapter Twenty

Blood, Sweat, and Tears

May 30th

The day shift dragged in from the fields and farmland surrounding the Spring Hill Refugee Center grimy and sticky from another day of labor in the near ninety-degree sun. The heat index had already pressed into the mid-nineties and summer hadn't remotely begun.

On this day both the temperature outside and tempers inside would combine to reach a fever pitch.

Lines quickly formed at the nearest water fountains as a grumbling mass discussed their options for getting out of the manual labor requirements of the facility. Many of the refugees were already getting disgruntled by the heat and humidity and were anxious to leave for more comfortable, and less demanding, surroundings.

Several had begun considering taking the opportunity for training to give themselves a skill to use outside the facility. If you were marketable, you could leave. They'd even set you up with a job and temporary housing. That had to be better than staying.

Others just wanted to go back to their easy life of government checks and government phones. Carter and his associates fell squarely into that camp.

As the teams would leave for the fields each morning, his group would often slip out of line and return to the bunks where they would scour the possessions of their fellow internees searching for anything of value that could be used to support their contraband business or perhaps be of value later on.

The PA system inside the massive building sounded the tone for dinner and throughout the former powertrain building lines of men began to head toward the central dining area. As they filed in from both sides a staff of men and women served up the final meal of the day.

In the main dining area, a somber, exhausted tone washed over the crowd as the men took their seats and began quietly cleaning their plates. On the upper mezzanine, where the office level was, the facility guards stood a casual watch. They all knew how the humid Tennessee heat could irritate more than just the skin, but the attitudes as well.

The last of the men wandered in, dirty and hungry. Among them was Alan Land, the confrontational would-be Robin Hood that had tangled with Carter a few days before. His arm still in a cast, he was a little cleaner than most of the rest. He was still on light duty until he healed or was relocated, whichever came first.

Land looked into the shadowy corner of the dining hall, under the mezzanine, knowing it was the preferred seat for Carter and his goons. Carter Country, as it had become known.

"It seems someone has been stealing stuff while everyone is on work detail," he announced,

"I don't suppose you'd know anything about that, would you, Carter?"

A tense silence filled the darkened corner. Slowly a muffled chuckle rose from the shadows.

"You accusing me of something, piss ant? Didn't you learn your lesson the other day?"

"Well, I can be kind of stupid sometimes. I figured since you and your boys were here all day, maybe you might have seen something."

"Me and my boys were out working, same as you."

Land took a long sniff around the area, his nostrils filling with the smell of perspiration and days old body odor mingled with the food on the dozens of tables around him.

"Do you smell that?" he asked.

Carter just sat quietly.

"I smell something. Do you?"

"All I smell is a bunch of nasty asses in here," Carter snapped.

"No," Land replied, "No, it's not that. It's….bullshit. That's what I smell. Pure, unfiltered bullshit and it's coming from…" he turned his gaze back to Carter, "over there. Imagine that."

"You little son of a bitch. How dare you call me a liar in front of all these good, hard-working people," Carter stood and kicked his chair behind him before he strode out into the full light of the room, "I think it's time I finished the lesson you didn't learn last time."

Land smiled broadly, "I called you a thieving liar, you ignorant bastard. If you're gonna call it, call it right."

Carter lunged from the corner as his men leapt to their feet, scrambling to form a perimeter around their leader and his prey. Tables quickly cleared of diners as the two men closed distance on each other. The guards upstairs quickly called for backup on their radios as they moved along the railings for a better vantage point if they needed to engage with their crowd control effects.

The state had chosen for them to be armed with non-lethal weapons rather than rifles and pistols since it would present a more positive and helpful image. After all, it wasn't a prison, but security did need to be maintained. This was a prime example of it.

Within a few seconds the two men were in a tangle with Carter having a definite advantage of the cast laden Land. Seeing the impending outcome, several men rallied to the side of Land and began attacking the men of Carter's detail. Within seconds the dining room began to resemble a saloon fight from an old western classic.

Staff members in the kitchen rushed to lock doors and close gates before anyone could grab any of the steel knives or forks from the drawers or prep areas before taking cover for themselves.

"Sting ball out!" One of the guards shouted as he released one of the CTS 9590 grenades into the fray below. A trail of smoke descended into the crowd and a loud BANG emanated from the group. Less than a second later came a louder explosion that sent a spray of .31 caliber rubber balls rocketing across the room in every direction. Men scrambled to cover faces, eyes, genitalia, and anything else exposed to the fury of the shot. Some responded by backing off, but others were too committed to the fight and carried on.

Doors on both sides of the cafeteria burst open as the room began to clear of the less ambitious while Carter, Land and their supporters fought on.

Already at a disadvantage, Land's arm became Carter's primary target. He knew it was a weak point and could use it to quickly gain the advantage in this fight. He'd rip it off, given the chance, but he'd settle for permanent disfigurement if nothing else.

"Sting ball out!" The second guard called as he pulled the safety pin on his grenade and tossed it over the railing. It struck the tile floor just beside Carter's right foot and bounced up about two feet before the initial explosion announced its arrival. The second explosion sent the rubber shrapnel directly into the faces of several men in the immediate vicinity, among them Land and Carter.

Land fell to the floor, his eye socket badly bruised from the impact of the shot as Carter stumbled backward, reeling from his own trauma. As he fumbled and staggered, he tried to find something, anything, he could use as a weapon to finish off Land. He never saw who it was, but someone placed a small blade in the palm of his hand. Not a plastic knife, but an actual metal blade.

Now he could finish it. Land would pay for his sins against Carter.

He gathered his senses about him and scanned the room, looking for his target. The fight continued to rage, but in smaller pockets rather than as a large amoeba-like mass as before. The sting balls had done their jobs, but not well enough.

Spying Land still lying on the floor Carter made his way back into the brawl. He stepped over Alan, filled with an unbridled rage at the man who would undo all his hard work here. As Land rolled over, still clutching the swollen eye socket, Carter struck.

The blade was small, but sharp. It wouldn't penetrate deeply enough to be fatal, but it would work well enough. Land screamed as the blade punctured his rib cage over and over.

Carter tried to get to the man's neck. He wanted Land dead, just like the cop. How dare these people not understand that they owed him. How dare they try to take things from him.

Someone had to pay. Someone else must be the example of how the world should work.

Land swung his arms up and protected his head and neck as best he could, but Carter continued the assault, slicing his arms like sticks of bologna as the doors burst open to the dining room.

Additional guards began to rush in, surrounding the room with gas masks on and truncheons out.

"Gas out!" came the call from one of the interlopers as a smoking cylinder arced high over the warring factions.

"Gas out!" again as another grenade was lobbed into the group.

"Sting ball out!" came another cry.

Soon the room was alive with the sound of small explosions and the hiss of belching tear gas. Fights began to break up as the participants scrambled for doors and fresh air, but they wouldn't make it.

Guards intercepted anyone that came near, slamming them to the ground and immediately applying zip cuffs as their captives lay choking and coughing on the acrid fumes.

Through his rage Carter looked up and saw the guards gaining the upper hand. It was time to back down. He was now risking everything. He quickly wiped his hands on another man's shirt before turning the corner into the restrooms.

He began to scrub the blood from his hands while trying to wash the gas from his eyes.

Outside, the guards would have their hands full for a couple of minutes. He needed a plan.

Grabbing the tiny blade, he realized he only had one option. With as much fortitude as he could muster, he plunged the blade into his abdomen and then across his own arm. Now bleeding, he wrapped the blade in paper towels and tossed it in the garbage can and returned to the sink. He made sure to wipe blood all over the handles and the basin and collected a large mass of paper towels which he promptly pressed hard into his own stomach, forcing the blood to flow. He plopped to the floor and awaited the guards.

The door swung open a minute later as two guards entered and cleared the room.

"We have a second man down in the bathroom. Need a medic in here too."

The guard made his way to Sean's side.

"Hey, buddy, you okay?"

Sean shook his head as he winced in pain. Blood trickled down his arm and had begun to pool on the floor tiles under his hand while the front of his shirt and pants displayed their own crimson stains.

A third guard entered the room with a medical kit and began inspecting his injuries.

"What happened?" the first guard asked, "Did you see who stabbed you?" Again, Carter shook his head. He was the victim here.

"Alright get him ready to move to primary medical. We'll get them all stable and start interviews."

Later, in the primary medical center in the old General Assembly plant, Sean was resting comfortably when Denise walked into the room.

She checked the beds on the opposite side from him, which gave him a few minutes to appreciate her beauty, head to toe, before she made it over to him.

"Back again, I see," she said without a shred of emotion on her gorgeous face.

"Couldn't stay away," he replied with a smile.

"I wish you had. It would have made my job so much easier," she studied his chart for a few seconds before continuing, "Considering some of the other people I've seen today, you are in surprisingly good shape. As long as you don't pull your stitches out you should be fine in a few days.

You know, you really need to stop all this fighting. It'll get you killed one day." Carter grunted as he tried to sit up in the bed.

"You should see the other guy," he said with a wincing grin.

"Oh, I did. He's at the medical center on the other side of town right now with about fifteen or twenty stab wounds on top of the bruises and lacerations from the fight and those damned 'less than lethal' weapons. You got lucky."

Carter thought about it for a minute. Land wasn't dead. And now he was off the property, where Carter couldn't reach him. If he talked, that would be the end game for Carter and his crew. No doubt that little turd would spill his guts and tell about the whole operation, well, as much as he knew of it, anyway. That would be enough, though. Once they started looking at him closer, someone would figure out that he was wanted for the murder of that damned cop back in Detroit. No, that wasn't going to happen. He couldn't go back there. He began evaluating his options over and over in his mind, totally tuning Denise out as he thought.

"Thanks to your little bar room brawl today, the word has just come from the Governor that he is sending the State Guard to replace our security forces. Now we'll have soldiers on the ground with *real* guns and bullets to make sure this doesn't happen again. Way to go, guys. You should all be so proud," She strode out of the room with an undeniable air of disgust and frustration about her.

"Wait, what did she say? They're bringing the military in as security? No, that's not good. That's not good at all," Carter thought to himself.

"You okay, Denise?" Mary, one of the nurses, asked as she slapped her clipboard on the counter and dragged up a stool. In many ways, not just appearance, Mary reminded Denise of Nurse Roberts from the old TV show *Scrubs*. Her dark brown skin concealed a razor-sharp wit and an attitude to go with it, while simultaneously housing a pure, caring heart.

"You know, I left California to get a break from idiocy like this. Just like this," she gestured toward the room where Carter and a number of other battered, bloody men now lay in various states of consciousness, "People trying to kill each other for stupid stuff. I spent my last dime trying to take a vacation to get away from it. When I got back, I couldn't go home because of it and now it's followed me *here*. I just want to help people. But people need to be worth helping. This is...bullshit. I want out. There has to be a place I can go. Somewhere I can do the job I love without all this bullshit." A small tear began to form at the corner of her eye and slowly stream down her cheek. She missed California and the clinic; the good times when the worst she'd see was a bad case of the flu or a nasty skateboarding accident.

She missed her old life, and she missed her comfort zone. She missed her friends and her apartment. As she sat there, she began to unravel and sob.

Mary slid her chair over to her side and draped a comforting arm around her friend.

"Hey, it's just a bad day, okay? We all have them. Today is just a little more intense than the rest. It's going to be alright."

"No. It's *another* bad day. That follows a *month* of bad days; that is becoming a *year* of bad days because people are stupid and I have to clean up their mess all the time. I just want to go home, Mary. I just want things the way they used to be. I just want out of here."

Mary gave her a tight hug and said quietly in her ear, "Look, you can see we need all the help we can get here. But, if you are serious about getting out, I can pull some strings and see what unravels, okay?"

Denise sat up and looked into Mary's face with tears and mascara smears from both eyes.

"What do you mean?"

"I have a little pull in some places and contacts through family and friends that might be able to get you transferred out of here. Let me see what I can do, okay?"

Denise smiled a shocked smile and hugged Mary around the neck so hard she thought she'd break.

"Mary, you're the greatest!"

"I know, child," she said with a grin, "but I don't make promises. All I can do is try. I hate to lose you. You have talent and skills, and we need that here but sometimes you have to consider your sanity first."

As Denise was changing out of her scrubs and coat Mary approached her in the locker room.

"Lewisburg."

"Excuse me?"

Mary stepped a little closer and repeated the word, "Lewisburg. There's a small hospital there and a few small clinics. All of them have been understaffed for years. It's a quiet location and not a lot seems to go on there. Sounds like just what you are looking for: Boredom Central."

"Seriously? You can get me there?"

"Say the word and you're on your way. Now, you need to understand that it's not a refined, economic powerhouse community like Spring Hill," she continued, "Lewisburg doesn't have all the fine restaurants and lavish shopping districts that we have here."

Denise smiled at the plug for the community since the restaurants and chain stores had all closed out or were almost closed due to a lack of available inventory.

"It's a manufacturing town that doesn't manufacture anymore. The biggest problems they have seen lately have been mainly from the drug trade. Apparently 'pharmaceutical agriculture' is a popular business there," Mary said with air quotes as she spoke.

"So, how does this work? How do I get there and when?"

"We can take you tomorrow if you're that anxious. It's about a half hour drive from here. From what I understand, there may be an opportunity to set you up with a house also. I'm not sure on the details of that, though."

Denise began to smile like a kid at a candy store with her wealthiest relative. She had never had her own house before. It was always a dream to live in a place with privacy and a yard of her own, but the price for that was always too prohibitive in California.

Denise gave a little hop for joy at the news and hugged Mary enthusiastically.

"Where do I sign up?" she asked.

"Let's get your paperwork started."

Chapter Twenty-One

In and Out

May 31st

Early in the morning a trio of camouflaged trucks rolled into the parking lot of the General Assembly building at SHRC. The canvas flaps swung open wide as the tailgates dropped. Uniformed men began to dispatch from the trucks and form ranks on the sidewalks in front of the building as a pair of officers pulled up in a Hummer and stepped out.

The enlisted men each carried a slung M-4 rifle on their shoulder and a holstered sidearm on their waist. Even a cursory glance would reveal that the magazines were in the weapons, indicating they were at least loaded, if not chambered.

The officers stepped out and addressed the troops before proceeding inside. They met with the facility administrator and the captain of the guards as a small detail of men followed through the doorway behind them.

"Gentlemen," the first officer said, "My name is Major Thomas. I have been sent here at the request of the governor to make sure that the incidents that occurred yesterday do not repeat themselves.

"With the condition of the nation being what it is, the governor is deeply concerned at the handling of this situation and the public image that it conveys. He does not want the reputation of the state to be tarnished by mismanagement of a humanitarian effort.

"To this end, the State Guard will immediately assume control of all security and safety measures on the site. A management review will commence this afternoon to verify that the program has not been compromised or corrupted and a determination of management of the facility will be made following that review. Do you understand?"

Both men nodded quietly as if they had been caught with hands in the cookie jar.

"Very good. I need a conference room and your men first, Captain."

Denise watched as the assembly of uniformed men entered the facility. She hated to see the military move in and take over, but she hated to see the insanity that had brought this on even worse. It didn't matter anymore. Soon she would be leaving this place and starting a whole new life.

She made one more pass through the infirmary to check on her patients before gathering her things. As she did a soldier entered the ward and began to take stock of the medical facility and the occupants within. He asked no questions and made no comments, but simply scanned the room slowly, absorbing the environment.

Denise finally made her way to Sean's bed and checked the reports from overnight on his condition.

"Good morning, Sunshine," Carter muttered. Clearly his pain meds were doing their job.

"Good morning," she replied flatly. She had already decided that her bedside manner would be as cold as ice that day. At least until she left for her new life. He looked the part of a victim, but she knew he had been in there before as a combatant, so she doubted his innocence this time.

Besides, there was just something…unwelcome about the way he looked at her.

"Feeling better this morning?"

"Oh, yeah, doc. Whatever you got me on has me feeling just fine. How are you feeling?" he asked with a sneer.

"I'll be feeling better in a couple of hours. Then I am out of here and I won't have to deal with this nonsense anymore."

"Mmm," he said groggily, "Shift change."

"Job change," she replied.

Carter's eyes opened and the confusion shone through the inebriation.

"Huh? You leaving me, doc?"

"Yep. I'm moving on. Take care of yourself. Your next fight might be your last."

She tucked the clip board under her arm and headed for the doorway. As she neared the armed guard, he leaned to address her.

"Ma'am," he said in a formal tone, "Would you happen to be Miss Shelby?"

"Yes. Is there something wrong?"

"No, ma'am. I was told you might be here. Whenever you're ready, I'll escort you to the Humvee for your new assignment."

"Oh," she said with a bit of a start, "I wasn't expecting a military escort. Are you going to Lewisburg?"

"Yes ma'am. There's a supply and maintenance group there that we will be picking up materials from. Since Mrs. Thomas suggested you were going that way as well, the Major decided we could save you some headache and give you a lift."

Mrs. Thomas? Mary. She didn't make the connection before, but now it made sense. Denise knew Mary's husband was a military man but never considered he might be the one in charge here today.

"Thank you. I'll be ready in just a little bit. It won't take long. I don't have much to get."

"Take your time, ma'am.

Carter rolled the name around in his mind, Lewisburg. Where was that? It had to be close, but he hadn't seen any maps or anything. Maybe he could get out of here and follow her to this new job. They could start a new life together. He certainly couldn't stay here. Not with the new management in control.

Denise shoved the last of her worldly possessions into the tiny suitcase and looked around her quarters. It was still strange to her that this tiny space inside of an old factory had been her "home" for the last few weeks. She came in with only a pair of suitcases and she was leaving with just that. That and a ton of experiences and memories, good and bad, that she never wanted.

She turned and made her way down the hallway toward the outer doors. She could already see Mary waiting up ahead along with most of the medical staff.

"I sure do hate to see you go, girl," Mary said with a smile, "but I don't blame you for leaving. Onward and upward, right?"

"Right," Denise replied with a grin. She looked at the faces of her coworkers. Some were local people that needed the job, others were like her. They had all become close over the past few weeks, and she was beginning to find it hard to let them go.

"If I don't get out of here, I'm never going to. It's been great meeting and working with you. All of you. Please take care of yourselves. And remember, I'm just going to be down the road a little."

She said hasty farewells to everyone as her eyes began to tear up, then grabbed her small bags and headed out the door.

Upstairs she found the corporal from earlier and they proceeded to the Hummer. He opened the rear door on the passenger side and gestured for Denise to have a seat. She slid in the confines of the vehicle, surprised at how compact the interior of such a large vehicle could be.

The central section of the vehicle was a raised platform that left almost no room for the seats on either side. Up front the instrument panel was a cluster of radios, indicators, ammo crates, shifter levers, and a big, ugly steering wheel that looked like it belonged in a big rig from the 1930's.

The driver's side door swung open as the corporal finished securing her luggage to the roof of the vehicle and he assumed his position as chauffeur. The passenger side front door also swung open as the captain slipped in and removed his cap.

"Good morning, Miss Shelby. I apologize for the rudimentary transportation. The government was never much on luxury in a combat vehicle," he smiled, "As soon as our gunner is in, we'll be on our way. Are you ready?"

Gunner? Why do we need a gunner?

"Um, I'm as ready as I'll ever be, I suppose. Can I ask a question?"

"Absolutely, Miss Shelby. What's on your mind?"

"Why do we need a gunner?"

The captain smiled a warm, disarming smile.

"Mostly it's just procedure, ma'am. I'd rather have one and not need one than to need one and not have one. In today's evolving world, well, we just never know if we'll need one."

The door across from her swung open as a third man entered, secured his weapon and stepped up onto the raised platform and out through the hole in the roof. With a couple of sharp raps on the roof the corporal started the engine, and they began moving out.

About twenty minutes after leaving the Spring Hill Refugee Center the Humvee approached the checkpoint at Pottsville. The corporal slowed to a stop as an officer approached the window and scanned the occupants.

"Can I help you?"

"Captain Watkins, Tennessee State Guard, en route to the 771st Supply in Lewisburg. We have a new staff member for your hospital as well," Watkins motioned to the back seat.

"Do you have travel papers, Captain?"

"Indeed, I do, son," the captain reached into a messenger bag at his feet and produced a small pack of papers which he promptly handed to the officer at the door.

After a quick glance at the paperwork, he returned them to the captain and leaned down into the window a bit more.

"Everything looks good. Miss Shelby, welcome to Marshall County. You should have a pretty boring ride in, captain, but I would suggest avoiding the back roads. We've had a little trouble here and there. I'd hate for your truck to get scratched up.

"The most direct path for you would be to turn left here and follow 99 all the way to the end. When it terminates at Nashville highway, hang a right. That will take you directly into Lewisburg. When you get to the first light, left will take you to the armory, right will take you to the hospital. Safe travels."

Watkins tucked the information packet back into the bag and returned it to the floorboard.

"Thank you, son. We'll see you again here in a couple of hours."

The corporal cut the wheel, and the Humvee was soon on its way.

Chapter Twenty-Two

Incoming

June 1st

Scott looked across the back yard of his family home. It was a warm summer day. The sky was a brilliant blue and the trees stood in stark contrast with their lush green foliage across the fields. He adjusted the tie around his neck and headed downstairs where a small group of friends waited near the back door of the home.

The men stepped back, allowing him an unobstructed aisle to the doorway. As he passed through, into the sunshine of the yard, he took notice of the dozens of men and women that sat in the chairs before him. Directly ahead was the massive oak tree he and his cousins used to play in as children and beneath stood the preacher, Bible in hand.

He took his position on the right side of the assembly as his friends lined themselves up to his right. Music began to play somewhere off to the side, and the guests began to rise from their seats. Everyone turned to face the house.

The back door to the home opened again and a radiant bride clad in white from head to toe stepped from the shadowy interior of the home out into the sunshine. The dress practically glowed as it reflected the summer sun.

As she neared Scott he strained to see through the veil, but the mesh was too dense to see her face. She took his hand and stepped beside him without a word as they turned to face the preacher. As the ceremony began, the words that were spoken were blurred and unintelligible; not so much words as sounds; a rising and falling of vocalization without form or meaning. He turned to his bride again and reached for the veil to see her face.

The ringing phone beside his bed shook him from his dream and nearly sent him to the floor.

He reached for the nightstand and checked the screen. It was Browning. It was also 5:30 in the morning.

"Yeah."

"Put your pants on. You need to get to the hospital. Now."

"What? Why? What's going on, man?"

"You'll see when you get there. Just get there. I'll meet you at the doors."

The ambulance arrived at the hospital ER entrance within a few minutes of the call from the checkpoint. The Chapel Hill station had responded to a call from the checkpoint on old Highway

96.

One adult male, one adult female, and two female children aged five and seven. All were badly dehydrated and malnourished. The adults had numerous lacerations, and the female had a broken wrist. The male appeared to have some sort of open wound to the left side of his torso. Both children were severely dehydrated, and one had a badly twisted ankle that had swollen to the point that walking was impossible.

The adults carried nearly empty packs on their backs with drained hydration bladders inside and water filtration gear, as if they had been hiking.

As the quartet approached the checkpoint the male had collapsed. The female fell beside him holding the five-year-old against her chest. They were spent.

Officers approached swiftly but cautiously and began to check the family out. Tucked in the waistbands of the adults they found each carried a handgun and spare magazines. Many rounds of which had been expended. Officers quickly secured the weapons and called the situation out over the radio. Within three minutes the ambulance had arrived and the EMTs started IVs on all four people. The adults were conscious enough to speak, but exhausted.

"Dave Browning," the man said.

"Hang on, sir, we'll get another ambulance and get you to the hospital ASAP," an officer
replied.

"We can all ride," the man said.

The officer looked at the EMT who shrugged his shoulder and motioned to load all four into the vehicle. The adults propped up against the walls of the ambulance while the kids occupied the gurney.

As they raced toward the medical center in Lewisburg the EMT turned to the mother.

"What happened to you all? Where did you come from?"

"Murfreesboro," she mumbled.

"Hey, ma'am, stay with me now. What's your name? What happened to you?"

Browning and Irwin raced into the ER. Without a word the charge nurse pointed down the hall. Browning quickly followed the finger and Irwin followed him.

Soon they stood at the foot of the bed where the five-year-old was fast asleep. In the bed beside her was the seven-year-old, also asleep. On the opposite side of the room were the parents.

Tom and Kim Richards were finally resting.

"What happened to them?" Scott asked.

"I don't know yet. They got to the checkpoint on Eagleville Highway and fell out. By the time I got the call they were all unconscious. EMTs were worried that they weren't going to make it."

"So, they've been out since they got here?"

"Yeah. They haven't been here long, though. I'll see if I can catch the doctor on call and find out any more information."

Dave stepped out of the room and Scott pulled up a chair beside his friend's bed. The sounds of the various monitors in the ER against an otherwise cold silence gave an ominous feel to the room.

"What the hell happened to you guys?" Scott muttered under his breath as he looked at the dozens of scratches and cuts along Tom's arms. His right hand was covered in lacerations, and the knuckles were swollen and red with dried blood and dirt.

Kim's hands were likewise filthy, her normally manicured nails chipped and broken with bits of hair and debris lodged in the cracks of one or two. Her cheeks were bruised, and she had a slender cut down her right cheek, about an inch and a half long, which ended just at the jaw line.

Scott carefully took notice of all the evidence he could, trying to see what tale their scars would tell while his friends still slept.

Dave came back in the room at a leisurely pace.

"Find out anything?"

"Yeah. Doc said they should all be fine. A few days of rest and fluids will take care of most of it. One of the girls has a pretty bad sprain that will take some time to get over and the obvious cuts and bruises will take some time to heal up, but they aren't in as bad of a shape as I thought."

"Any word on what happened to them?"

"Nope. Maybe we will find out tonight or tomorrow," Browning looked across at the girls and his mind quickly shifted to his own family.

Tom had been prepared. He had supplies and a plan. He wasn't a slacker when it came to comms or gear. His job had always given him an advantage when it came to being able to afford quality *and* quantity. What had happened?

As the pair sat silently wondering what had obviously gone awry in the Richards' bug out plan the nurse entered the room to check vitals. The young lady started on the opposite side with the children, making notes and minor adjustments here and there.

When she had finished there she moved across to the adults.

"Excuse me, guys. I need to work right where you're sitting."

"Oh, I'm sorry, ma'am. Let me get out of your way," Scott said as he and Dave quickly side stepped and gave her a wide swath of access.

The slender brunette noted the readings on Tom's monitors and checked the level of his IV solution. Dave immediately realized he didn't know the young lady despite being familiar with most of the staff here through his years on the force. "Ma'am?"

"Yes?" she replied without taking her eyes from the tasks at hand.

"I don't mean to be nosey, but are you new here? I know most of the staff by face if not by name through the police department, but you don't look familiar."

She turned and faced the pair who now had their attention fully on her.

"I just moved here a couple of days ago. I was working at the refugee center in Spring Hill, but I had to get out of there. It was getting to be too crazy up there for me." She extended her hand to Dave, "Denise Shelby," she said.

"Dave Browning. Glad to meet you."

She turned to Scott and again extended her hand.

"Scott Irwin. It's my pleasure, ma'am," he said. She was surprisingly attractive.

"I heard they had some trouble up there at the Center a few days ago. Is that why you left?" Dave didn't dance around issues often. He'd always subscribed to the military approach to things, bottom line up top. Tell what's important up front and worry about details later.

"Not to be too blunt, but yes. I was actually on my way home to California when everything fell apart. I ended up in Spring Hill. When they found out I was a nurse they gave me a job working at the facility. Everything was fine until more refugees started coming in and things got stupid. Fights started breaking out often and after the big one the other day I knew I didn't want to be there anymore. One of my nurses pulled some strings and got me moved here.

"You're both cops?"

"No ma'am," Browning said, "I am. Scott here is a pencil pushing nerd."

"That's the technical term for it. I'm actually an engineer with a firm in Nashville," Irwin corrected, "I had to move back home when things went off the rails myself. Now Browning has me attached to the local PD as part of a support program to help the officers."

She glanced back to the patients in her care, "So, are these people friends, victims, witnesses or suspects?"

"Friends," Scott said, "We haven't heard from them in several days and all of a sudden, they showed up at a check point early this morning like this. We've been trying to figure out what happened to them. Those are their daughters."

"Well, don't worry about them. They should be fine in a few days. They look pretty rough right now, but their injuries aren't as bad as they look," she smiled at the men, "I'll take good care of them. I promise."

The following day Scott returned to the hospital to check in on the Richards family. To his surprise, all four were awake and alert. He had unintentionally timed the visit with lunch, and they were all enjoying their meals.

"How about that," he said with a grin, "I've never seen anyone actually *enjoying* hospital food before."

"Hey, Scott," Tom began, "Man, it's good to see you. Browning just left a little while ago. I hear you guys dropped by yesterday, but we were 'unavailable.' Sorry about that." The man still managed a healthy grin to go with his comment despite looking like he had skirted the rim of Hell itself.

"Yeah, well, you looked like you were pretty tired, and I know how much you need your beauty sleep," the comment got a chuckle from Kim who almost spat a little yogurt out in the process.

Scott smiled at her. It was good to see them all awake and alert. They looked rough, to be sure, but it was great to see them, nonetheless.

"So, what happened? I mean, I know you probably already told Browning, but…"

"Communists," Tom said bluntly, "Communists, Socialists, Antifa. Whatever. Murfreesboro has been infested with them recently. It's a political thing that started on campus at the college.

When the economy tanked, it spread like wildfire.

"All these kids suddenly were slapped in the face with the reality that even if they did graduate, there would be no jobs to be had. No fine cars they could afford. No expensive homes they could finance themselves to death with. Their American Dream had been stolen from them, right before their eyes and they had nothing they could do about it.

"That's when these leftist groups started ramping up their propaganda machine, selling a new dream. A dream where capitalism was evil and had been the cause of what they saw before them. That the system had not just failed them but had abandoned them at the worst time."

"So, the movement grew pretty fast, huh?" Scott inquired.

"Their numbers exploded. Oh, there were a lot who didn't buy into it, but there were a lot more who did. Not all just college kids either. They hit up the projects and low-income neighborhoods too.

"When we decided to get out, they had already targeted our neighborhood for being 'too rich.' They intended to execute wealth redistribution in the only way they knew how: violently."

Tom shifted himself in the bed, trying to get comfortable, but not really succeeding. Kim picked up the story while he struggled with cords, cables and tubes.

"Part of the reason we didn't leave sooner was my fault. I really didn't think it had gotten that bad. Of course, since I left the agency, those two have been my purpose in life," she gestured to the girls who had gotten quiet and were listening intently.

"I hadn't been keeping up with things and didn't see the signs until it was too late. Tom kept saying that something bad was building, but I just dismissed it as his normal edginess. He's been expecting something to happen since before we met, so it was easy to think he was crying wolf.

"When Tom came home the other night he had already seen the people moving toward our side of town, even in our adjoining neighborhoods. They had begun to attack people and drag them into the streets from within their homes. The nicer the car in the driveway, the more likely it was going to be set ablaze. The nicer the home, well, you get the idea."

Scott's mind returned to the night he had to leave Franklin. It was the same situation, only a few weeks earlier.

"Okay, but you guys were prepared, right? I mean you always had a plan and everything, what happened? Why didn't you go to Knoxville?"

"You want the short version or the long version?" Tom asked.

"Short will work for me," Scott replied, "I'd hate for your…whatever that is…to get cold."

"We had the truck loaded and ready to go within thirty minutes of me getting home. All our gear was ready to roll. Comms online, mags loaded, everything. We rolled out of the garage and headed out of the subdivision when we ran dead on into them.

"These guys were pissed off and armed. Not like Hi Points and zip guns, man. I mean they had good gear and lots of it. Several of them had cocktails and stuff to throw, but a lot of them were toting some serious hardware. We tried to cut across a yard, but they had already decided that nobody was getting out of that neighborhood without going through them.

"So, we did."

"Did what? You bulldozed 'em?" Scott had a look of surprise on his face.

"Hey, man, state law says it is illegal to block a public thoroughfare for the purpose of unlawful assembly. They were being unlawful in their assembly, and I needed down the thoroughfare.

"We knocked several out of the way, some over and some to the side. One up on the roof for a few yards before he slid off into a cluster of garbage cans.

"The thing is, I was so pumped on adrenaline, I never heard the gunfire, I guess. The fuel tank had been hit and two tires had been shot out. I don't know how we managed to drive off without setting the truck on fire, throwing sparks off the rims like we had to be. We carried on until we couldn't go any farther and rolled the truck off into the bushes.

"There was no way to go back. No way to get to Knoxville, and no way to carry all the gear. We stayed with the truck the first night, then loaded up our packs with as much as we could and planned to go with Plan B; here. We torched the truck to keep anyone else from using it and hit the road on foot.

"What we didn't count on was having to go cross country as much as we did to avoid those idiots on the highways. When we left the truck, we had a van load of them come up on us about a quarter mile from the vehicle. We shoved the kids off the road and Kim and I exchanged lead with them before they finally left. I think I hit the driver. I'm pretty sure Kim hit their door gunner.

Unfortunately, I got grazed in the process." He motioned to the bandage on his side.

"A lot of the scratches and scrapes came from trying to move at night to avoid being seen. We'd stay low during the daytime and walk at night," Kim added, "It's not as easy to do when you don't have night vision gear and you aren't familiar with the terrain."

Denise came into the room to check on her patients about that time.

"Wow," she exclaimed, "I don't think I've ever seen anyone eat that much hospital food.

You guys must *really* like it!"

The girls giggled as Kim added, "I never knew hospital food could taste so good." Denise turned her attention to Scott.

"Back again, I see. I told you I'd take care of them, didn't I?"

"Yes ma'am, you did and I, for one, appreciate it. Now, if we can just get them out of your way I think they'd appreciate it too."

"One day at a time, Mr. Irwin."

Chapter Twenty-Three

Noobs

June 4th

The sun bore down on the hasty roadblock southeast of town. The strike team had just called in that they were ready to move in on the meth lab a few minutes earlier. Scott was close enough that he could respond quickly if anything went wrong, but far enough away to give a safe buffer zone for any traffic that he might have waiting on the narrow country road.

Traffic. Yeah, right. The only movement he had seen at all since blocking the lane had been the cattle that looked on across the fence with a casual curiosity.

At least the country road had plenty of shade so that the sunshine wasn't overbearing. The temperature was around 82 degrees with the heat index, so it was tolerable, but the dense canopy and foliage along the fence rows kept almost any air from moving. The shade picked up the slack.

After several minutes of silence, the radio crackled with the announcement that the scene was secure. Roadblocks were to be relieved, and all personnel were to report to the scene for cleanup.

Basically, that meant that they needed the roadblock vehicles to haul evidence and suspects back to the station while the crime scene was processed.

Scott sat in the driver's seat of the car and started the engine. This was his first experience with the auxiliary team since "training" a week ago. It was the most boring thing he could ever remember doing, and he had done some pretty boring things as an engineer.

Within a few seconds he pulled in what passed as a driveway at the lab. The rutted dirt trail across an overgrown front yard led almost directly to a small shed behind the main house. Scott could see officers carrying items out while four people were on the ground out front with hands behind their backs.

He rolled up and got out, making his way across the yard to the officer in charge and asked what his next task was going to be.

"Irwin, right?"

"Yeah," he replied, the hint of boredom evident in the tone

"I need you to take one of these idiots on in for me. We don't want them all in the same vehicle. When we question them, they don't need to have the chance to rehearse their stories with each other."

"Do you have a preference for who goes first?"

The lieutenant looked at the group and finally said, "Nope. Take your pick. If he starts telling you a sob story or anything just remind him that you're not a therapist and he's not on a couch." Scott walked over to the line of men who were now sitting upright on the ground.

"Okay fellas, who wants to go for a ride?" he asked in a tone as if talking to a pet. An officer close by heard the question and giggled quietly. None of the suspects responded.

"All right then," Scott said as he moved to the one closest to him, "Get your ass up and let's go. You're making me miss Family Feud."

He grabbed the man under the arm and hefted him to his feet before taking him to the back seat of the car.

Shortly after they arrived at the jail the second roadblock vehicle arrived with a passenger of its own. The support team member was Jeff Adams, the man from the first training session who had snorted at Simmons' naivety.

Jeff's man seemed to have a little more fight than Scott's as the two staggered about in the transfer bay.

Adams shoved the man into the holding cell and stepped back beside Scott.

"The other two are en route. Should be here soon. I'm gonna move my car. You might want to do the same."

"Yeah. They'll need the room if those two are as feisty as your guy," Scott commented.

"Yours didn't wanna fight?"

"Not a bit. Maybe he didn't like me."

Adams smiled as he headed to the vehicle.

Within a few minutes the four suspects were all inside and being processed. Across the street at the police department the officers were hauling in boxes of evidence from the trunks of a pair of patrol cars.

The lieutenant saw Adams and Irwin watching from across the street and motioned them over.

"Guys, I wanted to thank you for your help today. I know it wasn't a lot of excitement but having you two out there helped guarantee the safety of citizens that might have been caught in the middle if anything had happened. I appreciate that."

"You're welcome," they replied.

"Is there anything else we need to do today, Lieutenant?" Adams asked.

"No, as far as I know that's it for right now. Go home and enjoy Family Feud," he shot a grin at Scott, "We'll have something else before the week is out. I promise. In the meantime, I think you are scheduled for some firearms training tomorrow."

As the men turned to leave another patrol car pulled up and James Evans got out.

"What's up?" Scott asked, "Where have you been hiding today?"

James held up a handful of neatly folded papers, "Trying to hand these out but nobody seems to be home."

"Well, that's just inconsiderate, isn't it?" Scott smiled at his friend.

"What have you two been doing on such a lovely day?"

"Meth lab raid," Adams blurted out.

"Man, y'all get to have all the fun," Evans said with disappointment in his voice.

"Oh, yeah," Scott began, "it was just like you see in the movies, man, gunfight, car chase, massive explosions and fireballs. All that cool stuff."

"Yeah," Adams added, "Then he woke up and realized he was still standing in the middle of a dirt road listening to cows piss beside the car."

"That sounds more like my day," Evans quipped, "What are you about to do now?"

"Go home, I guess. Are you done for the day?"

"Yeah. We can't just leave the summons. They have to be hand delivered to the recipients so there is no doubt they got it. If we can't find them, we can't deliver them, so we're stopping for now.

Someone else will try again tonight."

Browning stepped outside the department door and headed for his friends on the sidewalk below.

"Simmons come in yet?"

"Haven't seen him, why?"

"He wanted me to keep an ear out for news from Washington. I may have something for him."

"I think he was on checkpoint duty at the interstate in Cornersville," Adams interjected,

"Want me to see if I can get him on the radio?"

"No. They should be rotating shifts about now. It can wait. Besides, he won't like what I heard."

"That bad?" Evans asked.

"It's pretty bad."

"I can try to call or text him if you want. I have his cell number," Scott suggested.

"Don't worry about it. Besides, there's no guarantee the message would go through since cell service is still so unreliable."

Since the Slip had taken place local utilities in the Southern States had remained relatively stable, but anything that required routing outside of the TVA area was, at best, a long shot. Cell phone service, long-distance calls, internet access, cable and satellite broadcasts; most all were unpredictable on a good day. Many times, they didn't work at all. When they did, there was little doubt that organizations such as the NSA and other federal agencies were watching and listening to feed the political camps.

"So, what are you hearing?" Adams asked.

"There have been extensive reports of rioting all around the Tacoma and Seattle areas. A lot of conservative businesses have been torched, and the state doesn't seem to be putting a lot of effort into investigating; or arresting, for that matter.

"It seems that the state is going pretty hard core on a conservative witch hunt. The transmission I heard mentioned something about a political camp being set up and a massive gun confiscation program being pushed. They are intentionally disarming their people to keep them under control.

"Things don't sound very pretty up there. It's not as bad as some other places, mind you, but still, it certainly doesn't sound like the open minded, tolerant, cries of a peaceful government to me."

"Sounds more like Nazism," Adams commented.

A truck pulled up near the group and began dispatching auxiliary and law enforcement team members. The checkpoint teams had begun rolling in.

A second truck arrived a few minutes later and one of the first over the tailgate was Simmons.

He stepped up to the cluster of men and exhaled sharply.

"Hey, guys. What's going on?"

"You got a minute?"

Chapter Twenty-Four

Trigger Time

June 5th

Neither the Police Department nor the Sheriff's office had an "official" firing range, but they did have access to a private one. A few miles outside of town, to the west, a former Navy man had set up a facility for his practical shooters club several years earlier. For a couple of decades, the place was only open to members, but he quickly saw the need for law enforcement to have a permanent place as well, so he made arrangements for their access.

It wasn't a fancy range, but it was isolated and adequate, nestled between the hills that formed a "C" shaped ridge line with sizeable berms pushed up to separate the individual bays on the lower levels. Most were ideal for pistol and shotgun use, but there was a long range that extended beyond one hundred yards for rifle applications as well. Following the road up to the top of the property afforded ranges out to a thousand yards, if you were that good.

The auxiliary team formed up on the firing line with the departmental instructor early in the morning. Downrange about ten yards stood a number of silhouette targets, one for each student.

Today would be handgun day. Scott didn't mind the practice; he just wished it was more…practical.

Each trainee loaded their sidearm and, on command, would fire a series of shots from a predetermined distance. It wasn't too dissimilar from the course of fire for the concealed carry permit that the state had established years earlier. It also didn't allow for any tactical aspects or movement. Stand. Shoot. Move to a new distance. Repeat.

At the end of the course the instructor tallied up their points. Each member had successfully passed the requirements for certification. Browning arrived as the scores were being announced.

He walked over to the instructor and asked if he could have some fresh targets and keep some of the trainees a bit longer. The instructor agreed and pulled a handful of rolled sheets out of his vehicle, handing them to Dave before stepping off to the side. He wasn't sure what Browning had in mind, but his curiosity was piqued.

"Irwin, Evans, Phillips, Adams, Simmons," Browning called out, "Step forward."

The men stepped back onto the range as the other trainees kept under the shade of the

shelter.

"We're going to run a few drills to sharpen your skills a bit. What you have done so far today is great and all…if you are ever faced with an angry mob of paper targets who intend to block your path."

The group chuckled quietly.

"How many rounds do you have left?"

The numbers ranged from fifty to "a couple hundred" from Evans.

"Tomorrow, you will bring extra ammunition to the range with you. You will need it. I would suggest a minimum of 100 rounds. The maximum is up to you. In a few days we will work on rifle drills. If you don't have one, you need one. See me later if you don't have access to one for regular use.

"For right now we are going to run some close-range drills. These will be unlike what some of you have done before. Speed is not the concern here. Don't shoot fast. Shoot careful."

Scott smiled at the quote from Clint Smith of Thunder Ranch. He and Browning had attended a few classes there years earlier, before careers and family obligations complicated things so much.

The men were released to load their magazines and return to the firing line. Each man stepped "toe to toe" with their targets. On command, each man would step back and punch forward with a palm strike to the face of their target while simultaneously drawing their sidearm and firing from the hip downward into the lower portion of the target. The distance and angle of the shot would have placed the round into the lower torso, legs, or genitalia of the target, had the situation been real. The whole time, the trainees were moving backward and raising the line of sight on their weapons to a more lethal center of mass.

After a series of repetitions, they began to work on shooting while moving. Rather than sidestepping to the right or the left, the trainees would turn their legs in the direction they needed to go while twisting their torsos to face the threat. Using the corner of the slide as an improvised sight allowed reasonably accurate shot placement even on the move.

It didn't take long before the trainees began to exhaust their ammunition for the day, but each was satisfied with their results and wished that they could continue the session.

Browning dismissed the class, and the departmental instructor approached him with a grin.

"That's some pretty nice techniques you were showing there, Dave. Where did you pick that up from?"

"We arranged for a close-range gunfighting class a few years ago. Evans, Phillips and Irwin were in the class, I just wanted to see how much they remembered."

"I noticed that those three seemed to pick it up pretty quickly. Was Adams in it as well?"

"No, he has prior military experience, so I figured he'd catch on fast." The instructor mulled the revelations over in his mind for a bit.

"Interesting. Say, would you mind if I sat in on the next session you cover with them?"

"Not at all. Maybe you can learn a thing or two," Browning said with a grin.

That night as the Irwins sat down to supper Scott noticed a vacancy at the table.

"Where's Whitney?"

"She found a place to stay in town," his mother said, "And a job."

"Really? Well, that's good. It's nice to see she's moving on and adjusting. I was really worried about her for a while."

"I wouldn't stop worrying just yet," Carol said, "She seems like the type to fall in with the wrong crowd, if you know what I mean."

Rachel came in and took what had become her usual seat beside Scott at the table. James, who had been spending the majority of the past few weeks at the Irwin home, had decided to go to his father's house and work on getting his HAM equipment set back up. It was uncannily quiet in the Irwin home for a change.

After a brief prayer from Ben, the foursome loaded plates and passed bowls until everyone was adequately filled. The portions had gotten smaller since the groceries were harder to come by, but the quality of the food had definitely improved.

Scott noticed that he had needed to tighten his belt a bit more in recent days. He had also noticed that he had extra energy that seemed to escape him when he was at the firm. All the increased activity, the training, and the dietary changes were beginning to get him into a lean condition like no gym membership ever had.

He had noticed a change in Rachel as well. She was attractive before, but now she was lithe and slender to a new level of sexy. She had essentially stopped wearing makeup since it was simply too hard to find, but her natural beauty was more than enough to turn Scott's head any day.

Rachel spent a lot of her time helping keep up with the business side of the farm. Ben had always disliked the paperwork side of farming and now that they had to deal with bartering as well as other currency it was a nuisance to him. Rachel had offered to help in order to earn her keep.

She would help with chores as well and quickly found that she fit in well around the homestead. She actually discovered that she enjoyed working the garden and the chickens quite a bit. Rachel never would have imagined that a few short weeks ago she would be enjoying farming, yet here she was.

"So," Scott said as he helped clear the dishes from the table, "Mom, you mentioned Whitney had found a job. What's she doing? I'm sure James would be interested." He smiled a bit of a dirty smile.

"She is helping out at one of the stores in town. You know Ginsberg's. Well, Mr. Ginsberg needed someone to help a few hours a day with customers and the like. Of course there's that apartment above the store, so he made a deal with her that she could stay there for free if she would help him with the business."

"That's good. It'll be good for her to stay busy. On top of that, Mr. Ginsberg could use the help, I'm sure. How old is he, anyway?"

"Oh, my," Carol said as she stopped washing dishes to consider the question, "I'd say he has to be in his nineties, wouldn't you, dear?"

"What?" Ben asked, "I wasn't listening."

"How old is Mr. Ginsberg? Do you have any idea?" Ben considered it briefly.

"Ninety-two, I think. He's been running that little store of his since he came to town over seventy years ago."

"Wow. I didn't realize he'd been here that long," Scott said, "It's amazing he's been able to stay in business with competition from the big chain stores like he has...well, had"

"Never underestimate the determination of the little guy, son."

"Speaking of little guys, Ben, don't forget we have to go to Spring Hill and trade for some honey with the Robertsons."

"I haven't forgotten, dear," Ben said with a small chuckle.

Mr. Robertson was a petite little fellow. His wife stood a full eight inches over him. They were good people and fair business folk. The Robertsons had a huge honey farm outside of Spring Hill and were always glad to barter for things they couldn't raise themselves. They had even talked at great length about putting some hives on the Irwin farm in exchange for honey rights, but the distance always became the deal breaker.

Harvesting honey was a time-consuming operation and to add the extra drive time and fuel costs only made it more expensive. When you factored in the maintenance and upkeep on the hives and bees over the course of the year it became more cost prohibitive. Had the economy not tanked, there would probably be several hives dotting the Irwin property already.

"Scott?" Rachel called from the dining room.

"Yes ma'am?"

"Don't call me that. It makes me feel old," she said with a smile.

"Just trying to be respectful. What's up?"

"Do you have to go to the department tomorrow?"

"Yeah, Dave is wanting us to run the range again tomorrow. Why? Do you need me to stick around here?"

"Actually, I was wondering if you could take me to the range again. I was thinking about it today and since I'm here on the farm all the time it would be a good idea if I was a little more proficient with…well…defense."

"Yeah, I can see that."

"Since you're going to be on the range anyway…"

"I don't know about that. It's not like we'll be on our property. I'd have to get it cleared with the department."

Rachel pouted her lip out just a little and tried her best at the sad puppy eyes. "Oh, now, that's just not fair."

The next day Rachel joined Scott, James, Andy, Jeff, Dale, and Dave on the firing line. The first order of business for Dave was a skills assessment of Rachel. He needed to know where she stood and how comfortable she was to determine whether or not she was ready to run with the others. He was pleasantly surprised.

"Do you have a pistol?"

"No."

Dave looked at the team and, without a word, Evans broke ranks and trotted to his range bag. He promptly stepped up with a Glock 22 in a simple Kydex holster and a full magazine of ammunition.

"I had a feeling *you* would have a spare," Dave said with a grin.

"Hey, two is one and one is none, right?"

Rachel clipped the holster in her waistband and press checked the pistol. She holstered the weapon and put on her eye and ear protection.

Her marksmanship was acceptable, and her grip and stance were actually very good. He could tell by the methodology in her presentation and recovery that either James or Scott, or both, had worked with her. She wasn't entirely up to their speed yet, but she had a good grasp of the fundamentals and that was something to work with.

"Okay, Rachel, I want you to sit back and watch for a few minutes. See what we do and how we do it. If you feel comfortable with what you see, let me know and we'll get you started on learning how to do it too."

Rachel nodded her head and pulled up a seat under the shelter where she could clearly see what was going on. Beside her stood the departmental instructor who smiled and nodded at her, recognizing her accomplishment.

The team began with a review of the day before and then proceeded to moving in different directions while engaging targets. She could see that Simmons was a bit awkward compared to the others, which made her feel a little better about being the newcomer to the firing line.

After an hour of watching, she couldn't stand it any longer and raised her hand, getting Dave's attention.

"Yes?"

"I'd like to give that a try."

Dave smiled. Scott had told him she was a bit on the competitive side when it came to pushing herself on new things.

"Take five, guys. Let the lady have a shot."

The team fell back for water and shade as Rachel stepped up. Dave quickly recited the drill from the day before and placed her in front of a target. He showed her the appropriate way to perform a palm strike, and they ran the drill dry a few times before he called to the rest of the group, "Range is hot!"

Dave stepped behind her and waited a few seconds to let her anxiety build a bit before shouting over her shoulder, "Go!"

She popped the target in the center of the head with the heel of her hand as she stepped back a half step and began to draw her weapon. The striking hand quickly moved to her chest, palm toward her as the pistol cleared the holster. She continued the step backward and pivoted the Glock toward the target, angling the barrel toward the lower part of the torso as her finger found the trigger. When her right foot planted firmly behind her and beside her left foot, she pulled the trigger twice, driving two .40 caliber rounds into the target and releasing the trigger. After a quick glance to either side she returned the pistol to the holster.

"Damn," the instructor said, "You boys had better watch out. She's a natural."

James and Scott both smiled and gave each other a goofy fist bump. From that point on Rachel was an integral part of any range time the group had.

Chapter Twenty-Five

Time to Shine

June 6th

"Gear up!" The lieutenant had called in his strike team for another raid. It hadn't been a full week yet and the auxiliary team members were on assignment again. This time they were supporting a raid on an illegal moonshine operation.

Now, in this part of the country, homemade alcohol was tradition. It always had been. Much of the American Revolution was funded by smugglers, bootleggers, and shiners and the recipes had only evolved with the nation. Under the prohibition era the tradition helped give rise to what would eventually become NASCAR. It was woven into the fabric of the culture. That didn't mean it was legal.

Under the new economy, the local governments didn't worry about dealing with the BATFE anymore and the brewers and shiners didn't worry about federal raids. There were no teeth in the ATF dog anymore, so there was no fear like in the old days of revenuers and gangsters.

To keep it under control, and to boost the local economies, many local governments offered licensing to the home brew community in exchange for taxes, revenues, and even products. In some cases, the still operators agreed to produce alcohol for medical applications in addition to that for consumption in exchange for licensing. Sometimes it was produced as fuel. It was all just semantics, really, but it made everyone happy. Everyone except the ones who didn't want to play by the rules.

There were always some.

For raids like this the strike team typically took the use of the MRAP donated by the feds years earlier. Team leaders would follow in the Humvee, and the auxiliary members would roll in ahead with standard unmarked patrol cars to set up the road blocks.

The militarization of local law enforcement was seen by many as a way to prepare the government for a civil uprising where all law enforcement agencies, under the oversight of Homeland Security, would work together to maintain peace and control. It didn't quite work out that way and departments around the country were left in possession of vehicles and equipment they had no use for to begin with. At least here they "blew the soot out" every now and then.

Adams lined his vehicle up on the narrow road and parked at a moderate angle to prevent anyone from getting by. On the opposite side of the target area Scott did the same. Simmons and Evans accompanied the lieutenant in the Humvee and parked just short of the suspect house. Their vehicle would act as a command and communication hub between all the assets on the ground.

The MRAP was called up and the strike team was quickly dispatched at the house. The building and occupants were quickly secured, but the main suspects were nowhere to be found.

The next phase led the team into the woods and across the hilltop behind the house. A freshwater stream bubbled along the valley floor, eventually passing in front of the house and onto the neighbor's property. They followed the flow of the water upstream where they got eyes on the still.

A radio call from the team leader alerted everyone that they were in sight of the still, but no suspects were in sight.

"Copy, Team Leader. Proceed with caution. Secure the equipment and arrest any individuals in the area. These men are known to be armed and should be considered dangerous.

"All team members be advised that we may have armed suspects on foot in the area. Stay alert and report any suspicious activity."

Back in the valley the strike team had fanned out across a large area and was slowly approaching the still. From up the hill a single rifle shot rang out and one of the members dropped.

The remaining men scrambled for cover as the team leader called over the radio, "Shots fired! Officer down!"

Another rifle crack echoed through the valley as a figure rose and broke cover near the top of the hill. Gunfire shredded leaves and bark as the man scampered over the crest of the hill and down toward the front of the property.

From the opposite side of the valley another shot rang out, dropping another officer who had taken cover behind a large, uprooted tree. His back was completely exposed to the new threat.

"Officer Down!" the call echoed over the radio as it blended with the background noise of sporadic gunfire.

The second figure ducked behind a large rock and made his escape. The team leader split the remaining officers into pursuit and cover elements as he called out descriptions and headings to his commander.

Adams scanned the hillside as the popping of rifle fire seemed to come from every angle before him. A flurry of movement to his right caught his attention.

"Stop!" he called, placing his hand on his sidearm. But the figure kept coming. In his hand the man bore a rifle, which he was beginning to bring up to his eye.

Adams quickly moved to the opposite side of the patrol car and called to the man again,

"Stop or I *will* shoot!"

The man replied with a pair of .30 caliber rounds from the lever action Marlin in his hands.

"*I warned you twice, you bastard,*" Adams muttered. Despite the distance, Jeff opened fire on the man who panicked and dodged behind a tree.

Following another pair of shots the man took a chance at moving up to within fifty yards of the patrol car. If he could take Adams out, he could get away in the car.

Adams popped a couple more rounds, narrowly missing the attacker who replied with another volley of his own. Soon the man was almost at the car.

Adams slipped back to the passenger side and jammed his SIG 226 through the open window where he fired another shot.

The man stumbled as the .40 caliber hollow point punched through the thin camouflage tee shirt and expanded in his left chest. His forward momentum kept him upright and moving forward as he drove on toward the getaway car.

A second round belched forth from the SIG, slamming the man almost in the centerline of the chest, just at the top of the sternum. Fragments of bone and tissue tore into the chest cavity as the bullet fragmented, spinning bits of copper jacket and lead bullet off into the heart and lungs and pulverizing his esophagus. He dropped face first into the dirt; the rifle slipping from his grip and bouncing ahead of the body.

Adams took a second to catch his breath and calm down before grabbing his radio. With an eerily calm voice he announced, "Suspect down."

The second suspect raced toward Scott's vehicle. He had the same plan as his partner.

Maybe he wouldn't have the same luck.

Scott radioed in that the second suspect was heading his way before drawing his own weapon and calling to the man, "Stop right there! I will shoot!"

Just like his partner the man plowed on through the ground cover and underbrush. Scott saw the man raise his rifle, an AR-15, and he ducked for cover behind the passenger side fender of his car.

The suspect opened with a barrage of .223 rounds that all flew well above the vehicle. He wasn't aiming, he was running. All he had to do was get to the car.

Scott popped his head around the front bumper and fired a three-round burst of his own slamming 9mm rounds into the dirt well in front of the fast-approaching man. As the man reached the bottom of the hill and hopped across the small ditch beside the road Scott fired two more shots.

Neither struck the man but were close enough to get his attention.

The suspect swung the rifle up to his shoulder and fired five more rounds at the fender of the car, not wanting to damage his means of escape, but not wanting to have to fight over it either.

Scott scooted back behind the wheel for extra protection. His adrenaline was pumping, and he was beginning to get tunnel vision.

"I've about had enough of this shit," he said and stood up behind the car, pointing the Glock directly at the man and firing as he himself broke into a run. It was a collision course that neither men had planned nor expected.

The suspect hesitated and was late bringing his rifle back up to engage. Scott was in a full run, and he was focused on the man, not his sights. Hollow point rounds sprayed all around the suspect without a single one striking home.

Time slowed as the two connected. Irwin brought the pistol up and clubbed the man along the left side of his head as he gripped the AR with his left hand and twisted the rifle upward.

Dazed by the sudden head strike, the man didn't have a response. As the rifle twisted from his possession he yanked the trigger, discharging another two rounds into the air that would fall harmlessly into the neighboring field.

Irwin then slammed the pistol down, striking the man on the neck with his forearm. It was an unintentional repeat of the move he'd used in Franklin on the home invaders at the Davis residence.

The man's eyes rolled white as he slumped to the ground in a heap. Scott dropped the rifle and quickly fished a pair of zip tie handcuffs from his pocket. He rolled the man over and cuffed him before collecting the rifle and clearing the chamber. A pair of officers jumped the ditch to assist but quickly realized it was all over.

"Suspect in custody," one of them called over the radio with a laugh.

"Damn, Irwin. That was awesome! We saw the whole thing coming down the hill!"

"Well, if you saw it, why didn't you shoot him?"

"We didn't have a clear shot," the second officer said, "We didn't want to hit you. Are you okay?"

Scott was shaking from the adrenaline rush.

"Yeah. I'm just pissed off is all."

Chapter Twenty-Six

Gold Stars

June 7th

The roll call was over, and the officers began to disperse to their respective patrol routes.

"What's on the schedule for us today, Dave?" Simmons asked.

"You, Phillips and Evans sit tight. Scott, you and Adams follow me. The Chief wants to talk to you for a bit."

The men looked nervously at each other as if they were back in school and the principal had called them into the office.

Evans' expression clearly questioned 'why' without uttering a word.

With a shrug of his shoulders Irwin turned to follow his friend down the hall.

Scott and Jeff stood outside the Chief's office, unsure of what to expect following the raid from earlier. Both men knew they were only to be there in a support role and wondered if they had exceeded their authority to support the team.

The door swung open, and Browning called the pair in. The lieutenant from the strike team stood to the right of the room and Browning moved to the left.

"Have a seat, gentlemen," he said as he motioned to the chairs in front of the Chief's desk.

"Boys," the elder officer began, "I understand that things went a little off track with this raid yesterday."

"Yes sir," they replied.

"Well, it's been my experience that sometimes things like that happen," he leaned back in his chair and glanced at Browning, then the lieutenant, "From what I understand, you two engaged and subdued two armed individuals who had already shot two of my men. Is that a fair summation?" Scott suddenly felt uneasy.

"Yes sir."

"And you both did this despite being told that you were only there in a support role, correct?"

"Yes sir."

"You, in fact, were not trained for this type of engagement, is that also correct?"

"Yes sir."

Scott shot a look at Browning who stood in silence. A slight smile cracked across his friend's face. Irwin began to wonder where this line of questioning was headed.

"Would either of you care to explain your actions?"

"Sir," Scott began, "We were there to support the team. When the team began taking fire and casualties, we were advised to be on the lookout for suspects who were on the move. We were not told to observe and report, and we were not told *not* to engage. Logically, it seemed that the best way to support our team was to engage and subdue."

"Lieutenant?"

"Yes sir?"

"Did you tell these men not to engage the suspects?"

"No sir."

The office fell silent for a lengthy few seconds.

"Well, thank God for that," he turned to face the pair across his desk, "I can only think of one thing to do, gentlemen." The elderly officer rose from his chair and stepped to the side of his desk.

"I'm going to recommend the two of you for the Medal of Appreciation for services rendered in support of this department."

Scott suddenly felt a wave of relief wash over him as Jeff cracked a smile.

"Now, we have certificates available, but I'm hoping we can actually get the medals themselves. If not, well, we'll cross that road when we come to it." He smiled a beaming smile at the pair and extended his hand to each of them.

As they left the office Adams was grinning from ear to ear.

"Man, I thought he was about to get all in our asses in there!"

"Yeah," Scott replied, "Me too. I'll take a commendation any day over a tail chewing."

"Congratulations, guys. You know, there aren't many civilian awards out there, so don't take this too lightly. Law enforcement doesn't hand these things out often. Even less lately, I'm sure," Browning added.

The three men rounded the corner where the other auxiliary team members waited.

"What happened to you guys?" Simmons asked.

"We got a raise," Adams popped back.

Evans and Simmons looked at each other doubtfully.

"What? What do you mean, 'a raise'? We don't get paid. How'd you get a raise?" Scott just laughed.

"So, what are we doing today, Dave?" Phillips finally asked.

"I think today we'll run rifles on the range. We need to work on our skills with long guns.

Everyone up for that?"

"Well, actually, I don't have a rifle," Simmons said awkwardly.

Adams shot him an odd look, "What? You have your carry permit but not a rifle? What's up with that?"

"I didn't get a permit to carry a *rifle*; I got a permit to carry a *pistol*. I don't hunt, so what did I need a rifle for? I never knew I was going to be playing policeman when all this started."

"Don't worry about it," Browning said, "We'll get you a rifle to use for the day. Firearms aren't easy to come by these days, but I'm trying to work on getting some lined up for you guys to use. Since the raid the other day I'm thinking we need to make sure you are properly equipped. "Meanwhile, grab your eye and ear protection and get ready to go to the range."

"Dave?" Scott piped up, "Would you mind if I called Rachel to sit in on the session? She could bring a spare rifle and ammo too."

"Sure. It's kind of nice having a cultured female around for a change, instead of looking at your ugly mugs all day," he laughed, "Besides, I'd much rather work on grip and stance with her than any of you any day."

Within about an hour the small team, the departmental instructor, the SWAT instructor, and Rachel had all arrived at the range. This time they worked on the one-hundred-yard range, beginning with a dry fire session to familiarize everyone with what they would be learning for the day.

The initial drills they ran weren't entirely dissimilar from those they had run with handguns before. They worked on cover versus concealment and tactical reloads as well as malfunctions, which was considerably more frustrating than with handguns.

"Wow," Rachel said during their first break, "I have to say I liked clearing jams a lot more when we shot pistols last time. All this with the rifles is a lot to handle if you try to do it fast."

"Yeah," Simmons agreed, "I don't think I'll ever get the hang of some of this stuff."

"Y'all are doing great," Dave said, "It's all about repetition. The more you practice, the better you'll get."

"I, for one, am very impressed by what I've seen out of you folks already," the SWAT instructor added, "It's hard to believe that you are all just civilians and have developed such a degree of capability."

"Well, Adams over there has a military background, so he's been through this before. That's why he's good at everything," Evans began, "You can blame Dave for Scott, Andy and me. Our little circle of friends used to come here a lot before we got jobs and families. We'd run the ranges with anything and everything we could. Rifles, pistols, shotguns; you name it, we shot it.   "Rachel has been practicing with Scott and me whenever time allows. She's a quick study and really picks up on things. I never thought I'd say it, but she's turning into a real threat."

The group laughed as a slight blush washed over Rachel's face.

"A few weeks ago, I had never even touched a firearm," she admitted, "Didn't want to, either, for that matter. Then everything got crazy, and Scott told me I was going to learn to shoot."

Adams commented, "Well, he's done a pretty good job. So far."

"That means a lot coming from an Army man," Scott quipped.

"Don't be so quick about my military background. I was a tanker. The gun I shot was 120 millimeters. I didn't get to play with the little stuff very often," he took a long sip of his water before continuing, "Little to me was a Ma Deuce."

"That reminds me," Dave said, "I've been working with the Chief and the Sheriff on trying to get access to some weapons you guys can use on these raids. The department doesn't have a bunch of issue weapons just lying around, but after recent events, we've been trying to figure out how we can get you guys 'up-armored' for the next one. I think we have a plan.

"In our evidence vault we have a number of weapons that have been confiscated from different suspects. Among them are some pretty good sidearms and rifles as well as some shotguns and a lot of blades. Most of these weapons are to be disposed of through either auctions or destruction. The suspects won't be able to get them back.

"Up until recently, public pressure would have demanded their destruction, and the ATF would have been on us to as well. Now that all that's changed, we aren't sure what to do with them. My suggestion was to issue them to you along with ammo and accessories that might have come in along with the arrest."

"Seriously?" Simmons asked, "What's the catch?"

"They would be considered issued weapons. If you quit the program, you turn everything back in. Other than that, you have to train with them and maintain them. That's it."

Rachel's jaw dropped a little, "Wait. You mean you get a 'free' rifle or pistol? And all you have to do is take care of it and train with it?"

"That's the plan."

"How do I get in on this plan?"

Chapter Twenty-Seven

Backstory

June 8th

"So, do you guys need anything?" Scott sat back in the chair in the hospital room beside Tom's bed.

"No. We're fine. I appreciate you dropping by and checking on us. Keeping us updated on what's going on outside, and everything. Hopefully we'll be out of here in another day or two."

Irwin smiled, "I know we'll be glad to see you all out of here."

Denise walked through the door as the words rolled off Scott's tongue.

"Hey, don't be rushing my best patients out of here. They're the most fun I've had at my job in a long time."

Kim laughed, "He has important obligations now, Denise. Scott just promised to take the girls to the farm and let them see the animals when we get out. I think they're ready to go now."

"Well, it won't be long, ladies," Denise said as she glanced at the tiny duo across the room.

"Speaking of ready to go, I guess I'd better get that way. I have to meet Dave in a little bit and cover our next assignment," Scott stood and stretched before making his way to the girls' side of the room, "You two stay out of trouble now. I don't want to hear of any wheelchair races down the hallways or anything, okay?"

The girls giggled and nodded.

"If you do, be sure to call me first. I might want to race too," he smiled, "Tom, you and Kim let me know if you think of anything you need. Any time. I'll see you tomorrow."

"We will," Kim said, "Oh, and by the way, congratulations on your medal. You must be really proud."

A sudden blush filled Irwin's cheeks.

"Oh, you heard about that, huh?"

"Dave told us about it," Tom added, "Congratulations. Maybe we'll be out of here for the presentation ceremony."

"Oh, it's not that big of a deal," he said as he stepped to the doorway, "Just, you know, doing the job."

With a wave he stepped out the doorway and proceeded down the hall.

Denise busied herself with the latest charts and reports for a second before checking the equipment readings on her patients.

"He seems really nice," she finally said, "What was all that about a medal?"

Tom quickly recounted the incident at the raid and told of the impending commendations that were to be awarded.

"He's really being modest about it. Dave said that the department doesn't hand out many tokens of appreciation to civilians," Kim added.

Denise turned her attention to the girls as she continued her conversation.

"Really? Well, that's pretty cool. Someone who's not afraid of doing the right thing in this day and time.

"His family must be really proud of him."

"Oh, I'm sure his parents haven't even heard anything about it. He wouldn't have said anything anyway. That's just the way Scott is," Tom said.

"I meant his wife and kids. Surely, they know."

"Oh, he's not married. Never has been. No kids either."

Denise studied the information for a second, "I just assumed with the way he plays and picks with the kids and everything…"

"No," Kim replied, "He married a career. Now that it's basically gone, I'm not sure what he's going to do. I can guarantee one thing, though, whoever or whatever gets his attention next will be treated with the same level of loyalty and dedication."

"Ladies," Tom said as he sat up on the bed, "Y'all will have to excuse me. This conversation sounds like it has reached the perfect point for me to go to the bathroom." He smiled as he eased out of the bed and across the room to the small bathroom at the far end.

Denise smiled as she resumed the conversation, "What do you mean?"

"Well, these guys, Tom included, are all high school buddies. They were called the 'Dirty Dozen' because there were twelve of them and they were always into something. I didn't meet Tom until college, but you could tell there was a certain…honor or fellowship among them.

"They all have different backgrounds and personalities; different senses of humor and so on, but they formed this kind of brotherhood that has always been incredibly strong. That loyalty extends to their families as well. You can always count on them to be there for you if you need them."

"I know Scott was an engineer, did all the rest go into law enforcement?"

"No. Most did or went into the military, but a few didn't. Scott was one of those. Tom was another.

"Dave, of course, did. Eric is a sniper with the Metro Nashville SWAT team. Donnie is a sheriff in L.A. now."

Denise perked up, "Los Angeles?"

"Lower Alabama. Sorry. Different L.A. around here," Kim said with a smile.

"Then there was Danny. He and Scott were almost like twins. They looked a little similar, but the real likeness was in their personalities. Both had this unbearably dry, sarcastic sense of humor and they would play off of each other and drive you nuts. They knew they did, and they loved every minute of it," Kim had a strange look on her face as she reminisced about the men.

"What happened to him? Is he a police officer too?"

"No. He joined the Army. I only met him a few times, but you would have thought he had known me all his life the way he picked.

"He was a Crew Chief of a helicopter crew. His chopper was shot down on a mission in Yemen about six years ago. No survivors."

"I didn't know we were ever at war with Yemen."

"We weren't. The 'official' story was that the crash was due to a mechanical failure, but we found out, off the record, of course, that his chopper had been sent in to extract a team of Special Forces operators when they were shot down. It was all whitewashed in the media and covered up to save the embarrassment of the White House.

"It makes you wonder, if they would go to those lengths to cover something like that up, how far would they go to cover something bigger up, you know?"

Denise really hadn't thought about it before. She typically had a narrow view of the world, like most people do. Go to work; pay bills; eat; sleep; repeat. She didn't care for politics or news or anything like that, but she was realizing that maybe she needed to pay more attention to the world around her. She would definitely be paying more attention to Scott Irwin.

Dave gathered all the team members in the courtroom at the station for an impromptu meeting. Among the regular team members sat Rachel. Despite not having her concealed carry permit, she had convinced Dave, the SWAT instructor and the regular instructor of her skills with firearms and gotten assigned to the team.

The Sheriff and the Chief had both reluctantly agreed to her admission, but only if she was to be used in a strictly supporting role. She was quickly brought up to speed on communications and radio operations and would be allowed to be a part of the next job.

She and Evans had spent the morning brushing up on her pistol skills while Scott had been visiting Tom and Kim in the hospital.

"Okay," Dave said with a sigh, "This morning, while you all were rolling around in your warm beds I was in here pulling teeth to get you what you need to do your jobs. Thanks to my charm and irrepressible political skills, we now have access to the confiscated weapons cache here at the station."

A few smiles spread across faces as Browning continued.

"Here in a few minutes, we will take you down and issue out firearms to those who need them. Each of you will be responsible for the maintenance and upkeep of these weapons. If you decide you are no longer interested in this line of work, you will be asked to turn them in.

"Now, before we go into the fine print and paperwork, I want to make it clear. These are not match grade guns. In most cases they are not even high-end. I refuse to issue garbage to you and expect you to defend yourself or anyone else with it. The turds will stay in the toilet, ladies and gentlemen. Having said that, there are some very nice items in the mix as well.

"When I call your name, please step up and form a line here. We will then go to the evidence room and begin signing these out to you."

Simmons and Rachel joined the small group of members and soon headed down the hallway and into the back. A clerk waited with a clipboard at the doorway to the evidence room. As each member stepped up, they provided their identification and verified name and address.

Simmons was issued a newer model Mini-14 that was collected with four of the Ruger brand magazines and a pair of cheaper copies. The clerk asked if he needed a knife as he motioned to an array of blades on a table just inside the door.

"Nah," he said, "I think I have one at home I can use."

Rachel was the last one in line. Dave stepped up with her and informed the clerk that hers was a special circumstance since she was not a local resident but was currently living at the same address as Scott.

"So, you're the one. I talked to Ben the other day and he said he'd had company living there for a few weeks. Glad to hear y'all made it out of Nashville and Franklin alright," the man smiled,

"Let's see what we have for you."

He checked his clipboard and stepped back into the room for a few seconds before returning with a Glock 22 in .40 caliber with a pair of factory magazines and a pair of Magpul magazines in pouches before disappearing to the back again.

Returning from the second trip he carried a 16" CMMG AR-15. The furniture was all Flat Dark Earth with Magpul back up sights on the flat top railing. Clamped onto the rail toward the rear was a small holographic sight. She would have to learn how to use the Vortex Strike Fire the next time she went to the range, but that was okay. Range time was next on the activity list for the day.

A broad smile crossed her face as she looked at the clerk and sheepishly said, "Thank you."

The man smiled back and said, "I feel like Santa now."

Chapter Twenty-Eight

Baptism

June 9th

Early in the morning, before the sun broke over the hills to the east, the strike team was assembled and en route to a significant drug bust. The larger group this time included Rachel who, along with Adams, would be assigned to the command Humvee as a communications technician and observer. Irwin, Evans, Phillips, and Simmons would be acting as containment and traffic safety elements to keep the public at a safe distance.

"Sweeps Week," as it had come to be known at the department, would conclude with this raid. One of the suspects from a previous arrest had sought to make a deal and spilled his guts about this location.

The property was a large, elegant older home on the west side of the county, not far from the interstate. It was being used as a hideout and a storage and distribution facility by a drug lord from Maury County. By keeping under the radar and being very discrete, he had managed to funnel drugs and even weapons through the place for years without being caught.

If the information was correct, the bust should put a decisive end to the traffic and be a major impact to the illicit industry in at least two counties. Due to the sensitive nature of the information, only a handful of people had been included in the planning of the job, to minimize the potential for a breach of security.

Since the house was situated on the side of a hill which overlooked the only road in or out of the area, care was taken to be sure the strike team members in the lead were walked in from adjoining properties.

The road was secured at both ends and the command vehicle moved into position just around the curve in the road that obscured it from the house. About halfway between the ends of the road and the house a second roadblock was set up to restrict access or movement further. Scott and his team would occupy these positions.

When the team members were all in position, the order was given to move in and secure the structure and occupants. Reserve members would immediately move in to a stand-by position for deployment if needed.

As the entry team approached the back of the house, down the hillside, movement inside the building let them know they had been compromised. Somewhere, somehow, they had been spotted.

It was too late to worry about how they would have to adjust their plan and make it work.

The wrap around porch on the southern downhill side of the structure was high enough off the ground as to prevent any easy access to the front of the house. It also helped to serve as an impressive sniper platform since the vantage from it overlooked the majority of the open driveway and nearly a 230° view of the surrounding area out to as much as 700 yards.

The backup team moved into their staging positions around the property while one of the SWAT snipers provided as much overwatch as he could from a barn loft next door. The second sniper position was behind the house in the woods, but visibility to the interior of the house was more restricted since that side lacked the large windows and sliding glass doors of the front side.

As the first of the strike team approached the house the chatter of gunfire erupted from a small storage building. Ducking behind trees and rocks, the team scrambled for cover and vantage points from which they could return fire.

From the west side of the main house came more gunfire as a second individual peered around the corner and brought his weapon to bear.

Phillips and Irwin listened to the echoing shots as they pierced the morning air. Both men considered keying the microphone to get a situation report, but knew that comms had to remain clear.

"Man, I wish I knew what was going on up there," Phillips muttered.

"I know. If they need us they'll call. Don't forget, we're just here for traffic control," Irwin reminded, "You *are* locked and loaded though, right?"

Phillips smiled and tightened his grip on the AR-15 in his hands.

"Keep your attention on the hilltops. I'll watch the road. I don't expect to see anyone coming in or out right now, but you never know," Irwin suggested.

On the opposite end of the gauntlet Evans and Simmons were focused on the sounds echoing across the hilltop as well.

"Sounds like the party has started," Simmons said.

"Yep. Sounds like a blowout too."

From up ahead they saw a flash of yellow orange from the barn loft. The sniper had taken one shot, but they didn't know if there was a kill to go with it or not. The radio remained quiet as a volley of gunfire echoed down the hill toward the red barn.

Evans gripped the AR as he strained through the early morning light to see what was happening down the road. He looked over to see Simmons watching through a pair of compact binoculars.

"Wha…where'd you get those?" Evans demanded.

"These? I brought these from home. I wasn't sure I'd be able to see what was going on since we were going to be on the outer edge, but at least I can see the barn from here."

"Can you tell what's happening?"

"I can make out the shooter in the loft. He's hunkered down behind the scope, but there's a lot of wood chipping away all over the wall around him. They know he's there."

Evans' mind briefly jumped to the old Monty Python skit of "How Not to be Seen" from their Flying Circus television show.

"Well, when you're in the only possible building around to take a shot from for a thousand yards in any direction, I don't guess it's too hard to figure out," Evans commented sarcastically.

Another shot rang from inside the barn and was followed by a brief lull from up the hill. He had either hit his mark or scared the crap out of his opposition.

The radio suddenly came to life as reports of a man down rang in the Humvee.

Rachel cut her eyes over to the Lieutenant, "What do we do?"

"Each team has an assigned medic. The area is too hot for more than that right now. I hate to say it, but we wait and let him do the job as best he can."

"*Well, that sucks*," Rachel thought as she turned her attention back to the hillside which was beginning to glow with the sunrise.

"Primary is on the move," came the call over the radio, "Red SUV."

Within seconds a red Ford Expedition came racing around the hillside and down the driveway. The sniper in the barn tried to maneuver into a good position, but the vehicle's speed and the angle of the building kept him from getting an effective shot off.

"He's headed toward the highway," the sniper called as gunfire slammed into the woodwork around him once again.

Rachel leaped from her seat in the Humvee and checked the chamber of her AR as she moved to a defensive position and leaned across the front fender of the vehicle.

The lieutenant and Adams also took up positions behind the protective barrier of the truck.

Their target was heading right for them.

Adams swung his rifle up and called to the others, "Heads up! Here they come!"

The engine revved louder as the SUV drew closer to the curve in the road. As it came within sight of their position a staccato of gunfire erupted from the passenger side window, pinging as rounds impacted the side of the Humvee and slapped the windows.

Adams immediately returned fire, sending a half dozen rounds of .308 ball into the passenger side of the windshield. The body behind suddenly went limp as the weapons dropped from the man's grip and bounced along the asphalt.

Rachel and the lieutenant simultaneously opened fire on the vehicle as it careened toward their position. Rachel put the glowing green aperture of the Strike Fire on the driver's windshield and began pressing the trigger repeatedly as glass turned to powder and the vehicle began to swerve.

A pair of rounds from the lieutenant struck the radiator and battery; beginning the process of shutting down the operational capability of the SUV while another volley from Adams shredded the left front tire.

The truck jogged hard to the right as the rim bit into the blacktop and the driver relinquished his grip on the wheel. The momentum of the heavy automobile caused an uncontrollable pitch as the rim dug deeper into the road and it began to flip.

Over and over it rolled, shredding the grassy narrow shoulder before rolling completely off the road and flipping into the small stream that ran parallel to the blacktop. It came to rest, upside down and suspended across the tributary, like some demented bridge. Smoke and leaking fluids poured from the engine compartment while the driver's body dangled from the open door, still strapped in by the seatbelt.

In the back, hanging upside down and semi-conscious, was the ringleader. Beneath him, lying on the headliner among thousands of cubes of shattered safety glass was his pistol. As he hung, dazed and confused about his situation, Adams, Rachel, and the Lieutenant approached the hulking mess.

"Keep your distance," the team leader said as he kept his sidearm trained on the vehicle.

The three spread out along the passenger side and scanned for movement. The sun hadn't quite cleared the ridge line to the east, so there were deep shadows still inside the vehicle which made visibility a challenge. With the back bumper facing east the shadows almost completely consumed the back seat and its occupant.

Slowly, deliberately, the man's hand eased to the grip of the pistol. From his precarious angle he could make out the figures as they began to encircle his position. He had already decided he would not go to jail. He would make his stand there and then. He might lose, but he would at least not die alone.

With as much speed as he could muster, he brought the pistol in line with his eye and pressed the trigger three times, one for each of his would-be captors.

The back seat suddenly exploded as bullets tore into the padding of the leather seats and carried on through his torso. He twitched and convulsed with each impact, feeling the hits, but unable to respond as the handgun slipped from his grip and fell back to the headliner with a thud.

The last image he saw before his vision turned cold and black was the first figure falling to the ground near the creek.

"I got one of 'em," he thought as a final shot was heard, and the darkness consumed him.

Chapter Twenty-Nine

Clean Up

June 9th

The fight continued at the house as the reserve team moved up to engage. The sniper in the barn hadn't fired a shot since the SUV had made a break, but he kept monitoring the house as best he could. On the hill behind, the second sniper had managed to drop one of the men inside through a small window. So far nobody else had tried to shoot from inside the house. That concerned him because if the entry team ran into problems inside, neither he nor the barn could support.

The corner of the small storage building looked as if some great starving beast had gnawed at it from the volume of bullet holes up and down its length.

Pressing his luck, the shooter behind still managed to get enough rounds out to keep heads down and prevent his capture. Popping out and firing quickly before retreating to the concealment of the wall was his only option, but he used it frequently and used it well enough that he was able to stay alive.

"You know, you can shoot through walls," one officer said to another as they evaluated their situation from the safety of their own cover.

"What?" Asked the second.

"You watch the corner. I'm going to try and flush him out by pumping rounds into the walls.

Ready?"

With a nod both men rolled out and targeted the small structure. One focused on the corner and watched for any movement while the second began systematically firing into the wall at intervals he thought would allow either a hit or would be close enough to drive their attacker out to the corner.

Inside the small building the bullets pierced not only walls, but contents. Bottles of motor oil, jugs of fuel for lawnmowers and string trimmers, swimming pool chemicals and even the equipment they serviced caught the volley of lead and copper as the rounds passed through.

The shooter on the other side quickly understood the tactic and dropped as low to the ground as he could, hoping the extra downhill grade and flooring material inside would afford him some added protection. Still, the rounds were getting closer.

Inside the little shed a bullet punctured a bag of granular swimming pool bleach, knocking it from its place on the shelving and spilling the contents across the floor in a wide spray and a considerable pile.

A few rounds later another shot ruptured the skin of a large bottle of brake fluid, also sending it tumbling onto the floor where it began to vomit a spreading pool of its own.

The shooter began to inch his way to the corner. He was compromised and knew it. He would have to surrender or make a final stand. Patting his pocket, he felt the familiar shape of his last magazine and prepared to roll up and kill the men who had him trapped. Neither he nor the officers opposite him had taken notice of the puffs of smoke seeping from the small, broken windows of the building.

Inside, the brake fluid and bleach had met and a subtle, but increasingly violent, chemical reaction began to take place. The mixture began to bubble slightly, belching small puffs of white smoke as it did before erupting into a brilliant ball of fire which spread quickly across the gritty mixture. Nearby, along the outer wall and at the edge of the puddle, sat the six gallons of gasoline and the smaller three-gallon fuel oil mixture for the lawn tools. Within seconds the containers exploded.

The building shook as siding dislodged from the studs and flames screamed from within, as if a great dragon had just been awakened.

The shooter outside, out of pure reflex, leapt forward, beyond the protection of his corner and out in the open as shards of splintered wood peppered him and a wave of heat washed over his body.

Jerking and lurching with each impact he fell to the ground as the officer's rounds found their mark. His fight was now over, and he had lost.

Gradually the sound of gunfire subsided, and the team cautiously approached the home.

Down the hill, the Lieutenant called out to Evans and Simmons over the radio to leave their positions and report to the Humvee. They quickly hopped in their car and raced to the location.

When they arrived, they saw Rachel at the overturned SUV waving her arms frantically and motioning them to come to her. The lieutenant was kneeling in the grass, but they couldn't tell what he was doing.

As the pair got out, Rachel yelled to them.

"Adams has been hit! Do you have your bag?"

Simmons reached back into the car and grabbed a small bag out of the back seat. They raced to the scene and found him conscious, but in considerable pain.

"Here," Simmons said as he tore into the pouch.

He produced a packet of Celox and began applying it to the wound on Jeff's side. Evans produced a roll of gauze from the pack and began to wrap the bloody gash on his right arm.

"Dammit!" Adams blurted out, "I knew the bastard wasn't dead. I knew it! Little shit got the drop on me!"

"That's alright, son," the Lieutenant said reassuringly, "Avery got him for you. He's done.

Now we just need to get you taken care of, Okay?"

"Thanks, Rach," he said trying to sit up and see his avenger.

"Anytime," was all she could think to say.

Within a few minutes they hefted Adams up from the grass and the lieutenant and Simmons gently escorted him to the Humvee.

Evans turned and looked over at the inverted SUV as Rachel stepped over to it with him.

"Girl," he began, "You made a mess," he said as he faced her.

Against the rising sun, she was radiant. He could clearly understand why Scott had constantly talked about asking her out.

Her beauty was bolstered by the fiercely independent look she sported just then, with her hair pulled back in a ponytail and tucked through the back of her cap, the rifle slung at low ready across her vest and the holstered Glock that jutted from her right side. She looked beautifully bad ass.

Rachel didn't say a word. The adrenaline was racing through her system, and she was shaky and wanted to scream. She wanted to run, or something; anything to calm down. Her hands began to tremble as Evans turned to face her.

"You okay?" he asked, taking her hand to get her attention off the scene of the vehicle.

She faced him and, without a word or even a thought, pulled him down to her and passionately kissed him. Evans was stunned and unsure what the appropriate response to such a sudden and unsolicited action should be. In the heat of the moment, he gave in to her and the pair fell into an ardent embrace as their rifles and gear clattered about them. The uneven ground and sudden clinch caused them to lose balance and tumble to the ground where her sudden enthusiasm continued to catch Evans off guard.

Suddenly, she pushed herself off of him and rolled to the side, up onto her hands and knees and began to throw up.

The adrenaline rush was subsiding, and the emotional roller coaster could manifest in many different ways. Nausea, increased energy, and a powerful sex drive were only three of several emotions experienced by those who had endured it. This was Rachel's first rush of this magnitude, and her body was in chaos.

Evans shot her a confused glance and propped himself up on his elbow.

"Well, that's a new one on me. I've never *actually* made a girl sick before," he quipped, "Is it my breath?"

"I'm sorry," she managed between heaves, "I'm so sorry."

"Entry team, on me," the team leader called over the mic.

The group moved up as the reserve unit fell in to cover them. Both snipers watched intently but knew their roles were limited at best at this point.

The point man moved in through the open back door and they began to sweep the house. Methodically clearing room after room, the officers quickly secured the main floor. From the sliding glass door on the front porch, there was a noticeable blood trail that led down the hallway to the basement door. The team stacked up and prepared to enter the basement space, unsure of what to expect.

As the door gently opened and light spilled down the steps the point man could clearly see the trail of blood drops as it meandered down the treads.

Without warning, he stumbled back amid a flurry of shots. Someone was still alive in the basement.

The officer fell against the opposite wall and dropped onto his butt, clenching the fresh dimple on his body armor as the other team members ducked for cover.

A second team member produced a flash bang grenade and gave a nod to the team leader who responded with a nod and a gesture down the stairwell.

Pulling the pin, the man tossed the Orbital ATK nine-banger grenade down the steps. One and a half seconds later a brilliant five million candela flash lit up the room which filled with 134 decibels of explosive noise. The discharge launched the grenade across the room where the cycle repeated. With each explosion the grenade would jump in a new direction; every half second the luminous noise maker was somewhere else. Until the fourth discharge.

The fourth time the grenade exploded it rocketed directly to the suspect's position. He was lying across from the bottom of the steps against a stack of large boxes and totes; his leg bleeding profusely as he tried to shield himself from the light and sound.

The grenade slid under his bent knee and bumped into the opposite leg, flipping upward as it impacted and discharged again. In his blinded fury the man began to fire wantonly in the general direction of the stairs, hoping he would hit someone, anyone, that waited to apprehend him.

The grenade dropped from eye level between his wounded leg and the wall, where it discharged again. Now in the confines of a small channel created by his leg and the concrete barrier, the grenade made itself at home and discharged three final times, each time burning and blinding the injured suspect as he continued to empty his magazine.

In his condition, he fired every round too high, slapping bullets into the subfloor above and coming nowhere near any of the officers who had already begun to race into the basement. As soon as he had eyes on the suspect, the point man took a shot, ending the desperate, but brief, standoff.

The team quickly moved to clear the room and secure it. While they encountered no more resistance, they were not alone.

Chapter Thirty

Surprise, Surprise

June 9th

Cautiously sweeping down the wooden stairwell, the entry team quickly cleared the main basement room and began to work their way through the remainder of the area.

Stacks of totes and boxes lined the walls of the main room, their contents unknown for a lack of labels or markings. It would all be catalogued later.

As they rounded the corner and stepped down a short hallway, they came to a pair of doors that opened into adjacent rooms. The first was a trashy, unkempt space that reeked of the odors of a drug den. A tattered old couch and chair sat along opposing walls and between them was a small coffee table. Paraphernalia was littered about the floor and tables inside, but otherwise the room was empty.

The second room contained much more than expected. As the door swung open the muzzles on the entry team rose to scan the multiple bodies huddled along the walls and laying in the floor and across another old couch.

Alive, but in various states of consciousness, these were apparently the guests to a party that weren't in a condition to leave. One pair, a boy and a girl, cowered in a corner, seemingly terrified of the men had that entered the room. Another young man lay sprawled against the wall with an ignorant grin across his face, his eyes barely slits, while a young lady was face down on the floor, totally oblivious to what was happening around her.

Unconscious but sitting more or less upright on the couch was another young lady; a rather well-endowed blonde with her hair and clothing in a considerably disheveled arrangement.

The team leader called the structure all clear and quickly the support members began to move in. Within a few minutes ambulances were on scene for the wounded, which were few and minor except for Adams' injuries.

EMTs moved in to stabilize the party goers from the basement as the auxiliary members began to arrive to execute their next instructions.

Evans and Simmons arrived at the house following Adams's transport to the ER and within only seconds Phillips and Irwin were on scene as well.

"Man, this place is a mess," Phillips said.

"No kidding," Irwin replied, "Let's find the team leader and see what they need us to do."

The four men moved toward the house, passing bodies of the defenders as they went before stepping inside and shuffling past the officers and medical techs escorting, no, dragging out the people from downstairs.

Evans suddenly stopped dead in his tracks and slapped Irwin on the chest, who had been watching the procession with a tinge of disgust.

"Wha..," he began to ask before his eyes met the sight of Whitney Anderson being carried out with the others.

Both of their hearts sank as her limp body was carried outside.

Without saying a word, both men knew they would have to follow up on her condition but now was not the time. They had work to do.

Simmons motioned to a corner of the living room where the team leader was standing, and the quartet made their way over to him.

"What do you need from us?" Irwin asked as the man's attention was finally directed their way.

"Get with the EMT's outside and see who is fit for transport to the hospital. If they are ready, we can go ahead and haul them in your vehicles. Some will have to go in an ambulance; they just aren't in a state to travel without restraints.

"Anyone not transporting can help us with evidence as soon as it is ready to be hauled out.

It'll be a while, though since we have a LOT to log in just in the basement.

"Meanwhile, go ahead and see who's ready to travel."

With that the four made their way outside again and lined up to talk to the EMT's

"Can I help you gentlemen?"

"We were told to check with you and see if anyone could be transported in our cruisers. The team leader said that some would have to go by ambulance, but we might be able to help move the others who didn't."

"Okay," the man said as he made some notes on his clipboard, "These two will have to ride with us. The other three should be ready here in a bit.

"I don't know for sure what these guys are on yet," he motioned to the paranoid boy and girl, "but it has them freaking out about everything. They're going to need restraints. If you want to stay and help, we'd be glad to have the extra muscle. Sometimes they tend to get a little wild when they're strung out like this."

"I'd be willing to say it's flakka again, boss," another EMT said.

"What's 'flakka'? I've never heard of that before," Simmons said.

"It's a derivative of the old bath salts that were banned years ago. The manufacturers change the formula a little to get it reclassified and mark the packaging as 'Not for Human Consumption' and sell it every day. Most of the time folks that are on it have wild delusions and hallucinations. They'll see dragons or zombies or whatever. They get really paranoid and think everyone is out to hurt or kill them. That's where these two are right now. They'll come down, but it could take a month before it's out of their systems."

"That sounds like some bad stuff," Irwin commented.

"It is. It's getting harder to find, thanks to the national situation, but there's always a substitute. If this stuff becomes totally unavailable, there will be something else to take its place. Guaranteed."

A few minutes later the EMTs helped load the patients into the back seats of three cruisers. Simmons would take the smiling man, Irwin would take the unconscious girl, and Evans would take Whitney. All would go to the hospital.

The paranoid girl and boy had already begun to resist the medics and were fighting restraint as best they could, kicking and biting to be left alone. Phillips looked back at Irwin with an expression of contempt as he wrangled the young man onto the gurney and tried to hold him down.

It didn't take long for the assembly of transports to begin arriving at the local hospital. As each vehicle pulled under the canopy of the ER entrance staff members would come out with wheelchairs or gurneys to move the patients in and begin stabilizing and treatment.

Scott was the last one to drop off his passenger, who sat silent and unconscious in the back seat. As the door opened and the medics began to remove her from the car he looked over to see Evans quietly watching Whitney being rolled through the doors and into the ER.

"You alright, man?" Scott asked his friend.

"Yeah, I'm fine," he replied, the frustration clear in his voice, "I'm just…disappointed. You know?"

Irwin nodded, "Yeah. But, hey, that's her baggage. Not yours, okay?"

"I know. She was probably hooked on something before we ever met her. It's just such a shame."

"I agree. But look at it like this; she has a chance to clean up and make some positive changes. Start over. That choice is hers to make, though. We can't make it for her. All we can do is be there and try to be a positive influence on her.”

Scott could hear the sirens approaching in the distance from the incoming ambulances.

“Hey, we need to move our rides. They’re probably going to need the space in a minute to fight these two again,” he smiled as the thought of Phillips’ expression from earlier crossed his mind.

Soon the last two patients were in the emergency room and were under control, albeit barely. Amid screaming and barking like dogs they were beginning to fatigue and become more controllable. With any luck it wouldn’t be long, and they would collapse from exhaustion. Maybe then the process of cleaning them up could begin.

Scott and Evans decided to take a moment to check on Adams while they were there and see how the Richards family was getting along as well.

Since he was in the emergency room, Adams was first on the list to visit.

“Hey, man,” Irwin said with a smile as he entered the room, “How are you feeling?”

“Not too bad. Just pissed. I can’t believe I let that sum bitch get the drop on me like that.”

Evans smiled, “Good thing Rachel was there to finish him off, huh?”

“Yeah. I guess,” Jeff said with a small smile, “She seriously never shot a gun before all this went off the rails?”

“Seriously,” Scott replied.

“Damn. For a hot chick, she’s got some balls.”

Evans didn't say a word, but his mind immediately leaped to the incident earlier and he wondered if he should say anything to Scott about it or not.

"What's the doc say?"

"Ah," Adams grunted, "Nothing serious. I'll be back on the job in a few days. One shot grazed my arm, but it's just a big scratch, really. The other was a through and through. Didn't hit anything vital, but it hurts like a bitch. I'll be fine in a couple of weeks. Mark my words." The three laughed at his optimistic appraisal.

"Well, I think we'll let you rest now. I have some other folks to check on before I go back to the scene and help with evidence. I'll be back to check on you later."

"Alright man. I appreciate the visit."

Evans and Irwin stepped out and began to head down the corridors toward the Richards' room. As they walked, they heard the familiar voice of Andy Phillips call from behind them.

"Wait up, guys."

Scott and James paused as Andy closed the distance between them.

"Did you already see Jeff?" he asked as he approached.

"Yeah, we just left. He's doing alright. I thought I'd check on Tom and his family before we head back," Scott said.

"How much fun was it loading those last two?" Evans asked with a grin.

"Man, they are seriously screwed up. The girl kept squealing some crap about monsters and witches and the dude was convinced we were all mutant aliens or something out to kill them both."

"Ha!" Evans chortled, "I'm so glad I didn't stay for that!"

"Speaking of staying, weren't you supposed to stay and help with evidence?"

"The medics asked if I could come along just in case they needed some help man handling those two again. The dude was pretty wild, but I got the girl calmed down enough that she was under control for the ride in."

"What did you do?"

"Well, she was so worried about monsters and witches I just quietly whispered in her ear that I was a warlock and if she didn't calm down I was going to cast a spell to turn her into a dog."

"Is that why we heard barking after they came in?"

"Probably," he said with a smile

The trio turned the last corner down the hallway where the Richards family was staying just as Denise stepped out of a room on the right.

"Well, good morning, gentlemen," she said with a smile. Her address was to all three, but her eyes were focused on Scott, "What brings you all around?"

"We have been busy bringing you new patients," Scott said with a reciprocal smile.

She slumped her shoulders and the smile faded, "What now?"

"One of my guys got shot in the side and arm. He says it's minor, so he shouldn't be too much trouble, but try to keep out of arm's reach," Scott said with a grin.

"Wonderful. Anything else?"

"Well, there are about five that we pulled out of a drug den this morning that are here to be cleaned up before they go to jail. Most of them are pretty much just taking up space, but there are a couple that should be fun," Phillips added.

"Well, you guys are just a bundle of good news, aren't you?"

Scott smiled at the brunette, "We don't want you to get bored."

"Please," she replied, "*Let* me be bored for a while." The men all chuckled at the request.

"We'll see what we can do, but no promises," Scott replied, "Well, before we have to go back to work, I think we're going to visit Tom and Kim for a minute."

"They aren't here," Denise said bluntly.

"No?"

"No, they discharged earlier this morning. I assumed you already knew."

"No, we've all been involved in this raid since before sunrise. I hadn't heard."

"The doctor said they were all fit enough to go home so he discharged them first thing this morning. I think they were going to Tom's parent's house, if I heard him correctly."

Chapter Thirty-One

Apothecary

June 11th

"Rachel," Carol called down the hallway of the farmhouse, "Can you come here for a minute?"

"Sure," came the reply as the echo of footsteps on the hardwood floors echoed through the house.

A few seconds later the young lady appeared at the kitchen doorway.

"Need some help?"

"In a way, yes," Carol said, "Do you have anything pressing today?"

"Not that I know of."

"Would you mind taking a little trip with me? I need to go pick up some medicine and things and Ben is tied up here. Of course, Scott is in town again, so that leaves you and me. What do you say to a little road trip? Just us girls. It's just better to have an extra pair of eyes when you travel these days, you know."

"Sure thing," Rachel said with a smile, "Let me grab my things and I'll be ready to go."

After a few minutes and a hasty goodbye to Ben, Carol and Rachel hopped in the pickup and began heading south. They passed through town and continued to head out into the southern part of the county.

"You said you had to pick up some medicine, right?" Rachel finally asked, "Wouldn't we need a pharmacy for that?"

"Yes," Carol answered with a smile, "But not all pharmacies are what you think they are."

Carol grinned at the confused expression across the younger girl's face before explaining a bit more.

"We're going to see a friend of mine from high school. She and her husband have run a farm down near Delina for years and she's a bit of an expert on herbal remedies and treatments. I need to barter with her for some items and then we'll be on our way."

"Oh," Rachel said with a notable tone of disbelief, "Okay. I thought we were going to pick up some prescriptions or something. You know, *real* medicine." Carol smiled but kept driving.

After a few miles down the twisting, turning back roads, they finally turned into a long driveway that led up to a rather stately old homestead situated at the foot of a small hill. The massive front porch of the home wrapped nearly three quarters of the outside of the house, and it was furnished with rocking chairs along the front and swings on either side.

Sitting in one of the rockers was Jenny Larwood. She stopped rocking for a second to see who her company was but instantly resumed her knitting as if the approaching pair of ladies were simply supposed to be there.

Carol parked the truck and got out, waving to Jenny as she did. Jenny set her knitting aside and stood to greet her guests.

"Good mornin'," Jenny said as the ladies approached the house, "How are you doin' today, Carol?"

"Fine, just fine," Carol said as she gestured to Rachel, "This is Rachel Avery. She agreed to ride shotgun with me this morning. She works with Scott…well, worked with Scott, at the firm in Nashville."

"It's a pleasure to meet you," Jenny said as she extended a hand.

"The pleasure's all mine."

"Well, what has been going on to bring you all the way down here?"

"Oh, I'm just running low on a few things and thought we could do a little trading. Do you happen to have any willow bark?"

"You know I do. I don't go a day without tending to my aches and pains," Jenny laughed as she made her way down the steps and headed toward her "pharmacy."

"Willow bark?"

Rachel's question immediately got the attention of Jenny who smiled broadly.

"Yes, dear. Willow bark contains salicin, which is basically the same as the main ingredient in aspirin. It's not exactly, but a very close natural alternative. It's great for those little aches and pains from time to time."

"Really?" Rachel seemed surprised.

"Honey, if you think about it, every modern medicine we have today had to come from somewhere. Now, these pharmaceutical companies will mess with them and make them more powerful or more able to deal with different things, but they all came from somewhere natural to begin with. God takes care of us. We just have to understand how."

Rachel hadn't considered it before, but it made sense. She took note of everything they discussed that morning and tried to remember the little pointers and advice on how best to prepare the herbs and plants.

The little building was absolutely packed with small bottles and bags of various items. Before long Carol had a pretty impressive list filled.

They had picked up a small bottle of willow root, for aches and pains; licorice root for congestion; bearberry for a sedative and for urinary tract infections; black haw for menstrual cramps; ginseng, for a great variety of issues; and sassafras for an antiseptic as well as a treatment for poison ivy rashes.

"Now," Jenny said as she looked to Rachel, "All these things are good for what we've talked about, but they can also be used for other problems too. You should study up on it some. You might be surprised at what you find out."

"I may do that," Rachel said, "Thanks for the education."

The three made their way to the truck where the payment process could begin. As they were exchanging items, Jenny noticed a box of honey in the corner of the bed.

"Who's honey, Carol?"

"The Robertson's up in Spring Hill," she replied.

"Oh," Jenny said, "If that had been some of the Cooke Farms honey I would have given you my eye teeth." The woman giggled.

"Honey's honey, right?" Rachel asked, a bit perplexed.

"Oh, no, dear. If you can get locally made honey close to your home, it's better for your allergies. It all helps with arthritis and such, but I like it for the allergy side of things, so I prefer to get it from closer to home. The Cooke's just don't have as many hives as the Robertson's, so they don't harvest as much."

"Okay, well, that's about the last we have of it to spare before we go see them here in the next few days. If you don't want it, I'll just hang on to it."

Jenny smiled, "Now I didn't say I didn't want *any*. I just don't want it *all*." She held her hands out almost like a child reaching for an over stacked ice cream cone.

Before long Carol and Rachel were on the way home. Rachel's mind was awash with the information she had just learned and couldn't help but wonder.

"Carol?"

"Yes?"

"How does Jenny know all that about the different plants and recipes and everything? She's like an encyclopedia of natural cures. I've never seen anything like it."

Carol smiled, "Jenny was raised by her grandmother. Her grandmother was part Cherokee and had learned all that from *her* mother and so on.

"The scary thing is, Jenny has probably forgotten more than she remembers."

Carol turned down another twisting back road and began heading east through the hills and valleys of the southern county area.

"Are we not going home yet?" Rachel asked quizzically.

"No, dear," Carol replied as she slowed to a stop and pulled her purse up onto the seat, "We have another stop to make." The elder lady produced a snub-nosed revolver from the confines of her pocketbook and laid it in her lap.

Rachel became a little concerned about their next appointment.

"You are carrying a weapon, aren't you?" Carol asked the young lady.

"Yes, ma'am."

"Good. That's why I wanted you along. I doubt we'll need them, but you just never know these days."

"Carol?"

"Yes?"

"Where, exactly, are we going?"

"Liquor store," the matriarch answered as she continued their course.

A few miles down the road, Carol began blowing the horn loudly on the truck. Rachel scanned the area but saw no houses or barns. No structures of any kind were in sight.

Other than the few rabbits and squirrels that panicked and ran from their approach, she didn't see any signs of life.

"Uh," Rachel started, "Why are you doing that?"

"It's like knocking on the door before you get to the house. The people we are going to see don't like unannounced visitors."

The truck slowed as they found the driveway and began to turn in. On the front porch of a small house stood a gray-haired lady in her gown tails and house shoes, with a notable pot belly. In her left hand she manipulated a cigarette to and from her lips as her right arm cradled a shotgun.

Carol rolled to an easy stop a few yards from the house and waved before stepping out of the truck. A pair of massive bloodhounds patrolled the yard, barking and sniffing as Carol opened the door.

"Good morning, Linda," Carol shouted to the woman on the porch.

"Mornin' Carol." Who's yer friend?"

"Linda, this is Rachel. She is one of Scott's friends from work. She's helping me run errands today."

The woman scanned Rachel up and down as she got out of the truck.

"Hi," Rachel said shyly, uncomfortable with the setting and unsure of the appropriate etiquette needed for the situation.

"Mmm," Linda said as she vented smoke from both nostrils, "What brangs ya out today, Carol?"

"I need to make up some flu medicine. We've almost run out after this last time. Can you help me out?"

"I reckon," Linda said as she eased toward the steps, "You want it on the books or off?"

"Off, if I can get it," Carol said in a lower tone.

Linda shot a glance at Rachel.

"I can do that fer ya. But she might wanna stay here."

Carol smiled and turned to Rachel, "Can you stay with the truck, Rachel. I won't be but a minute."

"Sure. Whatever you need."

The elder ladies disappeared around the corner of the house and out of sight. Rachel took her seat back in the truck as one of massive blue tick hounds made his approach, tail wagging and curious.

"Hey there, big guy," Rachel said as the dog filled the door to the truck absorbing her scent and slapping her forearm with ears and jowls.

Carefully she reached out her hand and began to scratch the dog's head, just behind the ears.

Her efforts were met with a series of low, satisfied grunts, and a wagging tongue.

As she stopped, he thanked her with a deafening bark that echoed off the interior of the pickup and almost made her ears ring. With that he was away, plodding across the yard with a giant loping stride.

It wasn't long before Carol and Linda appeared at the corner of the house again. This time each carried a gallon jug of clear liquid in glass bottles. They approached the truck, each woman smiling and giggling about some unheard joke or comment. They loaded the bottles into the truck and began to arrange payment.

Within a few minutes the jugs had been exchanged for three jars of honey, some of the bearberry and ginseng along with one 50 round box of .22 Long Rifle ammunition. The ladies shook hands and Carol hopped back in the truck.

"Tell Bob I hope the bearberry helps. And, Linda, if you need anything from us, you just let me know."

"I will, Carol. Thank y'all."

With the conclusion of their business Carol pointed the truck toward home. As they made their way through the narrow lanes Rachel was again curious about Carol's contacts.

"These people have been in the moonshine business around here for generations. They are very good at what they do, too," she said, "When the economy began looking ominous, the county offered an opportunity to anyone interested in going legitimate. They could use their stills to produce legal shine in exchange for charging a local tax on all of it they sold."

"Okay," Rachel said, "but if they're a legal operation, why the shotgun? Why blow the horn and everything?"

"Well, first off, as you could probably tell, they aren't the wealthiest bunch in the world and to my knowledge have never had a phone in the house. You can't call ahead to let them know you're coming, so you blow the horn before you get there.

"Second, the Harris family is unique in that they run both sides of the line. They charge taxes for all legal sales, and they can show the books for it all. But they also have a line of 'illegal' product that they sell cheaper, if you know about it."

"Off the books," Rachel muttered.

"Off the books," Carol confirmed, "That's how I was able to barter instead of giving them money. Knowing what people need is a big part of it too."

"Is this why you bartered for so many different things with Jenny?"

"You're catching on," Carol smiled, "See, Bob, Linda's husband, has trouble sleeping at night. Always has. The bearberry is a sedative. The ginseng is more of a stimulant and helps fight fatigue. Mary uses it for that and also as a mild antidepressant. They both have arthritis, and that's where the honey comes in."

"What about the bullets?"

"These woods are the grocery store. They hunt most everything they eat, so ammo is always a top barter tool. Since most of the animals you see around are small game, squirrels and rabbits, you don't need a big gun to kill them."

Rachel was still amazed at the new economy that had developed and the intricacies of it. Things weren't as simple as throwing down some paper currency and walking out with what you needed anymore or even swiping a plastic card to pay for what you wanted. Still, in some ways, she could see this system as being very effective since both parties got things they needed and not some overinflated pieces of paper. At the end of the day, regardless of the worth of the dollar, honey always held its value and bullets did too.

Chapter Thirty-Two

The Charge of the Homeless Brigade

June 11th

Chris Davis and his family arrived in Lewisburg just before lunch time and called Dave Browning to meet. Dave had been the one to get them through the security checkpoint at highway 50 earlier, so their arrival wasn't entirely unexpected. Entirely.

Chris dropped Miranda off at his parents' house and drove on in to meet Dave and the guys. As he pulled up outside the Gizmo, he saw the picnic table full of men as they were just beginning to sit down for a sack full of tiny burgers.

"Did you leave any for me?" he asked as he stepped out of the dark gray Trailblazer. The others happily greeted him with handshakes and pats on the back.

"Not many," Dave laughed as his friend approached the table, "How are you doing, man?"

"Well, we made it this far, so I guess we're doing alright."

"Miranda and the kids okay?"

"Yeah, I just dropped them off with Mom. It got…interesting."

The group silently acknowledged his experience before turning their attention back to lunch.

"I'll bet," Dave replied, "I hear the homeless situation up in Nashville has gotten crazy."

"You wouldn't believe it if I told you," Chris said, "That's why we finally left."

For years Nashville had been an unofficial destination for troublesome homeless people from across the nation. Thanks to the reputation Nashville had developed for compassionate treatment of vagrants and homeless people, many cities and states felt better about sending their problems to the Athens of the South to deal with.

Over time the problem had become so large that it was impossible to access the public computers in the local library due to the number of people maintaining their begging sites at the city's expense and they had grown from "tent cities" to actual structures. Some had even tapped into live power and water lines to provide themselves with very comfortable living conditions; again, at someone else's expense.

When the economy collapsed any public funding dried up quickly and many churches and private organizations tried to shoulder the immense cost of the destitute population. It couldn't be done on charitable donations alone and efforts crumbled quickly, leaving thousands of people already on the street facing starvation, sickness, and death in a very real way.

With nothing else to lose, they decided to simply take what they needed, and wanted.

"Home invasions and general looting have already been up, but when the money ran out to support the shelters it got worse. I had a guy come into the office one day with a machete and demand money," Chris said.

"What did you do?" Simmons asked.

"Well, first I kicked his ass and then I called Eric."

The other friends giggled at the idea while Simmons struggled to comprehend the situation.

"Eric is a friend of ours from high school," Dave added, "He's Metro SWAT and a fifth-degree black belt."

"By the time Eric got there the guy was pretty pissed off, but he wasn't ready for any more fighting. A little karate on top of a dose of Krav can make for a very bad day."

"Krav?" Simmons asked.

Evans spoke up, "Krav Maga. It's an Israeli self-defense form. Did you ever see any of the Bourne movies years ago?"

"Yeah."

"Well, a lot of the fighting moves are Krav. Chris here instructs in that and Brazilian Ju Jitsu.

When he's not kicking some homeless dude's ass, of course."

"Wow," Simmons said, "That would be kind of cool to learn. Could be handy these days."

"Well, I thought about trying to start a class up here since I apparently won't be in Nashville again for a while."

"Why did you leave? I mean, you had a guy come to the office, but that doesn't seem like enough to make you want to leave your house and everything," Irwin inquired.

"The guy at the office was just the first one. The four that broke into our house is what broke the camel's back."

"What happened?"

"Four?"

"What did they want?"

The questions came from all parts of the table.

"I don't know what they wanted, and I don't particularly care. They didn't get what they were after, I can guarantee that. Again, if it hadn't been for Eric being in the position he is, I would imagine that I wouldn't be here now."

"How so?"

"These guys came in through a broken window at the back and started rampaging through the house. I was upstairs with the kids. Miranda was downstairs getting ready for bed. I heard the window break and scrambled to get my shorty. By the time I got downstairs they were headed down the hallway to the bedroom. They had heard Miranda shut and lock the door and decided to find out who else was in the house, I guess.

"Anyway, when I called them out, one had a little snubby revolver in his hand, and the rest had bats and knives. The first dude took a shot at me but missed while his buddies decided to bum rush me."

"Did you drop 'em?" Andy asked with a stone-cold expression.

"Yeah. The cops came and took my shorty until I mentioned Eric's name. He backed me with a character reference and got it back for me, but I could tell it was time to go."

"What is the 'shorty' you keep talking about?" Simmons asked.

"A few years ago, I decided to build a truck gun, so I filed a Form 4 with the ATF and got the tax stamp for a Short-Barreled Rifle, or SBR.

"You know, even though I legally owned it and was in my house when all this happened, I really don't think they would have given it back if it hadn't been for Eric. Things have gotten kind of ignorant up there."

"What do you mean? Are they confiscating guns now?"

Evans' question was a concern to all at the table since Nashville was the state capital. Any legislation passed there could easily be pushed statewide.

"The mayor, in her infinite wisdom, hasn't started door to door confiscation yet. She *has* decided that if you are caught in public with a firearm, it is to be collected, for the public good, until such time as you can be proven not to be a threat. Even if you have a carry permit, they will take your weapon and hold onto it until they verify your background is clean. The thing is, they don't have a time limit to do their checks and even if you come back clean getting a gun back is essentially impossible."

"Wow," Scott said, "That is unbelievable. You know, I was thinking about making a trip to see how bad things are up there since I left, but I'm not going unarmed."

"That reminds me," Chris said, fumbling for his phone, "I have something to show you."

He navigated the apps on the screen until he came to the photo album and flipped it around to show everyone at the table, but mainly Scott.

On the screen was picture after picture of burned buildings and storefronts. Streets littered with debris and burned cars and homeless people by the score.

About halfway through the album was a picture of the "Batman Building." Scott shot a look at Chris when he saw it.

"We got a call from the property owners to give an estimate for repairs since we provide a lot of building supplies. They had a contractor, but he couldn't get materials cheap enough, so they asked us directly if we could provide what would be needed to repair the place. Keep looking."

Scott turned his attention back to the images. The lobby was completely trashed. Burn marks scarred the walls among all the spray-painted profanity. One image stopped Scott dead.

The lobby to Williams and Donovan looked as if a bomb had gone off. Rachel's desk was in splinters and several of the cubicles were nothing more than charred sheet metal frames surrounding heaps of blackened carpet and paper.

The conference room where he had been made a partner looked reasonably normal except for a large dark stain on the floor and the bar in the corner was clearly devoid of any refreshments.

"We think that the stain is blood. No body was found there, but unless it's analyzed we can't rule it out. Of course, the police never got a call from anyone, but there is a lot that has happened they don't know about, I'm sure."

Scott's mind immediately turned to the partners. He hadn't heard anything from them since the day he left Nashville. His heart sank at the thought of one of them being killed in the office.

As they were scrolling through the pictures another vehicle approached and parked beside Chris's. Tom Richards eased out of his father's pickup truck and made his way to the table still gingerly moving to avoid pulling stitches out.

"What about it, fellows?"

"Hey! You're still alive!" Evans quipped.

"Yeah, well, it'll take more than a few dozen entitlement punks to take me out."

His expression still displayed the discomfort of his injuries even though he didn't verbally acknowledge them.

"What's the hot topic today?"

Scott handed Tom the phone and he began scrolling through the images for himself.

"Man," he began, "That is seriously screwed up. You know, even though we've talked about this happening for years, I gotta say I'm still surprised at the level of damage that has already happened. It's just getting worse, too."

"What do you mean?"

"Since everything went off the rails the availability of a lot of drugs has dropped through the floor."

"Not around here," Andy snorted, "We just made a huge bust the other day."

"No, I don't mean illegal stuff. I'm talking prescription meds; pain killers and antibiotics, especially. Pharmacy robberies are epic, and addicts are desperate. That doesn't work well for the people who actually *need* the medicines. Before we left Murfreesboro, I had already been hearing that in some cities you couldn't find a syringe because of the heroin addicts. Diabetics were having their supplies stolen off their doorsteps just for the needles and we even heard of delivery trucks being robbed at the pharmacy doors. It's crazy."

"Well, to be fair," Dave replied, "A *lot* of what we confiscated the other day actually was prescription stuff. I don't know how much exactly, but a lot. Maybe I need to talk to the powers that be about handling that stuff discretely and getting it locked up."

"I'm just glad I started learning about options," Tom added, "There's a lot you can do without a prescription med."

Simmons felt awkwardly out of place. These men had apparently been anticipating the downfall of western civilization for most of their lives. Each had their own skill set that they brought to the table and he was seeing that many overlapped each other. Redundancy.

There was the law enforcement officer with access to non-public information who was also the tactical leader. The guitarist who had become a prominent communications officer, bringing news and information from outside that wasn't heard on the "official" broadcasts. Then there was the Hardware salesman with a background in self-defense instruction and hand to hand techniques. Now there was the healthcare professional with experience and knowledge about medical alternatives. He felt almost like a square wheel in their midst.

"Man," he began, "I wish I had some skill set to bring to the table."

"I'm sure you have something valuable that sets you apart," Dave suggested, "Any training or education you aren't using at the moment? Anything at all?" Simmons thought about it for a minute.

"Just my pilot's license. But I haven't flown in a few years. It's too expensive."

"Well, that's something none of the rest of us have. And you never know when it might come in handy."

"You got your license?" Scott asked, "I always wanted to get mine, but I never followed through. Like you said it got too expensive."

"Yeah," Dale smiled, "I actually got multi-engine certified about eight years ago. Work was going well, and I always wanted to learn, so I took a little time each week and knocked it out. Then the fuel and plane rental prices got ridiculous, and I just couldn't justify it anymore."

"Well, maybe one of these days we can barter a vacation somewhere and you can fly us all."

"I'd have to have a lot of apples and strawberries to cover the cost," he said with a laugh.

"Speaking of vacations," Tom began, "Who feels like taking a little road trip with me?"

"Where are you headed?"

"Back to Rutherford County. I need to get back to my truck." Evans and Browning shot each other a confused glance.

"I thought you said you left it a burnt-out hulk on the side of the road."

"I did. I emptied it first, though. Just because I didn't want anyone using my truck doesn't mean I was going to destroy all the gear that was in it too," he smiled.

"Wait, you stashed your gear? When? Where?" Browning asked.

"Remember I said we spent the first night in the truck? Well, while the kids and Kim were trying to sleep, I was dragging gear into the woods and burying what I could. I hid what I had to.

Now I need to go and collect it. There are a lot of things in there that could prove very useful," Richard said with a look that projected playful mischief.

"Count me in," Evans said.

"I'll go," Phillips added, "Could be fun."

Chapter Thirty-Three

Signs of the Times

June 12th

Denise had just finished her rounds when one of her fellow nurses stepped up to the station in a huff.

"What's wrong, Angie?"

The nurse flopped in the chair beside Denise and tossed a folder on the desktop with an audible sigh of frustration.

"Summer hasn't even started yet and we're already seeing tick fever and snake bites. I have a bad feeling about this year."

"Are you serious?"

Angie motioned to the paperwork, "I just checked on a sixteen-year-old with every textbook symptom of tick fever. In the room next door to his I have a twenty-three-year-old that met her first copperhead today. Apparently, *he* wasn't impressed."

"Copperhead?"

"Mean little snakes. They aren't fatal, but they aren't friendly. At least a rattler will give you fair warning before it strikes. A copperhead will just sit there quietly and wait for you and bite out of pure meanness."

Denise laughed at the suggestion.

"What? You don't have snakes where you're from?"

"I'm from Los Angeles. The snakes we have there walk around on two legs."

"Fair enough," Angie replied, "You know, it might not be a bad idea to brush up on the local plants and animals since you're new to the area. We have some unique things you might not have had to deal with before. Like copperheads."

Denise thought about it for a minute. That made sense. There were probably a lot of things she hadn't seen before, being from a large urban area like she was. The rural environment was a polar opposite to her home territory.

"So, what kinds of things do you see here? What should I learn about?" Angie leaned back in the chair for a minute.

"Well, snake bites can be pretty bad, but they aren't common. I think we've had maybe two rattler bites in the past twenty years. When they happen, they aren't what you'd expect. Copperheads are more aggressive, so you're more likely to see those, but even then, it's rare.

"Tick bites are a part of summer life in these parts. If you have a yard or trees, you'll have ticks. They usually aren't a problem if they are taken care of quick enough, but if you don't deal with them soon or in the right way, bad things can happen.

"The deer ticks are the main ones to watch out for. They have a little white dot on their backs that give them away and they are the most likely to carry the disease. I think they also call them dog ticks in other parts of the country.

"Mosquito borne sickness happens from time to time as well. We haven't seen it here as much as Nashville and other places have over the years. West Nile isn't a big headline now, but it was for a while. Zika still comes up from time to time too.

"You also have to keep your eyes out for poison oak and poison ivy rashes. Some people are highly allergic. We have one lady that can just look at the stuff and break out. She usually comes in a couple of times a summer for treatment."

"Why doesn't she just get rid of it?"

"It's not as easy as you'd think. She can't touch it because of her sensitivity to it, which means she can't uproot it. If you don't uproot it, it'll grow back."

"Why not burn it out? That should get it, right?"

"Nope. The oil droplets become vaporized, and you can actually breathe it in. That's a whole new kind of problem.

"In the cooler months you'll see the ever-popular sinus infections and bronchitis. I had a patient years ago that moved here and had never had sinus trouble before. His first winter he came into the ER and thought he was going to die. The pressure was so bad that his teeth had actually been pushed out of place as his gums moved and swelled. He couldn't breathe and his head throbbed all the time."

"Well, that sucks," Denise said with a snurled nose.

"Oh," Angie continued with a smile, "Marshall County's claim to fame; you can't forget kidney stones."

"Okay, but those happen everywhere. It's not just a local thing."

"That's true," Angie replied, "but around here we have the reputation of being the kidney stone capital of the world. The limestone here is so heavily concentrated in even the city water that stones happen constantly. I've even seen stones form inside the salivary glands in the mouth before."

"You've got to be kidding," Denise said with her jaw agape.

"Just another day around here," Angie said.

After a few minutes she continued along a totally different line of thought.

"I just hope something can change for the better with our pharmacy supplies. Otherwise, we're going to be hard pressed to treat some folks."

"What do you mean?"

"You haven't heard?"

"No, I guess not."

"We haven't gotten a shipment of medicine in nearly two weeks. Thankfully our patient load hasn't been too heavy, but the ones we've had already have drained our antibiotics, our pain killers, and a lot of our saline.

"Treating those people from that drug raid the other day has shorted us on other items as well. I'm just glad flu season is past."

"Why are we not getting medicine?"

"Well," Angie started, "We aren't a big hospital with a big patient demand, so I'm sure we aren't as high on the list for distribution as others. That's always been true, though.

"A lot of drugs are actually made out of the country and with the economy being in the shape it is, I'm going to guess we don't have the trade options to bring things in like we used to.

"Many of the things produced here in the states are manufactured in areas that are in a lot of trouble these days. They may not be able to produce or just don't want to give up their leverage to deal.

"Then again, I have heard that a number of shipments have been hijacked and pharmacies have been robbed.

"I'd say that a lot of people can't afford the medicines either now. Insurance companies have almost rolled over and closed their doors, leaving their customers hanging. Supply can't meet demand, and nobody can afford the supply."

After her shift ended Denise had Angie drop her off at her house. The notion of having her own home was still rather a new and foreign concept to her. Technically, it wasn't *her* house, but it was being provided by the hospital for her use in exchange for her employment.

Through some tough negotiations between the hospital, the city, and the developer, a deal was finally reached to provide housing in exchange for tax breaks and monetary compensation. The developer, after all, had several units sitting empty when the economy tanked and he would have lost a fortune if they had remained that way. He would have preferred to sell them outright and collect his cash, but that opportunity passed, and he was left to do what he could.

The subdivision was small and the houses in it were all two and three bedrooms with attached carports. Hers had a spacious living room area with a gas fireplace in the corner. The master bedroom was also large with a generous walk-in closet and attached master bath complete with a whirlpool tub. Most of the houses were built with tankless water heaters to avoid having to replace them when the steel tanks finally rusted through (they always did, some just took longer than others).

Just inside the door from the carport was the laundry room which was ideal because Denise found she could change into her comfortable "after work" clothes and go straight into relaxation mode.

It wasn't a mansion by any stretch, but it was big enough. It was much larger than her apartment back in California, by far. As she entered the laundry room, she pulled the door shut and locked it behind her, then stripped out of her work clothes and put her sleep shirt on that she had left on the washer that morning.

Soon she was in the kitchen boiling some green tea and looking forward to listening to some music.

The house was furnished, but only just. Arrangements with a local furniture company allowed her to get some items from their repo selection for free and other things were deeply discounted for people in her situation. She had a television that was actually installed by the developer when the house was built, but there was never anything on to watch, so Denise would most often relax to music on the radio or with a good book. Sometimes it was a combination.

She took her cup of tea and her book into the living room and curled up on the couch. Across the room, below the television, sat the little radio. With a press of the button on the remote the device came alive. She caught the evening news report about halfway through and, for a change, decided to listen to it rather than switch over to her own music collection.

She quickly realized it was one of the Nashville stations and her attention perked up a bit when they announced the weather forecast. She finally had the day off tomorrow and would love to be able to work on her tan. She had spent almost her entire time in Tennessee working and inside. "The forecast for tomorrow is clear and sunny with a high of about 85 and a low around 70.

The rest of the week should follow a similar pattern with highs in the mid 80's and lows in the upper 60's and low 70's. Just remember boys and girls that the heat index is going to put us at about 94, so if you plan on being outside stay hydrated."

Denise smiled to herself. Oh, yeah, she was definitely working on her tan. As she considered which swimsuit to wear, she became aware of the fact that she hadn't worn one since her trip, before the world went nuts.

Almost as if the radio was tuned to her thoughts, the news segment began. The main stories focused on the

Nashville and Middle Tennessee areas, which was logical. That was where the broadcast originated and where most of the listening audience would be.

Police were still working to get control of the worsening situation in Nashville with the homeless on a tear. Overnight an entire apartment building had been set ablaze in what was expected to be an associated incident. Police had been called in to another part of town to break up a group that had been obstructing traffic and assaulting motorists.

A meth lab explosion in an abandoned school building had left the entire property ablaze.

Before it was brought under control three people had died and the structure was a total loss.

News from Memphis was very brief and only said that police and state guard units had secured an area around the mayor's residence and were continuing to address the continued violence there. No other details were given.

In other news, the governor had just returned from a meeting in Texas with the governor there. The meeting was the first in an attempt to secure trade rights with the giant state. Rumors were circulating that Texas was moving toward reestablishing itself as an independent republic again and they had already announced the creation of a state currency, the Texas Dollar, or Longhorn, as it was being called.

The launch of the new tender would take place in the next few months, and it was expected that any state wishing to do business with Texas would be required to accept the money. That meant that Tennessee could potentially be trading with Texas Dollars very soon.

It also meant that certain goods, mainly fuels and petroleum-based products, could be secured at a cheaper rate than the rest of the nation was paying. Instead of $10 per gallon, the cost of gasoline could drop to $7 or maybe even less. Not enough to bring back the casual Sunday drive, but a definite improvement to be sure.

The thought crossed her mind about buying her own vehicle. She'd never owned her own car, despite having her license for years. Like buying your own house, it was just too expensive in California. With all the emissions testing and insurance requirements on top of the fuel prices and environmental taxes and fees, owning a personal vehicle was an enormous pain.

Maybe, if the Texas Dollar thing worked out, she would look into that a little more. Until then, her tea was getting cold, and her book was still unopened. She pressed another button on the remote and started her playlist.

Chapter Thirty-Four

Road Trip

June 13th

Phillips and Evans met Tom at his parents' house that morning to figure out the best approach to recovering his hidden gear. The trip would cost fuel, which hadn't been cheap for a while anyway, but now was almost prohibitive. The term 'liquid gold' was often applied to the mixture.

Tom's father had essentially given his pickup to Tom and Kim for their personal use since they had no vehicle of their own available. He would simply use his wife's car for what little travelling he needed to do and could always get the truck if he needed it.

"I stashed ten gallons of gas in the woods along with the gear. It may not be usable now, but I added some stabilizer to it before leaving the 'Boro, so we'll just have to see," Tom said, "I tried to hide it all far enough from the truck that it wouldn't be easy for anyone else to find, but close enough for me to find it easily enough."

Evans pulled out a road map of Tennessee that showed all the major highways and some of the more common secondary roads and spread it across the table.

"Okay, where are we going?"

Tom studied the map for a minute and stabbed his finger at a point along Highway 99.

"Right around here," he said, "We left the truck along this stretch of highway, but the gear is stashed in this area." He slid his finger across the map and up into the area south of Interstate 840 and east of Triune.

"That's not too far from the castle where they always had the renaissance festival, is it?"

"Right. The castle is over here, across this bridge and up this road. We hid the cache in the woods about here."

"Okay," Evans said, "We should be fine up through Chapel Hill. I doubt we'll run into any problems between there and Kirkland. I've never known what to expect through there."

"I think we'll be fine," Phillips said semi-confidently, "Kirkland is a small community, and I can't see there being many folks there who will give a crap about three dudes passing through."

"We didn't have any trouble through there on our way down, but we went through at night, so I'm not sure what goes on there during the day," Tom added.

"I'm thinking we go straight through. You know, just like we would any other time. I haven't heard anything over the radio about any trouble up that way recently. "If we need to, we can kick off to Patterson Road and take it to Rehobath Road. That brings us out really close to your cache. What do you think?" Evans suggested.

"Well, there's one way to find out," Phillips said.

"Are we ready to roll?" Richards asked.

The men checked their weapons and grabbed their bags. Evans and Phillips loaded into the cab while Richards bid his farewells to his family and soon, he was in the driver's seat.

The drive between Lewisburg and Chapel Hill was as uneventful as it had ever been. When they reached the checkpoint, the officer waved them forward. Seeing the Polo shirts on Phillips and Evans and the hardware they carried he was a bit surprised at first.

"What brings you up this way, gentlemen?"

"We're on our way to Triune. Picking up some supplies for the team," Evans said, "Any word on the traveling conditions up that way?"

"Most of the drive should be fine. Someone said there was a checkpoint at 41 and 31 that was trying to charge a toll to pass through. Tell them who you are, and they'll probably let you through without much trouble. I haven't heard anything about Triune," the officer said.

"Alright. Well, hopefully we'll be back in a couple of hours," Evans said, "Appreciate the info."

"No problem, sir. Be careful. Oh, and you might want to stay close to the Triune end of things. Murfreesboro is not a good place to be lately," He looked at the rifles they had slung and stored, "Then again, you seem to be a little better off than most who want to risk it."

He stepped back and waved the truck forward as Tom pressed down on the throttle.

Crossing through the rural farmland north of Chapel Hill proved as uneventful as the drive up from Lewisburg. As they passed through the tiny town of College Grove the trio began to think that the trip would be a cake walk.

Just up the road they came to the intersection of Highways 31 and 41A, at the community of Kirkland. Sur enough there was a short line of cars extending down each way from the awkward three-way convergence. Tom rolled to a stop as Evans and Phillips gripped their rifles.

An armed man approached the truck signaling for Tom to roll his window down. As he did the ninety-three-degree heat index flooded into the cab.

"Where you headed?" the man asked bluntly.

"Triune," Tom replied just as bluntly.

The man looked at the occupants and scanned their rifles quickly. After a hard swallow he noticed the insignia on their shirts.

"You cops?"

"Yeah," Evans replied, "That a problem?"

"Naw. You goin' to help out in Murfreesboro?"

"Not today," Richards said, "They need help?"

"What I hear. We don't go there. Sheriff told us to run this toll to keep folks out that they don't need addin' to the trouble. I hear it's pretty rough in places."

"Nah, we don't plan on going that far today."

"Alright. Y'all can go ahead. You comin' back today?"

"I hope so," Tom said with a smile.

The man smiled, exposing his crooked teeth, "Alright. We'll look for you later. Y'all be careful."

He stepped back and waved them forward. A few miles down the road the truck turned right onto Highway 96 at the little community of Triune. The "town" wasn't much, but it was a popular place each May when the Tennessee Renaissance Festival took place. It was the closest place on the map to get gas for many of the attendees and sat about halfway between Franklin and Murfreesboro.

Within a few minutes they had crossed Interstate 840 for the second time as it snaked eastward toward I-24. Less than a mile past it they pulled over to the shoulder.

"X marks the spot," Tom said, "The truck is just down there on the shoulder. The cache should be just through the woods over here." In the distance the friends could see a dark mass on the shoulder of the road. There seemed to be bright red or orange spray paint on the fenders.

"Alright, how do you want to work this?"

"I'm thinking one of us keeps watch while the other two grab the gear. It shouldn't take too long."

"Well, since you're the only one who knows where it is, I guess you won't be on lookout," Phillips said.

"I'll go with Tom and help get the stuff. Do you mind watching our backs?"

"No problem. If either of you need to swap out, let me know."

Evans and Richards disappeared into the underbrush and returned a few minutes later with a large tote. Judging by their faces it must have been a considerable load. When they hoisted it into the bed of the truck both men let out a resounding groan.

Quickly they hustled back to the trees to return with a second tote. Andy could tell this one was a beast as well by the way the handles seemed distorted by the weight.

"How in the hell did you manage these alone?" Evans asked.

"Like I said, I had all night."

They hefted the box into the bed and headed once again for the woods. When they returned, they each carried a jug of gasoline. They quickly loaded them in the corner and strapped them in by the handles.

"I think we can get the rest in one more load," Evans said with a huff.

"Do you need me to swap out?" Phillips asked.

"Nah, I'm good. Just a little warm to be hauling this much crap through that rough of terrain."

"Agreed," Tom said with a sigh of his own, "When I stashed it the temps were a lot cooler. Of course, it was well after dark, but still."

The pair vanished among the foliage once again and returned with a collection of ammo cans each. Judging by the amount of dirt on each one they must have been what Tom had buried.

"Ammo, first aid supplies, and communication gear," he said as he plopped the cans onto the tailgate and pushed them in, "That's all I have. We are ready to roll."

The three men again clamored into the cab and took their seats. Tom started the engine and checked his mirrors. His eyes came to rest on the charred remains of his SUV just down the road.

"You guys mind if I…," he gestured ahead.

"No. Go ahead," Phillips said, "I've been wondering what's painted on it myself."

The truck eased off the shoulder and down to the SUV. As they got closer, they could each see a large white circle with a roughly painted knife pointing to the lower left on the back door. The knife point was painted with a red tip, indicating blood. Across the back were the words 'Death to the USA.'

As they turned the truck around, Phillips took pictures of the graffiti. Across the passenger side doors the words 'Pray for Marxism' were painted with a large area painted out. Someone had tried to make it look like a red flag, but it didn't quite come out well.

"Probably couldn't spell Marxism," Evans snorted.

Tom turned the truck back toward Triune and home. Soon they reached the intersection at Kirkland. They could see the man that had stopped them before up ahead. He was drenched in sweat and still working the traffic stop.

Slowly they made their way up to him where he proceeded to wave them to a stop.

"I see you made it back. Did you get what you needed?"

Tom noticed that the man's shirt was soaked but his face was dry. He had essentially stopped sweating, and his arms showed goose bumps despite being in the sunlight all day. He seemed a bit disoriented at first.

"Yeah, we did," Tom said, "Sir? Are you feeling alright?"

"Yeah. I'm just a little hot's all."

"Tell you what, let me pull over here just a minute. Is that alright?"

"Sure," the man said with a bit of a slur to his voice.

Tom pulled to the shoulder and hopped out of the truck. He went to the bed while Evans and Phillips stepped out as well. The sight of heavily armed men getting out at the intersection put the other toll workers on edge. They had no idea who these men were or what they were doing.

Hands quickly moved to sidearms, and careful eyes monitored their every move.

Tom pulled a small bag out of one of the ammo cans and squeezed it until there was a small, but audible 'pop.'

"Here," he said as he approached the man twisting and squeezing the pack, "Put this on your neck and go sit under the awning of that gas station. Get inside where there's air conditioning if you can."

Phillips noticed the uneasy attention they were getting and turned his attention to Evans.

"Shoulder your rifle. Behind your back. These guys are looking nervous."

The two swung their rifles around in a less threatening position just as the older toll worker began to stumble.

"Guys!" Tom called.

Evans and Phillips quickly stepped over to the man and each grabbed him under an arm, hefting his weight while Tom recovered the chemical ice pack from the pavement.

Together they hauled him across the road to the awning and sat him down.

"Is there anything cold in there?" Tom shouted to the nearest man, "Air conditioning or cold water? Anything?"

The man ran to a nearby truck and flipped open a cooler. In a flash he was under the awning with two bottles of ice-cold water in his hands.

Tom proceeded to pour the liquid over the man's head and down his back.

"We need to get him cooled off. He's overheated already and on his way to heat exhaustion, if not heat stroke. Can we get him inside the store?"

"Yeah," the second man said. Together they moved him inside and got his temperature slowly under control.

"I don't know what his core temperature is, but he needs to cool down, otherwise he could have a heat stroke. Don't let him back on the pavement for a while, okay?"

"Yes sir," the man said.

Tom looked at the expression on the young man's face and a thought crossed his mind.

"You kin to him?"

"He's my dad," the man said, "I appreciate the help. I'll look after him."

"Does he take any medication?"

"Blood pressure meds. Why?"

"Sometimes that can affect your ability to stay hydrated. Does it have a diuretic in it? Makes him go piss a lot?"

"Yeah."

"I thought so. Keep his exposure to the heat limited. Get him in the shade every hour or so, if not more. He should be fine."

"Okay. Thanks. Are you a doctor or somethin'?"

Tom smiled, "Nah, I just know a lot of stuff."

The three men headed back to the truck and Tom reached to close up the ammo can when he noticed one of the cans was missing.

"Aww, man!" he snarled, "That figures. Try to help someone and some asshole takes your stuff."

The young man had followed them out to the truck and peered over Tom's shoulder.

"What are you missin'?"

"I had an ammo can like this full of handheld radios and chargers. Someone took it while we were inside with your dad. I should have known better than to leave the truck unattended."

The younger man turned and looked over the others working the intersection. Without warning, he yelled at the top of his lungs, "Alright. Which one of you took his stuff?"

Heads turned and eyes cut over, but nobody moved or raised a hand.

"I said, who took the ammo can from this truck?"

Finally, a slender man about five feet eleven inches walked over to an old Ford Ranger close by and grabbed the can out of the back. He carried it over, eyes cast down, and handed it to the young man, who promptly punched him in the face. The slender man fell to the ground holding his jaw. And shot a fearful look at his assailant.

"You know better'n 'at. Get your ass back to work." He placed the can back in the bed of the truck.

"Take a look and make sure it's all there. I'm sorry 'bout that. Sometimes he gets a little sticky fingered. He don't mean no harm, he's just ignorant like that." Tom just stared at the man for a second.

"I'm sure it's all there. I'm not worried about it. You guys have enough to handle as it is, so we'll just get on our way."

"Well, alright then. Thanks again for helpin' with Dad. I'll keep an eye on him. Y'all be careful."

"Yeah. You too. And watch the heat."

Tom, James and Andy all piled back in the cab and started south. About 45 minutes later they crossed the city limits of Lewisburg. The first order of business would be to pass on the information about the spray-painted truck. Dave would want to know about it for sure. Then they would unload the equipment and inspect it.

It was going to be a busy afternoon.

Chapter Thirty-Five

Checking Out

June 13th

Carter and his men had finally decided on a plan. Since the State Guard had assumed control of security at the Spring Hill Refugee Center, he had lost his contacts and suppliers for his "business venture" there.

The new security also kept him from maintaining his position as head bully of the complex. He had to keep his head down and play the game like everyone else. The only good thing was that Alan Land hadn't come back. As far as Carter knew the man was still unconscious in the hospital.

He and his men would slip out through one of the back doors of the building that they knew wouldn't latch. It had been used countless times already for sneaking ladies in and men out and would serve their needs just as well. The back of the plant faced west and, despite the gates, getting out was much simpler that way than climbing the sheer rock bluff on the east side of the facility.

There should have been no more than two guards to worry about before they got to the open ground leading across to Ephlin Parkway, the private road that encircled the entire complex. Once across it they would stick to the small row of trees that carried them almost all the way to the railroad tracks. A low fence would be all to stand between them and Cleburne Road.

There was a small stone shed on the opposite side of the road that they would use to catch their breath before moving south and then east. If necessary, they could stay there overnight, but it would be risky; especially if they had to kill the guards to get out.

After lights out they waited for nearly an hour before beginning to stir. In an effort to minimize the possibility of getting caught, Carter had only told a handful of his men the plan. The others would have to stay behind or figure their own way out. Quietly the men began to leave their bunks and head through the factory toward the rear of the plant.

Once at the southwest corner they gathered in the shadows near the doorway and waited for the patrol to get out of earshot. As the guards stepped away Carter made his way across the floor to the door and slowly cracked it open, peeking outside for any signs of movement. A few seconds later and he was out in the cool evening air.

It took several minutes for the others to slip out of the main building, but Carter had no intentions of waiting for anyone. The success of his plan was directly related to him staying on the move. Surviving worked much better if you were part of a group, but he was interested in saving his own skin first. Everyone else was just a plus.

He broke from the cover of the darkness and low ran across the open ground to the shadows of a nearby retaining wall which he followed to within a few yards of the first tree line. Scanning the building and the grounds closest to him, he decided to wait for a passing cloud to darken the moonlight for just a little more advantage.

Once the moonlight dimmed, he made a run for the trees. From there he could slow his pace and catch his breath as he moved toward the railroad tracks. Pausing in the cover of the foliage he turned back to the facility and saw silhouettes of three of the six men behind him, following in his steps. Carter turned his attention back to the path ahead.

He made his way down the tree line as quickly and quietly as he could until he faced open ground again. After another short dash he was at the outer perimeter fence. An old four-foot-tall cattle fence that separated the factory grounds from the railroad right of way. On the other side was the elevated railroad bed. As he crossed the fence he couldn't help but look back again at the massive factory.

Scattered among the trees he could barely make out the darkened shapes of his men, four this time, picking their way out. Carter hopped across the fence and was soon across the tracks. As he stepped onto the blacktop of Cleburne Road, he heard shouts coming from the direction of the factory. The shouts were followed by a pair of gunshots; rifles, by the sound of them.

The rest of the men scrambled through the trees and over the fence as Carter made for the shed. After several tense minutes the last of his five remaining men made it into the tiny stone structure. One had been shot in the escape, and his fate was unclear. One of the men stepped up onto the tracks and noticed that the lights had come on inside the building. They were no doubt doing a bed check to see how many had gotten out.

Hearing the report Carter decided it was imperative that they stay on the move. He began heading along the overgrown fence rows along Cleburne Road until it intersected Freehand Lane. Just down the road they came into a small subdivision that was a perfect source for fresh clothes and a little food and some weapons. Breaking into the homes was a risk, but it was a necessary one. Without the clothes they would be easily identified. Without the food they would run out of energy much faster. Without the weapons they couldn't get what they wanted later. Quick and quiet they stole what they needed and headed east.

Within an hour they had crossed Highway 31 and were on their way down Denning Lane. Soon they were passing in front of Oaklawn Manor, one of several pre-Civil War era plantation homes that still stood around Maury County. A large subdivision now occupied much of the surrounding farmland, but the original home and many of the supporting buildings remained as part of the historic registry. Carter found a secluded spot off the road where he could stop and get his bearings.

Reaching in his pocket he produced a cell phone. By the moonlight he began to scroll through the apps on the screen until he found what he was looking for.

"Whatcha got there? A phone?" one of the men asked.

"Yeah. I 'borrowed' this from somebody back at the camp. Anybody know what the name of this road is we're on?"

"I saw a sign way back there that said Dunning Lane or something like that."

Carter stared at the screen, swiping his finger left and right until he finally saw what he was looking for.

Scanning the map he finally saw a similar name.

"Denning Lane?" he asked.

"Yeah, maybe. I wasn't looking at signs so much as I was looking for cops. Where does that put us?"

"Not far enough away, but we're close to the main road we need to be on. We'll rest here for a little while before we head out. I don't want to be on the road in daylight until we are closer to Lewisburg."

"Maybe we should jack a car or something. I'm already tired of all this walking. How much farther do we have to go anyway?"

Carter chortled in a mocking child's voice, "Are we there yet?"

"Aw, shut up, man. I don't sound like that."

Major Thomas focused intently on the report of the breakout. He had already put an APB out for the men and given their photographs to law enforcement. Connecting dots to the reported burglaries south of the plant led him to believe that the men were either heading toward Columbia or the interstate in an attempt to get farther away.

To further complicate the issue, one of the homeowners had reported the theft of a .38 revolver and a .22 caliber rifle. His escapees were armed. The one that didn't make his escape was still in the medical ward but so far hadn't talked to anyone about the plan.

"Sir?" Captain Watkins said as he opened the door to the makeshift office.

"What is it, Captain?"

"We have a confirmed hit on one of the men."

Thomas looked up from the report before him, "Please tell me it isn't bad."

"I'd like to, sir, but I'd be lying."

Chapter Thirty-Six

Hot, Dry, and Boring

June 14th

"Sean Carter," Browning said with a sneer as he showed the mug shot to the officers in morning assembly, "This little bundle of joy is on the run from the Spring Hill Refugee Center. He and six of his best friends decided they no longer cared for the Governor's hospitality in their time of need, so they left last night. One of them made it as far as the parking lot before the State Guard shot him. The rest are still running.

"We have no reason to believe they will come here, but we don't know where they *are* headed, so keep your eyes peeled while at your posts. Especially at the border check points.

"Oh, one more thing," Browning said as he scanned the room of officers and auxiliary members, "Did I forget to mention that Mr. Carter is wanted in Detroit on a murder charge?

"It seems he shot a police officer in the face at a political protest that got out of hand several weeks back. He had kin in Spring Hill, which is why he ran here. Detroit would very much like him back and I, for one, would be glad to send him home…in a body bag.

"Heads on a swivel, folks. Be careful out there."

Scott and the rest of the team stepped up and looked the photos over again closely. He, Andy, Dale, and James were going to be on checkpoint duty today. With the temperature hitting around 86° and the impending flow bringing moisture up from the gulf the heat would feel like nearly 100°. Not the best conditions to be out in the sun with a dark shirt and pants and carrying rifles and ammo.

The men piled into their respective transports and headed out to relieve the officers and support staff that had been on duty all night.

Evans and Irwin managed to pull the same detail and were assigned the checkpoint on highway 50, just east of the I-65 exit at mile marker 37. It was situated along a long straight stretch of highway that allowed for plenty of advanced notice of approaching vehicles. Unfortunately, for as much as it offered in visibility, it lacked in shade, cover, or concealment. The road was basically wide open to fields on either side with little to nowhere to run in case anything bad should happen.

When they arrived on station there was a small line of cars waiting to be processed through.

The patrol cars were parked in a staggered configuration to allow traffic to flow, but very slowly.

Anyone wanting in or out would have to zigzag between the cars in order to reach the open road on the opposite side. The truck promptly dispatched the fresh troops onto the asphalt and began collecting the spent ones.

After a short briefing the security teams were exchanged and the night shift crew headed back toward town.

Normally, in the pre-Slip days, this was the busiest road into or out of the county. Thousands of workers would use this main highway every day and it was very convenient to the interstate as well, allowing commercial truck traffic a direct vein to the customers they served in town. In addition, it was a primary thoroughfare for intrastate traffic going to and from the larger cities to the north and south.

The new team quickly set to work, processing the traffic and soon the line had almost disappeared. Scott moved from his position on the road to an overwatch assignment on the shoulder where he would wait until they decided to rotate again. A few minutes later and Evans was operating in the same capacity on the opposite side of the road.

The morning dragged on slowly with mundane repetition of the same tasks. As the morning changed to midday the temperature corresponded with a peak of near ninety and a soul crushing heat index pushing 103°. They had been warned of the storm front working up from the gulf, but the rapid change still caught everyone off guard.

Scott stood among the swirling mirage that had begun to form along the surface of the road as sweat saturated his shirt and the band of his black ball cap.

"This sucks," he shouted across to Evans.

Evans smiled in response but didn't say a word. He was busy mopping his own brow as perspiration streamed across his face.

With five people manning the checkpoint lunch became a slight bit of an orchestration. Two would eat while two more took overwatch. The final team member would be responsible for the dubious honor of interfacing with the drivers and passengers.

Scott was given the task of checking the vehicles while Evans and the team leader acted as the overwatch elements during the first rotation. Whoever was eating also had to monitor radio traffic; a job usually handled by the appointed team leader. After thirty minutes the members would swap out and then finally the team leader would eat. It wasn't rocket science, but it served the purpose.

"Evans, Irwin, go eat," the leader called as the first pair returned to work.

"No argument from me," Evans said, "I'm about to starve to death."

The two made their way to one of the patrol cars and started the engine. The cost of fuel was prohibitive enough that letting the vehicle idle all day and night wasn't permitted, but a blind eye was generally turned to allow a little comfort and air conditioning from time to time. Besides, it helped keep the batteries charged since the radios were on 24-7.

"Man," Irwin began, "I sure do miss lunch at my old job."

"Tell me about it," Evans said as he indulged in a simple peanut butter sandwich.

"I'd love to have a big order of Cajun shrimp from the Steamer right now. Man, would that hit the spot!"

"Ooh," Evans said with a sigh, "You know what I'd like?"

"Chicken Fried Chicken from the Peaks?"

"You know me too well, my friend," he chuckled, "served with a side of their steamed vegetables…"

"With the bacon chunks in it for extra flavor," Scott added.

"Oh, yeah, and served up by Traci? That would be awesome!"

"Traci? Which one was that?"

"You remember. She was the one from Florida that was taking classes for business management."

Scott seemed to be at a loss.

"Blue eyes, long blonde hair?"

"Sorry dude. You just described half the girls that worked there."

"She had the tattoo of the Lord's Prayer on her lower back."

"Oh, yeah, okay," Irwin conceded, "I remember now. I never could figure out that one. You just can't find that level of class everyday, you know." Both men laughed.

"I never knew if it was proper to call that a 'tramp stamp' or not. I mean the location was right, but the verbiage was all wrong."

After a few seconds the men were back to inhaling their lunches. Evans was well into his apple while Irwin finished off the last of his sandwich.

"Scott?" Evans began.

"Yeah?"

"You mind if I ask you a personal question?"

"What's up?"

Evans kind of stammered about before deciding he was committed to the line of thought.

"You and Rachel…y'all have been in the house together for a few weeks now. Have you two….well, are you dating or what?"

Irwin thought for a minute. He hadn't considered how long they had been sharing the house.

"You know," he replied, "It's funny. All this time I've worked with her, and I always wanted to ask her out, but there was a strict policy of no interoffice dating. I never wanted to cross the line.

"Now that the world's out of whack, I guess I've just gotten used to that policy always being there and I haven't pushed. Maybe on a subconscious level I'm still thinking we'll be going back to work soon, and I just don't want to jeopardize the career situation…for either of us." Evans nodded sympathetically.

"Why? You lookin' to make a move on my woman?" Irwin jabbed at his friend.

"Me? I was just wondering. I mean. You guys have been in the same house and all. I thought maybe things might have gotten a little…intimate."

"Nah. Besides, it still feels weird having her in the house with Mom and Dad being there all the time. Almost like I'm back in high school again."

"Hey, I remember you in high school," Evans said with a smile, "That never stopped you back then."

"Alright, guys, break time's over. Time to let the boss eat," the lead called across the checkpoint.

The two friends quickly shut the engine off and headed back to their positions at the checkpoint.

Chapter Thirty-Seven

Rattle and Snap

June 15th – Early Morning

The evening temperature had dropped into the sixties around the mid-state area which, following the heat of the day before, was almost enough to give a bit of a chill to the air. With the moisture pushing in from the south the air was damp and juicy, adding to the extra cool feeling.

Carter and his men had settled down to rest and get their bearings in the early morning hours after crossing the interstate and decided to move onto the tertiary roads to reduce the possibility of being spotted by patrols.

They had managed to find a wooded area on the opposite side of an overgrown fence row which provided an excellent hiding place. The ground in the area was pretty rocky, but between the large stones were natural depressions that were large enough to lie down in and not be seen from ground level. They made a small campfire in one of the larger depressions to help stave off the cooling air and dampness and settled in to sleep.

All around the men were dozens of cedar trees whose resilience allowed them to thrive among the boulders and provided a wind break and extra cover from prying eyes.

As morning began to break, Carter was already stirring. He had found it impossible to sleep, despite his deficit. He was, after all, a "city-boy" and not used to being out in the wild like this. Every sound he heard had him staring into the darkness. He was exhausted and it was beginning to catch up to him. His temper was up, and he wanted to move on, but he didn't want to follow the main roads too much.

Carter reached into his pocket and produced the stolen phone. He quickly brought up the map application and waited for his position to be displayed. As he did some of the others began to stir.

"What's up, Sean?" Tommy, one of Carter's co-conspirators, asked groggily, "You been up long?"

"All night. Couldn't sleep. Too much noise out here," he said with a yawn

"Shit," the man replied, "That didn't bother me. My ass was dead to the world quick."

"Yeah, I noticed that."

The man began scratching vigorously at the small of his back as he woke up.

"What the hell...," he said as he raised his shirt tail up and felt along the skin, "What the hell is this?" The man pinched the small flat feature he found and promptly began to pull on it. With a small pop it released, leaving an irritation and small mound of inflamed tissue. Upon closer examination he realized he had been the unwitting victim of a tick bite. While he had managed to remove the body, the head remained in his flesh.

"Better check yourselves," he announced, "I just pulled a tick off me."

Within a few minutes all but one of the group was awake and doing self-assessments and examinations to see how many of the little parasites had come to visit in the night.

"Somebody wake Bobby's ass up," Carter sneered.

The man with the tick bite walked over and promptly kicked Bobby on the feet, ushering forth a tired groan.

"Bobby, man, get up. We got shit to do."

The slumbering Bobby slowly rolled over from his side onto his back and then, with a shout, leapt to his feet.

"Shit!" he screamed, "Shit, shit shit!" He was jumping about in a circle grasping for the back of his upper arm. Nobody else had noticed the small Timber Rattler that had curled up beside him for warmth near the coals of the fire in the cool overnight hours.

When he rolled over, he had unknowingly pinned the serpent beneath his arm. Defensively, the creature had bitten back only to be slung off into the undergrowth when Bobby jumped to his feet.

"What the hell's wrong with you, man?"

Bobby quickly dropped onto his knees in the dirt and began to remove his shirt.

"Damn, dude!" Tommy exclaimed

The bite was already streaming a small trickle of blood, but the damage was all on the inside. The hemotoxin was already making its way through his body and soon would be wreaking havoc on his organs.

"Yo, I don't know no whole lot, but that's a snake bite. I know that much." Another of the men said.

"What kind was it?"

"I don't know," Bobby said, "I didn't know he was even there until he bit me."

With most of the men from urban backgrounds, none were familiar with treatments for snake bites. The ones from smaller towns all had come from areas with little to no suitable habitat for pit vipers. They had all seen the westerns and decided that the proper course of action was to cut between the fang marks and suck the poison out. After all, it worked in the movies, so it had to be true, right?

"What do we do, Sean?"

Carter considered it for a minute. He refused to turn back for the man. He had to get to Lewisburg. That was his goal.

"There's a hospital back in Spring Hill. If one of you want to carry him back there, go ahead.

I have to keep moving south."

The group began to murmur amongst themselves. Going back meant getting caught. There was no doubt about it. Leaving him here meant that Bobby would die. The only one that didn't seem to be bothered by that was Carter. His mind was made up and his choice didn't include Bobby coming along.

Finally, Tommy spoke up.

"I'll take him. Maybe they can give me something for this tick bite too. It's itching like a bastard anyway."

Carter looked the pair over. Bobby was clearly in a lot of pain and seemed to be getting sick looking.

"Alright. Head back to the main road. From there go back across the interstate and when you get to Saturn Parkway the hospital is on the other side, somewhere.

"If anyone asks, you tell them we got separated and you decided to get him some help. As far as you know I'm heading to Florida or some shit. You understand?"

"Yeah," Tommy said, "I understand. Don't worry about it."

Carter and the others quickly grabbed what little possessions they had among them and headed down the fence row in the direction of Lewisburg. Tommy looked at Bobby and tried to figure out how he was going to manage to get the man back to civilization in his current condition.

A few yards away he spotted some large limbs from a cedar that had apparently broken off under high winds. He looked at Bobby and a plan began to come together.

Grabbing Bobby's discarded shirt, he stretched it across the two tree limbs and made a sort of improvised stretcher. Placing his own shirt on it as well made for a decent sized area to cradle the man's torso and upper legs. He would use the setup as a drag not too unlike the old Native American method: grabbing it by the ends of the limbs and lifting Bobby off the ground, then dragging him along supported on the opposite ends of the limbs. It was crude but would be much easier than bearing the entire weight of the man for several miles under the summer sun.

Getting started was the most difficult problem he faced since he had to manhandle Bobby across the fence row and then place him on the improvised stretcher in order to even begin dragging him toward help.

As he dragged the assembly, he became aware that Bobby had begun struggling with breathing and would from time to time roll himself over and throw up on the road, or the stretcher, or himself. He was sweating profusely, but that could have been from the sweltering humidity.

"How you feelin' man?"

Bobby's response was muddled and unintelligible. His face had already begun to go numb. "What's that? I couldn't hear you."

"Shit," was all he said.

Tommy glanced back at his companion and noticed that his arm had swollen considerably, even to the point that the ring on his right hand was almost cutting the finger off.

After several minutes they made it to Kedron Road and turned back to the west. It was still several miles to the hospital, but maybe, just maybe, they could catch a ride from a passerby. Even a cop would take them to the hospital first, wouldn't they?

Chapter Thirty-Eight

Barter Town

June 15th – 9:30 a.m.

Ben and Carol had loaded the truck full of cases of canned vegetables and fresh items alike.

They also carried several boxes of empty honey jars which the Robertsons would clean and reuse.

That counted as credit toward the bartering process.

Rachel busied herself with the accounting side of the farm to estimate what they had taken for trade and made notes of what they hoped to bring back. She still had to remind herself that the world no longer revolved around the mighty dollar, so estimating profits and expenses was…different these days.

It was just another day in the new world.

About 9:30 the couple hopped in the truck and headed out to Spring Hill. Within just a few minutes they had passed through the checkpoint at Highway 99 and were soon through Pottsville and on the way to Rally Hill. Their bartering adventures for the day would be extensive, and they were already regretting such a late start.

Hanging a left onto Kedron Road the pickup bounced along the blacktop, steadily making progress toward the Robertson honey farm.

Being the bartering master mind of the family, Carol began to offer Ben suggestions about what she felt were acceptable arrangements of exchange among all the supplies they had brought.

Some things would be bartered, as was the herbal medicine, in order to be exchanged again for other necessary items. It was like an intricate ballet of monetary movement and Carol was unequalled.

Rounding a bend in the road, Ben suddenly jammed on the brakes.

"What in the hell?"

"Ben!"

"Sorry, honey."

Tommy had heard the approach of the truck before he could see it. Struggling with Bobby's limp and swollen body on the drag had taken a toll on him and he couldn't move out of the road fast enough, so he was hoping whoever was coming would be able to stop before running them both down.

Forgetting his predicament, he turned and raised a hand to flag the vehicle down, in turn dumping Bobby onto the pavement face down. He flagged the pickup to a stop and rushed to the driver's side door.

Ben gripped the .357 in his hand tightly as he watched the man approach. On the other side of the cab, Carol had her .38 out and hidden behind her purse. "Thank you!" Tommy cried, "I need help!" Ben cautiously rolled the window down.

"What's the problem, son?"

"My friend here. He was bitten by a snake this morning and I don't have a good way to get him to the hospital. Can we catch a ride?"

Ben glanced at Carol and then down to the revolver in her hand. She nodded and he turned his attention to the man in the road.

"Alright. Let's see what you've got here," he said as he opened the door.

Ben Irwin stepped out into the road and tucked the revolver into his waistband, causing Tommy to stop dead in his tracks.

"Don't do anything stupid, son and you've got nothing to worry about."

The men approached the drag and looked over the situation. Carol watched as Ben motioned to the bed of the truck and Tommy nodded in agreement. They collected Bobby and drug him to the bed of the truck where it took both of them to load him up.

"You stay back here with him," Ben said, "I'll get you to the hospital as quick as I can." He turned to get in the cab as Tommy clamored over the tailgate.

"Is that man dead, Ben?"

"Not yet. He could be pretty soon, though. If he *doesn't* die, he's in for a rough life."

Ben put the truck in gear and hit the gas pedal. Within a few minutes the group was pulling under the awning at the hospital emergency room.

Ben left his revolver on the seat beside Carol and ran to the doors. Seconds later he returned with a pair of orderlies and a wheelchair followed by the charge nurse.

As they stepped out into the June heat Tommy was already out of the bed and trying to maneuver Bobby to the back of the vehicle.

Within a couple of minutes, they had Bobby out of the truck and wheeled into the building.

Tommy turned to thank the Irwins for their help.

"I don't know what would have happened if you hadn't come along," he said with a smile.

"That's alright, son. He's not out of the woods yet. That bite happen today?"

"Yes. This morning. Why?"

"Hmm," Ben said, "You might want to keep him in your prayers. If he lives through this, it's gonna hurt."

Ben got back in the cab of the truck and, with a friendly wave, headed back to the tasks at hand. Tommy headed back through the doors to see what the doctors had to say about Bobby. As he passed by the nurse's station, he failed to realize that the charge nurse was on the phone.

Within ten minutes Major Thomas and four of his men strolled through the doors. The charge nurse stood to address them immediately.

"Where can I find them," Thomas said.

"The one with the bite is in exam 4. His friend was with him a few minutes ago."

"Thank you," he said as he headed into the exam area.

Tommy straightened up as soon as the major walked through the doorway. He knew he was in trouble, but he knew that before he ever got to the hospital.

"Alright, son," Thomas began, "You know what I need to know. Where's Carter?"

Tommy stared at Bobby in silence, considering his options. He'd promised to not give away Carter's destination. He didn't want to jeopardize anything by going back on his word. After all, Lewisburg wasn't *that* far away.

"I don't know," he finally mumbled.

"Now, see, that's what I like to call 'a lie,' Tommy. We know you were one of the six men that slipped out the other night with him. We also know that he only told six of you about his plan. That means you're in his inner circle. A confidant," Thomas pulled over a chair and sat down facing the man, "Care to try it again?"

"All I know is we were leaving and heading south," he finally muttered, "I don't know what the final stop was."

"Okay," Thomas said as he leaned back in the chair, "How?"

"How what?"

"How was he planning on getting there, wherever 'there' is? Did he have a map?"

Tommy picked through his words carefully.

"Yeah."

"Alright. Where did he get a map from? Did he steal one from a car, or maybe a gas station?

Is he using a cell phone or GPS?"

When 'cell phone' emerged into the conversation Thomas noticed a slight, almost imperceptible twitch in Tommy's demeanor. He began to suspect that this man was no professional criminal; he just fell in with the wrong bunch and rode the coat tails for what he could get.

"A cell phone? We don't have a record of him having a cell phone. Where did he get it?"

Again, Tommy sat silently. He wasn't used to being questioned about things. He wasn't used to being in this kind of situation. He was afraid any answer he gave would be the wrong one. He was sure of it, actually.

"Son," Thomas said flatly, "I have a tough situation here. I have a man who is wanted for murder on the loose in my jurisdiction. One of his men is in this hospital being treated for a gunshot wound he received from my men while attempting to escape a refugee center after a particularly violent fight. Another is lying here unconscious being treated for a snake bite and the only one I'm able to get any answers from won't talk to me.

"That puts me in a spot I don't want to be in. Talk to me and I'll see what we can do about putting you somewhere else, because I'll tell you, I'm willing to lay money down that if I put you back in *my* facility, you'll be dead by morning. I gotta be honest, I just don't want to deal with that any more."

Tommy sat stone faced. Internally he was struggling with options, but didn't know what to say, or not to.

"The only thing I know to do is either put you in an actual jail or send you back home." The thought of being sent back to Chicago immediately drew a response.

"No," he said, "You can't send me back there. That place is…is…a war zone. They've lost their minds up there. I can't go back. Don't send me back."

Thomas crossed his legs and looked at the young man. Now he had the leverage he wanted.

"Then you need to tell me what you know."

"Did he really kill someone?"

"Yep. A cop. Shot him in the face and then ran here. That's who your friend really is, Tommy. I can't have him on the loose, understand?"

"But, if I tell you, he might come back and kill me. I don't want to die."

"Son, look beside you. He doesn't care if you die or not. He's already decided that, otherwise he wouldn't have left this fool behind.

"I don't think you're on the same level as Carter. I can't say that you're the greatest fellow I've ever met, but I don't think you're a hardened killer, either. I think, deep down, you want to do the right thing. If that leads us to him, you don't have to worry about him coming back for you." After another minute or so of silence Tommy finally opened up.

"He took the phone from one of the other refugees. I don't know who. He just pulled it out of his pocket and started using it for the maps when we got away from the camp."

"Yeah, we had a report that one had been stolen," Thomas nodded to one of his men,

"What else?"

The soldier quietly stepped out of the room as Thomas continued the conversation.

"He said something about going to Florida," Tommy blurted out, "I don't know if he

actually will, but he said something about it." It wasn't technically a lie. After all, Carter *did* say to tell them he was going to Florida.

The bartering had gone better than Ben had expected, and he was still smiling from the exchange. Carol wasn't as enthusiastic. She thought they could have done even better, but it was still a very good arrangement.

"I'm glad we left as early as we did," Ben said, "I didn't think we'd ever get away from them."

Carol laughed, "That little man certainly does love to talk. I'm just ready to get back home."

"Well, we can't go just yet," Ben replied, "We still have a couple more stops to make. We'll be home in time for supper. After all, it isn't every day we can justify the cost of gas to come up here, so I want to get as much done as I can before we go back." Carol nodded her head in agreement.

"I can't believe how expensive gas has gotten. Remember when it first hit $1.00 a gallon?"

"Oh, yes," Ben recalled, "I think I ranted for a week. It cost me $10.00 to go to Nashville and back then. I was furious.

"Of course, I was just out of high school and only making about $4.00 an hour working part time. It took a lot of my check just to fill up the truck each week."

"Yeah," Carol smiled, "Those were the good ole days."

A couple of hours later the Irwins had done all the running they could in Spring Hill and were finally on their way home. The truck was laden with all sorts of honey, sugar, salt, nails, and other various supplies and materials that were needed for maintenance and barter back home, plus a little extra for the personal pantry and workshop.

As the truck headed back down Kedron Road Ben tucked the .357 Revolver in the center console of the seat and Carol slid over beside her husband. They snuggled up in the cab and enjoyed the peace and quiet of the ride for a while as the sun began to set. The sky behind them was turning a deep blue with a swath of purple and crimson that seemed to divide night from day.

Despite his desire to get home quickly, Ben didn't want to burn fuel unnecessarily, so he kept the speed down and took the drive easy.

Soon they arrived at the intersection of Kedron Road and Highway 431 at Rally Hill and turned south toward Pottsville. They proceeded through the checkpoint without issue and within a couple of minutes were around the corner and almost to Hardison Mill. The road home was just ahead, but first they would have to cross the river. In the fading light Carol noticed movement on the side of the road halfway or so across the bridge.

"What's that up ahead, Ben?" Carol asked.

Chapter Thirty-Nine

Sadie Hawkins Day

June 15th – 4:00 p.m.

Range day concluded with the members of the team tired and sweaty. They had run drills alone and as partners as well as a few working as a cohesive unit. While they weren't perfect, they were beginning to gel into a fairly functional group. One of the SWAT instructors sat in, giving suggestions on how to make communications easier and less confusing.

Rather than using terms like "cover" to indicate a problem during a firefight, he suggested "red." It was much shorter and easily understood. If you heard "red" it meant something had gone wrong, please cover my targets while I straighten things out.

As opposed to saying "clear" when the issue was resolved the term "green" was used. This was of particular use when entering a building since the term "clear" was used to inform the rest of the squad that the room was secure and could be a source of confusion if used in the wrong context. "Green" simply meant that whatever problem had occurred was resolved and that member was back in the fight.

Simple things like that served to smooth the drills out and make the members more organized. They were coming together as a group, and it was showing. Even the SWAT instructor commented on how well they had evolved over the previous several days, especially considering that the entire auxiliary unit was only a couple of weeks old.

As the team broke for the afternoon various topics of discussion came up. Some were curious about the direction of the support team. Had things changed since the raid? Would they be expected to take a more active role in raids and arrest procedures?

Others wanted to know about less mission critical things such as news from outside the area.

"I heard that there was a fire in Birmingham last night. A propane facility burned to the ground. Lots of damage. A few people badly burned. Did you hear anything over the wire about it?" The SWAT instructor choked down a piece of fried chicken before updating the news.

"Yeah, I heard about that. Birmingham has been having a lot of problems since the Slip. They have reason to believe that last night was the work of a political group they've had trouble with. They're trying to push a socialist agenda down there and are really pressing hard."

"What group is it? Any names?"

"My contact down there didn't mention individual names, but the organization used to be associated with Antifa. They broke away to form a more radical group, if you can believe that. They call themselves the Hammer and Sickle."

"Any chance they might gain influence in this area?"

"Nah. Right now they're pretty small, but crazy. My contact said they have strong intel on the leadership and are planning to cut the head off soon. Hopefully it will send a clear message to other groups to stand down or even dissolve. Time will tell."

Evans piped up, "I finally got my equipment set up over the weekend and have been trying to monitor some radio traffic here and there regularly. Lots of stuff going on around the country.

Not all of it good.

"One interesting thing I heard about was the 'I miss America' graffiti popping up across the Washington state area. It kind of reminded me of the old stories about Killroy from World War Two. From what I gathered the feds are trying really hard to maintain control up there, but they are losing the rural areas. Metro areas are a mess, but the feds and the state have a strong presence there.

Out in the country, not so much. It'll be interesting to see how this all plays out."

Browning added onto Evans' commentary, "It's like that all over. Most of the bigger cities have been falling apart due to the entitlement groups and strong control of liberal politicians. Outside the wire people don't rely on government support as much so they seem to handle things better on their own."

"Word is," the SWAT instructor continued, "Chicago has been essentially turning from a combat zone into a containment zone. They're not trying to retake the city. Just letting it burn itself out. Nobody in or out."

"That's crazy," Simmons said, "Why would they do that?"

"Picking their battles. I'd say for it to have gotten that bad they've already invested more than they wanted to and got nothing out of it. It's time to cut losses and clean up whatever's left later," Browning suggested.

After a few minutes of contemplation, Irwin finally said rhetorically, "I wonder what New

York and D.C. have turned into."

His comment was largely met with silence or grunts of consideration. Finally, he looked at his watch and announced, "Well, fellas, it's been real and it's been fun, but it hasn't been real fun. I need to get on the road."

"What's the hurry? Hot date?" Browning jabbed.

"Nah, got some things to take care of before I get home. I'm going to run by the hospital and check on Adams, too."

"I think you're going to run by the hospital to check out that little brunette," Browning prodded again, "What's her name? Denise?"

Irwin smiled broadly, "She *is* hard to ignore, isn't she?"

"So," Evans chimed in, "You aren't going to do Krav with me, Davis and Rachel?"

"Not today, man. Y'all have fun. You can bring me up to speed later."

Scott gathered his gear and began to load up the Jeep. He popped a fresh magazine into the well of his AR pistol and folded the buffer tube to the side before laying it on the passenger seat and climbing in. He had finally managed to sight it in at the farm a couple of weeks earlier, but today was the first day to run it on the range. He liked it even more now as his "truck gun" than before.

"I'll join you guys for the hand to hand," Richards spoke up, "It's been a while since I've had the opportunity and after our trip here, I can use the practice."

"The more the merrier," Davis said with a grin.

"Anybody need a ride into town before I go?"

"Hang on," Simmons said, "I'll ride along."

"I guess I need to go myself," Phillips added, "Pulling night shift at the checkpoint up at Pottsville tonight."

"Ugh," some of the team groaned, "Lucky you."

"Well, at least it will be cooler than it is right now, and I can get a couple of hours of sleep before I have to be there. It all works out."

Soon the range was almost devoid of life as a small caravan headed east toward Lewisburg.

Gradually the vehicles peeled off the main highway and veered toward each particular destination.

Scott dropped Simmons off by his house and then continued on to the downtown area.

Evans had to meet Rachel at the Irwin farm and bring her to town to meet Davis and Richards. Browning broke off to go home and see his own family before beginning the evening rituals of tending gardens, chickens, and tuning in the radio to gather news and information.

After dropping Simmons off and finishing his errands for the day Scott headed to the hospital. Adams was already looking better yesterday, and he had been told that he was recuperating well. Faster than anticipated, actually, but he would still have to take it easy for a while. Recovery from gunshot wounds wasn't like in the movies. Rarely is anything ever like in the movies. Things in real life tend to be more...complicated.

As he strolled into the room, he found Adams asleep in the bed with reruns of Family Feud playing quietly on the television.

Irwin silently eased into the chair in the corner and watched his teammate...his friend...resting across the room. His mind was filled with thoughts and unanswered questions about what went wrong and how to avoid getting his men caught off guard like this again. His men. *His* men. They weren't his men. They were friends and colleagues. They were no more his than anything else he had at his disposal. The only thing that was his anymore was the weapons he had and the shoes on his feet. He even owed his clothes to his family for providing them. The world had completely changed for Scott Irwin. He was simultaneously humbled and frustrated to be thrust into such a position. He was a bit embarrassed to be so far off target on things he should have expected.

Things he used to keep track of.

He began to wonder, if he hadn't focused on material things like new cars, nice homes, and technology, would he have spent more time and attention to the world around him, to prepping and training? How much money had he invested in that house and car that were both now burnt-out hunks of debris? How much of that could have gone into medical training to help someone like Adams? How much could have gone into supplies for a better, more complete trauma kit?

"You look like a man with a lot on his mind," a voice said from the doorway as Denise walked in.

"Hmm? Oh, yeah, sorry. Just…well…thinking about things. You know?"

"No worries. We all do that these days. Stopping by to check on Mr. Adams again, I see."

"Nah. I just like to watch Family Feud reruns, and we don't get this channel on the farm," Irwin said sarcastically.

Denise smiled and giggled a little, "Most patients don't care what's on, as long as it's something to break the silence. Something normal. We've found that most of them prefer the old game show reruns to anything else because it isn't spewing the biased media rhetoric of all the other channels."

"My grandmother, before she passed away several years ago, used to be obsessed with this show," Scott admitted, "She was also hard of hearing, so when we'd go visit, you could hear the TV all the way out in the driveway, even to the mailbox, with the doors and windows closed.

"For years I couldn't stand to have a game show of any kind on. It drove me nuts. Especially this one. I never realized how many different episodes of it were out there; and they would play back-to-back for hours at a time, every day."

Denise carefully pointed the remote at the television and turned it off.

"There you go. We don't want you traumatized, do we?" Scott smiled.

"How's he doing?" he asked, motioning to Adams.

"He's fine. I wouldn't be surprised if he gets sent home in a couple of days. He's been fighting a little infection, but it's under control. He's tough. You've got a fighter here."

"Yeah, I know. They're all good guys. I just wish I could have been there to keep him out of

the firing line."

Denise stepped over to Scott's side of the room and looked him square in the eyes.

"I know it's none of my business," she began, "but you don't need to dwell on things like that. Do what you can with what you have. Trust them to make the right decisions. That's all you can do. At the end of the day, it's all anyone can do. These days, that's hard enough."

"You're a pretty sharp lady, you know?"

Denise smiled again. She wanted to press the conversation, but the moment felt awkward.

Finally, she decided to cast her reservations aside.

"I know this may seem a bit, well, unorthodox," she stammered, "but would you happen to have any interest in getting together some time? I mean, I would love to tonight if you're not busy, but I have a few hours left on my shift and I'd rather clean up first…"

"Are you asking me out on a date?" Scott smiled back.

"Yeah, I guess I am. It's just that you seem like a really interesting person and I'd like to get to know you better. I mean, if you already have a girlfriend or something, I understand, I just thought…"

"No," Scott said, but his mind was filling with thoughts of Rachel, "Nobody right now. I've been kind of preoccupied with all this.

"I'm not busy tonight, but I do have a lot to do tomorrow, so I need to get some rest, and I'll need to help my family unload all their trading when I get home, so what about tomorrow night?"

"Well, I'm off tomorrow night. Would that be okay? We can meet somewhere in town. I don't know my way around very well, but there must be something we can do or someplace we can go."

"I'll tell you what," Scott said, "write down your address and I'll come and pick you up. I'm sure we can figure something out."

Denise scrambled for a pen and paper and began writing her contact information down. "Thank God," a grouchy voice rumbled from the bed.

Scott looked over to see Adams smiling back at him, "How long have you been awake?"

"Ever since someone turned off the TV. She's been badgering the piss out of me about you every day. It's about damn time one of you made a move."

Chapter Forty

Cross Country

June 15th – 9:30 a.m.

As the men made their way down the narrow one-lane roads of Eastern Maury County, Carter began reconsidering his approach to Lewisburg. According to the map on the phone, they were just north of an intersection of highways around a little community called Pottsville. The county line ran close by the community, and the Duck River was just south of the town as well. With so much potential traffic in one small area, the possibility of being spotted was considerably higher than he was comfortable with.

He began to think it might be best to avoid road travel completely and make their way across the fields and farms in the area instead. It would be more difficult to be found and would allow them to cut a lot of travel off their distance. Of course, they wouldn't be able to travel as fast as if they were on established roads, but that was a price he could accept over being caught.

Soon he called the group to a stop and huddled in the underbrush.

"Ok, I'm thinking we might be going about this wrong," he said.

"What do you mean, Sean?"

"Look," he pulled the phone out of his pocket and opened the map application, "Here's where we are now, right?" He pointed a dirty finger at the small OLED screen, indicating a pulsing blue circle.

"Now, look down here," he slid the finger across to show the intersection and the nearby community, "This is what's just down the road. We have three highways coming together in this little town here. The county line is nearby, and the interstate isn't too far to the west. I'm thinking this is a perfect place to get caught."

"Yeah," one of the men replied, "but it could also be a good place to pick up some food and something to drink, too."

"He does have a point, Carter. We've been walking all morning in this heat and I'm starting to feel it, man. A good cool drink of something don't sound bad. If we're careful…"

"I'm not willing to take that chance yet," Carter snapped, "Once we're past this intersection and south of this little flea speck, we can stop. Until then, I say we cut across country and avoid the roads altogether. It would be a shorter distance, off the main roads, so we'd be harder to spot, and it would put us past all this before dark. I think this is a better way to go."

The other two men considered the logic. Carter did make a valid point. Both of them were already thinking with their stomachs, though, and sought a compromise.

"Okay, I'll give you that," one began, "but what if we took a minute just to slip over there and check out what we're willing to bypass? If there's no danger, I say we just ease through and see what's available. If it's too risky, we go ahead and follow your plan." Carter considered the option for a minute.

"Alright. You go ahead and see what's going on around the place. If it looks to be a clean shot, one of you come back and get me. If not, we go my way. I'll wait here for you. If I don't hear anything back from either of you in…three hours, I'm going on without you.

"You both have watches?"

The first man pointed to his wrist, showing a battered digital watch and band. Carter looked at the second man.

"Lost mine in a poker game three nights ago. Sorry."

"Dumbass," was all Carter said.

Within a few minutes the pair had made for the town. Navigating the woods was time-consuming since neither had been allowed to take the phone or had any idea where they were headed. They tried to remember landmarks as best as they could and listen for the sounds of any traffic in the distance, but the trees and breeze obscured most, if not all, vehicles from earshot.

Within an hour they arrived at the northernmost leg of Highway 99 and crouched down to watch for traffic. Feeling confident that they had plenty of time, they strolled south across the pavement and into the woods on the opposite side before turning east and heading toward the large intersection.

As they got closer to the community, they began to realize it wasn't so much a town as it was a cluster of houses and a Dollar store that had been allowed to exist at an intersection. Save for a small restaurant and a church, the entire area was farmhouses and an intersection with flashing lights.

To the north they heard an approaching car and deftly dropped from view behind a small barn. They could hear the car begin to decelerate as it passed, but they didn't hear it stop. Finally, when it was in sight again, they could tell the driver was slowing down, but no signal was on to indicate it was leaving the road. They decided to investigate further and moved south in the direction of the car.

Soon they were overlooking the security checkpoint near the county line. Since it was a county line checkpoint there were officers from two different departments on station, and they were carrying some pretty serious hardware. As they watched a third department arrived from the east.

The side of the car read Chapel Hill.

The Chapel Hill vehicle pulled alongside a car on the shoulder that had apparently come through the checkpoint but was waiting on an escort. The officer checked licenses and talked to the occupants for a minute before returning to his own car. Within a few seconds both vehicles were heading back east.

"Looks like we'll be taking the nature trail," one of the men said. The second nodded in agreement and they began their careful withdrawal from the area.

Finding their way back to Carter was not an easy task. They tried to remember all the landmarks they had mentally noted on the way in, but so many features in the area looked remarkably similar. They finally spotted him moving toward the highway just off to their right.

Apparently, their time had run out and he wasn't joking about not waiting.

"Hey," they called. "Sean. Hey, man, wait up."

Carter heard them and stopped, slipping his hand gingerly to the butt of the revolver at first, but realizing who it was and recovering just as quickly.

"I thought you two had been caught. I guess the way isn't clear?"

"Nah. The town isn't much of a town, and there's a big police checkpoint at the other side of it. Your plan seems like the best way to go."

"I tried to tell you that earlier, but you wouldn't listen," Carter remarked, "How is the traffic? Heavy?"

"Nope," the other man replied, "We only saw one or two cars the whole time, other than patrol cars. But they are stopping everyone at the roadblock.

"We can cross the highway up ahead pretty easy, though. Ain't nobody comin' from the interstate."

"Alright. We just need to get across this highway here and then we can ease up a bit until we get to Hardison Mill Road. That will bypass the checkpoint and bring us around to the river. There's bound to be a house or something on that road we can get something to eat at."

The men made their way back to the shoulder of Highway 99 and carefully listened for traffic before stepping onto the pavement. A few strides across the black top and they were all safely across the road. They followed Flat Creek until it intersected with Duck River and then turned east, following the riverbank from the tree line as much as possible to conceal their presence.

Within a few minutes they were far enough away from the highways that they were strolling at a comfortable pace and beginning to relax a little, despite the hunger pangs that gnawed and the thirst from the heat and humidity.

Travel along the riverbank proved highly uneventful and they had quickly made it past Tugas Bend and were almost to Cheeks Bend when Carter noticed a lone house trailer situated a few yards from the river at the end of a narrow, wooded driveway. He stopped and carefully observed the location for several minutes before turning his attention to the other men.

"I think we need to take a closer look at this one," he said, "Could be something in there worth having. You never know."

"Why didn't you want to stop at the others about a half mile up river? They were a lot nicer; could have had more worth the taking."

"Nah, they were too close together. Too easy for a neighbor to hear us and see us. Look, this place is out of sight and out of earshot of anyone for probably miles in every direction. Now, look at the truck in the driveway. Can you see the rifle rack in the back window?"

Carter began to smile, "C'mon. Let's go see if anybody's home."

The trio cautiously approached the single wide trailer from the concealment of the riverbank tree line and soon ducked behind the truck. A quick look at the back glass had Carter smiling broadly now. A series of decals on the bottom left-hand corner stated proudly, "You've got your family, I've got mine," and was comprised of a series of firearm silhouettes ranging from AR's and scoped bolt actions on the left to pistols and revolvers on the right. The owner was clearly a "gun guy."

Carter quickly surmised that he was one of those right-wing radicals who had voted to take away all the programs people like himself had come to depend on for their daily survival. He hoped the person was at home. He was a bit surprised that there wasn't one of those racist Confederate flags blowing in the wind on the front porch or, even worse, one of those yellow flags with the snake on it.

Carter eased over to the wall of the trailer and listened near the windows to see if there were any sounds of life emanating from within. Silence. No sound of any movement or television, or radio met his ears.

Slowly he eased himself around to peer in the window and stood up slightly. Through the sheer curtains at the back of the living room he could see the furnishings inside. An old wooden framed couch with a gaudy wildlife pattern on it and a matching chair sat at ninety degrees to each other, directing the focus of the room onto the 42" television on the interior wall. A pair of symmetrically mounted deer heads flanked the set while there, along the opposite wall from his vantage point, was the grand prize: a large wooden gun cabinet with etched glass doors. Inside he could see the bolt action Remington 700. Beside that was a pump shotgun, probably a Maverick or Mossberg 12 gauge. Beside that was the AR-15 and next to it sat a squat little underfold AK-47. On hooks dangled two revolvers, and two pistols.

He could see several boxes of ammunition on the floor of the cabinet as well and some cleaning supplies too. There was no sign of a wife or girlfriend in sight. Everything was very masculine about the room. No toys were on the floor to indicate children lived there either. This was going to be easy.

The three men cautiously circled the trailer, peering in through every window to see where the owner might be. On such a hot day they had assumed that he would be asleep under a fan or air conditioner. That's what they would have been doing had the world not gone sideways.

Nonetheless, there was no sign of life in the structure except for a dirty plate in the kitchen sink and a slow drip in the faucet. It was time to get inside.

The front door had a three-light arrangement of small windows in a slight stair step configuration. Carter figured he could reach the doorknob from the lowest one and promptly broke it out with the revolver. Reaching inside he managed to unlock the front door and swung it wide open. The storm door latch was broken, so that was never an issue.

"So much for hiding out in the woods, huh?" he said with a small chuckle as he stepped inside, "I guess this guy thought nobody would come looking to steal anything all the way out here. Otherwise, he might have been more careful."

As Carter ransacked the gun cabinet and collected ammo, the other two raided the refrigerator, swilling cheap beer and grabbing whatever food they could find first. They loaded pockets with everything from Vienna Sausages to .22 Long Rifle ammo and made their way back outside.

They started to take the truck as a getaway vehicle but soon realized why it was there. Despite the keys being in the ignition, the old four-wheel drive sat there immobile; the battery was gone.

"Looks like we're still walking," someone commented.

The three quickly headed down the driveway toward Hardison Mill Road once again.

They decided to once again hug the riverbank as much as possible, sometimes taking them well below road level and out of sight of prying eyes completely.

Carter had tucked one of the revolvers in his waistband and a pistol in the small of his back while one of the others carried the AR. The last man carried the shotgun and a pistol in his own waistband.

Carter wasn't very knowledgeable when it came to firearms, they were essentially banned in Detroit long before things went crazy, but he knew how simple a revolver could be to use. If something doesn't go "bang" when you squeeze the trigger the first time, you simply squeeze it again. No complicated magazine changes to worry about; no extra moving parts to break. They just worked. Of course, there was always the issue with round count, but in reality, he didn't expect to *need* that many anyway.

About a half hour after leaving the little trailer, the trio found the boat ramp alongside the bridge at Hardison Mill. Overhead was the only way across without a boat; the bridge at highway 431. They slowly crept up the steep incline of gravel until they finally neared road level. Giving a listen they couldn't hear any cars approaching, so they stepped out on the asphalt and began to cross the river carefully.

About halfway across the expanse, and with nowhere to go, the three suddenly stopped as the glare of headlight beams broke over the hill behind them.

Chapter Forty-One

Good Help Is Hard to Find

June 15th – 6:00 p.m.

Ben slowed the truck down to a crawl along the bridge as they neared the three men. Each carried a rifle or shotgun, but they were south of the security checkpoint, so he assumed they had already been cleared or were residents of the area. There was no way the officers would have let them through otherwise, especially with weapons.

As they closed the distance, one of the men waved his hands to get the Irwins to slow down. Ben slipped the magnum back into his lap and slowly rolled the window down as he neared the young man.

"Can I help you?"

"Yes, sir. I don't mean to be a bother, but you wouldn't happen to be going into Lewisburg, would you?"

Ben glanced at Carol. The look on her face confirmed that she had her revolver ready, just in case.

"Well, no, son, we aren't. Is that where you're headed?"

"Yes sir. Our truck broke down back at the house and we need to get there tonight, if we can. I'm sorry to bother you. Thanks for stopping. Y'all have a good night."

The young man turned and began to trot back toward the others. They were on the far side of the bridge by now and seemed intent on maintaining their course.

"What do you think, Carol?"

"I don't know, Ben," she said, "The checkpoint back there wouldn't have let them through if they were trouble. I know Andy wouldn't have, anyway."

Ben considered the situation. If the men lived close by, they wouldn't have had to cross the checkpoint. Of course, they didn't seem to be too concerned with causing trouble, since each of them far outgunned Ben and Carol combined. If they had intended to steal the truck, there was little they could do to stop them. That didn't seem to be their goal.

"Let's find out what's going on," Ben said as he eased on the accelerator.

He hung his head out the window and called to the young man again, "Son?"

The man turned again, a slight look of confusion crossed his face, "Yes, sir?"

"You say you all are headed to Lewisburg?"

"Yes, sir."

"Getting kind of a late start, aren't you?"

"Uh, yeah. Well, we didn't get the call until about an hour ago. Daddy got hurt and they took him to the ER down there. We're just trying' to get there and check on him. We don't know how bad he's hurt or anything. Since the truck died on us, we got no choice but walkin' so, we're walkin'."

Ben thought about it for a minute. He didn't know these men, but his instincts drove him to offer help to those in need. It was a character flaw prominent among older generations of Southern men, some said.

"I'll tell you what. If you can give us a few minutes to unload some of this stuff, I'll drive you all into town. Can you wait for me to do that?"

The man's face brightened as if he had won the lottery.

"Really? Shoot yeah. I mean, we'll help you unload it if you need us to. Anything beats

walkin' all the way there. 'Specially carryin' all this to boot!" he gestured to the rifle slung across his shoulder, "Hang on, lemme tell my brothers!"

The man ran ahead and caught up to the other two and explained the situation. Carter looked back at the truck with a sly grin.

"Brothers, huh?" he said with a smile, "Yeah, that'll work."

"I hope you know what you're doing, Ben," Carol said as the smiling trio approached the

truck.

Soon the men were situated in the back, and the truck was meandering along the narrow black top lane toward the Irwin farm.

6:10 p.m.

Scott poured himself a glass of sweet tea as he looked out the kitchen window of the homestead. The farm was like a living monument to his family. It had always been there. It had always provided for them, and many others, in time of need. He knew every square inch of the property and what grew best in the soil of each field. Growing up as his father's number one farm hand had taught him that. It also revealed the fact that he had no desire to be a farmer.

His eyes scanned the backyard and came to rest on the huge oak tree that he and his cousins had spent so much of their youth in. Seeing it reminded him of the dream he had about getting married. It still perplexed him since he never got to see the face of his bride. It was most likely Rachel, but the phone had rung and he couldn't be sure. Not one to dwell on things like that, he just dismissed it and continued to drink his tea.

As the sun sank lower over the horizon, the shadows of the tree lines began to stretch and darken the fields. His parents should be along soon. It wouldn't be long before night finally set in fully and he was ready for a solid night's sleep. Between the heat and the activity of the day, he was tired.

Browning liked to push the guys in their training much more than the state required. He had always found the minimum to be unacceptable, and that didn't only apply to range time. It was amazing to see how much that man could cram into a day. Dave had a level of self-discipline that Scott and most of the others only dreamt of, or feared.

His attention was drawn to the sound of an approaching vehicle. The engine noise and slow speed told him, without even looking, that his parents were home.

Quickly he chugged the last of the tea and headed toward the door, right past the chair that cradled his AR and Glock.

The truck drove directly to the back yard and out to the workshop where it slowed to a stop. Before Scott stepped outside Carter and his men were already out of the bed and Ben was opening the door to the building.

The men stacked their weapons against the bed of the truck as Ben and Carol began to direct the supplies to their respective locations.

Scott stepped out the back door and immediately took note of the extra hands. Figuring that his parents had picked up some relatives to help with their haul, he made his way toward the truck.

About halfway across the yard he looked up to see Sean Carter step out of the dimmed interior of the workshop and into the fading sunlight. Scott came to an abrupt halt. He stood there staring at the same face he had seen in the photos from the Spring Hill Refugee Center files. It couldn't be. It just couldn't, but it was. His parents had brought a murderer home…with friends.

A quick about face put Scott on the path back to the house as he fumbled for his cell phone. As he lifted the device to his ear, he prayed silently that the network was working and he could get a call through.

Carter emerged from the workshop to collect his next load. This was, by far, the most physical work he had ever done. Well, it felt like it, anyway. They had unloaded almost half of the traded goods when he looked up and saw a silhouette of a man with a phone to his ear heading toward the house.

"Who's that?" he asked.

Craning his head around the corner of the cab Ben replied, "Oh, that's Scott, our son. He'll be along in a minute. Probably talking to Rachel or one of his buddies."

Carter shot a glance at one of the other men who quickly conjured an excuse.

"I hate to be a bother, but do you have a bathroom I could use?"

"Oh, yes," Carol replied, "Inside the house. Scott can show you where, just go and ask."

"Thanks. I appreciate it," the man said as he put the case of honey back on the tailgate.

Scott's temper began to rise as the phone failed time after time to connect to the network. Finally, out of frustration, he decided to try sending a text. He knew texts were a better way to communicate during emergency situations than phone calls because they didn't rely on the volume of data like a voice conversation and that freed up the network. He hoped that the system was at least stable enough to get the message through.

He opened his messaging application and began a group text to all of the team members.

"Carter here. My house. 3 men. Backup ASAP."

The message was blunt and simple. He hoped it would be a small enough data burst to get through. As he neared the house, he heard footsteps approaching from behind.

He turned to see the man approaching with a smile on his face.

"Hey, man," he said, "You're Scott, right?"

"Yeah."

"Your mom said you could show me where the bathroom is."

Irwin stopped and glanced back at the truck. His mother was heading into the workshop with a small tote of something. Beside her was Carter.

"So," Carter started, "Your son work the farm for you?"

Carol chuckled, "Scott? No, he never was much for farming. He's an engineer. Well, he was an engineer until everything went crazy."

"So, he's not an engineer anymore? What's he do all day?"

"Don't misunderstand, Scott was raised on the farm and knows everything about it. He'd make an excellent farmer, if he wanted to. He just never really wanted to. Since he's come back home, he still helps around here, but most of his time is working with the police department."

"Really," Carter mused, "I'd like to talk to him."

Chapter Forty-Two

Flash Traffic

June 15th – 6:12 p.m.

Major Thomas was sitting in his office at the Spring Hill Refugee Center scanning the inventory reports for the facility. To his left, in a disheveled heap, sat the files for Carter and the other men.

Captain Watkins had been working diligently to try and capture transmission data from the stolen telephone that Carter had to establish a location. The biggest problem was that the service provider for the phone didn't recognize the legal authority of the recently formed State Guard to allow access to their data.

Watkins had brought in the local Sheriff to bridge the gap and get the data they needed, but it was still a trying process. He stuck his head in briefly to update the Major concerning the effort. "Sir?"

"Yes, Captain?"

"We've managed to make a little progress on the data collection, but we don't have any recent information. A triangulation overnight put them east of Interstate 65, in a wooded area near the Old Rally Hill Cutoff Road. They are trying to get more updated information now, but it appears they are not following the main roads at all."

"Show me," Thomas said.

Watkins made his way to a map that Thomas had pinned to the wall of his office showing the immediate area.

"The first ping we got showed him here," he pointed to a location to the west of Kedron Road, "Next hit came from around here." The Major slid his finger across the map to a point on Kedron Road itself.

"This latest hit was here," he said indicating the wooded camp area where the snake bite had taken place.

Thomas considered the information momentarily.

"He's not headed to Florida, that's for damn sure," he grumbled, "Isn't there a police checkpoint along the line there?"

"Yes, sir. It's here, just south of Pottsville," Watkins again slid his finger along the map, coming to rest at the intersection.

"Get on the horn to the folks at that checkpoint. See if they've seen anything. I doubt they have. I'm willing to bet he's going off road. He'll avoid that highway if he can."

"Yes, sir," Watkins began, "He'll have to come up at least once, though. He will have to cross the river here, and the only bridge to do that on is here at Hardison Mill. The only problem is that our information is so old he could have easily crossed by now."

6:18 p.m.

Browning was in the garden working a fresh patch of chicken manure into the soil when his phone chimed. Wiping the sweat from his brow he dug into his pocket and pulled the device out. As he flipped it over, he saw the text was from Scott and included the other team members.

Immediately he passed it along to the Chief and the Sheriff and made for his truck.

6:21 p.m.

"Major!" Watkins called as he raced across the office space, "We have his location!"

"Where?" Thomas leapt to his feet and stepped around the desk.

"I'll tell you on the way."

"Radio ahead to the checkpoint. We need to get there ASAP."

"Already done, sir. They have a man standing by to take us in."

The pair clamored into the closest Humvee just as the gunner took his position up top.

"Permission to go hot, sir?"

"Not yet, son. Let's see how this plays out first."

Within minutes the truck was barreling down Kedron Road toward the Pottsville checkpoint.

6:22 p.m.

Scott escorted the man into the house and pointed him in the direction of the bathroom.

"Yeah, I thought I had to go," the man said with a sneer, "but I guess the urge has passed."

Scott took a half step away and began to size up his options. He knew the man was probably going to get aggressive, but so far he hadn't shown any indicators. Suddenly he remembered that he had left both his Glock and AR pistol in the living room chair. He had decided to disarm since he was in the security of his own home. Had he really become *that* careless? Yes. Yes, he had.

"Funny how that happens," Scott replied, "You and your friends there, you headed somewhere?"

"Yeah. We were headed to Lewisburg when your mom and dad were kind enough to offer us a ride."

"Well, Dad can be a little old fashioned like that. He likes to give folks the benefit of the doubt…especially if they look to be in need. "Can I get you something to drink?"

After being in the heat of the Middle Tennessee sunshine all day he wavered and almost took the offer. The thought just made him thirstier.

"Nah. I'd better pass. See, we are in a bit of a hurry, and we'd like to be back on the road as soon as we can. Places to go and people to see, you know.

"Now, if you will cooperate, we can be out of here and on our way in just a few minutes. You can go back to life on the farm like we were never here. Otherwise, well, it could get…complicated. See?"

Scott felt the hairs on the back of his neck rise as the thinly veiled threat came out.

"Is that a threat?"

"No, Scott. It's a promise."

"I see," Irwin said as he tightened his muscles and tried to decide what response he needed to take. He could probably take the man in a fair fight, but Scott didn't want a fair fight. He wanted one decidedly in his favor.

The man pulled his shirt tail up slightly to reveal the pistol tucked in his waistband.

"Nobody needs to know we were ever here. Understand? Now, who were you on the phone with earlier?"

"Yeah, see that's the thing," Scott said as he looked and felt around him for a weapon of his own, "I texted my co-workers to let them all know you were here, Robert. They're coming over to say 'hello' right now."

"*Robert? How did he know my name,*" the man thought, "*I never told him who I was.*"

Suddenly the realization began to sink in that Scott somehow had information about all three of them. Was he a cop? Was he military? It didn't matter at this point. Their plan was now compromised, and they had to leave immediately.

Robert reached for the shirt tail again, but as his hand swept to grab the butt of the pistol Irwin slammed his fist into Robert's forearm, knocking the hand away and sending a stabbing pain up and down his arm. A tingly numbness settled in as he tried to hold Irwin off and get to the gun again.

With his numbness he fumbled with the shirt and dropped the pistol. Irwin, knowing he couldn't reach the weapon for his own use, kicked it across the room and drew back for a power punch to Robert's face.

Robert twisted his body as he watched the pistol sliding farther from his grip. Realizing he was exposed, he jabbed back with his arm, striking Scott squarely in the abdomen and knocking the breath out of him.

Irwin foundered and fell against the wall as Robert changed direction and stumbled toward the pistol. Grabbing the closest thing he could find, Scott hurled a small vase at his opponent, striking him in the neck and jaw on his left side. Robert dropped to the floor within reach of the pistol.

Seeing he couldn't get to the gun before Robert, Scott dashed to the living room to retrieve his own weapons.

Hearing the breaking glass outside Carter motioned for the second man to go check it out.

"What was that, dear?" Carol asked.

"I don't know," Ben replied, "I'll go take a look."

"That's alright. Tim will go and check it out. It was probably Bob. Sometimes his blood sugar gets low, and he gets kind of clumsy. I'd rather help you get the rest of this unloaded so we can get out of your hair, if you don't mind," Carter suggested.

The second man scurried back toward the house, unsure of what to expect when he got there, but hoping it was nothing significant.

As Tim was reaching for the door, Robert was lifting the pistol from the floor. In the front room, Scott was press checking the AR and heading for cover. As he neared the doorway to the dining room the casing splintered as a 115-grain full metal jacket slammed into it.

Scott dropped low and brought the AR around to engage as another round slapped the wall just beside his head.

At the back door Tim heard the gunshots and dropped low to the ground as well. He reached around and pulled the pistol from the small of his back and began to rush around the side of the house toward the front door.

Before Carter could react, Ben and Carol both had their revolvers out and trained on him.

"Son," Ben said, "Just take it easy and step over to the truck. Hands up and on the roof. Don't move. And we'll figure out what's going on."

6:32 p.m.

Andy paced back and forth at the checkpoint, constantly staring into the tree line at the riverbank. On the other side, a few hundred yards across the fields, Scot was toe to toe with a known murderer and his friends. He kept straining to hear if there were any gunshots, but the countryside was stone silent.

"ETA?" he asked with a tone of frustration in his voice.

The team leader shrugged his shoulders and replied, "Same as it was two minutes ago,

Phillips. It'll take them a little bit to get here. Just hang on."

Finally, they could hear the approach of the Humvee as it raced down Franklin Pike toward them. With adrenaline already pumping, Andy began to move toward the sound. If he could, he would have jumped in the truck from where he was.

Suddenly, from across the river he heard it, a single gunshot. He snapped his head around to face the farm just as he heard a second one, then a third. Two different calibers.

The Humvee rolled up and slowed in front of him as he grabbed for the door handle.

"Major Thomas? I'm Andy Phillips. We have to go NOW."

Hearing the pop of gunfire echo across the nearby river the Major motioned for Phillips to take a seat. In seconds the truck was under full throttle again and racing toward the farm.

"Once we cross the river take the first road to the left. It's a crooked bastard, but it's a shorter route to the house than the next road."

The driver nodded as he focused his eyes on the pavement ahead.

"You're familiar with the place?" Thomas asked.

"Practically grew up there. The Irwin's are almost like a second family to a lot of us. We probably spent as much time on this farm as we did at home; especially when we were in high school."

The truck slowed and hung a hard left onto a narrow one lane blacktop road. As they bumped along Andy checked his weapons and quickly muttered a short prayer.

Chapter Forty-Three

End Game

June 15th – 6:42 p.m.

Tim stepped up onto the front porch of the Irwin home. He could hear movement inside, but there hadn't been any more gunfire in a minute or two. Carefully, he opened the front door. As the door swung open, Robert turned and prepared to shoot but quickly realized it was Tim and returned his attention to a nearby doorway.

A series of booming shots rang out inside the living room as Robert and Tim both jumped for cover. As he fell Robert felt a burning sensation across his calf as a 55-grain full metal jacket ripped across his flesh, tearing a gash across the muscle as it went.

The frame of the front door shuddered as two rounds ran wide and almost caught Tim as he dropped, without a shred of grace or style, onto the porch and belly crawled to the edge. He flopped into the dirt and huddled next to the old stone foundation trying to figure out what he should do.

Robert heard Scott's fleeting steps and rose to pursue, finding his leg painful and bleeding. His pursuit would be slow, but it would happen. He limped through the dining room and heard the slamming of the back door. Was that Tim or Scott? He'd have to find out, but he really didn't want to.

Scott low ran to the oak tree and crouched down. He could see his parents had Carter under control, but he didn't know if they could keep him there until help arrived. With two people on him, he'd have to do something to put the odds more in his favor.

Ben strained to see what was happening at the house. The light was fading fast, and he couldn't tell who had just come outside. Carol let herself be distracted as well when she heard the door slam.

Carter realized he had an opportunity, and he took it.

Quickly turning he punched Ben as hard as he could in the chest, knocking the old man backward and sending him stumbling to the ground.

Carol squeezed the trigger on her revolver but in her excited state she sent the round wide and left, passing over Carter's shoulder as he drew his own revolver.

Almost instinctively, he cranked the trigger and the snub little handgun belched forth a 158-grain jacketed hollow point that found its way directly into Carol's right shoulder. The shock wave of the impact caused her to immediately drop her own revolver as the shoulder blade shattered, and the cavitation tore tendons and tissues all across her upper right torso.

As Carol screamed in pain Scott quickly turned his attention back to the truck. He could see his mother holding her shoulder and the blood stain spreading from it. Where was his father?

He looked around the truck and finally saw the man lying on the ground on his back. He was struggling to get up, but he was getting up. Scott decided that his priority needed to be Carter and set out to put him down immediately.

"Look, I didn't want any trouble. I just wanted to go to Lewisburg. That's all. You people…this is all your fault. I just wanted to have my life back. Well, since you are screwing it all up, you're going to get it all back!" Carter was practically screaming with rage now. He was on the verge of losing control and Scott needed him to keep his tunnel vision for just a few more seconds until he could close the distance.

"You!" he screamed at Carol, "Get in the truck! NOW!" She sheepishly crawled in the driver's seat and slid across. As she did, she tried to see what kind of shape Ben was in. He had a small trickle of blood from the corner of his mouth, but he was slowly getting back to his feet.

6:47 p.m.

"Turn in right here," Andy shouted as he pointed to the gate, "It's a long driveway, but it's pretty easy to drive so you can open it up if you want."

The driver stomped the pedal as a cloud of dust and small gravel flew up behind the truck. As they rounded the final bend in the driveway they could see a man in the front yard but couldn't tell who it was.

In the back yard Scott was racing to his parents' truck. His focus was on Carter, so he didn't pay attention to his father yelling at him.

"Scott! Behind you!" Ben shouted.

Robert had come out and was raising his pistol at Scott. Ben quickly reached over and grabbed the AR that

Tim had brought and ran the bolt, flipping a round out onto the ground beside his right foot.

Ben brought the rifle to bear and fired a volley of shots, striking Robert in the torso, upper leg, hip, and chest. The would-be assassin dropped to the ground instantly without firing another shot.

Scott skidded to a halt, unsure of who had fired or who the intended target was. As he tried to assess the situation, Carter was in the cab of the truck doing the same thing. He quickly divined that Ben was now an immediate threat and swung his revolver to engage the elder.

Before Ben could bring the rifle around, Carter fired two rounds at the elder man, striking him once in the lower abdomen and once in the chest. As Ben fell to the ground Carter fired a third shot which entered Ben's torso low and traveled upward through the abdominal cavity to the lower chest cavity, shredding organs as it went.

"NO!" Scott screamed as his father fell to the ground again. He couldn't get a clear shot at the man, but when he could, he would make sure Carter never killed again.

Carol took advantage of the opportunity and, using the only weapon she had left at her disposal, stabbed Carter in the kidney with her ink pen, driving it deep into his side. She withdrew the makeshift dagger and prepared to go for the neck as Carter swung around and blocked her stab with a swipe of his arm. He slid toward the door and brought his revolver up, pressing the trigger once.

Time slowed as Scott saw the passenger side window suddenly change to a dark crimson and his mother slump against the door.

His heart was pounding in his chest, and the adrenaline rush was in full effect. As he drew closer to the man who just killed his parents his focus became singular. Carter's death would be brutal.

Realizing that the truck was useless without keys, Carter stumbled out of the cab and drug himself over to Ben's body. He knew the man had the keys. He must have put them in his pocket when they stopped.

Scott opened fire with his AR pistol, not even focusing on the sights or optics at first. His rage was jeopardizing his own vengeance.

The rounds went wide, and high, and low, and everywhere except into the body of Carter.

Tim heard the exchange and stepped around the corner. He saw Scott running full bore toward the truck. As Irwin swung his little AR up and opened fire, Tim brought his pistol up and was about to shoot him in the back, or try to.

Suddenly, he became aware of a fast-moving vehicle approaching. He turned to see the Humvee racing directly at him and began firing at the vehicle desperately.

"Light 'em up!" Thomas called to the gunner.

With a hefty tug, the gunner racked the bolt on the M2 .50 caliber then swung it at Tim.

It only took a single hit to almost completely separate Tim's torso from his hips. The second round was really not necessary as his digestive tract was mostly a reddish spray against the white wall of the house.

The driver then pointed the truck to the side yard where they would head to the workshop.

Hearing the thunderous blasts from the Ma Deuce, Carter and Irwin were both shaken momentarily. They looked to see who the new participant in their death match was, but quickly knew it was down to the two of them, regardless.

Carter brought his revolver up and fired hitting Scott in the lower abdomen, but missing any vital organs.

Scott regained his focus, fighting through the adrenaline and pain as he put the red dot of his optic squarely on Carter's chest and began to press the trigger.

The first round hit low on the right lung. The second hit low on the left lung, the third punched through the spleen.

Carter's fifth round in the cylinder grazed Scott's left arm and the sixth barely missed his head.

Scott's fourth and fifth rounds severed the spinal column at the T-6 and T-10 vertebrae.

Carter dropped like a stone as he continued to press the trigger of his own weapon. The revolver replied with the resounding click of a hammer falling on a spent primer as Irwin rounded the bed of the truck.

Scott rushed to the fallen man and kicked the revolver out of his reach. Blood saturated Carter's shirt and a mix of spittle and blood began to trickle from his lips.

The Humvee rolled to a top behind Scott as he raised the muzzle to Carter's head.

"Stand Down!" Thomas shouted, "It's over! We've got him! Stand down, son!"

Son? Who called him son? Scott lowered his muzzle and turned to look at his father, then up to the Major.

"It's alright, Scott. You've done it. You stopped him. It's time to stand down now and let us take it from here. Okay?"

Phillips stepped around the bumper of the Humvee with a trauma kit and the driver in tow. They immediately rushed to Ben to check his condition as Thomas looked at the pile that was Carter.

Scott dropped his AR as he knelt down beside his father. Tears began to well in his eyes as the emotion of the situation began to manifest itself.

"Your dad's a tough guy, Mr. Irwin. He's not done yet. We need to get him ambulatory, okay?"

Scott nodded as Andy stood to escort his friend away from the scene.

"C'mon, man. Let 'em work," he said.

The two men stepped away as the gunner moved in and began to apply Quick Clot to Ben's wounds.

In the distance the sound of sirens could be heard on highway 99 from Chapel Hill. The ambulances were on their way.

Andy looked at Scott and realized there was a large red stain forming on his shirt and he was beginning to look washed out.

"Aw, shit. C'mon. I'm taking you to the hospital."

"No," Scott said, "I'm gonna stay with Dad."

"Your dad is coming later. You need to come with me now. We need to get you checked out as soon as possible. I don't want Ben to lose you too, now get your ass in the Jeep. Where are the keys?"

Scott dug reluctantly in his pocket and produced the keys to his Jeep. He handed them over to Andy and slumped to the ground.

"Major?" Andy called, "I'm taking Scott ahead. He's been hit."

"Go. We've got this."

Andy rushed to the Jeep and drove it around the house to Scott. He loaded his friend up and tore down the driveway passing the ambulances and patrol cars as they came in.

Chapter Forty-Four

Hello and Goodbye

June 15th – 7:38 p.m.

Andy slid under the awning of the emergency room entrance and shoved the gear shift into Park. A group of nurses and orderlies were already waiting thanks to a radio call from the teams at the farm. Within seconds of their arrival, Scott was inside and being prepped to remove the bullet from his gut.

Fresh bandages were applied to his arm and butterfly stitches held the gash closed for the time being. An IV was started and vitals were being monitored when the first ambulance arrived.

Ben was wheeled directly into surgery as a groggy, beaten Scott looked on.

"Is he gonna be okay?" he asked one of the nurses as she sped by.

"I don't know. We'll do all we can, but it's pretty bad. Keep him in your prayers," she said as she hurried after the gurney.

A few minutes later the second ambulance arrived and dispatched a bloody, but living, Sean Carter. The sheets were blotched with massive red patches as the first responders wheeled him past Scott.

He could feel the anger welling inside as he thought about his mother. He wanted to finish the job that the Major wouldn't allow. He wanted to get out of the room and rip Carter's heart out like Carter had done to him, only he wanted it to be literal.

While he was still stewing in his rage Denise ran into the Emergency Room and found him.

"Scott! Thank God you're okay," she cried, "I heard you had been shot and I thought the worst. What happened?"

"I got the bad guys."

Denise looked at him with a curious gaze. He had lost a good bit of blood and was probably still wrestling with the emotional crash of the adrenaline high. She decided to let the questions go until later when he was a bit more himself.

"He shot my dad," he finally muttered, "And he killed my mom."

Denise's jaw dropped open a little bit as she searched for the proper response.

"But I got him," he continued, "and his friend. Only problem is they wouldn't let me finish it."

"Who? Who did you get?"

"Carter. Sean Carter. They're prepping the bastard for surgery right now."

As Denise heard the name the shock of it hit her like a ton of bricks. She left the exam room and went directly to surgery. Peering through the door she saw Ben Irwin on the table as the surgical team worked at a fever pitch to get him stable.

Next door, in the second surgical bay, was a gurney with a bloody Sean Carter on top. The team was preparing the instruments and equipment when Denise burst into the room.

"You can't come in here! This is a sterile environment! Get out!"

Denise ignored the orders and walked directly to Carter's side. As she stepped up beside his face, he turned a weary eye to her and a slight smile began to form.

"I found you," he whispered, "Now you can take care of me, like before. You always took good care of me." His voice was straining, and his eyes were beginning to blur, but the smile remained.

Denise leaned in close to his ear.

"I told you before that one day fighting was going to get you killed. You can die and go straight to Hell."

Carter never lost his smile. His hearing had stopped with all the gunfire. Long before she ever entered the room and all that was left was the comfort of knowing that the woman of his dreams was at his side once again. As Denise stormed out of the room the heart monitor flat-lined, and Sean Carter slipped into darkness.

By the time Denise walked back into Scott's exam room she found him struggling to get off the bed and find Carter.

"What are you doing?" she demanded.

"I gotta go," he replied.

"And do what, exactly?"

"Kill that son of a bitch."

"He's already dead."

Scott stopped his escape attempt and stared back at the beautiful brunette.

"What?"

"He's dead. I just left the O.R. and I heard the monitor flatline as I walked out. Like you said, you got him."

"They'll probably revive him. Send the bastard back to Michigan where he'll get a slap on the wrist and walk."

"Scott," Denise said softly, "I saw him. There is no reviving. I don't care if they shove an extension cord up his ass, he's not coming back. The damage was too great. He was dead before he got here. His body just hadn't accepted the fact yet.

"Bringing him to the hospital was just a formality to say they tried. If anyone asks, they can honestly say they tried to revive and operate, but he was too far gone. It's over."

Scott thought about it for a minute, then began to shuffle to get up again.

"Scott," the tone was a bit more authoritarian now, "What are you doing?"

"I need to see my dad."

"You can't. He's in surgery."

Irwin stopped and slumped his shoulders back to the mattress.

"I'll tell you what. Let me go and talk to the surgical staff. We'll get you updates as they go through the operation and keep you in the loop, okay?"

"Yeah, I'd appreciate that."

As Denise again left the room Scott struggled to keep his composure. Over and over his mind played back the images of his parents as they were both viciously gunned down. He never heard Browning and Evans come in the room.

"Hey, man," Evans said cautiously, "How are you feeling?" Scott quickly turned his head to face his company.

"Oh, hey. I'm, uh, I'm doing alright. They say they're going to take me in as soon as they get a room ready."

Dave glanced at the large bandage taped to Irwin's abdomen. Blood still seeped through the fabric, forming a circular patch about the size of a quarter.

"Well, we're going to step out so they can take care of you, alright? We just wanted to check in on you."

"Yeah, okay. Thanks guys."

As they turned to step out an orderly came in.

"Alright, Mr. Irwin, looks like it's show time for you," the man said as he unlocked the wheels of the bed and wheeled Scott out of the room.

Irwin awoke the following morning to find Denise sitting beside the bed. She was dozing quietly in the chair, still wearing her scrubs from the night before.

Scott fumbled around for the remote. There was no clock in the room, so he had no idea what time it was. He would try to catch the news on one of the Nashville stations. They usually had the time stamped in the corner of the screen during the morning shows.

As he pressed the button the television roared to life with the jarring theme music to Family Feud.

"Oh, dammit," he spluttered. Frantically he pressed the volume button, and the television slowly became more tolerable, but the damage was done. Denise was now wide awake and staring at him.

"Sorry. I didn't know it would be that loud."

She smiled at him with a tired look and glanced at the screen.

"Yeah, I know. I'm changing it now. Just hush."

"How do you feel?" she asked as she began to stand.

"Like a huge pile of crap. My arm is sore and my gut just plain hurts."

"It should. That bullet did more damage than they expected. You're lucky nothing important got hit. Most of the pain is going to be from general soreness, but there is some patchwork going on in there you should be mindful of. No doing anything stupid for a while, young man."

"Yes, ma'am," he replied with a subtle hint of sarcasm, "Any word on Dad?" She took a deep breath and braced herself.

"He made it through the surgery last night alright, but he's not out of the woods yet. There is extensive damage in his abdominal cavity and into his chest cavity. He's on life support and that's keeping him stable, but he's in too fragile of a state to go through another surgery right now.

"Even if they manage to repair all the damage, he may still not make it."

Irwin sat there considering her words in silence. On one level it made him mad to know that, despite everything, he may still lose his father. On another, he couldn't help but wonder what kind of life the man could expect given his condition. At the very least he probably wouldn't last long without his wife. Scott had known several couples who would pass within days, or weeks, of each other's passing. As close as his parents were, he fully expected his dad to be gone within a year without his mother being there. Call it Broken Heart Syndrome or whatever you wanted, he knew it happened.

"Do you want to go see him?"

"Yeah. Yeah, I do."

Denise left the room and returned moments later with a wheelchair. She eased him up out of the bed and into the seat with a proven and professional touch.

"I'd say you've done that before," Irwin quipped.

"More than you can guess," she said with a smile as she turned him toward the door.

A couple of minutes later they entered the Critical Care Unit and she pushed him alongside his father's bed.

"Is he conscious?" Scott asked.

"It comes and goes," she said, "He's on a lot of medication to manage the pain and fight infection, but they said they were really surprised when he started talking early this morning."

"What did he say?"

"I'm not sure. I think it was like when someone talks in their sleep; garbled and mumbling, you know?"

"Yeah."

Denise watched Scott for a minute before deciding it was time to give him some privacy.

"Hey, I'm going to grab something to snack on and maybe a drink. Do you want anything?"

"Um, no. I'm good. Thanks though."

"Anytime, Scott. I'll be right back."

As she turned to leave, she caressed his shoulders with her hand. The contact instantly registered as affectionate with Scott and he found himself watching her as she left. She was gorgeous. More than that, she was intelligent and seemed to truly care about him. That's when it hit him.

"Shit. We were supposed to go out tonight."

"Language, son."

The voice was rough and weak, but it was definitely his father. Scott looked up to see his dad looking back at him.

"Your mother would have a fit if she heard you cuss like that."

"Dad! Hey! Yeah, I know. I just wasn't thinking. It slipped out."

"That's alright, buddy. I won't tell her."

Scott smiled at the man in the bed. Despite all the tubes and monitors and equipment that surrounded him he was still cracking jokes.

"How are you feeling, Dad?"

Ben struggled with his breathing for a second as he formulated his reply.

"I'll be fine, son. Don't worry about me."

"Good. I'm glad to hear it. You know we never did finish that deer stand up in the northwest corner. We need to get on that when you get out of here." Ben managed a tiny smile.

"I don't think I'm going to worry about that, Scott. That deer stand is yours. You fix it up however you want."

He tried to collect a deep breath, but his lungs were aching just to keep up as it was.

"As a matter of fact, the whole farm is yours now. Take care of it, okay?"

"What are you talking about? You have to get better and come back home…"

"Take care of it and it'll take care of you, son."

Ben's breathing became more laborious as Scott noticed the numbers on the heart monitor began to drop.

"I'm gonna go see your mom now, Scott. Don't worry. I won't tell her."

"Dad?"

The heart rate dropped more as his breathing began to slow.

"Don't worry, son. Take care of it."

The heart monitor echoed forth a monotone alert as Ben gently closed his eyes. Soon the room was filling with staff as the crash cart was wheeled in, and Scott was wheeled out.

Chapter Forty-Five

Visitations

June 16th

That evening, as Scott was working his way through his liquid diet, Dave, Evans, Phillips, Rachel, Simmons, and the Richards knocked on his door.

"Are you decent?" Browning asked.

"Has he ever been?" Evans commented.

"Come on in, guys," Scott replied, "I'm just drinking my supper and enjoying the Game Show Network."

As the group filtered into the room, they spread themselves around and occupied the few chairs that were available.

Andy looked at the television and began to smile, "Are you turning into your grandmother?"

Scott smiled back, "Nah. I don't have the volume up to 100 yet."

"How are you feeling?" Kim asked.

"Honestly?"

She nodded silently.

"I feel like someone punched me in the stomach with a freight train. The good news is nothing important was hit, but the bad news is I have to stay here for a little while longer."

"Any ideas on how long?" Simmons asked.

"If no infections set in or anything they say I might be out in a week, but I won't be able to be up and around much for about two to three weeks. I think I'll try to push that a little. I can't stand this liquid diet crap."

"Yeah, it sucks, doesn't it?" Adams commented as he rolled through the door.

"Hey, man! What are you doing out of bed?" Scott grinned at his friend.

"Shhh. They don't know I'm gone yet. Somebody left this sweet ride just outside my door and I thought I might as well see the sights. Go get yours and we'll race," he said with a devilish grin.

"I would," Scott grinned back, "but Dave would get me for DUI right now. I'll need to wait until he's gone."

A nurse stepped into the doorway with her hands on her hips.

"I found him," she called down the hallway, "Mr. Adams, you know you are not supposed to be taking off like that. Come on, back to bed."

"Wow, either they're getting better at this or I'm getting worse. Looks like visiting hours are over. See ya later, Scott!"

The nurse pushed Adams back down the hallway toward his room, scolding him for his ambitious joyriding the whole way.

"I thought he was kidding," Scott said with a chuckle.

"He ain't right," Phillips snapped.

The friends talked for a while before a nurse entered the room with his next round of medication.

She handed the tiny cup off to Scott who snurled his nose and swallowed the capsules and tablets.

"Well, that tasted worse than the broth, but at least it had texture," he said.

"Maybe you could get them to put the pills in the broth and make soup," Evans commented.

"Now that's a thought," Irwin said with a smile.

"Well, we don't want to take up your whole evening, but we did want to check on you and see how you were doing. Is there anything you need?" Browning asked.

"Nah. I'm good. I just want to be out of here. I hate being in the hospital."

"Okay. But if you think of anything, you let me know, okay?"

"You got it."

The friends exchanged handshakes and hugs and bid Scott a farewell until the next day. As they walked out the door, he noticed that Rachel and Evans were sticking very closely together and seemed to be enjoying a lively conversation of their own.

Denise entered a few minutes later. She had finally managed to make it home and change out of her scrubs and into something a little less…medical.

"*One door opens as another door closes,*" Scott thought.

"Hey," she said with a radiant smile, "How are you feeling?"

"Better by the minute," he replied.

"Ah, they just brought your meds, didn't they?"

"Yeah, but that's not why."

"Oh, really?"

"Really. You know, we were supposed to have a date tonight."

"I know. I've gotta say, I don't think I've ever known *anyone* who went this far to get out of a date before."

Scott smiled, "Who says I want to get out of it? Maybe this is exactly where I wanted to go tonight. I mean, we have quality entertainment," he motioned to the television, "five-star room service, and, if you're one of those 'fast women' I'm already in the bed. You didn't think about it like that, did you?"

She giggled aloud at the absurdity of the comment.

"You are crazy, you know that?"

"I've been told that before. It helps."

The next morning, as Scott was trying to quickly power through his gelatin breakfast, he had a knock at the door.

"Scott?"

"Yeah."

The door pushed open to reveal the smiling face of John Hardin, the preacher at Ben and Carol's church. John had turned to a life of preaching after a long run in the military. Graduating with Scott and the others, John had known them well growing up. Scott and John weren't terribly close, but they were friendly acquaintances.

"How are you doing, man?"

"Hey, John. I'm doing pretty well, all things considered, you know? How are you?"

"I'm fine. Doing fine. Hey, I just wanted to stop by and visit for a bit if you don't mind."

"No, that's good. Pull up a chair."

John stepped across the room and sat down in the chair beside the bed that Denise had slept in the first night Scott was in the room.

"I'm so sorry to hear about your mom and dad. That is terrible. I just want you to know that everyone at church is just devastated by this. If there's anything you need, you just let us know, okay?"

"I appreciate it, John. I just need some time to process it all and deal with it, you know?"

"Yeah, I do. More than you realize."

The comment struck Scott as a bit odd, but he didn't dwell on it.

"Not to keep bringing it up, but I did want you to know that your parents had a burial policy in place. All of their funeral arrangements have been taken care of years ago."

"Yeah, I remember Mom talking about that when they took the policies out."

"Well, the only thing is that they didn't specify a plot and we're not sure where they would have wanted to be buried. Do you know?"

Scott considered it for a few minutes. There was only one place that seemed logical: under the oak tree on the farm.

"Yeah, I think so. I'll have someone dig the graves out back of the house and we'll bury them under the old oak tree in the back yard. They used to love sitting under the shade of that tree and enjoying their life together. It's the only place that fits.

"Are you doing the service?"

"Yeah, they asked me to a couple of years ago, and I agreed, so unless you have an objection…"

"No. No, I wouldn't dream of anyone else taking care of it, John. Besides, I'd be worried of what they would think if I changed their plans."

Both men smiled at the thought of going against either of the Irwins when their minds were made up.

"You know, I hadn't seen much of them since everything went sideways. I had been meaning to drop in on them and see how they were doing, but with all the chaos we've had since May, well, I just haven't had time to do it all."

"I know they missed being in church on a regular basis, but the cost of fuel went nuts and they decided that they would cut their expenses and tune in the service on the evening radio broadcast."

"Oh, I know. We've had several members to do that. It's just too expensive to go anywhere these days; too dangerous as well.

"Well, I don't want to take your breakfast time up. You look like you were really enjoying that gelatin, so I'll let you get back to it," John smiled.

"Well, you know, looks can be deceiving, right?"

John thought about the statement for a second before he responded.

"Yeah. They certainly can be. Hey, I'll catch up with you later, alright? Again, if you need anything, you let me know."

"Sounds good, John. Thanks for stopping by."

Hardin pulled the door to as he left, leaving Scott alone again with his liquid diet, game shows, and a mind full of memories about his parents.

Chapter Forty-Six

"It looks just like him."

June 18th

The arrangements called for a simple, graveside service. Ben and Carol had matching caskets that were arranged so that John could stand between them and deliver his eulogy.

Greg, the director of the funeral home, had made sure that there were awnings set up for additional shade for anyone who couldn't get a seat under the massive limbs of the oak tree. Since the Irwin family was so well known, the turnout was considerable.

Some people sent their condolences and flowers, resigning to allow the family some privacy.

Others thought it best to be there and show support in person.

To Scott's surprise he noticed that Major Thomas and Captain Watkins were both present and in full dress uniforms. The mayors, county and city, mingled among the crowd while Browning, the Sheriff, and the Chief of Police chatted off to the side with a few members of the team.

Scott sat in his wheelchair by the foot of his mother's casket, shaking hands and talking to friends and acquaintances, old and new.

During a short lull in activity Denise stepped up beside him.

"How are you doing?"

"I'm good," he said.

"You're not getting too hot, are you?"

"No, I'm fine." He glanced over his shoulder at his mother, then at his father. They both looked so peaceful and serene. Scott couldn't help but crack a smile as a memory flashed in his mind.

"What?" Denise asked, "What's so funny?"

"I just remembered going to a funeral once when I was a kid. I couldn't have been more than, I don't know eight, maybe. Anyway, we were in the line to view the body and give our condolences and everything and my aunt was with us. She was one of those people that would go to a funeral just to have something to do, you know?

"So, we get up to the casket and my aunt says, 'They did a really good job. It looks just like him.'

"Now, I'm eight and I'm not much of one to think before I speak, so I blurted out, 'It ought to; it's him.'

"I thought my mom was going to have a meltdown and beat me senseless. She was so mad, and my aunt could have crawled under a rock."

"That's horrible," Denise said with a chuckle, "Did anyone else hear you?"

"I did," Cousin Alan said with a laugh, "I thought I was gonna die myself, right there."

"Hey, Alan," Scott said, "How are you doing?"

"Doing pretty well, Scott. How are you holding up?"

Before the conversation could go much farther John Hardin stepped up and asked if Scott was ready to begin the service. He agreed and Denise wheeled him back to the front row of chairs.

The service was simple, as John explained the Irwins had wanted. Nothing fancy because, quite simply, they weren't fancy people.

Following the eulogy the caskets were lowered into the ground and the workers began to cover them with dirt. Scott sat quietly as some people made their way to their cars and trucks.

A few would hang around and socialize and some paid their respects to him again as they announced their departure. Before long the crowd had thinned considerably, and the Chief of Police made his way over.

"Scott?"

"Yes, sir?"

"When you get back on your feet, I'd like it if you could stop by my office. I have some things to discuss with you. No rush. You get to feeling better."

"Yes, sir. I'll do that."

The Chief extended his hand and shook Scott's firmly.

"Your folks were good people. They don't make 'em like that much anymore," he smiled slyly, "but you can find some running around here and there."

"Thank you, sir," Scott replied with a smile of his own.

As he walked off Major Thomas and Captain Watkins approached.

"Scott," the Major began, "I'm sorry for your loss. If there's *anything* you ever need from me, don't hesitate to ask. Understand?"

Scott looked at the man curiously, "Yes, sir. I appreciate it. Thanks for all your help."

"I wish we could have done more, son."

The officers shook hands with him and Thomas stepped off to the side where his wife and Denise were engrossed in shop talk. Denise brought Mary up to speed on her new situation while Mary told of the increase in refugees and the conditions of the center since Denise had left.

After a while the farm was empty of cars and chairs. The awnings had been broken down and removed and the graves rustled with the sound of floral arrangements in a gentle summer breeze.

Denise sat down beside Scott and took his hand.

"Hey, you ready to go?"

Scott sat silently for a minute.

"Yeah," he finally said with a crack to his voice. As he glanced across the farm he could still clearly see the bullet holes in the wall of the workshop where his shots at Carter had missed their mark.

"I've got a lot to fix around here," he said.

"Don't worry about that right now," Denise said.

"We'll work on it for you," Evans said as he and Rachel walked up to the pair, "Don't think anything about it. It'll be good as new when you get out."

"Thanks, guys," Scott muttered, "I appreciate it."

As Denise stood and turned the wheelchair in the direction of the driveway, Scott could see the tailgate of the pickup truck behind the workshop. He certainly had a lot to work on.

Chapter Forty-Seven

Gettin' Paper

June 30th

Scott arrived at the police department that morning curious about why the Chief needed to see him. His recovery had been coming along smoothly, but the doctors still wanted him to be on "light duty" for a few more days. Adams had gotten a similar treatment and was doing quite well. Of course, his idea of light duty was not exactly the same as what the doctors had in mind. Still, he was doing well.

As he stepped into the lobby of the small department, the dispatcher smiled and slid the window open to his radio area.

"Hey! You made it! How are you feeling, man?"

"Pretty good. Sore. Really sore, but I'll be fine."

"Good. Glad to hear it," the dispatcher said, "The Chief is expecting you. Head on in. Glad to see you're up and about."

Scott smiled as the man slid the glass closed and returned to his duties. He turned the corner and stepped into the administrative office where the Chief's assistant usually sat at her desk. She was curiously absent but could have been practically anywhere. He stepped across the small office and knocked on the door.

"Come in."

Scott opened the door to reveal the Sheriff and Browning already inside.

"Scott! Good to see you, son. Take a seat."

"No offense, sir, but sitting isn't exactly my favorite thing lately. The soreness is a lot more tolerable if I'm standing up."

"Oh, well, suit yourself, then. We wanted to talk to you for just a minute before we have to go to the courtroom."

"Yes, sir."

"The mayors, the Sheriff and I have been talking a lot with Browning here lately and we've decided that your group has become much more than we anticipated."

"I'm not sure I understand," Scott said.

"We feel like the Auxiliary Support Group has outgrown its original intent, Scott," the Sheriff interjected, "We feel like your team, specifically, needs to step out of that capacity. We have a new job for you."

Browning stood silently smiling at Scott as the other officers continued.

"Your group will be re-designated as the Tactical Support Unit, and you will be responsible for smaller special operations across both city and county jurisdictions as an individual unit as well as primary support for our SWAT team.

"Browning will act as Team Leader, and you will take position as second in command. You will continue to report to myself and the Sheriff directly and indirectly to the city and county mayors."

"How does that sound to you, Scott?" the Chief asked.

"Uh, yeah, thanks. Thank you. I'll do my best not to disappoint."

Suddenly Scott felt almost like he did in the meeting with Williams and Donovan when they made him a partner.

"Great. I'm glad to hear it," the Chief continued, "Now, if you can, we have a little something to attend to. Can you follow me?"

The men stood and headed out the office door and down the hallway into the courtroom. As the door swung open Scott became aware of the room being filled with dozens of people. In the front row of chairs sat the entire team with their "uniforms" on.

Adams, Simmons, Rachel, Evans, Phillips, Richards, and Davis all smiled broadly as the men entered. Behind them sat an array of people, some were local business owners, family members, and residents while others were apparently reporters of some sort or another with accompanying photographers.

As they began to cross the floor, the attendees began to stand and clap. Scott was a bit taken off guard and confused but simply smiled as he looked at his teammates. The expression on his face was clearly that of, "what the hell is going on?" which made Rachel smile even more and got a thumbs up from Phillips.

The entrants stopped in the middle of the room where Bill Thomas, the County Mayor, stepped up to a rostrum that had been arranged front and center and gestured for them to each take a seat.

"Ladies and gentlemen," he began, "Let me begin by first thanking you for taking your time to come out for this special occasion.

"Only a few short weeks ago, on the heels of a devastating economic crash, our communities saw a phenomenal increase in crime. Our situation was not unique. In fact, we fared much better than many areas across the nation, but it strained our law enforcement resources to a breaking point.

"As a result, the leadership of this county and the city of Lewisburg, decided to try an experiment. We reached out to our citizens and asked for help. Through a careful selection process and screening of candidates we formed what would be called the Auxiliary Support Program.

"These volunteers would take on the less demanding roles often associated with law enforcement and free up our officers to do their job of fighting crime and keeping our streets safe.

"What we did not expect was that in the execution of their duties, some of these people would become more deeply involved in law enforcement than we had intended. What we also didn't expect was that, not only would they rise to the challenges they encountered, but they would accomplish what they have.

"As a result of their selfless, quick reaction to situations lives were saved and criminal elements have been removed from our streets." Thomas scanned the faces of the men and women of the room before settling on the front row of black Polo clad team members.

"Scott Irwin and Jeff Adams, would you please step up here?"

Scott stood and stepped forward as Jeff moved to a position beside him. An officer stepped up beside Thomas with a small wooden box.

"These two men were assigned to a traffic detail during a sting operation on June sixth when two suspects opened fire on our tactical team, seriously injuring two of our officers. As these suspects fled the scene, they approached the roadblocks where Irwin and Adams were acting as a safety element to keep the public safe.

"Knowing the suspects were armed and desperate, Irwin and Adams selflessly put themselves in harm's way in order to stop them and prevent their escape.

"For their courage under fire and their selfless valor, it is my pleasure to award these two men the Medal of Appreciation."

Cameras began to rise, and shutters click as the small assortment of media cashed in on their photo opportunity.

He stepped up to Adams and placed the ribbon around his neck before shaking his hand and handing him a framed copy of the accompanying certificate.

Next, he draped a medal around Scott's neck and shook his hand before handing over a second certificate.

Irwin and Adams promptly returned to their seats as Thomas again faced the assembly.

"In addition, the mayor of Lewisburg, the Sheriff, the Chief of Police, and myself have all discussed the phenomenal performance of this group and have come to the conclusion that, under the guidance and training of Lieutenant Dave Browning, they will be reorganized into our first Tactical Support Unit. Scott Irwin will assume the role of second in command as soon as his injuries will allow."

"Finally, since the actions of this entire team have been exemplary and on more than one occasion they have gone above and beyond their responsibilities to support our officers and others, we are recognizing them with a departmental commendation."

The team members had known about the awards for Adams and Irwin and a couple had even known about the leadership designations, but none knew about this. Thomas motioned for them to rise and step forward as the assembly again began to clap.

Sheepishly, they took their places before the crowd as Irwin and Browning assumed their places alongside. Another photo opportunity was hard to pass up as the cameras clicked away. It wasn't national news, but it was positive news for the local area, and that was in short supply.

While the mainstream media outlets droned on about the economy or the fictitious recovery of it, people were dying. All across the former United States bad news was abundant. Here, at least in this community, there was something positive taking place. Maybe, just maybe it would inspire other communities to take a more aggressive stance to bring things back online. At least it was a start.

After the ceremony concluded and the crowd had gone the team members gathered together to give each other congratulations and discuss the new structure. As they talked, Browning walked in with a large cardboard box in his arms and a smile on his face.

"Heads up, folks. Got some new duds for you."

He opened the flaps on the box and began handing out brand new black ball caps to each team member. Embroidered across the back were the words Tactical Support Unit in a light gray thread. A patch of Velcro was attached to the front for the application of custom patches or name badges.

"Tactical Support Unit," Adams said, "Man, that sounds formal. I was hoping for something a little more...high speed and low drag, you know?"

"How about the Black Caps? I think that sounds good," Rachel suggested, "Plus, it's part of the uniform, right?"

A few nods and some mumbles indicated that the suggestion wasn't being dismissed out of hand, anyway.

"I kind of like 'Rock Creek Hooligans' myself," Phillips said with a grin.

"Now that has a nice ring to it," Adams said with a laugh, "Y'all call it what you want, I'm having that put on my shirts."

They all had a good chuckle at the suggestion.

"Which brings me to our next prize," Browning said.

Reaching back into the box, he began to pull out brand new Polo shirts with their names stitched across the right chest and the Tactical Support Unit text embroidered just above the cuff on the left sleeve in the same gray thread as the caps. On the left chest was a logo in the shape of the county with a shield behind it and the letters T.S.U. beneath.

"Wow. Classy," Richards said with a smile.

"That almost makes us look official," Evans popped.

"One more thing," Browning interjected, "We think it would be a good idea to standardize our weapons. Now, before we had to use what was available and that hasn't changed. What has changed is what has become available.

"Following the drug raid a few weeks ago we managed to confiscate several AR-15's. That will be your new issue rifle. Everyone will have interchangeable calibers, magazines, and parts, if necessary. The team will have an inventory provided by the department to work with along with ammunition that came from the same raid and the allotment we already maintain.

"Sidearms will still be your own, unless you want to try something from what we have available. If you want to standardize there, I understand. If you are comfortable with what you have, carry on."

He looked at the group in front of him and saw smiles. They had become a team. Now the hard part would start: keeping them that way.

Epilogue

Carry On

July 19ᵗʰ

Browning and Scott stepped into the spacious expanse of Bill Thomas' office. His request had been frantic and urgent. The man was visibly shaken and a bundle of nerves as they took their seats across the desk from him.

"Gentlemen, thank you for seeing me on such a short notice. I know you are both very busy with the and all…"

"What's the problem, Mayor?" Dave asked.

"My daughter. She is enrolled in college in Arkansas. We have been keeping in touch with her constantly ever since the economy fell apart. Recently, she told me that things where she lives have been rapidly deteriorating. She and her roommate, another local girl from Cornersville, had decided to leave and come back home."

"Um, no offense, sir, but we're not really a taxi service and I don't think anyone in Arkansas is going to recognize our authority there…"

"No," he snarled, "Listen, that's not the problem. She left Arkansas two days ago and we haven't heard from her until today. She's in danger and I need you to go and get her before something terrible happens to her, okay?"

"Okay, so, where is she?" Irwin asked bluntly.

"Memphis."